The
MINORITY
REPORT

The Collected Stories of Philip K. Dick available from Citadel Press

The Short Happy Life of the Brown Oxford and Other Classic Stories
ISBN 0-8065-1153-2

We Can Remember It For You Wholesale and Other Classic Stories
ISBN 0-8065-1209-1

Second Variety and Other Classic Stories
ISBN 0-8065-1226-1

The Minority Report and Other Classic Stories
ISBN 0-8065-2379-4

The Eye of Sybil and Other Classic Stories
ISBN 0-8065-1328-4

The Philip K. Dick Reader
ISBN 0-8065-1856-1

The MINORITY REPORT

AND OTHER CLASSIC STORIES BY

Philip K. Dick

WITH AN INTRODUCTION BY JAMES TIPTREE, JR.

CITADEL PRESS
Kensington Publishing Corp.
www.kensingtonbooks.com

CITADEL PRESS BOOKS are published by

Kensington Publishing Corp.
850 Third Avenue
New York, NY 10022

All Kensington titles, imprints, and distributed lines are available at special
quantity discounts for bulk purchases for sales promotions, premiums,
fund-raising, educational, or institutional use. Special book excerpts or
customized printings can also be created to fit specific needs. For details,
write or phone the office of the Kensington special sales manager:
Kensington Publishing Corp., 850 Third Avenue, New York, NY 10022,
attn: Special Sales Department, phone 1-800-221-2647.

Citadel Press and the Citadel Logo are trademarks of Kensington Publishing
Corp.

First Kensington printing: May 2002

10   9   8

Printed in the United States of America

Cataloging data may be obtained from the Library of Congress.

ISBN 0-8065-2379-4

Contents

INTRODUCTION

By James Tiptree, Jr.

I think, first and pervasively, it was the strangeness. Strange, Dick was and is. I think it was that which kept me combing the SF catalogs for more by him, waiting for each new book to come out. One hears it said, "X just doesn't *think* like other people." About Dick, it was true. In the stories, you can't tell what's going to happen next.

And yet his characters are seemingly designed to be ordinary people — except for the occasional screaming psychotic female who is one of Dick's specialties, and is always treated with love. They are ordinary people caught up in wildly bizarre situations, running a police force with the help of the mumblings of precognitive idiots, facing a self-replicating factory that has taken over the earth. Indeed, one of the factors in the strangeness is the care Dick takes to set his characters in the world of reality, an aspect most other writers ignore.

In how many other science fiction stories do you know what the hero does for a living when he isn't caught up in the particular plot? Oh, he may be a member of a space crew, or, vaguely, a scientist. Or Young Werther. In Dick, you are introduced to the hero's business concerns on page one. That's not literally true of the short stories in this volume (I went back and checked), but the impression of the pervasiveness of "grubby" business concerns is every-where, especially in the novels. The hero is in the antique business, say; as each new marvel turns up, he ruminates as to whether it is saleable. When the dead talk, they offer business advice. Dick never sheds his concern that we know how his characters earn their bread and butter. It is a part of the peculiar "grittiness" of Dick's style.

Another part of the grittiness is the jerkiness of the dialog. I can never decide whether Dick's dialog is purely unreal, or more real than most. His people do not interact as much as they deliver monologs to carry on the plot, or increase the reader's awareness of a situation.

And the situations are purely Dick. His "plots" are like nothing else in SF. If Dick writes a time-travel story, say, it will have a twist on it that makes it *sui generis*. Quite typically, the central gee-whiz marvel will *not* be centered, but will come at you obliquely, in the course, for instance, of a political election.

And any relation between Dick and a nuts-and-bolts SF writer is a pure coincidence. In my more sanguine moments, I concede that he probably knows what happens when you plug in a lamp and turn it on, but beyond that there is little evidence of either technology or science. His science, such as it is, is all engaged in the technology of the soul, with a smattering of abnormal psychology.

So far I have perhaps emphasized his oddities at the expense of his merits. What keeps you reading Dick? Well, for one thing, the strangeness, as I said, but within it there is always the atmosphere of *striving*, of men desperately trying to get some necessary job done, or striving at least to understand what is striking at them. A large percentage of Dick's heroes are tortured men; Dick is expert at the machinery of despair.

And another beauty is the desolations. When Dick gives you a desolation, say after the bomb, it is a desolation unique of its kind. There is one such in this book. But amid the desolation you often find another of Dick's characteristic touches, the *little animals*.

The little animals are frequently mutants, or small robots who have taken on life. They are unexplained, simply noted by another character in passing. And what are they doing? They are striving, too. A freezing sparrow hugs a rag around itself, a mutant rat plans a construction, "peering and planning." This sense of the ongoing busy-ness of life, however doomed, of a landscape in which every element has its own life, is *trying to live*, is typically and profoundly Dick. It carries the quality of compassion amid the hard edges and the grit, the compassion one suspects in Dick, but that never appears frontally. It is this quality of love, always quickly suppressed, that gleams across Dick's rubbled plains and makes them unique and memorable.

James Tiptree, Jr.
December, 1986

I used to believe the universe was basically hostile. And that I was misplaced in it, I was different from it...fashioned in some other universe and placed here, you see. So that it zigged while I zagged. And that it had singled me out only because there was something weird about me. I didn't really groove with the universe.

I had a lot of fears that the universe would discover just how different I was from it. My only suspicion about it was that it would find out the truth about me, and its reaction would be perfectly normal: it would get me. I didn't feel that it was malevolent, just perceptive. And there's nothing worse that a perceptive universe if there's something weird about you.

But this year I realized that that's not true. That the universe is perceptive, but it's friendly...I just don't feel that I'm different from the universe anymore.

— Philip K. Dick in an interview, 1974.
(from *ONLY APPARENTLY REAL*)

THE MINORITY REPORT

AUTOFAC

I

TENSION hung over the three waiting men. They smoked, paced back and forth, kicked aimlessly at weeds growing by the side of the road. A hot noonday sun glared down on brown fields, rows of neat plastic houses, the distant line of mountains to the west.

"Almost time," Earl Perine said, knotting his skinny hands together. "It varies according to the load, a half second for every additional pound."

Bitterly, Morrison answered, "You've got it plotted? You're as bad as it is. Let's pretend it just *happens* to be late."

The third man said nothing. O'Neill was visiting from another settlement; he didn't know Perine and Morrison well enough to argue with them. Instead, he crouched down and arranged the papers clipped to his aluminum checkboard. In the blazing sun, O'Neill's arms were tanned, furry, glistening with sweat. Wiry, with tangled gray hair, horn-rimmed glasses, he was older than the other two. He wore slacks, a sports shirt and crepe-soled shoes. Between his fingers, his fountain pen glittered, metallic and efficient.

"What're you writing?" Perine grumbled.

"I'm laying out the procedure we're going to employ," O'Neill said mildly. "Better to systemize it now, instead of trying at random. We want to know what we tried and what didn't work. Otherwise we'll go around in a circle. The problem we have here is one of communication; that's how I see it."

"Communication," Morrison agreed in his deep, chesty voice. "Yes, we can't get in touch with the damn thing. It comes, leaves off its load and goes on — there's no contact between us and it."

"It's a machine," Perine said excitedly. "It's dead — blind and deaf."

1

2 PHILIP K. DICK

"But it's in contact with the outside world," O'Neill pointed out. "There has to be some way to get to it. Specific semantic signals are meaningful to it; all we have to do is find those signals. Rediscover, actually. Maybe half a dozen out of a billion possibilities."

A low rumble interrupted the three men. They glanced up, wary and alert. The time had come.

"Here it is," Perine said. "Okay, wise guy, let's see you make one single change in its routine."

The truck was massive, rumbling under its tightly packed load. In many ways, it resembled conventional human-operated transportation vehicles, but with one exception — there was no driver's cabin. The horizontal surface was a loading stage, and the part that would normally be the headlights and radiator grill was a fibrous spongelike mass of receptors, the limited sensory apparatus of this mobile utility extension.

Aware of the three men, the truck slowed to a halt, shifted gears and pulled on its emergency brake. A moment passed as relays moved into action; then a portion of the loading surface tilted and a cascade of heavy cartons spilled down onto the roadway. With the objects fluttered a detailed inventory sheet.

"You know what to do," O'Neill said rapidly. "Hurry up, before it gets out of here."

Expertly, grimly, the three men grabbed up the deposited cartons and ripped the protective wrappers from them. Objects gleamed: a binocular microscope, a portable radio, heaps of plastic dishes, medical supplies, razor blades, clothing, food. Most of the shipment, as usual, was food. The three men systematically began smashing objects. In a few minutes, there was nothing but a chaos of debris littered around them.

"That's that," O'Neill panted, stepping back. He fumbled for his checksheet. "Now let's see what it does."

The truck had begun to move away; abruptly it stopped and backed toward them. Its receptors had taken in the fact that the three men had demolished the dropped-off portion of the load. It spun in a grinding half circle and came around to face its receptor bank in their direction. Up went its antenna; it had begun communicating with the factory. Instructions were on the way.

A second, identical load was tilted and shoved off the truck.

"We failed," Perine groaned as a duplicate inventory sheet fluttered after the new load. "We destroyed all that stuff for nothing."

"What now?" Morrison asked O'Neill. "What's the next strategem on our board?"

"Give me a hand." O'Neill grabbed up a carton and lugged it back to the truck. Sliding the carton onto the platform, he turned for another. The other two men followed clumsily after him. They put the load back onto the truck. As the truck started forward, the last square box was again in place.

The truck hesitated. Its receptors registered the return of its load. From within its works came a low sustained buzzing.

"This may drive it crazy," O'Neill commented, sweating. "It went through its operation and accomplished nothing."

The truck made a short, abortive move toward going on. Then it swung purposefully around and, in a blur of speed, again dumped the load onto the road.

"Get them!" O'Neill yelled. The three men grabbed up the cartons and feverishly reloaded them. But as fast as the cartons were shoved back on the horizontal stage, the truck's grapples tilted them down its far-side ramps and onto the road.

"No use," Morrison said, breathing hard. "Water through a sieve."

"We're licked," Perine gasped in wretched agreement, "like always. We humans lose every time."

The truck regarded them calmly, its receptors blank and impassive. It was doing its job. The planetwide network of automatic factories was smoothly performing the task imposed on it five years before, in the early days of the Total Global Conflict.

"There it goes," Morrison observed dismally. The truck's antenna had come down; it shifted into low gear and released its parking brake.

"One last try," O'Neill said. He swept up one off the cartons and ripped it open. From it he dragged a ten-gallon milk tank and unscrewed the lid. "Silly as it seems."

"This is absurd," Perine protested. Reluctantly, he found a cup among the littered debris and dipped it into the milk. "A kid's game!"

The truck has paused to observe them.

"Do it," O'Neill ordered sharply. "Exactly the way we practiced it."

The three of them drank quickly from the milk tank, visibly allowing the milk to spill down their chins; there had to be no mistaking what they were doing.

As planned, O'Neill was the first. His face twisting in revulsion, he hurled the cup away and violently spat the milk into the road.

"God's sake!" he choked.

The other two did the same; stamping and loudly cursing, they kicked over the milk tank and glared accusingly at the truck.

"It's no good!" Morrison roared.

Curious, the truck came slowly back. Electronic synapses clicked and whirred, responding to the situation; its antenna shot up like a flagpole.

"I think this is it," O'Neill said, trembling. As the truck watched, he dragged out a second milk tank, unscrewed its lid and tasted the contents. "The same!" he shouted at the truck. "It's just as bad!"

From the truck popped a metal cylinder. The cylinder dropped at Morrison's feet; he quickly snatched it up and tore it open.

STATE NATURE OF DEFECT

The instruction sheets listed rows of possible defects, with neat boxes by each; a punch-stick was included to indicate the particular deficiency of the product.

"What'll I check?" Morrison asked. "Contaminated? Bacterial? Sour? Rancid? Incorrectly labeled? Broken? Crushed? Cracked? Bent? Soiled?"

Thinking rapidly, O'Neill said, "Don't check any of them. The factory's undoubtedly ready to test and resample. It'll make its own analysis and then ignore us." His face glowed as frantic inspiration came. "Write in that blank at the bottom. It's an open space for further data."

"Write what?"

O'Neill said, "Write: *the product is thoroughly pizzled.*"

"What's that?" Perine demanded, baffled.

"Write it! It's a semantic garble — the factory won't be able to understand it. Maybe we can jam the works."

With O'Neill's pen, Morrison carefully wrote that the milk was pizzled. Shaking his head, he resealed the cylinder and returned it to the truck. The truck swept up the milk tanks and slammed its railing tidily into place. With a shriek of tires, it hurtled off. From its slot, a final cylinder bounced; the truck hurriedly departed, leaving the cylinder lying in the dust.

O'Neill got it open and held up the paper for the others to see.

A FACTOR REPRESENTATIVE
WILL BE SENT OUT.
BE PREPARED TO SUPPLY COMPLETE DATA
ON PRODUCT DEFICIENCY.

For a moment, the three men were silent. Then Perine began to giggle. "We did it. We contacted it. We got across."

"We sure did," O'Neill agreed. "It never heard of a product being pizzled."

Cut into the base of the mountains lay the vast metallic cube of the Kansas City factory. Its surface was corroded, pitted with radiation pox, cracked and scarred from the five years of war that had swept over it. Most of the factory was buried subsurface, only its entrance stages visible. The truck was a speck rumbling at high speed toward the expanse of black metal. Presently an opening formed in the uniform surface; the truck plunged into it and disappeared inside. The entrance snapped shut.

"Now the big job remains," O'Neill said. "Now we have to persuade it to close down operations — to shut itself off."

II

Judith O'Neill served hot black coffee to the people sitting around the living room. Her husband talked while the others listened. O'Neill was as close to being an authority on the autofac system as could still be found.

In his own area, the Chicago region, he had shorted out the protective fence of the local factory long enough to get away with data tapes stored in its posterior brain. The factory, of course, had immediately reconstructed a better type of fence. But he had shown that the factories were not infallible.

"The Institute of Applied Cybernetics," O'Neill explained, "had complete control over the network. Blame the war. Blame the big noise along the lines of communication that wiped out the knowledge we need. In any case, the Institute failed to transmit its information to us, so we can't transmit our information to the factories — the news that the war is over and we're ready to resume control of industrial operations."

"And meanwhile," Morrison added sourly, "the damn network expands and consumes more of our natural resources all the time."

"I get the feeling," Judith said, "that if I stamped hard enough, I'd fall right down into a factory tunnel. They must have mines everywhere by now."

"Isn't there some limiting injunction?" Perine asked nervously. "Were they set up to expand indefinitely?"

"Each factory is limited to its own operational area," O'Neill said, "but the network itself is unbounded. It can go on scooping up our resources forever. The Institute decided it gets top priority; we mere people come second."

"Will there be *anything* left for us?" Morrison wanted to know.

"Not unless we can stop the network's operations. It's already used up half a dozen basic minerals. Its search teams are out all the time, from every factory, looking everywhere for some last scrap to drag home."

"What would happen if tunnels from two factories crossed each other?"

O'Neill shrugged. "Normally, that won't happen. Each factory has its own special section of our planet, its own private cut of the pie for its exclusive use."

"But it *could* happen."

"Well, they're raw material-tropic; as long as there's anything left, they'll hunt it down." O'Neill pondered the idea with growing interest. "It's something to consider. I suppose as things get scarcer — "

He stopped talking. A figure had come into the room; it stood silently by the door, surveying them all.

In the dull shadows, the figure looked almost human. For a brief moment,

O'Neill thought it was a settlement latecomer. Then, as it moved forward, he realized that it was only quasi-human: a functional upright biped chassis, with data-receptors mounted at the top, effectors and proprioceptors mounted in a downward worm that ended in floor-grippers. Its resemblance to a human being was testimony to nature's efficiency; no sentimental imitation was intended.

The factory representative had arrived.

It began without preamble. "This is a data-collecting machine capable of communicating on an oral basis. It contains both broadcasting and receiving apparatus and can integrate facts relevant to its line of inquiry."

The voice was pleasant, confident. Obviously it was a tape, recorded by some Institute technician before the war. Coming from the quasi-human shape, it sounded grotesque; O'Neill could vividly imagine the dead young man whose cheerful voice now issued from the mechanical mouth of this upright construction of steel and wiring.

"One word of caution," the pleasant voice continued. "It is fruitless to consider this receptor human and to engage it in discussions for which it is not equipped. Although purposeful, it is not capable of conceptual thought; it can only reassemble material already available to it."

The optimistic voice clicked out and a second voice came on. It resembled the first, but now there were no intonations or personal mannerisms. The machine was utilizing the dead man's phonetic speech-pattern for its own communication.

"Analysis of the rejected product," it stated, "shows no foreign elements or noticeable deterioration. The product meets the continual testing-standards employed throughout the network. Rejection is therefore on a basis outside the test area; standards not available to the network are being employed."

"That's right," O'Neill agreed. Weighing his words with care, he continued, "We found the milk substandard. We want nothing to do with it. We insist on more careful output."

The machine responded presently. "The semantic content of the term 'pizzled' is unfamiliar to the network. It does not exist in the taped vocabulary. Can you present a factual analysis of the milk in terms of specific elements present or absent?"

"No," O'Neill said warily; the game he was playing was intricate and dangerous. " 'Pizzled' is an overall term. It can't be reduced to chemical constituents."

"What does 'pizzled' signify?" the machine asked. "Can you define it in terms of alternate semantic symbols?"

O'Neill hesitated. The representative had to be steered from its special inquiry to more general regions, to the ultimate problem of closing down the network. If he could pry it open at any point, get the theoretical discussion started ...

" 'Pizzled,' " he stated, "means the condition of a product that is manufactured when no need exists. It indicates the rejection of objects on the grounds that they are no longer wanted."

The representative said, "Network analysis shows a need of high-grade pasteurized milk-substitute in this area. There is no alternate source; the network controls all the synthetic mammary-type equipment in existence." It added, "Original taped instructions describe milk as an essential to human diet."

O'Neill was being outwitted; the machine was returning the discussion to the specific. "We've decided," he said desperately, "that we don't *want* any more milk. We'd prefer to go without it, at least until we can locate cows."

"That is contrary to the network tapes," the representative objected. "There are no cows. All milk is produced synthetically."

"Then we'll produce it synthetically ourselves," Morrison broke in impatiently. "Why can't we take over the machines? My God, we're not children! We can run our own lives!"

The factory representative moved toward the door. "Until such time as your community finds other sources of milk supply, the network will continue to supply you. Analytical and evaluating apparatus will remain in this area, conducting the customary random sampling."

Perine shouted futilely, "How can we find other sources? You have the whole setup! You're running the whole show!" Following after it, he bellowed, "You say we're not ready to run things — you claim we're not capable. How do you know? You don't give us a chance! We'll never have a chance!"

O'Neill was petrified. The machine was leaving; its one-track mind had completely triumphed.

"Look," he said hoarsely, blocking its way. "We want you to shut down, understand. We want to take over your equipment and run it ourselves. The war's over with. Damn it, you're not needed anymore!"

The factory representative paused briefly at the door. "The inoperative cycle," it said, "is not geared to begin until network production merely duplicates outside production. There is at this time, according to our continual sampling, no outside production. Therefore network production continues."

Without warning, Morrison swung the steel pipe in his hand. It slashed against the machine's shoulder and burst through the elaborate network of sensory apparatus that made up its chest. The tank of receptors shattered; bits of glass, wiring and minute parts showered everywhere.

"It's a paradox!" Morrison yelled. "A word game — a semantic game they're pulling on us. The Cyberneticists have it rigged." He raised the pipe and again brought it down savagely on the unprotesting machine. "They've got us hamstrung. We're completely helpless."

The room was in uproar. "It's the only way," Perine gasped as he pushed past O'Neill. "We'll have to destroy them — it's the network or us." Grabbing down a lamp, he hurled it in the "face" of the factory representative. The lamp and the intricate surface of plastic burst; Perine waded in, groping blindly for the machine. Now all the people in the room were closing furiously around the upright cylinder, their impotent resentment boiling over. The machine sank down and disappeared as they dragged it to the floor.

Trembling, O'Neill turned away. His wife caught hold of his arm and led him to the side of the room.

"The idiots," he said dejectedly. "They can't destroy it; they'll only teach it to build more defenses. They're making the whole problem worse."

Into the living room rolled a network repair team. Expertly, the mechanical units detached themselves from the half-track mother-bug and scurried toward the mound of struggling humans. They slid between people and rapidly burrowed. A moment later, the inert carcass of the factory representative was dragged into the hopper of the mother-bug. Parts were collected, torn remnants gathered up and carried off. The plastic strut and gear was located. Then the units restationed themselves on the bug and the team departed.

Through the open door came a second factory representative, an exact duplicate of the first. And outside in the hall stood two more upright machines. The settlement had been combed at random by a corps of representatives. Like a horde of ants, the mobile data-collecting machines had filtered through the town until, by chance, one of them had come across O'Neill.

"Destruction of network mobile data-gathering equipment is detrimental to best human interests," the factory representative informed the roomful of people. "Raw material intake is at a dangerously low ebb; what basic materials still exist should be utilized in the manufacture of consumer commodities."

O'Neill and the machine stood facing each other.

"Oh?" O'Neill said softly. "That's interesting. I wonder what you're lowest on — and what you'd really be willing to fight for."

Helicopter rotors whined tinnily above O'Neill's head; he ignored them and peered through the cabin window at the ground not far below.

Slag and ruins stretched everywhere. Weeds poked their way up, sickly stalks among which insects scuttled. Here and there, rat colonies were visible: matted hovels constructed of bone and rubble. Radiation had mutated the rats, along with most insects and animals. A little farther, O'Neill identified a squadron of birds pursuing a ground squirrel. The squirrel dived into a carefully prepared crack in the surface of slag and the birds turned, thwarted.

"You think we'll ever have it rebuilt?" Morrison asked. "It makes me sick to look at it."

"In time," O'Neill answered. "Assuming, of course, that we get industrial control back. And assuming that anything remains to work with. At best, it'll be slow. We'll have to inch out from the settlements."

To the right was a human colony, tattered scarecrows, gaunt and emaciated, living among the ruins of what had once been a town. A few acres of barren soil had been cleared; drooping vegetables wilted in the sun, chickens wandered listlessly here and there, and a fly-bothered horse lay panting in the shade of a crude shed.

"Ruins-squatters," O'Neill said gloomily. "Too far from the network — not tangent to any of the factories."

"It's their own fault," Morrison told him angrily. "They could come into one of the settlements."

"That was their town. They're trying to do what *we're* trying to do — build up things again on their own. But they're starting now, without tools or machines, with their bare hands, nailing together bits of rubble. And it won't work. We need machines. We can't repair ruins; we've got to start industrial production."

Ahead lay a series of broken hills, chipped remains that had once been a ridge. Beyond stretched out the titanic ugly sore of an H-bomb crater, half filled with stagnant water and slime, a disease-ridden inland sea.

And beyond that — a glitter of busy motion.

"There," O'Neill said tensely. He lowered the helicopter rapidly. "Can you tell which factory they're from?"

"They all look alike to me," Morrison muttered, leaning over to see. "We'll have to wait and follow them back, when they get a load."

"*If* they get a load," O'Neill corrected.

The autofac exploring crew ignored the helicopter buzzing overhead and concentrated on its job. Ahead of the main truck scuttled two tractors; they made their way up mounds of rubble, probes burgeoning like quills, shot down the far slope and disappeared into a blanket of ash that lay spread over the slag. The two scouts burrowed until only their antennas were visible. They burst up to the surface and scuttled on, their treads whirring and clanking.

"What are they after?" Morrison asked.

"God knows." O'Neill leafed intently through the papers on his clipboard. "We'll have to analyze all our back-order slips."

Below them, the autofac exploring crew disappeared behind. The helicopter passed over a deserted stretch of sand and slag on which nothing moved. A grove of scrub-brush appeared and then, far to the right, a series of tiny moving dots.

A procession of automatic ore carts was racing over the bleak slag, a string of rapidly moving metal trucks that followed one another nose to tail. O'Neill turned the helicopter toward them and a few minutes later it hovered above the mine itself.

Masses of squat mining equipment had made their way to the operations. Shafts had been sunk; empty carts waited in patient rows. A steady stream of loaded carts hurled toward the horizon, dribbling ore after them. Activity and the noise of machines hung over the area, an abrupt center of industry in the bleak wastes of slag.

"Here comes that exploring crew," Morrison observed, peering back the way they had come. "You think maybe they'll tangle?" He grinned. "No, I guess it's too much to hope for."

"It is this time," O'Neill answered. "They're looking for different substances, probably. And they're normally conditioned to ignore each other."

The first of the exploring bugs reached the line of ore carts. It veered slightly and continued its search; the carts traveled in their inexorable line as if nothing had happened.

Disappointed, Morrison turned away from the window and swore. "No use. It's like each doesn't exist for the other."

Gradually the exploring crew moved away from the line of carts, past the mining operations and over a ridge beyond. There was no special hurry; they departed without having reacted to the ore-gathering syndrome.

"Maybe they're from the same factory," Morrison said hopefully.

O'Neill pointed to the antennas visible on the major mining equipment. "Their vanes are turned at a different vector, so these represent two factories. It's going to be hard; we'll have to get it exactly right or there won't be any reaction." He clicked on the radio and got hold of the monitor at the settlement. "Any results on the consolidated back-order sheets?"

The operator put him through to the settlement governing offices.

"They're starting to come in," Perine told him. "As soon as we get sufficient samplings, we'll try to determine which raw materials which factories lack. It's going to be risky, trying to extrapolate from complex products. There may be a number of basic elements common to the various sublots."

"What happens when we've identified the missing element?" Morrison asked O'Neill. "What happens when we've got two tangent factories short on the same material?"

"Then," O'Neill said grimly, "we start collecting the material ourselves — even if we have to melt down every object in the settlements."

III

In the moth-ridden darkness of night, a dim wind stirred, chill and faint. Dense underbrush rattled metallically. Here and there a nocturnal rodent prowled, its senses hyper-alert, peering, planning, seeking food.

The area was wild. No human settlements existed for miles; the entire region had been seared flat, cauterized by repeated H-bomb blasts. Somewhere in the murky darkness, a sluggish trickle of water made its way among slag and weeds, dripping thickly into what had once been an elaborate labyrinth of sewer mains. The pipes lay cracked and broken, jutting up into the night darkness, overgrown with creeping vegetation. The wind raised clouds of black ash that swirled and danced among the weeds. Once an enormous mutant wren stirred sleepily, pulled its crude protective night coat of rags around it and dozed off.

For a time, there was no movement. A streak of stars showed in the sky overhead, glowing starkly, remotely. Earl Perine shivered, peered up and huddled closer to the pulsing heat-element placed on the ground between the three men.

"Well?" Morrison challenged, teeth chattering.

O'Neill didn't answer. He finished his cigarette, crushed it against a mound of decaying slag and, getting out his lighter, lit another. The mass of tungsten — the bait — lay a hundred yards directly ahead of them.

During the last few days, both the Detroit and Pittsburgh factories had run short of tungsten. And in at least one sector, their apparatus overlapped. This sluggish heap represented precision cutting tools, parts ripped from electrical switches, high-quality surgical equipment, sections of permanent magnets, measuring devices — tungsten from every possible source, gathered feverishly from all the settlements.

Dark mist lay spread over the tungsten mound. Occasionally, a night moth fluttered down, attracted by the glow of reflected starlight. The moth hung momentarily, beat its elongated wings futilely against the interwoven tangle of metal and then drifted off, into the shadows of the thick-packed vines that rose up from the stumps of sewer pipes.

"Not a very damn pretty spot," Perine said wryly.

"Don't kid yourself," O'Neill retorted. "This is the prettiest spot on Earth. This is the spot that marks the grave of the autofac network. People are going to come around here looking for it someday. There's going to be a plaque here a mile high."

"You're trying to keep your morale up," Morrison snorted. "You don't believe they're going to slaughter themselves over a heap of surgical tools and light-bulb filaments. They've probably got a machine down in the bottom level that sucks tungsten out of rock."

"Maybe," O'Neill said, slapping at a mosquito. The insect dodged cannily and then buzzed over to annoy Perine. Perine swung viciously at it and squatted sullenly down against the damp vegetation.

And there was what they had come to see.

O'Neill realized with a start that he had been looking at it for several minutes without recognizing it. The search-bug lay absolutely still. It rested at the crest of a small rise of slag, its anterior end slightly raised, receptors fully extended. It might have been an abandoned hulk; there was no activity of any kind, no sign of life or consciousness. The search-bug fitted perfectly into the wasted, fire-drenched landscape. A vague tub of metal sheets and gears and flat treads, it rested and waited. And watched.

It was examining the heap of tungsten. The bait had drawn its first bite.

"Fish," Perine said thickly. "The line moved. I think the sinker dropped."

"What the hell are you mumbling about?" Morrison grunted. And then he, too, saw the search-bug. "Jesus," he whispered. He half rose to his feet, massive body arched forward. "Well, there's *one* of them. Now all we need is a unit from the other factory. Which do you suppose it is?"

O'Neill located the communication vane and traced its angle. "Pittsburgh, so pray for Detroit ... pray like mad."

Satisfied, the search-bug detached itself and rolled forward. Cautiously approaching the mound, it began a series of intricate maneuvers, rolling first one way and then another. The three watching men were mystified — until they glimpsed the first probing stalks of other search-bugs.

"Communication," O'Neill said softly. "Like bees."

Now five Pittsburgh search-bugs were approaching the mound of tungsten products. Receptors waving excitedly, they increased their pace, scurrying in a sudden burst of discovery up the side of the mound to the top. A bug burrowed and rapidly disappeared. The whole mound shuddered; the bug was down inside, exploring the extent of the find.

Ten minutes later, the first Pittsburgh ore carts appeared and began industriously hurrying off with their haul.

"Damn it!" O'Neill said, agonized. "They'll have it all before Detroit shows up."

"Can't we do anything to slow them down?" Perine demanded helplessly. Leaping to his feet, he grabbed up a rock and heaved it at the nearest cart. The rock bounced off and the cart continued its work, unperturbed.

O'Neill got to his feet and prowled around, body rigid with impotent fury. Where were they? The autofacs were equal in all respects and the spot was the exact same linear distance from each center. Theoretically, the parties should have arrived simultaneously. Yet there was no sign of Detroit — and the final pieces of tungsten were being loaded before his eyes.

But then something streaked past him.

He didn't recognize it, for the object moved too quickly. It shot like a bullet among the tangled vines, raced up the side of the hill-crest, poised for an instant to aim itself and hurtled down the far side. It smashed directly into the lead cart. Projectile and victim shattered in an abrupt burst of sound.

Morrison leaped up. "What the hell?"

"That's it!" Perine screamed, dancing around and waving his skinny arms. "It's Detroit!"

A second Detroit search-bug appeared, hesitated as it took in the situation, and then flung itself furiously at the retreating Pittsburgh carts. Fragments of tungsten scattered everywhere — parts, wiring, broken plates, gears and springs and bolts of the two antagonists flew in all directions. The remaining carts wheeled screechingly; one of them dumped its load and rattled off at top speed. A second followed, still weighed down with tungsten. A Detroit search-bug caught up with it, spun directly in its path and neatly overturned it. Bug and cart rolled down a shallow trench, into a stagnant pool of water. Dripping and glistening, the two of them struggled, half submerged.

"Well," O'Neill said unsteadily, "we did it. We can start back home." His legs felt weak. "Where's our vehicle?"

As he gunned the truck motor, something flashed a long way off, something large and metallic, moving over the dead slag and ash. It was a dense clot of carts, a solid expanse of heavy-duty ore carriers racing to the scene. Which factory were they from?

It didn't matter, for out of the thick tangle of black dripping vines, a web of counter-extensions was creeping to meet them. Both factories were assembling their mobile units. From all directions, bugs slithered and crept, closing in around the remaining heap of tungsten. Neither factory was going to let needed raw material get away; neither was going to give up its find. Blindly, mechanically, in the grip of inflexible directives, the two opponents labored to assemble superior forces.

"Come on," Morrison said urgently. "Let's get out of here. All hell is bursting loose."

O'Neill hastily turned the truck in the direction of the settlement. They began rumbling through the darkness on their way back. Every now and then, a metallic shape shot by them, going in the opposite direction.

"Did you see the load in that last cart?" Perine asked, worried. "It wasn't empty."

Neither were the carts that followed it, a whole procession of bulging supply carriers directed by an elaborate high-level surveying unit.

"Guns," Morrison said, eyes wide with apprehension. "They're taking in weapons. But who's going to use them?"

"They are," O'Neill answered. He indicated a movement to their right. "Look over there. This is something we hadn't expected."

They were seeing the first factory representative move into action.

As the truck pulled into the Kansas City settlement, Judith hurried breathlessly toward them. Fluttering in her hand was a strip of metal-foil paper.

"What is it?" O'Neill demanded, grabbing it from her.

"Just come." His wife struggled to catch her breath. "A mobile car — raced up, dropped it off — and left. Big excitement. Golly, the factory's — a blaze of lights. You can see it for miles."

O'Neill scanned the paper. It was a factory certification for the last group of settlement-placed orders, a total tabulation of requested and factory-analyzed needs. Stamped across the list in heavy black type were six foreboding words:

ALL SHIPMENTS SUSPENDED UNTIL FURTHER NOTICE

Letting out his breath harshly, O'Neill handed the paper over to Perine. "No more consumer goods," he said ironically, a nervous grin twitching across his face. "The network's going on a wartime footing."

"Then we did it?" Morrison asked haltingly.

"That's right," O'Neill said. Now that the conflict had been sparked, he felt a growing, frigid terror. "Pittsburgh and Detroit are in it to the finish. It's too late for us to change our minds, now — they're lining up allies."

IV

Cool morning sunlight lay across the ruined plain of black metallic ash. The ash smoldered a dull, unhealthy red; it was still warm.

"Watch your step," O'Neill cautioned. Grabbing hold of his wife's arm, he led her from the rusty, sagging truck, up onto the top of a pile of strewn concrete blocks, the scattered remains of a pillbox installation. Earl Perine followed, making his way carefully, hesitantly.

Behind them, the dilapidated settlement lay spread out, a disorderly checkerboard of houses, buildings and streets. Since the autofac network had closed down its supply and maintenance, the human settlements had fallen into semibarbarism. The commodities that remained were broken and only partly usable. It had been over a year since the last mobile factory truck had appeared, loaded with food, tools, clothing and repair parts. From the flat expanse of dark concrete and metal at the foot of the mountains, nothing had emerged in their direction.

Their wish had been granted — they were cut off, detached from the network.

On their own.

Around the settlement grew ragged fields of wheat and tattered stalks of sun-baked vegetables. Crude handmade tools had been distributed, primitive artifacts hammered out with great labor by the various settlements. The settlements were linked only by horsedrawn carts and by the slow stutter of the telegraph key.

They had managed to keep their organization, though. Goods and services were exchanged on a slow, steady basis. Basic commodities were produced and distributed. The clothing that O'Neill and his wife and Earl Perine wore was coarse and unbleached, but sturdy. And they had managed to convert a few of the trucks from gasoline to wood.

"Here we are," O'Neill said. "We can see from here."

"Is it worth it?" Judith asked, exhausted. Bending down, she plucked aimlessly at her shoe, trying to dig a pebble from the soft hide sole. "It's a long way to come, to see something we've seen every day for thirteen months."

"True," O'Neill admitted, his hand briefly resting on his wife's limp shoulder. "But this may be the last. And that's what we want to see."

In the gray sky above them, a swift circling dot of opaque black moved. High, remote, the dot spun and darted, following an intricate and wary course. Gradually, its gyrations moved it toward the mountains and the bleak expanse of bomb-rubbled structure sunk in their base.

"San Francisco," O'Neill explained. "One of those long-range hawk projectiles, all the way from the West Coast."

"And you think it's the last?" Perine asked.

"It's the only one we've seen this month." O'Neill seated himself and began sprinkling dried bits of tobacco into a trench of brown paper. "And we used to see hundreds."

"Maybe they have something better," Judith suggested. She found a smooth rock and tiredly seated herself. "Could it be?"

Her husband smiled ironically. "No. They don't have anything better."

The three of them were tensely silent. Above them, the circling dot of black drew closer. There was no sign of activity from the flat surface of metal and concrete; the Kansas City factory remained inert, totally unresponsive. A few billows of warm ash drifted across it and one end was partly submerged in rubble. The factory had taken numerous direct hits. Across the plain, the furrows of its subsurface tunnels lay exposed, clogged with debris and the dark, water-seeking tendrils of tough vines.

"Those damn vines," Perine grumbled, picking at an old sore on his unshaven chin. "They're taking over the world."

Here and there around the factory, the demolished ruin of a mobile extension rusted in the morning dew. Carts, trucks, search-bugs, factory representatives, weapons carriers, guns, supply trains, subsurface projectiles, indiscriminate parts of machinery mixed and fused together in shapeless piles. Some had been destroyed returning to the factory; others had been contacted as they emerged, fully loaded, heavy with equipment. The factory itself — what remained of it — seemed to have settled more deeply into the earth. Its upper surface was barely visible, almost lost in drifting ash.

In four days, there had been no known activity, no visible movement of any sort.

"It's dead," Perine said. "You can see it's dead."

O'Neill didn't answer. Squatting down, he made himself comfortable and prepared to wait. In his own mind, he was sure that some fragment of automation remained in the eroded factory. Time would tell. He examined his wrist-watch; it was eight thirty. In the old days, the factory would be starting its daily routine. Processions of trucks and varied mobile units would be coming to the surface, loaded with supplies, to begin their expeditions to the human settle-ment.

Off to the right, something stirred. He quickly turned his attention to it.

A single battered ore-gathering cart was creeping clumsily toward the factory. One last damaged mobile unit trying to complete its task. The cart was virtually empty; a few meager scraps of metal lay strewn in its hold. A scavenger ... the metal was sections ripped from destroyed equipment encountered on the way. Feebly, like a blind metallic insect, the cart approached the factory. Its progress was incredibly jerky. Every now and then, it halted, bucked and quivered, and wandered aimlessly off the path.

"Control is bad," Judith said, with a touch of horror in her voice. "The factory's having trouble guiding it back."

Yes, he had seen that. Around New York, the factory had lost its high-fre-quency transmitter completely. Its mobile units had floundered in crazy gyra-tions, racing in random circles, crashing against rocks and trees, sliding into gullies, overturning, finally unwinding and becoming reluctantly inanimate.

The ore cart reached the edge of the ruined plain and halted briefly. Above it, the dot of black still circled the sky. For a time, the cart remained frozen.

"The factory's trying to decide," Perine said. "It needs the material, but it's afraid of that hawk up there."

The factory debated and nothing stirred. Then the ore cart again resumed its unsteady crawl. It left the tangle of vines and started out across the blasted open plain. Painfully, with infinite caution, it headed toward the slab of dark concrete and metal at the base of the mountains.

The hawk stopped circling.

"Get down!" O'Neill said sharply. "They've got those rigged with the new bombs."

His wife and Perine crouched down beside him and the three of them peered warily at the plain and the metal insect crawling laboriously across it. In the sky, the hawk swept in a straight line until it hung directly over the cart. Then, without a sound or warning, it came down in a straight dive. Hands to her face, Judith shrieked, "I can't watch! It's awful! Like wild animals!"

"It's not after the cart," O'Neill grated.

As the airborne projectile dropped, the cart put on a burst of desperate speed. It raced noisily toward the factory, clanking and rattling, trying in a last futile attempt to reach safely. Forgetting the menace above, the frantically eager factory opened up and guided its mobile unit directly inside. And the hawk had what it wanted.

Before the barrier could close, the hawk swooped down in a long glide parallel with the ground. As the cart disappeared into the depths of the factory, the hawk shot after it, a swift shimmer of metal that hurtled past the clanking cart. Suddenly aware, the factory snapped the barrier shut. Grotesquely, the cart struggled; it was caught fast in the half-closed entrance.

But whether it freed itself didn't matter. There was a dull rumbling stir. The ground moved, billowed, then settled back. A deep shock wave passed beneath the three watching human beings. From the factory rose a single column of black smoke. The surface of concrete split like a dried pod; it shriveled and broke, and dribbled shattered bits of itself in a shower of ruin. The smoke hung for a while, drifting aimlessly away with the morning wind.

The factory was a fused, gutted wreck. It had been penetrated and destroyed.

O'Neill got stiffly to his feet. "That's all. All over with. We've got what we set out after — we've destroyed the autofac network." He glanced at Perine. "Or was that what we were after?"

They looked toward the settlement that lay behind them. Little remained of the orderly rows of houses and streets of the previous years. Without the network, the settlement had rapidly decayed. The original prosperous neatness had dissipated; the settlement was shabby, ill-kept.

"Of course," Perine said haltingly. "Once we get into the factories and start setting up our own assembly lines ... "

"Is there anything left?" Judith inquired.

"There must be something left. My God, there were levels going down miles!"

"Some of those bombs they developed toward the end were awfully big," Judith pointed out. "Better than anything we had in our war."

"Remember that camp we saw? The ruins-squatters?"

"I wasn't along," Perine said.

"They were like wild animals. Eating roots and larvae. Sharpening rocks, tanning hides. Savagery, bestiality."

"But that's what people like that want," Perine answered defensively

"Do they? Do we want this?" O'Neill indicated the straggling settlement. "Is this what we set out looking for, that day we collected the tungsten? Or that day we told the factory truck its milk was — " He couldn't remember the word.

"Pizzled," Judith supplied.

"Come on," O'Neill said. "Let's get started. Let's see what's left of that factory — left for us."

They approached the ruined factory late in the afternoon. Four trucks rumbled shakily up to the rim of the gutted pit and halted, motors steaming, tailpipes dripping. Wary and alert, workmen scrambled down and stepped gingerly across the hot ash.

"Maybe it's too soon," one of them objected.

O'Neill had no intention of waiting. "Come on," he ordered. Grabbing up a flashlight, he stepped down into the crater.

The sheltered hull of the Kansas City factory lay directly ahead. In its gutted mouth, the ore cart still hung caught, but it was no longer struggling. Beyond the cart was an ominous pool of gloom. O'Neill flashed his light through the entrance; the tangled, jagged remains of upright supports were visible.

"We want to get down deep," he said to Morrison, who prowled cautiously beside him. "If there's anything left, it's at the bottom."

Morrison grunted. "Those boring moles from Atlanta got most of the deep layers."

"Until the others got their mines sunk." O'Neill stepped carefully through the sagging entrance, climbed a heap of debris that had been tossed against the slit from inside, and found himself within the factory — an expanse of confused wreckage, without pattern or meaning.

"Entropy," Morrison breathed, oppressed. "The thing it always hated. The thing it was built to fight. Random particles everywhere. No purpose to it."

"Down underneath," O'Neill said stubbornly, "we may find some sealed enclaves. I know they got so they were dividing up into autonomous sections, trying to preserve repair units intact, to re-form the composite factory."

"The moles got most of them, too," Morrison observed, but he lumbered after O'Neill.

Behind them, the workmen came slowly. A section of wreckage shifted ominously and a shower of hot fragments cascaded down.

"You men get back to the trucks," O'Neill said. "No sense endangering any more of us than we have to. If Morrison and I don't come back, forget us — don't risk sending a rescue party." As they left, he pointed out to Morrison a descending ramp still partially intact. "Let's get below."

Silently, the two men passed one dead level after another. Endless miles of dark ruin stretched out, without sound or activity. The vague shapes of darkened machinery, unmoving belts and conveyer equipment were partially visible, and the partially completed husks of war projectiles, bent and twisted by the final blast.

"We can salvage some of that," O'Neill said, but he didn't actually believe it. The machinery was fused, shapeless. Everything in the factory had run together, molten slag without form or use. "Once we get it to the surface ... "

"We can't," Morrison contradicted bitterly. "We don't have hoists or winches." He kicked at a heap of charred supplies that had stopped along its broken belt and spilled halfway across the ramp.

"It seemed like a good idea at the time," O'Neill said as the two of them continued past vacant levels of machines. "But now that I look back, I'm not so sure."

They had penetrated a long way into the factory. The final level lap spread out ahead of them. O'Neill flashed the light here and there, trying to locate undestroyed sections, portions of the assembly process still intact.

It was Morrison who felt it first. He suddenly dropped to his hands and knees; heavy body pressed against the floor, he lay listening, face hard, eyes wide. "For God's sake — "

"What is it?" O'Neill cried. Then he, too, felt it. Beneath them, a faint, insistent vibration hummed through the floor, a steady hum of activity. They had been wrong; the hawk had not been totally successful. Below, in a deeper level, the factory was still alive. Closed, limited operations still went on.

"On its own," O'Neill muttered, searching for an extension of the descent lift. "Autonomous activity, set to continue after the rest is gone. How do we get down?"

The descent lift was broken off, sealed by a thick section of metal. The still-living layer beneath their feet was completely cut off; there was no entrance.

Racing back the way they had come, O'Neill reached the surface and hailed the first truck. "Where the hell's the torch? Give it here!"

The precious blowtorch was passed to him and he hurried back, puffing, into the depths of the ruined factory where Morrison waited. Together, the two of them began frantically cutting through the warped metal flooring, burning apart the sealed layers of protective mesh.

"It's coming," Morrison gasped, squinting in the glare of the torch. The plate fell with a clang, disappearing into the level below. A blaze of white light burst up around them and the two men leaped back.

In the sealed chamber, furious activity boomed and echoed, a steady process of moving belts, whirring machine-tools, fast-moving mechanical supervisors. At one end, a steady flow of raw materials entered the line; at the far end, the final product was whipped off, inspected and crammed into a conveyer tube.

All this was visible for a split second; then the intrusion was discovered. Robot relays came into play. The blaze of lights flickered and dimmed. The assembly line froze to a halt, stopped in its furious activity.

The machines clicked off and became silent.

At one end, a mobile unit detached itself and sped up the wall toward the hole O'Neill and Morrison had cut. It slammed an emergency seal in place and expertly welded it tight. The scene below was gone. A moment later the floor shivered as activity resumed.

Morrison, white-faced and shaking, turned to O'Neill. "What are they doing? What are they making?"

"Not weapons," O'Neill said.

"That stuff is being sent up" — Morrison gestured convulsively — "to the surface."

Shakily, O'Neill climbed to his feet. "Can we locate the spot?"

"I — think so."

"We better." O'Neill swept up the flashlight and started toward the ascent ramp. "We're going to have to see what those pellets are that they're shooting up."

The exit valve of the conveyor tube was concealed in a tangle of vines and ruins a quarter of a mile beyond the factory. In a slot of rock at the base of the mountains the valve poked up like a nozzle. From ten yards away, it was invisible; the two men were almost on top of it before they noticed it.

Every few moments, a pellet burst from the valve and shot up into the sky. The nozzle revolved and altered its angle of deflection; each pellet was launched in a slightly varied trajectory.

"How far are they going?" Morrison wondered.

"Probably varies. It's distributing them at random." O'Neill advanced cautiously, but the mechanism took no note of him. Plastered against the towering wall of rock was a crumpled pellet; by accident, the nozzle had released it directly at the mountainside. O'Neill climbed up, got it and jumped down.

The pellet was a smashed container of machinery, tiny metallic elements too minute to be analyzed without a microscope.

"Not a weapon," O'Neill said.

The cylinder had split. At first he couldn't tell if it had been the impact or deliberate internal mechanisms at work. From the rent, an ooze of metal bits was sliding. Squatting down, O'Neill examined them.

The bits were in motion. Microscopic machinery, smaller than ants, smaller than pins, working energetically, purposefully — constructing something that looked like a tiny rectangle of steel.

"They're building," O'Neill said, awed. He got up and prowled on. Off to the side, at the far edge of the gully, he came across a downed pellet far advanced on its construction. Apparently it had been released some time ago.

This one had made great enough progress to be identified. Minute as it was, the structure was familiar. The machinery was building a miniature replica of the demolished factory.

"Well," O'Neill said thoughtfully, "we're back where we started from. For better or worse ... I don't know."

"I guess they must be all over Earth by now," Morrison said, "landing everywhere and going to work."

A thought struck O'Neill. "Maybe some of them are geared to escape velocity. That would be neat — autofac networks throughout the whole universe."

Behind him, the nozzle continued to spurt out its torrent of metal seeds.

SERVICE CALL

IT WOULD BE WISE to explain what Courtland was doing just before the door-bell rang.

In his swank apartment on Leavenworth Street where Russian Hill drops to the flat expanse of North Beach and finally to the San Francisco Bay itself, David Courtland sat hunched over a series of routine reports, a week's file of technical data dealing with the results of the Mount Diablo tests. As research director for Pesco Paints, Courtland was concerning himself with the comparative durability of various surfaces manufactured by his company. Treated shingles had baked and sweated in the California heat for five hundred and sixty-four days. It was now time to see which pore-filler withstood oxidation, and to adjust production schedules accordingly.

Involved with his intricate analytical data, Courtland at first failed to hear the bell. In the corner of the living room his high-fidelity Bogen amplifier, turntable, and speaker were playing a Schumann symphony. His wife, Fay, was doing the dinner dishes in the kitchen. The two children, Bobby and Ralf, were already in their bunk beds, asleep. Reaching for his pipe, Courtland leaned back from the desk a moment, ran a heavy hand through his thinning gray hair ... and heard the bell.

"Damn," he said. Vaguely, he wondered how many times the demure chimes had sounded; he had a dim subliminal memory of repeated attempts to attract his attention. Before his tired eyes the mass of report sheets wavered and receded. Who the hell was it? His watch read only nine-thirty; he couldn't really complain, yet.

"Want me to get it?" Fay called brightly from the kitchen.

"I'll get it." Wearily, Courtland got to his feet, stuffed his feet into his shoes, and plodded across the room, past the couch, floor lamp, magazine

21

rack, the phonograph, the bookcase, to the door. He was a heavy-set middle-aged technologist, and he didn't like people interrupting his work.

In the halls stood an unfamiliar visitor. "Good evening, sir," the visitor said, intently examining a clipboard; "I'm sorry to bother you."

Courtland glared sourly at the young man. A salesman, probably. Thin, blond-haired, in a white shirt, bow tie, single-breasted blue suit, the young man stood gripping his clipboard in one hand and a bulging black suitcase with the other. His bony features were set in an expression of serious concentration. There was an air of studious confusion about him; brow wrinkled, lips tight together, the muscles of his cheeks began to twitch into overt worry. Glancing up he asked, "Is this 1846 Leavenworth? Apartment 3A?"

"That's right," Courtland said, with the infinite patience due a dumb animal.

The taut frown on the young man's face relaxed a trifle. "Yes, sir," he said, in his urgent tenor. Peering past Courtland into the apartment, he said, "I'm sorry to bother you in the evening when you're working, but as you probably know we've been pretty full up the last couple of days. That's why we couldn't answer your call sooner."

"My call?" Courtland echoed. Under his unbuttoned collar, he was beginning to glow a dull red. Undoubtedly something Fay had got him mixed up in; something she thought he should look into, something vital to gracious living. "What the hell are you talking about?" he demanded. "Come to the point."

The young man flushed, swallowed noisily, tried to grin, and then hurried on huskily, "Sir, I'm the repairman you asked for; I'm here to fix your swibble."

The facetious retort that came to Courtland's mind was one that later on he wished he had used. "Maybe," he wished he had said, "I don't want my swibble fixed. Maybe I like my swibble the way it is." But he didn't say that. Instead, he blinked, pulled the door in slightly, and said, "My *what?*"

"Yes, sir," the young man persisted. "The record of your swibble installation came to us as a matter of course. Usually we make an automatic adjustment inquiry, but your call preceded that — so I'm here with complete service equipment. Now, as to the nature of your particular complaint ... " Furiously, the young man pawed through the sheaf of papers on his clipboard. "Well, there's no point in looking for that; you can tell me orally. As you probably know, sir, we're not officially a part of the vending corporation ... we have what is called an *insurance*-type coverage that comes into existence automatically, when your purchase is made. Of course, you can cancel the arrangement with us." Feebly, he tried a joke. "I have heard there're a couple of competitors in the service business."

Stern morality replaced humor. Pulling his lank body upright, he finished,

"But let me say that we've been in the swibble repair business ever since old R.J. Wright introduced the first A-driven experimental model."

For a time, Courtland said nothing. Phantasmagoria swirled through his mind: random quasi-technological thoughts, reflex evaluations and notations of no importance. So swibbles broke right down, did they? Big-time business operations... send out a repairman as soon as the deal is closed. Monopoly tactics... squeeze out the competition before they have a chance. Kickback to the parent company, probably. Interwoven books.

But none of his thoughts got down to the basic issue. With a violent effort he forced his attention back onto the earnest young man who waited nervously in the hall with his black service kit and clipboard. "No," Courtland said emphatically, "no, you've got the wrong address."

"Yes, sir?" the young man quavered politely, a wave of stricken dismay crossing his features. "The wrong address? Good Lord, has dispatch got another route fouled up with that new-fangled — "

"Better look at your paper again," Courtland said, grimly pulling the door toward him. "Whatever the hell a swibble is, I haven't got one; and I didn't call you."

As he shut the door, he perceived the final horror on the young man's face, his stupefied paralysis. Then the brightly painted wood surface cut off the sight, and Courtland turned wearily back to his desk.

A swibble. What the hell was a swibble? Seating himself moodily, he tried to take up where he had left off... but the direction of his thoughts had been totally shattered.

There was no such thing as a swibble. And he was on the in, industrially speaking. He read *U.S. News*, the *Wall Street Journal*. If there was a swibble he would have heard about it — unless a swibble was some pip-squeak gadget for the home. Maybe that was it.

"Listen," he yelled at his wife as Fay appeared momentarily at the kitchen door, dishcloth and blue-willow plate in her hands. "What is this business? You know anything about swibbles?"

Fay shook her head. "It's nothing of mine."

"You didn't order a chrome-and-plastic a.c.-d.c. swibble from Macy's?"

"Certainly not."

Maybe it was something for the kids. Maybe it was the latest grammar-school craze, the contemporary bolo or flip cards or knock-knock-who's-there? But nine-year-old kids didn't buy things that needed a service man carrying a massive black tool kit — not on fifty cents a week allowance.

Curiosity overcame aversion. He had to know, just for the record, what a swibble was. Springing to his feet, Courtland hurried to the hall door and yanked it open.

The hall was empty, of course. The young man had wandered off. There was a faint smell of men's cologne and nervous perspiration, nothing more.

Nothing more, except a wadded-up fragment of paper that had come unclipped from the man's board. Courtland bent down and retrieved it from the carpet. It was a carbon copy of a route-instruction, giving code-identification, the name of the service company, the address of the caller.

> 1846 Leavenworth Street S.F. v-call rec'd Ed Fuller 9:20 P.M. 5-28. Swibble 30s15H (deluxe). Suggest check lateral feedback & neural replacement bank. AAw3-6.

The numbers, the information, meant nothing to Courtland. He closed the door and slowly returned to his desk. Smoothing out the crumpled sheet of paper, he reread the dull words again, trying to squeeze some meaning from them. The printed letterhead was:

ELECTRONIC SERVICE INDUSTRIES
455 Montgomery Street, San Francisco 14. Ri8-4456n
Est. 1963

That was it. The meager printed statement: Established in 1963. Hands trembling, Courtland reached mechanically for his pipe. Certainly, it explained why he had never heard of swibbles. It explained why he didn't own one ... and why, no matter how many doors in the apartment building he knocked on, the young repairman wouldn't find anybody who did.

Swibbles hadn't been invented yet.

After an interval of hard, furious thought Courtland picked up the phone and dialed the home number of his subordinate at the Pesco labs.

"I don't care," he said carefully, "what you're doing this evening. I'm going to give you a list of instructions and I want them carried out right away."

At the other end of the line Jack Hurley could be heard pulling himself angrily together. "Tonight? Listen, Dave, the company isn't my mother — I have some life of my own. If I'm supposed to come running down — "

"This has nothing to do with Pesco. I want a tape recorder and a movie camera with infrared lens. I want you to round up a legal stenographer. I want one of the company electricians — you pick him out, but get the best. And I want Anderson from the engineering room. If you can't get him, get any of our designers. And I want somebody off the assembly line; get me some old mechanic who knows his stuff. Who really knows machines."

Doubtfully, Hurley said, "Well, you're the boss; at least, you're boss of research. But I think this will have to be cleared with the company. Would you mind if I went over your head and got an okay from Pesbroke?"

"Go ahead." Courtland made a quick decision. "Better yet, I'll call him myself; he'll probably have to know what's going on."

"What *is* going on?" Hurley demanded curiously. "I never heard you sound this way before ... has somebody brought out a self-spraying paint?"

Courtland hung up the phone, waited out a torturous interval, and then dialed his superior, the owner of Pesco Paint.

"You have a minute?" he asked tightly, when Pesbroke's wife had roused the white-haired old man from his after-dinner nap and got him to the phone. "I'm mixed up in something big; I want to talk to you about it."

"Has it got to do with paint?" Pesbroke muttered, half humorously, half seriously. "If not — "

Courtland interrupted him. Speaking slowly, he gave a full account of his contact with the swibble repairman.

When Courtland had finished, his employer was silent. "Well," Pesbroke said finally, "I guess I could go through some kind of routine. But you've got me interested. All right, I'll buy it. But," he added quietly, "if this is an elaborate time-waster, I'm going to bill you for the use of the men and equipment."

"By time-waster, you mean if nothing profitable comes out of this?"

"No," Pesbroke said. "I mean, if you *know* it's a fake; if you're consciously going along with a gag. I've got a migraine headache and I'm not going along with a gag. If you're serious, if you really think this might be something, I'll put the expenses on the company books."

"I'm serious," Courtland said. "You and I are both too damn old to play games."

"Well," Pesbroke reflected, "the older you get, the more you're apt to go off the deep end; and this sounds pretty deep." He could be heard making up his mind. "I'll telephone Hurley and give him the okay. You can have whatever you want ... I suppose you're going to try to pin this repairman down and find out what he really is."

"That's what I want to do."

"Suppose he's on the level ... what then?"

"Well," Courtland said cautiously, "then I want to find out what a swibble is. As a starter. Maybe after that — "

"You think he'll be back?"

"He might be. He won't find the right address; I know that. Nobody in *this* neighborhood called for a swibble repairman."

"What do you care what a swibble is? Why don't you find out how he got from his period back here?"

"I think he knows what a swibble is — and I don't think he knows how he got here. He doesn't even know he's here."

Pesbroke agreed. "That's reasonable. If I come over, will you let me in? I'd sort of enjoy watching."

"Sure," Courtland said, perspiring, his eye on the closed door to the hall.

"But you'll have to watch from the other room. I don't want anything to foul this up ... we may never have another chance like this."

Grumpily, the jury-rigged company team filed into the apartment and stood waiting for Courtland to instruct. Jack Hurley, in aloha sports shirt, slacks, and crepe-soled shoes, clodded resentfully over to Courtland and waved his cigar in his face. "Here we are; I don't know what you told Pesbroke, but you certainly pulled him along." Glancing around the apartment, he asked, "Can I assume we're going to get the pitch now? There's not much these people can do unless they understand what they're after."

In the bedroom doorway stood Courtland's two sons, eyes half-shut with sleep. Fay nervously swept them up and herded them back into the bedroom. Around the living room the various men and women took up uncertain positions, their faces registering outrage, uneasy curiosity, and bored indifference. Anderson, the designing engineer, acted aloof and blasé. MacDowell, the stoop-shouldered, pot-bellied lathe operator, glared with proletarian resentment at the expensive furnishings of the apartment, and then sank into embarrassed apathy as he perceived his own work boots and grease-saturated pants. The recording specialist was trailing wire from his microphones to the tape recorder set up in the kitchen. A slim young woman, the legal stenographer, was trying to make herself comfortable in a chair in the corner. On the couch, Parkinson, the plant emergency electrician, was glancing idly through a copy of *Fortune*.

"Where's the camera equipment?" Courtland demanded.

"Coming," Hurley answered. "Are you trying to catch somebody trying out the old Spanish Treasure bunco?"

"I wouldn't need an engineer and an electrician for that," Courtland said dryly. Tensely, he paced around the living room. "Probably he won't even show up; he's probably back in his own time, by now, or wandering around God knows where."

"Who?" Hurley shouted, puffing gray cigar smoke in growing agitation. "What's going on?"

"A man knocked on my door," Courtland told him briefly. "He talked about some machinery, equipment I never heard of. Something called a swibble."

Around the room blank looks passed back and forth.

"Let's guess what a swibble is," Courtland continued grimly. "Anderson, you start. What would a swibble be?"

Anderson grinned. "A fish hook that chases down fish."

Parkinson volunteered a guess. "An English car with only one wheel."

Grudgingly, Hurley came next. "Something dumb. A machine for housebreaking pets."

"A new plastic bra," the legal stenographer suggested.

"I don't know," MacDowell muttered resentfully. "I never heard of anything like that."

"All right," Courtland agreed, again examining his watch. He was getting close to hysteria; an hour had passed and there was no sign of the repairman. "We don't know; we can't even guess. But someday, nine years from now, a man named Wright is going to invent a swibble, and it's going to become big business. People are going to make them; people are going to buy them and pay for them; repairmen are going to come around and service them."

The door opened and Pesbroke entered the apartment, overcoat over his arm, crushed Stetson hat clamped over his head. "Has he showed up again?" His ancient, alert eyes darted around the room. "You people look ready to go."

"No sign of him," Courtland said drearily. "Damn it — I sent him off; I didn't grasp it until he was gone." He showed Pesbroke the crumpled carbon.

"I see," Pesbroke said, handing it back. "And if he comes back you're going to tape what he says, and photograph everything he has in the way of equipment." He indicated Anderson and MacDowell. "What about the rest of them? What's the need of them?"

"I want people here who can ask the right questions," Courtland explained. "We won't get answers any other way. The man, if he shows up at all, will stay only a finite time. During that time, we've got to find out — " He broke off as his wife came up beside him. "What is it?"

"The boys want to watch," Fay explained. "Can they? They promise they won't make any noise." She added wistfully, "I'd sort of like to watch, too."

"Watch, then," Courtland answered gloomily. "Maybe there won't be anything to see."

While Fay served coffee around, Courtland went on with his explanation. "First of all, we want to find out if this man is on the level. Our first questions will be aimed at tripping him up; I want these specialists to go to work on him. If he's a fake, they'll probably find it out."

"And if he isn't?" Anderson asked, an interested expression on his face. "If he isn't, you're saying ... "

"If he isn't, then he's from the next decade, and I want him pumped for all he's worth. But — " Courtland paused. "I doubt if we'll get much theory. I had the impression that he's a long way down on the totem pole. The best we probably can do is get a run-down on his specific work. From that, we may have to assemble our picture, make our own extrapolations."

"You think he can tell us what he does for a living," Pesbroke said cannily, "but that's about it."

"We'll be lucky if he shows up at all," Courtland said. He settled down on the couch and began methodically knocking his pipe against the ashtray. "All we can do is wait. Each of you think over what you're going to ask. Try to figure out the questions you want answered by a man from the future who doesn't know he's from the future, who's trying to repair equipment that doesn't yet exist."

"I'm scared," the legal stenographer said, white-faced and wide-eyed, her coffee cup trembling.

"I'm about fed up," Hurley muttered, eyes fixed sullenly on the floor. "This is all a lot of hot air."

It was just about that time that the swibble repairman came again, and once more timidly knocked on the hall door.

The young repairman was flustered. And he was getting perturbed. "I'm sorry, sir," he began without preamble. "I can see you have company, but I've rechecked my route instructions and this is *absolutely* the right address." He added plaintively, "I tried some other apartments; nobody knew what I was talking about."

"Come in," Courtland managed. He stepped aside, got himself between the swibble repairman and the door, and ushered him into the living room.

"Is this the person?" Pesbroke rumbled doubtfully, his gray eyes narrowing.

Courtland ignored him. "Sit down," he ordered the swibble repairman. Out of the corner of his eye he could see Anderson and Hurley and Mac-Dowell moving in closely; Parkinson threw down his *Fortune* and got quickly to his feet. In the kitchen, the sound of tape running through the recording head was audible ... the room had begun moving into activity.

"I could come some other time," the repairman said apprehensively, eyeing the closing circle of people. "I don't want to bother you, sir, when you have guests."

Perched grimly on the arm of the couch, Courtland said, "This is as good a time as any. In fact, this is the best time." A wild flood of relief spilled over him: now they had a chance. "I don't know what got into me," he went on rapidly. "I was confused. Of course I have a swibble; it's set up in the dining room."

The repairman's face twitched with a spasm of laughter. "Oh, really," he choked. "In the dining room? That's about the funniest joke I've heard in weeks."

Courtland glanced at Pesbroke. What the hell was so funny about that? Then his flesh began to crawl; cold sweat broke out on his forehead and the palms of his hands. What the hell was a swibble? Maybe they had better find out right away — or not at all. Maybe they were getting into something deeper than they knew. Maybe — and he didn't like the thought — they were better off where they were.

"I was confused," he said, "by your nomenclature. I don't think of it as a swibble." Cautiously, he finished, "I know that's the popular jargon, but with that much money involved, I like to think of it by its legitimate title."

The swibble repairman looked completely confused; Courtland realized that he had made another mistake; apparently *swibble* was its correct name.

Pesbroke spoke up. "How long have you been repairing swibbles, Mr. ... " He waited, but there was no response from the thin, blank face. "What's your name, young man?" he demanded.

"My *what?*" The swibble repairman pulled jerkily away. "I don't understand you, sir."

Good Lord, Courtland thought. It was going to be a lot harder than he had realized — than any of them had realized.

Angrily, Pesbroke said, "You must have a name. Everybody has a name."

The young repairman gulped and stared down red-faced at the carpet. "I'm still only in service group four, sir. So I don't have a name yet."

"Let it go," Courtland said. What kind of a society gave out names as a status privilege? "I want to make sure you're a competent repairman," he explained. "How long have you been repairing swibbles?"

"For six years and three months," the repairman asserted. Pride took the place of embarrassment. "In junior high school I showed a straight-A record in swibble-maintenance aptitude." His meager chest swelled. "I'm a born swibble-man."

"Fine," Courtland agreed uneasily; he couldn't believe the industry was that big. They gave tests in junior high school? Was swibble maintenance considered a basic talent, like symbol manipulation and manual dexterity? Had swibble work become as fundamental as musical talent, or as the ability to conceive spatial relationships?

"Well," the repairman said briskly, gathering up his bulging tool kit, "I'm all ready to get started. I have to be back at the shop before long ... I've got a lot of other calls."

Bluntly, Pesbroke stepped up squarely in front of the thin young man. "What is a swibble?" he demanded. "I'm tired of this damn fooling around. You say you work on these things — *what are they?* That's a simple enough question; they must be something."

"Why," the young man said hesitantly, "I mean, that's hard to say. Suppose — well, suppose you ask me what a cat or a dog is. How can I answer that?'

"We're getting nowhere," Anderson spoke up. "The swibble is manufactured, isn't it? You must have schematics, then; hand them over."

The young repairman gripped his tool kit defensively. "What in the world is the matter, sir? If this is your idea of a joke — " He turned back to Courtland. "I'd like to start work; I really don't have much time."

Standing in the corner, hands shoved deep in his pockets, MacDowell said slowly, "I've been thinking about getting a swibble. The missus thinks we ought to have one."

"Oh, certainly," the repairman agreed. Color rising in his cheeks, he rushed on, "I'm surprised you don't have a swibble already; in fact, I can't imagine what's wrong with you people. You're all acting — oddly. Where, if I may ask, do you come from? Why are you so — well, so uninformed?"

"These people," Courtland explained, "come from a part of the country where there aren't any swibbles."

Instantly, the repairman's face hardened with suspicion. "Oh?" he said sharply. "Interesting. What part of the country is that?"

Again, Courtland had said the wrong thing; he knew that. While he floundered for a response, MacDowell cleared his throat and inexorably went on. "Anyhow," he said, "we've been meaning to get one. You have any folders with you? Pictures of different models?"

The repairman responded. "I'm afraid not, sir. But if you'll give me your address I'll have the sales department send you information. And if you want, a qualified representative can call on you at your convenience and describe the advantages of owning a swibble."

"The first swibble was developed in 1963?" Hurley asked.

"That's right." The repairman's suspicions had momentarily lulled. "And just in time, too. Let me say this — if Wright hadn't got his first model going, there wouldn't be any human beings left alive. You people here who don't own swibbles — you may not know it — and you certainly act as if you didn't know it — but you're alive right now because of old R.J. Wright. It's swibbles that keep the world going."

Opening his black case, the repairman briskly brought out a complicated apparatus of tubes and wiring. He filled a drum with clear fluid, sealed it, tried the plunger, and straightened up. "I'll start out with a shot of dx — that usually puts them back into operation."

"What is dx?" Anderson asked quickly.

Surprised at the question, the repairman answered, "It's a high-protein food concentrate. We've found that ninety per cent of our early service calls are the result of improper diet. People just don't know how to care for their new swibble."

"My God," Anderson said feebly. "It's alive."

Courtland's mind took a nose dive. He had been wrong; it wasn't precisely a repairman who had stood gathering his equipment together. The man had come to fix the swibble, all right, but his capacity was slightly different than Courtland had supposed. He wasn't a repairman; he was a veterinarian.

Laying out instruments and meters, the young man explained: "The new swibbles are a lot more complex than the early models; I need all this before I can even get started. But blame the War."

"The War?" Fay Courtland echoed apprehensively.

"Not the early war. The big one, in '75. That little war in '61 wasn't really much. You know, I suppose, that Wright was originally an Army engineer, stationed over in — well, I guess it was called Europe. I believe the idea came to him because of all those refugees pouring across the border. Yes, I'm sure that's how it was. During that little war, back in '61, they came across by the millions. And they went the other way, too. My goodness, people were shifting back and forth between the two camps — it was revolting."

"I'm not clear on my history," Courtland said thickly. "I never paid much attention in school ... the '61 war, that was between Russia and America?"

"Oh," the repairman said, "it was between everybody. Russia headed the Eastern side, of course. And America the West. But everybody was in it. That was the little war, though; that didn't count."

"Little?" Fay demanded, horrified.

"Well," the repairman admitted, "I suppose it looked like a lot at the time. But I mean, there were buildings still standing, afterward. And it only lasted a few months."

"Who — won?" Anderson croaked.

The repairman tittered. "Won? What an odd question. Well, there were more people left in the Eastern bloc, if that's what you mean. Anyhow, the importance of the '61 war — and I'm *sure* your history teachers made that clear — was that swibbles appeared. R.J. Wright got his idea from the camp-changers that appeared in that war. So by '75, when the *real* war came along, we had plenty of swibbles." Thoughtfully, he added, "In fact, I'd say the real war was a war over swibbles. I mean, it was the last war. It was the war between the people who wanted swibbles and those who didn't." Complacently, he finished, "Needless to say, *we* won."

After a time Courtland managed to ask, "What happened to the others? Those who — didn't want swibbles."

"Why," the repairman said gently, "the swibbles got them."

Shakily, Courtland started his pipe going. "I didn't know about that."

"What do you mean?" Pesbroke demanded hoarsely. "How did they get them? What did they do?"

Astonished, the repairman shook his head. "I didn't know there was such ignorance in lay circles." The position of pundit obviously pleased him; sticking out his bony chest, he proceeded to lecture the circle of intent faces on the fundamentals of history. "Wright's first A-driven swibble was crude, of course. But it served its purpose. Originally, it was able to differentiate the camp-shifters into two groups: those who had really seen the light, and those who were insincere. Those who were going to shift back ... who weren't really loyal. The authorities wanted to know which of the shifters had really come over to the West and which were spies and secret agents. That was the original swibble function. But that was nothing compared to now."

"No," Courtland agreed, paralyzed. "Nothing at all."

"Now," the repairman said sleekly, "we don't deal with such crudities. It's absurd to wait until an individual has accepted a contrary ideology, and then hope he'll shift away from it. In a way, it's ironic, isn't it? After the '61 war there was really only one contrary ideology: those who opposed the swibbles."

He laughed happily. "So the swibbles differentiated those who didn't want to be differentiated by swibbles. My, that was quite a war. Because that wasn't a messy war, with a lot of bombs and jellied gasoline. That was a *scientific* war — none of that random pulverizing. That was just swibbles going down into cellars and ruins and hiding places and digging out those Contrapersons one by one. Until we had all of them. So now," he finished, gathering up his equipment, "we don't have to worry about wars or anything of that sort. There won't be any more conflicts, because we don't have any contrary ideologies. As Wright showed, it doesn't really matter what ideology we have; it isn't important whether it's Communism or Free Enterprise or Socialism or Fascism or Slavery. What's important is that every one of us agrees completely; that we're all absolutely loyal. And as long as we have our swibbles — "
He winked knowingly at Courtland. "Well, as a new swibble owner, you've found out the advantages. You know the sense of security and satisfaction in being *certain* that your ideology is exactly congruent with that of everybody else in the world. That there's no possibility, no chance whatsoever that you'll go astray — and that some passing swibble will feed on you."

It was MacDowell who managed to pull himself together first. "Yeah," he said ironically. "It certainly sounds like what the missus and I want."

"Oh, you ought to have a swibble of your own," the repairman urged. "Consider — if you have your own swibble, it'll adjust you automatically. It'll keep you on the right track without strain or fuss. You'll always know you're not going wrong — remember the swibble slogan: Why be *half* loyal? With your own swibble, your outlook will be corrected by painless degrees ... but if you wait, if you just *hope* you're on the right track, why, one of these days you may walk into a friend's living room and his swibble may just simply crack you open and drink you down. Of course," he reflected, "a passing swibble may still get you in time to straighten you out. But usually it's too late. Usually — "
He smiled. "Usually people go beyond redemption, once they get started."

"And your job," Pesbroke muttered, "is to keep the swibbles working?"

"They do get out of adjustment, left to themselves."

"Isn't it a kind of paradox?" Pesbroke pursued. "The swibbles keep us in adjustment, and we keep them in adjustment ... it's a closed circle."

The repairman was intrigued. "Yes, that's an interesting way of putting it. But we must keep control over the swibbles, of course. So they don't die." He shivered. "Or worse."

"Die?" Hurley said, still not understanding. "But if they're built — "
Wrinkling his brows he said, "Either they're machines or they're alive. Which is it?"

Patiently, the repairman explained elementary physics. "Swibble-culture is an organic phenotype evolved in a protein medium under controlled conditions. The directing neurological tissue that forms the basis of the swibble is alive, certainly, in the sense that it grows, thinks, feeds, excretes waste. Yes, it's definitely alive. But the swibble, as a functioning whole, is a manufactured item. The organic tissue is inserted in the master tank and then sealed. I certainly don't repair *that*; I give it nutriments to restore a proper balance of diet, and I try to deal with parasitic organisms that find their way into it. I try to keep it adjusted and healthy. The balance of the organism, is, of course, totally mechanical."

"The swibble has direct access to human minds?" Anderson asked, fascinated.

"Naturally. It's an artificially evolved telepathic metazoan. And with it, Wright solved the basic problem of modern times: the existence of diverse, warring ideological factions, the presence of disloyalty and dissent. In the words of General Steiner's famous aphorism: War is an extension of the disagreement from the voting booth to the battlefield. And the preamble of the World Service Charter: war, if it is to be eliminated, must be eliminated from the minds of men, for it is in the minds of men that disagreement begins. Up until 1963, we had no way to get into the minds of men. Up until 1963, the problem was unsolvable."

"Thank God," Fay said clearly.

The repairman failed to hear her; he was carried away by his own enthusiasm. "By means of the swibble, we've managed to transform the basic sociological problem of loyalty into a routine technical matter: to the mere matter of maintenance and repair. Our only concern is keep the swibbles functioning correctly; the rest is up to them."

"In other words," Courtland said faintly, "you repairmen are the only controlling influence over the swibbles. You represent the total human agency standing above these machines."

The repairman reflected. "I suppose so," he admitted modestly. "Yes, that's correct."

"Except for you, they pretty damn well manage the human race."

The bony chest swelled with complacent, confident pride. "I suppose you could say that."

"Look," Courtland said thickly. He grabbed hold of the man's arm. "How the hell can you be sure? Are you really in control?" A crazy hope was rising up inside him: as long as men had power over the swibbles there was a chance to roll things back. The swibbles could be disassembled, taken apart piece by piece. As long as swibbles had to submit to human servicing it wasn't quite hopeless."

"What, sir?" the repairman inquired. "Of course we're in control. Don't you worry." Firmly, he disengaged Courtland's fingers. "Now, where is your swibble?" He glanced around the room. "I'll have to hurry; there isn't much time left."

"I haven't got a swibble," Courtland said.

For a moment it didn't register. Then a strange, intricate expression crossed the repairman's face. "No swibble? But you told me — "

"Something went wrong," Courtland said hoarsely. "There aren't any swibbles. It's too early — they haven't been invented. Understand? You came too soon!"

The young man's eyes popped. Clutching his equipment, he stumbled back two steps, blinked, opened his mouth and tried to speak. "Too — soon?" The comprehension arrived. Suddenly he looked older, much older. "I wondered. All the undamaged buildings ... the archaic furnishings. The transmission machinery must have misphased!" Rage flashed over him. "That instantaneous service — I knew dispatch should have stuck to the old mechanical system. I told them to make better tests. Lord, there's going to be hell to pay; if we ever get this mix-up straightened out I'll be surprised."

Bending down furiously, he hastily dropped his equipment back in the case. In a single motion he slammed and locked it, straightened up, bowed briefly at Courtland.

"Good evening," he said frigidly. And vanished.

The circle of watchers had nothing to watch. The swibble repairman had gone back to where he came from.

After a time Pesbroke turned and signaled to the man in the kitchen. "Might as well shut off the tape recorder," he muttered bleakly. "There's nothing more to record."

"Good Lord," Hurley said, shaken. "A world run by machines."

Fay shivered. "I couldn't believe that little fellow had so much power; I thought he was just a minor official."

"He's completely in charge," Courtland said harshly.

There was silence.

One of the two children yawned sleepily. Fay turned abruptly to them and herded them efficiently into the bedroom. "Time for you two to be in bed," she commanded, with false gaiety.

Protesting sullenly, the two boys disappeared, and the door closed. Gradually, the living room broke into motion. The tape-recorder man began rewinding his reel. The legal stenographer shakily collected her notes and put away her pencils. Hurley lit up a cigar and stood puffing moodily, his face dark and somber.

"I suppose," Courtland said finally, "that we've all accepted it; we assume it's not a fake."

"Well," Pesbroke pointed out, "he vanished. That ought to be proof enough. And all the junk he took out of his kit — "

"It's only nine years," Parkinson, the electrician, said thoughtfully. "Wright must be alive already. Let's look him up and stick a shiv into him."

"Army engineer," MacDowell agreed. "R.J. Wright. It ought to be possible to locate him. Maybe we can keep it from happening."

"How long would you guess people like him can keep the swibbles under control?" Anderson asked.

Courtland shrugged wearily. "No telling. Maybe years ... maybe a century. But sooner or later something's going to come up, something they didn't expect. And then it'll be predatory machinery preying on all of us."

Fay shuddered violently. "It sounds awful; I'm certainly glad it won't be for a while."

"You and the repairman," Courtland said bitterly. "As long as it doesn't affect you — "

Fay's overwrought nerves flared up. "We'll discuss it later on." She smiled jerkily at Pesbroke. "More coffee? I'll put some on." Turning on her heel, she rushed from the living room into the kitchen.

While she was filling the Silex with water, the doorbell quietly rang.

The roomful of people froze. They looked at each other, mute and horrified.

"He's back," Hurley said thickly.

"Maybe it's not him," Anderson suggested weakly. "Maybe it's the camera people, finally."

But none of them moved toward the door. After a time the bell rang again, longer, and more insistently.

"We have to answer it," Pesbroke said woodenly.

"Not me," the legal stenographer quavered.

"This isn't my apartment," MacDowell pointed out.

Courtland moved rigidly toward the door. Even before he took hold of the knob he knew what it was. Dispatch, using its new-fangled instantaneous transmission. Something to get work crews and repairmen directly to their stations. So control of the swibbles would be absolute and perfect; so nothing would go wrong.

But something had gone wrong. The control had fouled itself up. It was working upside down, completely backward. Self-defeating, futile: it was too perfect. Gripping the knob, he tore the door open.

Standing in the hall were four men. They wore plain gray uniforms and caps. The first of them whipped off his cap, glanced at a written sheet of paper, and then nodded politely at Courtland.

"Evening, sir," he said cheerfully. He was a husky man, wide-shouldered, with a shock of thick brown hair hanging over his sweat-shiny forehead. "We — uh — got a little lost, I guess. Took a while to get here."

Peering into the apartment, he hitched up his heavy leather belt, stuffed his route sheet into his pocket, and rubbed his large, competent hands together.

"It's downstairs in the trunk," he announced, addressing Courtland and the whole living room of people. "Tell me where you want it, and we'll bring it right up. We should have a good-sized space — that side over there by the window should do." Turning away, he and his crew moved energetically toward the service elevator. "These late-model swibbles take up a lot of room."

CAPTIVE MARKET

SATURDAY MORNING, about eleven o'clock, Mrs. Edna Berthelson was ready to make her little trip. Although it was a weekly affair, consuming four hours of her valuable business time, she made the profitable trip alone, preserving for herself the integrity of her find.

Because that was what it was. A find, a stroke of incredible luck. There was nothing else like it, and she had been in business fifty-three years. More, if the years in her father's store were counted — but they didn't really count. That had been for the experience (her father made that clear); no pay was involved. But it gave her the understanding of business; the feel of operating a small country store, dusting pencils and unwrapping fly paper and serving up dried beans and chasing the cat out of the cracker barrel where he liked to sleep.

Now the store was old, and so was she. The big heavy-set, black-browed man who was her father had died long ago; her own children and grandchildren had been spawned, had crept out over the world, were everywhere. One by one they had appeared, lived in Walnut Creek, sweated through the dry, sun-baked summers, and then gone on, leaving one by one as they had come. She and the store sagged and settled a little more each year, became a little more frail and stern and grim. A little more themselves.

That morning very early Jackie said: "Grandmaw, where are you going?" Although he knew, of course, where she was going. She was going out in her truck as she always did; this was the Saturday trip. But he liked to ask; he was pleased by the stability of the answer. He liked having it always the same.

To another question there was another unvarying answer, but this one didn't please him so much. It came in answer to the question: "Can I come along?"

The answer to that was always *no.*

Edna Berthelson laboriously carried packages and boxes from the back of the store to the rusty, upright pickup truck. Dust lay over the truck; its red-metal sides were bent and corroded. The motor was already on; it was wheezing and heating up in the mid-day sun. A few drab chickens pecked in the dust around its wheels. Under the porch of the store a plump white shaggy sheep squatted, its face vapid, indolent, indifferently watching the activity of the day. Cars and truck rolled along Mount Diablo Boulevard. Along Lafayette Avenue a few shoppers strolled, farmers and their wives, petty businessmen, farm hands, some city women in their gaudy slacks and print shirts, sandals, bandanas. In the front of the store the radio tinnily played popular songs.

"I asked you a question," Jackie said righteously. "I asked you where you're going."

Mrs. Berthelson bent stiffly over to lift the last armload of boxes. Most of the loading had been done the night before by Arnie the Swede, the hulking white-haired man who did the heavy work around the store. "What?" she murmured vaguely, her gray, wrinkled face twisting with concentration. "You know perfectly well where I'm going."

Jackie trailed plaintively after her, as she re-entered the store to look for her order book. "Can I come? Please, can I come along? You never let me come — you never let *anybody* come."

"Of course not," Mrs. Berthelson said sharply. "It's nobody's business."

"But I *want* to come along," Jackie explained.

Slyly, the little old woman turned her gray head and peered back at him, a worn, colorless bird taking in a world perfectly understood. "So does everybody else." Thin lips twitching in a secret smile, Mrs. Berthelson said softly: "But nobody can."

Jackie didn't like the sound of that. Sullenly, he retired to a corner, hands stuck deep in the pockets of his jeans, not taking part in something that was denied him, not approving of something in which he could not share. Mrs. Berthelson ignored him. She pulled her frayed blue sweater around her thin shoulders, located her sunglasses, pulled the screen door shut after her, and strode briskly to the truck.

Getting the truck into gear was an intricate process. For a time she sat tugging crossly at the shift, pumping the clutch up and down, waiting impatiently for the teeth to fall into place. At last, screeching and chattering, the gears meshed; the truck leaped a little, and Mrs. Berthelson gunned the motor and released the hand brake.

As the truck roared jerkily down the highway, Jackie detached himself from the shade by the house and followed along after it. His mother was nowhere in sight. Only the dozing sheep and the two scratching chickens were visible. Even Arnie the Swede was gone, probably getting a cold coke. Now was a fine time. Now was the best time he had ever had. And it was going to be sooner or later anyhow, because he was determined to come along.

Grabbing hold of the tailboard of the truck, Jackie hoisted himself up and landed face-down on the tightly-packed heaps of packages and boxes. Under him the truck bounced and bumped. Jackie hung on for dear life; clutching at the boxes he pulled his legs under him, crouched down, and desperately sought to keep from being flung off. Gradually the truck righted itself, and the torque diminished. He breathed a sigh of relief and settled gratefully down.

He was on his way. He was along, finally. Accompanying Mrs. Berthelson on her secret weekly trip, her strange covert enterprise from which — he had heard — she made a fabulous profit. A trip which nobody understood, and which he knew, in the deep recesses of his child's mind, was something awesome and wonderful, something that would be well worth the trouble.

He had hoped fervently that she wouldn't stop to check her load along the way.

With infinite care, Tellman prepared himself a cup of "coffee." First, he carried a tin cup of roasted grain over to the gasoline drum the colony used as a mixing bowl. Dumping it in, he hurried to add a handful of chicory and a few fragments of dried bran. Dirt-stained hands trembling, he managed to get a fire started among the ashes and coals under the pitted metal grate. He set a pan of tepid water on the flames and searched for a spoon.

"What are you up to?" his wife demanded from behind him.

"Uh," Tellman muttered. Nervously, he edged between Gladys and the meal. "Just fooling around." In spite of himself, his voice took on a nagging whine. "I have a right to fix myself something, don't I? As much right as anybody else."

"You ought to be over helping."

"I was. I wrenched something in my back." The wiry middle-aged man ducked uneasily away from his wife; tugging at the remains of his soiled white shirt, he retreated toward the door of the shack. "Damn it, a person has to rest, sometimes."

"Rest when we get there." Gladys wearily brushed back her thick dark-blonde hair. "Suppose everybody was like you."

Tellman flushed resentfully. "Who plotted our trajectory? Who's done all the navigation work?"

A faint ironic smile touched his wife's chapped lips. "We'll see how your charts work out," she said. "Then we'll talk about it."

Enraged, Tellman plunged out of the shack, into the blinding late-afternoon sunlight.

He hated the sun, the sterile white glare that began at five in the morning and lasted until nine in the evening. The Big Blast had sizzled the water vapor from the air; the sun beat down pitilessly, sparing nobody. But there were few left to care.

To his right was the cluster of shacks that made up the camp. An eclectic hodge-podge of boards, sheets of tin, wire and tar paper, upright concrete blocks, anything and everything dragged from the San Francisco ruins, forty miles west. Cloth blankets flapped dismally in doorways, protection against the vast hosts of insects that swept across the camp site from time to time. Birds, the natural enemy of insects, were gone. Tellman hadn't seen a bird in two years — and he didn't expect to see one again. Beyond the camp began the eternal dead black ash, the charred face of the world, without features, without life.

The camp had been set up in a natural hollow. One side was sheltered by the tumbled ruins of what had once been a minor mountain range. The concussion of the blast had burst the towering cliffs; rock had cascaded into the valley for days. After San Francisco had been fired out of existence, survivors had crept into the heaps of boulders, looking for a place to hide from the sun. That was the hardest part: the unshielded sun. Not the insects, not the radioactive clouds of ash, not the flashing white fury of the blasts, but the sun. More people had died of thirst and dehydration and blind insanity than from toxic poisons.

From his breast pocket, Tellman got a precious package of cigarettes. Shakily, he lit up. His thin, claw-like hands were trembling, partly from fatigue, partly from rage and tension. How he hated the camp. He loathed everybody in it, his wife included. Were they worth saving? He doubted it. Most of them were barbarians, already; what did it matter if they got the ship off or not? He was sweating away his mind and life, trying to save them. The hell with them.

But then, his own safety was involved with theirs.

He stalked stiff-legged over to where Barnes and Masterson stood talking. "How's it coming?" he demanded gruffly.

"Fine," Barnes answered. "It won't be long, now."

"One more load," Masterson said. His heavy features twitched uneasily. "I hope nothing gets fouled up. She ought to be here any minute."

Tellman loathed the sweaty, animal-like scent that rolled from Masterson's beefy body. Their situation wasn't an excuse to creep around filthy as a pig ... on Venus, things would be different. Masterson was useful, now; he was an experienced mechanic, invaluable in servicing the turbine and jets of the ship. But when the ship had landed and been pillaged ...

Satisfied, Tellman brooded over the re-establishment of the rightful order. The hierarchy had collapsed in the ruins of the cities, but it would be back strong as ever. Take Flannery, for example. Flannery was nothing but a foul-mouthed shanty-Irish stevedore ... but he was in charge of loading the ship, the greatest job at the moment. Flannery was top dog, for the time being ... but that would change.

It had to change. Consoled, Tellman strolled away from Barnes and Masterson, over to the ship itself.

The ship was huge. Across its muzzle the stenciled identification still remained, not yet totally obliterated by drifting ash and the searing heat of the sun.

U. S. ARMY ORDNANCE

SERIES A-3 (B)

Originally, it had been a high-velocity "massive retaliation" weapon, loaded with an H-warhead, ready to carry indiscriminate death to the enemy. The projectile had never been launched. Soviet toxic crystals had blown quietly into the windows and doors of the local command barracks. When launching day arrived, there was no crew to send it off. But it didn't matter — there was no enemy, either. The rocket had stood on its buttocks for months ... it was still there when the first refugees straggled into the shelter of the demolished mountains.

"Nice, isn't it?" Patricia Shelby said. She glanced up from her work and smiled blearily at Tellman. Her small, pretty face was streaked with fatigue and eye-strain. "Sort of like the trylon at the New York World's Fair."

"My God," Tellman said, "you remember that?"

"I was only eight," Patricia answered. In the shadow of the ship she was carefully checking the automatic relays that would maintain the air, temperature, and humidity of the ship. "But I'll never forget it. Maybe I was a precog — when I saw it sticking up I knew someday it would mean a lot to everybody."

"A lot to the twenty of us," Tellman corrected. Suddenly he offered her the remains of his cigarette. "Here — you look like you could use it."

"Thanks." Patricia continued with her work, the cigarette between her lips. "I'm almost done — Boy, some of these relays are tiny. Just think." She held up a microscopic wafer of transparent plastic. "While we're all out cold, this makes the difference between life and death." A strange, awed look crept into her dark-blue eyes. "To the human race."

Tellman guffawed. "You and Flannery. He's always spouting idealistic twaddle."

Professor John Crowley, once head of the history department at Stanford, now the nominal leader of the colony, sat with Flannery and Jean Dobbs, examining the suppurating arm of a ten-year-old boy. "Radiation," Crowley was saying emphatically. "The overall level is rising daily. It's settling ash that does it. If we don't get out soon, we're done."

"It's not radiation," Flannery corrected in his ultimately-certain voice.

"It's toxic crystalline poisoning; that stuff's knee-deep up in the hills. He's been playing around up there."

"Is that so?" Jean Dobbs demanded. The boy nodded his head, not daring to look at her. "You're right," she said to Flannery.

"Put some salve on it," Flannery said. "And hope he'll live. Outside of sulfathiazole there's not much we have." He glanced at his watch, suddenly tense. "Unless she brings the penicillin, today."

"If she doesn't bring it today," Crowley said, "she'll never bring it. This is the last load; as soon as it's stored, we're taking off."

Rubbing his hands, Flannery suddenly bellowed: "Then get out the money!"

Crowley grinned. "Right." He fumbled in one of the steel storage lockers and yanked out a handful of paper bills. Holding a sheaf of bills up to Tellman he fanned them out invitingly. "Take your pick. Take them all."

Nervously, Tellman said, "Be careful with that. She's probably raised the price on everything, again."

"We've got plenty." Flannery took some and stuffed it into a partly-filled load being wheeled by, on its way to the ship. "There's money blowing all over the world, along with the ash and particles of bone. On Venus we won't need it — she might as well have it all."

On Venus, Tellman thought, savagely, things would revert to their legitimate order — with Flannery digging sewers where he belonged. "What's she bringing mostly?" he asked Crowley and Jean Dobbs, ignoring Flannery. "What's the last load made up of?"

"Comic books," Flannery said dreamily, wiping perspiration from his balding forehead; he was a lean, tall, dark-haired young man. "And harmonicas."

Crowley winked at him. "Uke picks, so we can lie in our hammocks all day, strumming *Someone's in the Kitchen with Dinah*."

"And swizzle sticks," Flannery reminded him. "In order that we may all the more properly flatten the bubbles of our vintage '38 champagne."

Tellman boiled. "You — degenerate!"

Crowley and Flannery roared with laughter, and Tellman stalked off, smoldering under this new humiliation. What kind of morons and lunatics were they? Joking at a time like this ... He peered miserably, almost accusingly, at the ship. Was this the kind of world they were going to found?

In the pitiless white-hot sun, the huge ship shimmered and glowed. A vast upright tube of alloy and protective fiber mesh rising up above the tumble of wretched shacks. One more load, and they were off. One more truckful of supplies from their only source, the meager trickle of uncontaminated goods that meant the difference between life and death.

Praying that nothing would go wrong, Tellman turned to await the arrival of Mrs. Edna Berthelson and her battered red pickup truck. Their fragile umbilical cord, connecting them with the opulent, undamaged past.

On both sides of the road lay groves of lush apricot trees. Bees and flies buzzed sleepily among the rotting fruit scattered over the soil; every now and then a roadside stand appeared, operated by somnambulistic children. In driveways stood parked Buicks and Oldsmobiles. Rural dogs wandered here and there. At one intersection stood a swank tavern, its neon sign blinking on and off, ghostly pale in the mid-morning sun.

Mrs. Edna Berthelson glared hostilely at the tavern, and at the cars parked around it. City people were moving out into the valley, cutting down the old oak trees, the ancient fruit orchards, setting up suburban homes, stopping in the middle of the day for a whiskey sour and then driving cheerfully on. Driving at seventy-five miles an hour in their swept-back Chryslers. A column of cars that had piled up behind her truck suddenly burst forth and swung past her. She let them go, stony-faced, indifferent. Served them right for being in such a hurry. If she always hurried like that, she would never have had time to pay attention to that odd ability she had found in her introspective, lonely drives; never have discovered that she could look "ahead," never had discovered that hole in the warp of time which enabled her to trade so easily at her own exorbitant prices. Let them hurry if they wanted. The heavy load in the back of the truck jogged rhythmically. The motor wheezed. Against the back window a half-dead fly buzzed.

Jackie lay stretched out among the cartons and boxes, enjoying the ride, gazing complacently at the apricot trees and cars. Against the hot sky the peak of Mount Diablo rose, blue and white, an expanse of cold rock. Trails of mist clung to the peak; Mount Diablo went a long way up. He made a face at a dog standing indolently at the side of the road, waiting to cross. He waved gaily at a Pacific Telephone Co. repairman, stringing wire from a huge reel.

Abruptly the truck turned off the state highway and onto a black-surfaced side road. Now there were fewer cars. The truck began to climb ... the rich orchards fell behind and gave way to flat brown fields. A dilapidated farm house lay to the right; he watched it with interest, wondering how old it was. When it was out of sight, no other man-made structures followed. The fields became unkempt. Broken, sagging fences were visible occasionally. Torn signs, no longer legible. The truck was approaching the base of Mount Diablo ... almost nobody came this way.

Idly, the boy wondered why Mrs. Berthelson's little trip took her in this direction. Nobody lived here; suddenly there were no fields, only scrub grass and bushes, wild countryside, the tumbled slope of the mountain. A rabbit hopped skillfully across the half-decayed road. Rolling hills, a broad expanse of trees and strewn boulders ... there was nothing here but a State fire tower, and maybe a water shed. And an abandoned picnic area, once maintained by the State, now forgotten.

An edge of fear touched the boy. No customers lived out this way ... he had been positive the battered red pickup truck would head directly into town, take him and the load to San Francisco or Oakland or Berkeley, a city where he could get out and run around, see the interesting sights. There was nothing here, only abandoned emptiness, silent and foreboding. In the shadow of the mountain, the air was chill. He shivered. All at once he wished he hadn't come.

Mrs. Berthelson slowed the truck and shifted noisily into low. With a roar and an explosive belch of exhaust gases, the truck crept up a steep ascent, among jagged boulders, ominous and sharp. Somewhere far off a bird cried shrilly; Jackie listened to its thin sounds echoing dismally away and wondered how he could attract his grandmother's attention. It would be nice to be in front, in the cabin. It would be nice —

And then he noticed it. At first he didn't believe it ... but he *had* to believe it.

Under him, the truck was beginning to fade away.

It faded slowly, almost imperceptibly. Dimmer and dimmer the truck grew; its rusty red sides became gray, then colorless. The black road was visible underneath. In wild panic, the boy clutched at the piles of boxes. His hands passed through them; he was riding precariously on an uneven sea of dim shapes, among almost invisible phantoms.

He lurched and slid down. Now — hideously — he was suspended momentarily halfway *through* the truck, just above the tail pipe. Groping desperately, he struggled to catch hold of the boxes directly above him. "Help!" he shouted. His voice echoed around him; it was the only sound ... the roar of the truck was fading. For a moment he clutched at the retreating shape of the truck; then, gently, gradually, the last image of the truck faded, and with a sickening crunch, the boy dropped to the road.

The impact sent him rolling into the dry weeds beyond the drainage ditch. Stunned, dazed with disbelief and pain, he lay gasping, trying feebly to pull himself up. There was only silence; the truck, Mrs. Berthelson, had vanished. He was totally alone. He closed his eyes and lay back, stupefied with fright.

Sometime later, probably not much later, he was aroused by the squeal of brakes. A dirty, orange State maintenance truck had lurched to a stop; two men in khaki work clothes were climbing down and hurrying over.

"What's the matter?" one yelled at him. They grabbed him up, faces serious and alarmed. "What are you doing here?"

"Fell," he muttered. "Off the truck."

"What truck?" they demanded. "How?"

He couldn't tell them. All he knew was that Mrs. Berthelson had gone. He hadn't made it, after all. Once again, she was making her trip alone. He would never know where she went; he would never find out who her customers were.

Gripping the steering wheel of the truck, Mrs. Berthelson was conscious that the transition had taken place. Vaguely, she was aware that the rolling brown fields, rocks and green scrub bushes had faded out. The first time she had gone "ahead" she had found the old truck floundering in a sea of black ash. She had been so excited by her discovery that day that she had neglected to "scan" conditions on the other side of the hole. She had known there were customers ... and dashed headlong through the warp to get there first. She smiled complacently ... she needn't have hurried, there was no competition here. In fact, the customers were so eager to deal with her, they had done virtually everything in their power to make things easier for her.

The men had built a crude strip of road out into the ash, a sort of wooden platform onto which the truck now rolled. She had learned the exact moment to "go ahead"; it was the instant that the truck passed the drainage culvert a quarter mile inside the State park. Here, "ahead," the culvert also existed ... but there was little left of it, only a vague jumble of shattered stone. And the road was utterly buried. Under the wheels of the truck the rough boards thumped and banged. It would be bad if she had a flat tire ... but some of them could fix it. They were always working; one little additional task wouldn't make much difference. She could see them, now; they stood at the end of the wooden platform, waiting impatiently for her. Beyond them was their jumble of crude, smelly shacks and beyond that, their ship.

A lot she cared about their ship. She knew what it was: stolen Army property. Setting her bony hand rigidly around the gearshift knob, she threw the truck into neutral and coasted to a stop. As the men approached, she began pulling on the hand brake.

"Afternoon," Professor Crowley muttered, his eyes sharp and keen as he peered eagerly into the back of the truck.

Mrs. Berthelson grunted a noncommittal answer. She didn't like any of them ... dirty men, smelling of sweat and fear, their bodies and clothes streaked with grime, and the ancient coating of desperation that never seemed to leave them. Like awed, pitiful children they clustered around the truck, poking hopefully at the packages, already beginning to pluck them out onto the black ground.

"Here now," she said sharply. "You leave those alone."

Their hands darted back as if seared. Mrs. Berthelson sternly climbed from the truck, grabbed up her inventory sheet, and plodded up to Crowley.

"You just wait," she told him. "Those have to be checked off."

He nodded, glanced at Masterson, licked his dry lips, and waited. They all waited. It had always been that way; they knew, and she knew, that there was no other way they could get their supplies. And if they didn't get their supplies, their food and medicine and clothing and instruments and tools and raw materials, they wouldn't be able to leave in their ship.

In this world, in the "ahead," such things didn't exist. At least, not so anybody could use them. A cursory glance had told her that; she could see the ruin with her own eyes. They hadn't taken very good care of their world. They had wasted it all, turned it into black ash and ruin. Well, it was their business, not hers.

She had never been much interested in the relationship between their world and hers. She was content to know that both existed, and that she could go from one to the other and back. And she was the *only* one who knew how. Several times, people from this world, members of this group, had tried to go "back there" with her. It had always failed. As she made the transition, they were left behind. It was her power, her faculty. Not a shared faculty — she was glad of that. And for a person in business, quite a valuable faculty.

"All right," she said crisply. Standing where she could keep her eye on them, she began checking off each box as it was carried from the truck. Her routine was exact and certain; it was a part of her life. As long as she could remember she had transacted business in a distinct way. Her father had taught her how to live in a business world; she had learned his stern principles and rules. She was following them now.

Flannery and Patricia Shelby stood together at one side; Flannery held the money, payment for the delivery. "Well," he said, under his breath, "now we can tell her to go leap in the river."

"Are you sure?" Pat asked nervously.

"The last load's here." Flannery grinned starkly and ran a trembling hand through his thinning black hair. "Now we can get rolling. With this stuff, the ship's crammed to the gills. We may even have to sit down and eat some of that *now*." He indicated a bulging paste-board carton of groceries. "Bacon, eggs, milk, real coffee. Maybe we won't shove it in deep-freeze. Maybe we ought to have a last-meal-before-the-flight orgy."

Wistfully, Pat said, "It would be nice. It's been a long time since we've had food like that."

Masterson strode over. "Let's kill her and boil her in a big kettle. Skinny old witch — she might make good soup."

"In the oven," Flannery corrected. "Some gingerbread, to take along with us."

"I wish you wouldn't talk like that," Pat said apprehensively. "She's so — well, maybe she *is* a witch. I mean, maybe that's what witches were ... old women with strange talents. Like her — being able to pass through time."

"Damn lucky for us," Masterson said briefly.

"But she doesn't understand it. Does she? Does she know what she's doing? That she could save us all by sharing her ability. Does she know what's happened to our world?"

Flannery considered. "Probably she doesn't know — or care. A mind like hers, business and profit — getting exorbitant rates from us, selling this stuff to us at an incredible premium. And the joke is that money's worth nothing to us. If she could see, she'd know that. It's just paper, in this world. But she's caught in a narrow little routine. Business, profit." He shook his head. "A mind like that, a warped, miserable flea-sized mind ... and *she* has that unique talent."

"But she can *see*," Pat persisted. "She can see the ash, the ruin. How can she not know?"

Flannery shrugged. "She probably doesn't connect it with her own life. After all, she'll be dead in a couple of years ... she won't see the war in her real time. She'll only see it this way, as a region into which she can travel. A sort of travelogue of strange lands. She can enter and leave — but we're stuck. It must give you a damn fine sense of security to be able to walk out of one world, into another. God, what I'd give to be able to go back with her."

"It's been tried," Masterson pointed out. "That lizard-head Tellman tried it. And he came walking *back*, covered with ash. He said the truck faded out."

"Of course it did," Flannery said mildly. "She drove it back to Walnut Creek. Back to 1965."

The unloading had been completed. The members of the colony were toiling up the slope, lugging the cartons to the check-area beneath the ship. Mrs. Berthelson strode over to Flannery, accompanied by Professor Crowley.

"Here's the inventory," she said briskly. "A few items couldn't be found. You know, I don't stock all that in my store. I have to send out for most of it."

"We know," Flannery said, coldly amused. It would be interesting to see a country store that stocked binocular microscopes, turret lathes, frozen packs of antibiotics, high-frequency radio transmitters, advanced text books in all fields.

"So that's why I have to charge you a little dearer," the old woman continued, the inflexible routine of squeeze. "On items I bring in — " She examined her inventory, then returned the ten-page typewritten list that Crowley had given her on the previous visit. "Some of these weren't available. I marked them back order. That bunch of metals from those laboratories back East — they said maybe later." A cunning look slid over the ancient gray eyes. "And they'll be very expensive."

"It doesn't matter," Flannery said, handing her the money. "You can cancel all the back orders."

At first her face showed nothing. Only a vague inability to understand.

"No more shipments," Crowley explained. A certain tension faded from them; for the first time, they weren't afraid of her. The old relationship had ended. They weren't dependent on the rusty red truck. They had their shipment; they were ready to leave.

"We're taking off," Flannery said, grinning starkly. "We're full up."

Comprehension came. "But I placed orders for those things." Her voice was thin, bleak. Without emotion. "They'll be shipped to me. I'll have to pay for them."

"Well," Flannery said softly, "isn't that too damn bad."

Crowley shot him a warning glance. "Sorry," he said to the old woman. "We can't stick around — this place is getting hot. We've got to take off."

On the withered face, dismay turned to growing wrath. "You ordered those things! You *have* to take them!" Her shrill voice rose to a screech of fury. "What am I supposed to do with them?"

As Flannery framed his bitter answer, Pat Shelby intervened. "Mrs. Berthelson," she said quietly, "you've done a lot for us, even if you wouldn't help us through the hole into your time. And we're very grateful. If it wasn't for you, we couldn't have got together enough supplies. But we really have to go." She reached out her hand to touch the frail shoulder, but the old woman jerked furiously away. "I mean," Pat finished awkwardly, "we can't stay any longer, whether we want to or not. Do you see all that black ash? It's radioactive, and more of it sifts down all the time. The toxic level is rising — if we stay any longer it'll start destroying us."

Mrs. Edna Berthelson stood clutching her inventory list. There was an expression on her face that none of the group had ever seen before. The violent spasm of wrath had vanished; now a cold, chill glaze lay over the aged features. Her eyes were like gray rocks, utterly without feeling.

Flannery wasn't impressed. "Here's your loot," he said, thrusting out the handful of bills. "What the hell." He turned to Crowley. "Let's toss in the rest. Let's stuff it down her goddamn throat."

"Shut up," Crowley snapped.

Flannery sank resentfully back. "Who are you talking to?"

"Enough's enough." Crowley, worried and tense, tried to speak to the old woman. "My God, you can't expect us to stay around here forever, can you?"

There was no response. Abruptly, the old woman turned and strode silently back to her truck.

Masterson and Crowley looked uneasily at each other. "She sure is mad," Masterson said apprehensively.

Tellman hurried up, glanced at the old woman getting into her truck, and then bent down to root around in one of the cartons of groceries. Childish greed flushed across his thin face. "Look," he gasped. "Coffee — fifteen pounds of it. Can we open some? Can we get one tin open, to celebrate?"

"Sure," Crowley said tonelessly, his eyes on the truck. With a muffled roar, the truck turned in a wide arc and rumbled off down the crude platform, toward the ash. It rolled off into the ash, slithered for a short distance, and then faded out. Only the bleak, sun-swept plain of darkness remained.

"Coffee!" Tellman shouted gleefully. He tossed the bright metal can high in the air and clumsily caught it again. "A celebration! Our last night — last meal on Earth!"

It was true.

As the red pickup truck jogged metallically along the road, Mrs. Berthelson scanned "ahead" and saw that the men were telling the truth. Her thin lips writhed; in her mouth an acid taste of bile rose. She had taken it for granted that they would continue to buy — there was no competition, no other source of supply. But they were leaving. And when they left, there would be no more market.

She would never find a market that satisfactory. It was a perfect market; the group was a perfect customer. In the locked box at the back of the store, hidden down under the reserve sacks of grain, was almost two hundred and fifty thousand dollars. A fortune, taken in over the months, received from the imprisoned colony as it toiled to construct its ship.

And *she* had made it possible. She was responsible for letting them get away after all. Because of her short-sightedness, they were able to escape. She hadn't used her head.

As she drove back to town she meditated calmly, rationally. It was totally because of her: she was the only one who had possessed the power to bring them their supplies. Without her, they were helpless.

Hopefully, she cast about, looking this way and that, peering with her deep inner sense, into the various "aheads." There was more than one, of course. The "aheads" lay like a pattern of squares, an intricate web of worlds into which she could step, if she cared. But all were empty of what she wanted.

All showed bleak plains of black ash, devoid of human habitation. What she wanted was lacking: they were each without customers.

The patterns of "aheads" was complex. Sequences were connected like beads on a string; there were chains of "aheads" which formed interwoven links. One step led to the next ... but not to alternate chains.

Carefully, with great precision, she began the job of searching through each of the chains. There were many of them ... a virtual infinity of possible "aheads." And it was her power to select; she had stepped into that one, the particular chain in which the huddled colony had labored to construct its ship. She had, by entering it, made it manifest. Frozen it into reality. Dredged it up from among the many, from among the multitude of possibilities.

Now she needed to dredge another. That particular "ahead" had proven unsatisfactory. The market had petered out.

The truck was entering the pleasant town of Walnut Creek, passing bright stores and houses and supermarkets, before she located it. There were so many, and her mind was old ... but now she had picked it out. And as soon as she found it, she knew it was the one. Her innate business instinct certified it; the particular "ahead" clicked.

Of the possibilities, this one was unique. The ship was well-built, and thoroughly tested. In "ahead" after "ahead" the ship rose, hesitated as automatic machinery locked, and then burst from the jacket of atmosphere, toward the morning star. In a few "aheads," the wasted sequences of failure, the ship exploded into white-hot fragments. Those, she ignored; she saw no advantage in that.

In a few "aheads" the ship failed to take off at all. The turbines lashed; exhaust poured out... and the ship remained as it was. But then the men scampered out, and began going over the turbines, searching for the faulty parts. So nothing was gained. In later segments along the chain, in subsequent links, the damage was repaired, and the take-off was satisfactorily completed.

But one chain was correct. Each element, each link, developed perfectly. The pressure-locks closed, and the ship was sealed. The turbines fired, and the ship, with a shudder, rose from the plain of black ash. Three miles up, the rear jets tore loose. The ship floundered, dropped in a screaming dive, and plunged back toward the Earth. Emergency landing jets, designed for Venus, were frantically thrown on. The ship slowed, hovered for an agonizing instant, and then crashed into the heap of rubble that had been Mount Diablo. There the remains of the ship lay, twisted metal sheets, smoking in the dismal silence.

From the ship the men emerged, shaken and mute, to inspect the damage. To begin the miserable, futile task all over again. Collecting supplies, patching the rocket up ... The old woman smiled to herself.

That was what she wanted. That would do perfectly. And all she had to do — such a little thing — was select that sequence when she made her next trip. When she took her little business trip, the following Saturday.

Crowley lay half buried in the black ash, pawing feebly at a deep gash in his cheek. A broken tooth throbbed. A thick ooze of blood dripped into his mouth, the hot salty taste of his own body-fluids leaking helplessly out. He tried to move his leg, but there was no sensation. Broken. His mind was too dazed, too bewildered with despair, to comprehend.

Somewhere in the half-darkness, Flannery stirred. A woman groaned; scattered among the rocks and buckled sections of the ship lay the injured and dying. An upright shape rose, stumbled, and pitched over. An artificial light flickered. It was Tellman, making his way clumsily over the tattered remains of their world. He gaped foolishly at Crowley; his glasses hung from one ear and part of his lower jaw was missing. Abruptly he collapsed face-forward into a smoking mound of supplies. His skinny body twitched aimlessly.

Crowley managed to pull himself to his knees. Masterson was bending over him, saying something again and again.

"I'm all right," Crowley rasped.

"We're down. Wrecked."

"I know."

On Masterson's shattered face glittered the first stirrings of hysteria. "Do you think — "

"No," Crowley muttered. "It isn't possible."

Masterson began to giggle. Tears streaked the grime of his cheeks; drops of thick moisture dripped down his neck into his charred collar. "She did it. She fixed us. She wants us to stay here."

"No," Crowley repeated. He shut out the thought. It couldn't be. It just couldn't. "We'll get away," he said. "We'll assemble the remains — start over."

"She'll be back," Masterson quavered. "She knows we'll be here waiting for her. Customers!"

"No," Crowley said. He didn't believe it; he made himself not believe it. "We'll get away. We've *got* to get away!"

THE MOLD OF YANCY

LEON SIPLING GROANED and pushed away his work papers. In an organization of thousands he was the only employee not putting out. Probably he was the only yance-man on Callisto not doing his job. Fear, and the quick pluckings of desperation, made him reach up and wave on the audio circuit to Babson, the over-all office controller.

"Say," Sipling said hoarsely, "I think I'm stuck, Bab. How about running the gestalt through, up to my spot? Maybe I can pick up the rhythm ... " He grinned weakly. "The hum of other creative minds."

After a speculative moment, Babson reached for the impulse synapsis, his massive face unsympathetic. "You holding up progress, Sip? This has to be integrated with the daily by six tonight. The schedule calls for the works to be on the vidlines during the dinner-hour stretch."

The visual side of the gestalt had already begun to form on the wall screen; Sipling turned his attention to it, grateful of a chance to escape Babson's cold glare.

The screen showed a 3-D of Yancy, the usual three quarter view, from the waist up. John Edward Yancy in his faded workshirt, sleeves rolled up, arms brown and furry. A middle-aged man in his late fifties, his face sunburned, neck slightly red, a good-natured smile on his face, squinting because he was looking into the sun. Behind Yancy was a still of his yard, his garage, his flower garden, lawn, the back of his neat little white plastic house. Yancy grinned at Sipling: a neighbor pausing in the middle of a summer day, perspiring from the heat and the exertion of mowing his lawn, about to launch into a few harmless remarks about the weather, the state of the planet, the condition of the neighborhood.

"Say," Yancy said, in the audio phones propped up on Sipling's desk. His

53

voice was low, personal. "The darndest thing happened to my grandson Ralf, the other morning. You know how Ralf is; he's always getting to school half an hour early ... says he likes to be in his seat before anybody else."

"That eager-beaver," Joe Pines, at the next desk, cat-called.

From the screen, Yancy's voice rolled on, confident, amiable, undisturbed. "Well, Ralf saw this squirrel; it was just sitting there on the sidewalk. He stopped for a minute and watched." The look on Yancy's face was so real that Sipling almost believed him. He could, almost, see the squirrel and the tow-headed youngest grandson of the Yancy family, the familiar child of the familiar son of the planet's most familiar — and beloved — person.

"This squirrel," Yancy explained, in his homey way, "was collecting nuts. And by golly, this was just the other day, only the middle of June. And here was this little squirrel — " with his hands he indicated the size, "collecting these nuts and carrying them off for winter."

And then, the amused, anecdote-look on Yancy's face faded. A serious, thoughtful look replaced it: the meaningful-look. His blue eyes darkened (good color work). His jaw became more square, more imposing (good dummy-switch by the android crew). Yancy seemed older, more solemn and mature, more impressive. Behind him, the garden-scene had been jerked and a slightly different backdrop filtered in; Yancy now stood firmly planted in a cosmic landscape, among mountains and winds and huge old forests.

"I got to thinking," Yancy said, and his voice was deeper, slower. "There was that little squirrel. How did he know winter was coming? There he was, working away, getting prepared for it." Yancy's voice rose. "Preparing for a winter he'd never seen."

Sipling stiffened and prepared *himself*; it was coming. At his desk, Joe Pines grinned and yelled: "Get set!"

"That squirrel," Yancy said solemnly, "had faith. No, he never saw any sign of winter. But he knew winter was coming." The firm jaw moved; one hand came slowly up ...

And then the image stopped. It froze, immobile, silent. No words came from it; abruptly the sermon ended, in the middle of a paragraph.

"That's it," Babson said briskly, filtering the Yancy out. "Help you any?"

Sipling pawed jerkily at his work papers. "No," he admitted, "actually it doesn't. But — I'll get it worked out."

"I hope so." Babson's face darkened ominously and his small mean eyes seemed to grow smaller. "What's the matter with you? Home problems?"

"I'll be okay," Sipling muttered, sweating. "Thanks."

On the screen a faint impression of Yancy remained, still poised at the word *coming*. The rest of the gestalt was in Sipling's head: the continuing slice of words and gestures hadn't been worked out and fed to the composite.

Sipling's contribution was missing, so the entire gestalt was stopped cold in its tracks.

"Say," Joe Pines said uneasily, "I'll be glad to take over, today. Cut your desk out of the circuit and I'll cut myself in."

"Thanks," Sipling muttered, "but I'm the only one who can get this damn part. It's the central gem."

"You ought to take a rest. You've been working too hard."

"Yes," Sipling agreed, on the verge of hysteria. "I'm a little under the weather."

That was obvious: everybody in the office could see that. But only Sipling knew why. And he was fighting with all his strength to keep from screaming out the reason at the top of his lungs.

Basic analysis of the political milieu at Callisto was laid out by Niplan computing apparatus at Washington, D.C.; but the final evaluations were done by human technicians. The Washington computers could ascertain that the Callisto political structure was moving toward a totalitarian make-up, but they couldn't say what that indicated. Human beings were required to class the drift as malign.

"It isn't possible," Taverner protested. "There's constant industrial traffic in and out of Callisto; except for the Ganymede syndicate they've got out-planet commerce bottled up. We'd know as soon as anything phony got started."

"How would we know?" Police Director Kellman inquired.

Taverner indicated the data-sheets, graphs and charts of figures and percentages that covered the walls of the Niplan Police offices. "It would show up in hundreds of ways. Terrorist raids, political prisons, extermination camps. We'd hear about political recanting, treason, disloyalty ... all the basic props of a dictatorship."

"Don't confuse a totalitarian society with a dictatorship," Kellman said dryly. "A totalitarian state reaches into every sphere of its citizens' lives, forms their opinions on every subject. The government can be a dictatorship, *or* a parliament, *or* an elected president, *or* a council of priests. That doesn't matter."

"All right," Taverner said, mollified. "I'll go. I'll take a team there and see what they're doing."

"Can you make yourselves look like Callistotes?"

"What are they like?"

"I'm not sure," Kellman admitted thoughtfully, with a glance at the elaborate wall charts. "But whatever it is, they're all beginning to turn out alike."

* * *

Among its passengers the interplan commercial liner that settled down at Callisto carried Peter Taverner, his wife, and their two children. With a grimace of concern, Taverner made out the shapes of local officials waiting at the exit hatch. The passengers were going to be carefully screened; as the ramp descended, the clot of officials moved forward.

Taverner got to his feet and collected his family. "Ignore them," he told Ruth. "Our papers will get us by."

Expertly prepared documents identified him as a speculator in nonferric metals, looking for a wholesale outlet to handle his jobbing. Callisto was a clearing-point for land and mineral operations; a constant flood of wealth-hungry entrepreneurs streamed back and forth, carting raw materials from the underdeveloped moons, hauling mining equipment from the inner planets.

Cautiously, Taverner arranged his topcoat over his arm. A heavyset man, in his middle thirties, he could have passed for a successful business operator. His double-breasted business suit was expensive, but conservative. His big shoes were brightly shined. All things considered, he'd probably get by. As he and his family moved toward the exit ramp, they presented a perfect and exact imitation of the out-planet business-class.

"State your business," a green-uniformed official demanded, pencil poised. I-d tabs were being checked, photographed, recorded. Brain pattern comparisons were being made: the usual routine.

"Nonferric enterprises," Taverner began, but a second official cut him abruptly off.

"You're the third cop this morning. What's biting you people on Terra?" The official eyed Taverner intently. "We're getting more cops than ministers."

Trying to maintain his poise, Taverner answered evenly: "I'm here to take a rest. Acute alcoholism — nothing official."

"That's what your cohorts said." The official grinned humorously. "Well, what's one more Terran cop?" He slid the lockbars aside and waved Taverner and his family through. "Welcome to Callisto. Have fun — enjoy yourselves. Fastest-growing moon in the system."

"Practically a planet," Taverner commented ironically.

"Any day now." The official examined some reports. "According to our friends in your little organization, you've been pasting up wall graphs and charts about us. Are we that important?"

"Academic interest," Taverner said; if three spots had been made, then the whole team had been netted. The local authorities were obviously primed to detect infiltration ... the realization chilled him.

But they were letting him through. Were they *that* confident?

Things didn't look good. Peering around for a cab, he grimly prepared to undertake the business of integrating the scattered team members into a functioning whole.

That evening, at the *Stay-Lit* bar on the main street of the commercial district of town, Taverner met with his two team members. Hunched over their whiskey sours, they compared notes.

"I've been here almost twelve hours," Eckmund stated, gazing impassively at the rows of bottles in the gloomy depths of the bar. Cigar smoke hovered in the air; the automatic music box in the corner banged away metallically. "I've been walking around town, looking at things, making observations."

"Me," Dorser said, "I've been at the tape-library. Getting official myth, comparing it to Callistote reality. And talking to the scholars — educated people hanging around the scanning rooms."

Taverner sipped his drink. "Anything of interest?"

"You know the primitive rule-of-thumb test," Eckmund said wryly. "I loafed around on a slum street corner until I got in a conversation with some people waiting for a bus. I started knocking the authorities: complaining about the bus service, the sewage disposal, taxes, everything. They chimed right in. Heartily. No hesitation. And no fear."

"The legal government," Dorser commented, "is set up in the usual archaic fashion. Two-party system, one a little more conservative than the other — no fundamental difference of course. But both elect candidates at open primaries, ballots circulated to all registered voters." A spasm of amusement touched him. "This is a model democracy. I read the text books. Nothing but idealistic slogans: freedom of speech, assembly, religion — the works. Same old grammar school stuff."

The three of them were temporarily silent.

"There are jails," Taverner said slowly. "Every society has law violations."

"I visited one," Eckmund said, belching. "Petty thieves, murderers, claim-jumpers, strong-arm hoods — the usual."

"No political prisoners?"

"No." Eckmund raised his voice. "We might as well discuss this at the top of our lungs. Nobody cares — the authorities don't care."

"Probably after we're gone they'll clap a few thousand people into prison," Dorser murmured thoughtfully.

"My God," Eckmund retorted, "people can leave Callisto any time they want. If you're operating a police state you have to keep your borders shut. And these borders are wide open. People pour in and out."

"Maybe it's a chemical in the drinking water," Dorser suggested.

"How the hell can they have a totalitarian society without terrorism?" Eckmund demanded rhetorically. "I'll swear to it — there are no thought-control cops here. There is absolutely no fear."

"Somehow, pressure is being exerted," Taverner persisted.

"Not by cops," Dorser said emphatically. "Not by force and brutality. Not by illegal arrest and imprisonment and forced labor."

"If this were a police state," Eckmund said thoughtfully, "there'd be some kind of resistance movement. Some sort of 'subversive' group trying to overthrow the authorities. But in this society you're free to complain; you can buy time on the TV and radio stations, you can buy space in the newspapers — anything you want." He shrugged. "So how can there be a clandestine resistance movement? It's silly."

"Nevertheless," Taverner said, "these people are living in a one-party society with a party line, with an official ideology. They show the effects of a carefully controlled totalitarian state. They're guinea pigs — whether they realize it or not."

"Wouldn't they realize it?"

Baffled, Taverner shook his head. "I would have thought so. There must be some mechanism we don't understand."

"It's all open. We can look everything over."

"We must be looking for the wrong thing." Idly, Taverner gazed at the television screen above the bar. The nude girlie song-and-dance routine had ended; now the features of a man faded into view. A genial, round-faced man in his fifties, with guileless blue eyes, an almost childish twitch to his lips, a fringe of brown hair playing around his slightly prominent ears.

"Friends," the TV image rumbled, "it's good to be with you again, tonight. I thought I might have a little chat with you."

"A commercial," Dorser said, signalling the bartending machine for another drink.

"Who is that?" Taverner asked curiously.

"That kindly-looking geezer?" Eckmund examined his notes. "A sort of popular commentator. Name of Yancy."

"Is he part of the government?"

"Not that I know of. A kind of home-spun philosopher. I picked up a biography of him on a magazine stand." Eckmund passed the gaily-colored pamphlet to his boss. "Totally ordinary man, as far as I can see. Used to be a soldier; in the Mars-Jupiter War he distinguished himself — battlefield commission. Rose to the rank of major." He shrugged indifferently. "A sort of talking almanac. Pithy sayings on every topic. Wise old saws: how to cure a chest cold. What the trouble is back on Terra."

Taverner examined the booklet. "Yes, I saw his picture around."

"Very popular figures. Loved by the masses. Man of the people — speaks for them. When I was buying cigarettes I noticed he endorses one particular brand. Very popular brand, now; just about driven the others off the market. Same with beer. The Scotch in this glass is probably the brand Yancy endorses. The same with tennis balls. Only he doesn't play tennis — he plays croquet. All the time, every weekend." Accepting his fresh drink Eckmund finished, "So now everybody plays croquet."

"How can croquet be a planet-wide sport?" Taverner demanded.

"This isn't a planet," Dorser put in. "It's a pipsqueak moon."

"Not according to Yancy," Eckmund said. "We're supposed to think of Callisto as a planet."

"How?" Taverner asked.

"Spiritually, it's a planet. Yancy likes people to take a spiritual view of matters. He's strong on God and honesty in government and being hardworking and clean-cut. Warmed-over truisms."

The expression on Taverner's face hardened. "Interesting," he murmured. "I'll have to drop by and meet him."

"Why? He's the dullest, most mediocre man you could dream up."

"Maybe," Taverner answered, "that's why I'm interested."

Babson, huge and menacing, met Taverner at the entrance of the Yancy Building. "Of course you can meet Mr. Yancy. But he's a busy man — it'll take a while to squeeze in an appointment. Everybody wants to meet Mr. Yancy."

Taverner was unimpressed. "How long do I have to wait?"

As they crossed the main lobby to the elevators, Babson made a computation. "Oh, say four months."

"Four *months*!"

"John Yancy is just about the most popular man alive."

"Around here, maybe," Taverner commented angrily, as they entered the packed elevator. "I never heard of him before. If he's got so much on the ball, why isn't he piped all around Niplan?"

"Actually," Babson admitted, in a hoarse, confidential whisper, "I can't imagine what people see in Yancy. As far as I'm concerned he's just a big bag of wind. But people around here enjoy him. After all, Callisto is — provincial. Yancy appeals to a certain type of rural mind — to people who like their world simple. I'm afraid Terra would be too sophisticated for Yancy."

"Have you tried?"

"Not yet," Babson said. Reflectively, he added: "Maybe later."

While Taverner was pondering the meaning of the big man's words, the elevator ceased climbing. The two of them stepped off into a luxurious, carpeted hall, illuminated by recessed lights. Babson pushed open a door, and they entered a large, active office.

Inside, a screening of a recent Yancy gestalt was in progress. A group of yance-men watched it silently, faces alert and critical. The gestalt showed Yancy sitting at his old-fashioned oak desk, in his study. It was obvious that he had been working on some philosophical thoughts: spread out over the desk were books and papers. On Yancy's face was a thoughtful expression; he sat with his hand against his forehead, features screwed up into a solemn study of concentration.

"This is for next Sunday morning," Babson explained.

Yancy's lips moved, and he spoke. "Friends," he began, in his deep, personal, friendly, man-to-man voice, "I've been sitting here at my desk — well, about the way you're sitting around your living rooms." A switch in camera work occurred; it showed the open door of Yancy's study. In the living room was the familiar figure of Yancy's sweet-faced middle-aged homey wife; she was sitting on the comfortable sofa, primly sewing. On the floor their grandson Ralf played the familiar game of jacks. The family dog snoozed in the corner.

One of the watching yance-men made a note on his pad. Taverner glanced at him curiously, baffled.

"Of course, I was in there with them," Yancy continued, smiling briefly. "I was reading the funnies to Ralf. He was sitting on my knee." The background faded, and a momentary phantom scene of Yancy sitting with his grandson on his knee floated into being. Then the desk and the book-lined study returned. "I'm mighty grateful for my family," Yancy revealed. "In these times of stress, it's my family that I turn to, as my pillar of strength." Another notation was made by a watching yance-man.

"Sitting here, in my study, this wonderful Sunday morning," Yancy rumbled on, "I realize how lucky we are to be alive, and to have this lovely planet, and the fine cities and houses, all the things God has given us to enjoy. But we've got to be careful. We've got to make sure we don't lose these things."

A change had come over Yancy. It seemed to Taverner that the image was subtly altering. It wasn't the same man; the good humor was gone. This was an older man, and larger. A firm-eyed father, speaking to his children.

"My friends," Yancy intoned, "there are forces that could weaken this planet. Everything we've built up for our loved ones, for our children, *could be taken away from us overnight*. We must learn to be vigilant. We must protect our liberties, our possessions, our way of life. If we become divided, and fall to bickering among each other, we will be easy prey for our enemies. We must work together, my friends.

"That's what I've been thinking about this Sunday morning. *Cooperation. Teamwork*. We've got to be secure, and to be secure, we must be one united people. That's the key, my friends, the key to a more abundant life." Pointing out the window at the lawn and garden, Yancy said: "You know, I was ... "

The voice trailed off. The image froze. Full room lights came on, and the watching yance-men moved into muttering activity.

"Fine," one of them said. "So far, at least. But where's the rest?"

"Sipling, again," another answered. "His slice still hasn't come through. What's wrong with that guy?"

Scowling, Babson detached himself. "Pardon me," he said to Taverner.

"I'll have to excuse myself — technical matters. You're free to look around, if you care to. Help yourself to any of the literature — anything you want."

"Thanks," Taverner said uncertainly. He was confused; everything *seemed* harmless, even trivial. But something basic was wrong.

Suspiciously, he began to prowl.

It was obvious that John Yancy had pontificated on every known subject. A Yancy opinion on every conceivable topic was available ... modern art, or garlic in cooking, or the use of intoxicating beverages, or eating meat, or socialism, or war, or education, or open-front dresses on women, or high taxes, or atheism, or divorce, or patriotism — every shade and nuance of opinion possible.

Was there any subject that Yancy *hadn't* expressed himself on?

Taverner examined the voluminous tapes that lined the walls of the offices. Yancy's utterances had run into billions of tape feet ... could one man have an opinion on everything in the universe?

Choosing a tape at random, he found himself being addressed on the topic of table manners.

"You know," the miniature Yancy began, his voice tinny in Taverner's ears, "at dinner the other night I happened to notice how my grandson Ralf was cutting his steak." Yancy grinned at the viewer, as an image of the six-year-old boy sawing grimly away floated briefly into sight. "Well, I got to thinking, there was Ralf working away at that steak, not having any luck with it. And it seemed to me — "

Taverner snapped the tape off and returned it to the slot. Yancy had definite opinions on everything ... or *were* they so definite?

A strange suspicion was growing in him. On some topics, yes. On minor issues, Yancy had exact rules, specific maxims drawn from mankind's rich storehouse of folklore. But major philosophical and political issues were something else again.

Getting out one of the many tapes listed under War, Taverner ran it through at random.

" ... I'm against war," Yancy pronounced angrily. "And I ought to know; I've done my share of fighting."

There followed a montage of battle scenes: the Jupiter-Mars War in which Yancy had distinguished himself by his bravery, his concern for his comrades, his hatred of the enemy, his variety of proper emotions.

"But," Yancy continued staunchly, "I feel a planet must be strong. We must not surrender ourselves meekly ... weakness invites attack and fosters aggression. By being weak we promote war. We must gird ourselves and protect those we love. With all my heart and soul I'm against useless wars; but I say again, as I've said many times before, a man must come forward and fight a *just* war. He must not shrink from his responsibility. War is a terrible thing. But sometimes we must ... "

As he restored the tape, Taverner wondered just what the hell Yancy *had* said. What were his views on war? They took up a hundred separate reels of tape; Yancy was always ready to hold forth on such vital and grandiose subjects as War, the Planet, God, Taxation. But did he *say* anything?

A cold chill crawled up Taverner's spine. On specific — and trivial — items there were absolute opinions: dogs are better than cats, grapefruit is too sour without a dash of sugar, it's good to get up early in the morning, too much drinking is bad. But on big topics ... an empty vacuum, filled with the vacant roll of high-sounding phrases. A public that agreed with Yancy on war and taxes and God and planet agreed with absolutely nothing. And with everything.

On topics of importance, they had no opinion at all. They only *thought* they had an opinion.

Rapidly, Taverner scanned tapes on various major subjects. It was the same all down the line. With one sentence Yancy gave; with the next he took away. The total effect was a neat cancellation, a skillful negation. But the viewer was left with the illusion of having consumed a rich and varied intellectual feast. It was amazing. And it was professional: the ends were tied up too slickly to be mere accident.

Nobody was as harmless and vapid as John Edward Yancy. He was just too damn good to be true.

Sweating, Taverner left the main reference room and poked his way toward the rear offices, where busy yance-men worked away at their desks and assembly tables. Activity whirred on all sides. The expression on the faces around him was benign, harmless, almost bored. The same friendly, trivial expression that Yancy himself displayed.

Harmless — and in its harmlessness, diabolical. And there wasn't a damn thing he could do. If people liked to listen to John Edward Yancy, if they wanted to model themselves after him — what could the Niplan Police do about it?

What crime was being committed?

No wonder Babson didn't care if the police prowled around. No wonder the authorities had freely admitted them. There weren't any political jails of labor gangs or concentration camps ... there didn't have to be.

Torture chambers and extermination camps were needed only when persuasion failed. And persuasion was working perfectly. A police state, rule by terror, came about when the totalitarian apparatus began to break down. The earlier totalitarian societies had been incomplete; the authorities hadn't really gotten into every sphere of life. But techniques of communication had improved.

The first really successful totalitarian state was being realized before his eyes: harmless and trivial, it emerged. And the last stage — nightmarish, but perfectly logical — was when all the newborn boys were happily and voluntarily named John Edward.

Why not? They already lived, acted, and thought like John Edward. And there was Mrs. Margaret Ellen Yancy, for the women. She had her full range of opinions, too; she had her kitchen, her taste in clothes, her little recipes and advice, for all the women to imitate.

There were even Yancy children for the youth of the planet to imitate. The authorities hadn't overlooked anything.

Babson strolled over, a genial expression on his face. "How's it going, officer?" he chuckled wetly, putting his hand on Taverner's shoulder.

"Fine," Taverner managed to answer; he evaded the hand.

"You like our little establishment?" There was genuine pride in Babson's thick voice. "We do a good job. An artistic job — we have real standards of excellence."

Shaking with helpless anger, Taverner plunged out of the office and into the hall. The elevator took too long; furiously, he turned toward the stairs. He had to get out of the Yancy Building; he had to get away.

From the shadows of the hall a man appeared, face pale and taut. "Wait. Can — I talk to you?"

Taverner pushed past him. "What do you want?"

"You're from the Terran Niplan Police? I — " The man's Adam's apple bobbed. "I work here. My name's Sipling, Leon Sipling. I have to do something — I can't stand it anymore."

"Nothing can be done," Taverner told him. "If they want to be like Yancy — "

"But there isn't any Yancy," Sipling broke in, his thin face twitching spasmodically. "We made him up ... we invented him."

Taverner halted. "You *what?*"

"I've decided." Voice quavering excitedly, Sipling rushed on: "I'm going to do something — and I know exactly what." Catching hold of Taverner's sleeve he grated: "You've got to help me. I can stop all this, but I can't do it alone."

In Leon Sipling's attractive, well-furnished living room, the two of them sat drinking coffee and watching their children scramble around on the floor, playing games. Sipling's wife and Ruth Taverner were in the kitchen, drying the dishes.

"Yancy is a synthesis," Sipling explained. "A sort of composite person. No such individual actually exists. We drew on basic prototypes from sociological records; we based the gestalt on various typical persons. So it's true to life. But we stripped off what we didn't want, and intensified what we did want."

Broodingly, he added: "There could be a Yancy. There are a lot of Yancy-like people. In fact, that's the problem."

"You deliberately set out with the idea of remolding people along Yancy's line?" Taverner inquired.

"I can't precisely say what the idea is, at top level. I was an ad writer for a mouth wash company. The Callisto authorities hired me and outlined what they wanted me to do. I've had to guess as to the purpose of the project."

"By authorities, you mean the governing council?"

Sipling laughed sharply. "I mean the trading syndicates that own this moon: lock, stock, and barrel. But we're not supposed to call it a moon. It's a planet." His lips twitched bitterly. "Apparently, the authorities have a big program built up. It involves absorbing their trade rivals on Ganymede — when that's done, they'll have the out-planets sewed up tight."

"They can't get at Ganymede without open war," Taverner protested. "The Medean companies have their own population behind them." And then it dawned. "I see," he said softly. "They'd actually start a war. It would be worth a war, to them."

"You're damn right it would. And to start a war, they have to get the public lined up. Actually, the people here have nothing to gain. A war would wipe out all the small operators — it would concentrate power in fewer hands — and they're few enough already. To get the eighty million people here behind the war, they need an indifferent, sheep-like public. *And they're getting that.* When this Yancy campaign is finished, the people here on Callisto will accept anything. Yancy does all their thinking for them. He tells them how to wear their hair. What games to play. He tells the jokes the men repeat in their back rooms. His wife whips up the meal they all have for dinner. All over this little world — millions of duplicates of Yancy's day. Whatever he does, whatever he believes. We've been conditioning the public for eleven straight years. The important thing is the unvarying monotony of it. A whole generation is growing up looking to Yancy for an answer to everything."

"It's a big business, then," Taverner observed. "This project of creating and maintaining Yancy."

"Thousands of people are involved in just writing the material. You only saw the first stage — and it goes into every city. Tapes, films, books, magazines, posters, pamphlets, dramatic visual and audio shows, plants in the newspapers, sound trucks, kids' comic strips, word-of-mouth report, elaborate ads ... the works. A steady stream of Yancy." Picking up a magazine from the coffee table he indicated the lead article. " 'How is John Yancy's Heart?' Raises the question of what would we do without Yancy? Next week, an article on Yancy's stomach." Acidly, Sipling finished: "We know a million approaches. We turn it out of every pore. We're called yance-men; it's a new art-form."

"How do you — the corps, feel about Yancy?"

"He's a big sack of hot air."

"None of you is convinced?"

"Even Babson has to laugh. And Babson is at the top; after him come the boys who sign the checks. God, if we ever started believing in Yancy ... if we got started thinking that trash *meant* something — " An expression of acute agony settled over Sipling's face. "That's it. That's why I can't stand it."

"Why?" Taverner asked, deeply curious. His throat-mike was taking it all in, relaying it back to the home office at Washington. "I'm interested in finding out why you broke away."

Sipling bent down and called his son. "Mike, stop playing and come on over here." To Taverner he explained: "Mike's nine years old. Yancy's been around as long as he's been alive."

Mike came dully over. "Yes, sir?"

"What kind of marks do you get in school?" his father asked.

The boy's chest stuck out proudly; he was a clear-eyed little miniature of Leon Sipling. "All A's and B's."

"He's a smart kid," Sipling said to Taverner. "Good in arithmetic, geography, history, all that stuff." Turning to the boy he said: "I'm going to ask you some questions; I want this gentleman to hear your answers. Okay?"

"Yes, sir," the boy said obediently.

His thin face grim, Sipling said to his son: "I want to know what you think about war. You've been told about war in school; you know about all the famous wars in history. Right?"

"Yes, sir. We learned about the American Revolution, and the First Global War, and then the Second Global War, and then the First Hydrogen War, and the War between the colonists on Mars and Jupiter."

"To the schools," Sipling explained tightly to Taverner, "we distribute Yancy material — educational subsidies in packet form. Yancy takes children through history, explains the meaning of it all. Yancy explains natural science. Yancy explains good posture and astronomy and every other thing in the universe. But I never thought my own son ... " His voice trailed off unhappily, then picked up life. "So you know all about war. Okay, what do you think of war?"

Promptly, the boy answered: "War is bad. War is the most terrible thing there is. It almost destroyed mankind."

Eying his son intently, Sipling demanded: "Did anybody tell you to say that?"

The boy faltered uncertainly. "No, sir."

"You really believe those things?"

"Yes, sir. It's true, isn't it? Isn't war bad?"

Sipling nodded. "War is bad. But what about *just* wars?"

Without hesitation the boy answered: "We have to fight just wars, of course."

"Why?"

"Well, we have to protect our way of life."

"Why?"

Again, there was no hesitation in the boy's reedy answer. "We can't let them walk over us, sir. That would encourage aggressive war. We can't permit a world of brute power. We have to have a world of — " He searched for the exact word. "A world of *law.*"

Wearily, half to himself, Sipling commented: "I wrote those meaningless, contradictory words myself, eight years ago." Pulling himself together with a violent effort he asked: "So war is bad. But we have to fight just wars. Well, maybe this — *planet*, Callisto, will get into a war with ... let's pick Ganymede, at random." He was unable to keep the harsh irony from his voice. "Just at random. Now, we're at war with Ganymede. Is it a *just* war? Or only a war?"

This time, there was no answer. The boy's smooth face was screwed up in a bewildered, struggling frown.

"No answer?" Sipling inquired icily.

"Why, uh," the boy faltered. "I mean ... " He glanced up hopefully. "When the time comes won't somebody say?"

"Sure," Sipling choked. "Somebody will say. Maybe even Mr. Yancy."

Relief flooded the boy's face. "Yes, sir. Mr. Yancy will say." He retreated back toward the other children. "Can I go now?"

As the boy scampered back to his game, Sipling turned miserably to Taverner. "You know what game they're playing? It's called Hippo-Hoppo. Guess whose grandson just loves it. Guess who invented the game."

There was silence.

"What do you suggest?" Taverner asked. "You said you thought something could be done."

A cold expression appeared on Sipling's face, a flash of deeply-felt cunning. "I know the project ... I know how it can be pried apart. But somebody has to stand with a gun at the head of the authorities. In nine years I've come to see the essential key to the Yancy character ... the key to the new type of person we're growing, here. It's simple. It's the element that makes that person malleable enough to be led around."

"I'll bite," Taverner said patiently, hoping the line to Washington was good and clear.

"All Yancy's beliefs are insipid. The key is *thinness.* Every part of his ideology is diluted: nothing excessive. We've come as close as possible to *no* beliefs ... you've noticed that. Wherever possible we've cancelled attitudes out, left the person apolitical. Without a viewpoint."

"Sure," Taverner agreed. "But with the illusion of a viewpoint."

"All aspects of personality have to be controlled; we want the total person. So a specific attitude has to exist for each concrete question. In every respect, our rule is: *Yancy believes the least troublesome possibility.* The most shallow. The simple, effortless view, the view that fails to go deep enough to stir any real thought."

Taverner got the drift. "Good solid lulling views." Excitedly he hurried on, "But if an extreme original view got in, one that took real effort to work out, something that was hard to live ... "

"Yancy plays croquet. So everybody fools around with a mallet." Sipling's eyes gleamed. "But suppose Yancy had a preference for — Kriegspiel."

"For *what?*"

"Chess played on two boards. Each player has his own board, with a complete set of men. He never sees the other board. A moderator sees both; he tells each player when he's taken a piece, or lost a piece, or moved into an occupied square, or made an impossible move, or checked, or is in check himself."

"I see," Taverner said quickly. "Each player tries to infer his opponent's location on the board. He plays blind. Lord, it would take every mental faculty possible."

"The Prussians taught their officers military strategy that way. It's more than a game: it's a cosmic wrestling match. What if Yancy sat down in the evening with his wife and grandson, and played a nice lively six-hour game of Kriegspiel? Suppose his favorite books — instead of being western gun-toting anachronisms — were Greek tragedy? Suppose his favorite piece of music was Bach's *Art of the Fugue*, not *My Old Kentucky Home?*"

"I'm beginning to get the picture," Taverner said, as calmly as possible. "I think we can help."

Babson squeaked once. "But this is — illegal!"

"Absolutely," Taverner acknowledged. "That's why we're here." He waved the squad of Niplan secret-servicemen into the offices of the Yancy Building, ignoring the stunned workers sitting bolt-upright at their desks. Into his throat-mike he said, "How's it coming with the big-shots?"

"Medium," Kellman's faint voice came, strengthened by the relay system between Callisto and Earth. "Some slipped out of bounds to their various holdings, of course. But the majority never thought we'd taken action."

"You can't!" Babson bleated, his great face hanging down in wattles of white dough. "What have we done? What law — "

"I think," Taverner interrupted, "we can get you on purely commercial grounds alone. You've used the name Yancy to endorse various manufactured products. There's no such person. That's a violation of statutes governing ethical presentation of advertising."

Babson's mouth closed with a snap, then slid feebly open. "No — such — person? But everybody knows John Yancy. Why, he's — " Stammering, gesturing, he finished, "He's everywhere."

Suddenly a wretched little pistol appeared in his pulpy hand; he was waving it wildly as Dorser stepped up and quietly knocked it skidding across the floor. Babson collapsed into fumbling hysterics.

Disgusted, Dorser clamped handgrapples around him. "Act like a man," he ordered. But there was no response; Babson was too far gone to hear him.

Satisfied, Taverner plunged off, past the knot of stunned officials and workers, into the inner offices of the project. Nodding curtly, Taverner made his way up to the desk where Leon Sipling sat surrounded by his work.

The first of the altered gestalts was already flickering through the scanner. Together, the two men stood watching it.

"Well?" Taverner said, when it was done. "You're the judge."

"I believe it'll do," Sipling answered nervously. "I hope we don't stir up too much ... it's taken eleven years to build it up; we want to tear it down by degrees."

"Once the first crack is made, it should start swaying." Taverner moved toward the door. "Will you be all right on your own?"

Sipling glanced at Eckmund who lounged at the end of the office, eyes fixed on the uneasily working yance-men. "I suppose so. Where are you going?"

"I want to watch this as it's released. I want to be around when the public gets its first look at it." At the door, Taverner lingered. "It's going to be a big job for you, putting out the gestalt on your own. You may not get much help, for a while."

Sipling indicated his co-workers; they were already beginning to pick up their tempo where they had left off. "They'll stay on the job," he disagreed. "As long as they get full salaries."

Taverner walked thoughtfully across the hall to the elevator. A moment later he was on his way downstairs.

At a nearby street corner, a group of people had collected around a public vid-screen. Anticipating the late-afternoon TV cast of John Edward Yancy.

The gestalt began in the regular way. There was no doubt about it: when Sipling wanted to, he could put together a good slice. And in this case he had done practically the whole pie.

In rolled-up shirt sleeves and dirt-stained trousers, Yancy crouched in his garden, a trowel in one hand, straw hat pulled down over his eyes, grinning into the warm glare of the sun. It was so real that Taverner could hardly believe no such person existed. But he had watched Sipling's sub-crews laboriously and expertly constructing the thing from the ground up.

"Afternoon," Yancy rumbled genially. He wiped perspiration from his steaming, florid face and got stiffly to his feet. "Man," he admitted, "it's a hot day." He indicated a flat of primroses. "I was setting them out. Quite a job."

So far so good. The crowd watched impassively, taking their ideological nourishment without particular resistance. All over the moon, in every house, schoolroom, office, on each street corner, the same gestalt was showing. And it would be shown again.

"Yes," Yancy repeated, "it's really hot. Too hot for those primroses — they like shade." A fast pan-up showed he had carefully planted his primroses in the shadows at the base of his garage. "On the other hand," Yancy continued, in his smooth, good-natured, over-the-back-fence conversational voice, "my dahlias need lots of sun."

The camera leaped to show the dahlias blooming frantically in the blazing sunlight.

Throwing himself down in a striped lawnchair, Yancy removed his straw hat and wiped his brow with a pocket handkerchief. "So," he continued genially, "if anybody asked me which is better, shade or sun, I'd have to reply it depends on whether you're a primrose or a dahlia." He grinned his famous guileless boyish grin into the cameras. "I guess I must be a primrose — I've had all the sun I can stand for today."

The audience was taking it in without complaint. An inauspicious beginning, but it was going to have long-term consequences. And Yancy was starting to develop them right now.

His genial grin faded. That familiar look, that awaited serious frown showing that deep thoughts were coming, faded into place. Yancy was going to hold forth: wisdom was on the way. But it was nothing ever uttered by him before.

"You know," Yancy said slowly, seriously, "that makes a person do some thinking." Automatically, he reached for his glass of gin and tonic — a glass which up until now would have contained beer. And the magazine beside it wasn't *Dog Stories Monthly*; it was *The Journal of Psychological Review*. The alteration of peripheral props would sink in subliminally; right now, all conscious attention was riveted on Yancy's words.

"It occurs to me," Yancy orated, as if the wisdom were fresh and brand-new, arriving just now, "that some people might maintain that, say, sunlight is *good* and shade is *bad*. But that's down-right silly. Sunlight is good for roses and dahlias, but it would darn well finish off my fuchsias."

The camera showed his ubiquitous prize fuchsias.

"Maybe you know people like that. They just don't understand that — " And as was his custom, Yancy drew on folklore to make his point. "That one man's meat," he stated profoundly, "is another man's poison. Like for instance, for breakfast I like a couple of eggs done sunny-side up, maybe a few stewed prunes, and a piece of toast. But Margaret, she prefers a bowl of cereal. And Ralf, he won't take either. He likes flapjacks. And the fellow down the street, the one with the big front lawn, he likes a kidney pie and a bottle of stout."

Taverner winced. Well, they would have to feel their way along. But still the audience stood absorbing it, word after word. The first feeble stirrings of a radical idea: that each person had a different set of values, a unique style of life. That each person might believe, enjoy, and approve of different things.

It would take time, as Sipling said. The massive library of tapes would have to be replaced; injunctions built up in each area would have to be broken down. A new type of thinking was being introduced, starting with a trite observation about primroses. When a nine-year-old-boy wanted to find out if a war was just or unjust, he would have to inquire into his own mind. There would be no ready answer from Yancy; a gestalt was already being prepared on that, showing that every war had been called just by some, unjust by others.

There was one gestalt Taverner wished he could see. But it wouldn't be around for a long time; it would have to wait. Yancy was going to change his taste in art, slowly but steadily. One of these days, the public would learn that Yancy no longer enjoyed pastoral calendar scenes.

That now he preferred the art of that fifteenth century Dutch master of macabre and diabolical horror, Hieronymus Bosch.

THE MINORITY REPORT

I

THE FIRST THOUGHT Anderton had when he saw the young man was: *I'm getting bald. Bald and fat and old.* But he didn't say it aloud. Instead, he pushed back his chair, got to his feet, and came resolutely around the side of his desk, his right hand rigidly extended. Smiling with forced amiability, he shook hands with the young man.

"Witwer?" he asked, managing to make this query sound gracious.

"That's right," the young man said. "But the name's Ed to you, of course. That is, if you share my dislike for needless formality." The look on his blond, overly-confident face showed that he considered the matter settled. It would be Ed and John: Everything would be agreeably cooperative right from the start.

"Did you have much trouble finding the building?" Anderton asked guardedly, ignoring the too-friendly overture. *Good God, he had to hold on to something.* Fear touched him and he began to sweat. Witwer was moving around the office as if he already owned it — as if he were measuring it for size. Couldn't he wait a couple of days — a decent interval?

"No trouble," Witwer answered blithely, his hands in his pockets. Eagerly, he examined the voluminous files that lined the wall. "I'm not coming into your agency blind, you understand. I have quite a few ideas of my own about the way Precrime is run."

Shakily, Anderton lit his pipe. "How is it run? I should like to know."

"Not badly," Witwer said. "In fact, quite well."

Anderton regarded him steadily. "Is that your private opinion? Or is it just cant?"

71

Witwer met his gaze guilelessly. "Private and public. The Senate's pleased with your work. In fact, they're enthusiastic." He added, "As enthusiastic as very old men can be."

Anderton winced, but outwardly he remained impassive. It cost him an effort, though. He wondered what Witwer *really* thought. What was actually going on in that closecropped skull? The young man's eyes were blue, bright — and disturbingly clever. Witwer was nobody's fool. And obviously he had a great deal of ambition.

"As I understand it," Anderton said cautiously, "you're going to be my assistant until I retire."

"That's my understanding, too," the other replied, without an instant's hesitation.

"Which may be this year, or next year — or ten years from now." The pipe in Anderton's hand trembled. "I'm under no compulsion to retire. I founded Precrime and I can stay on here as long as I want. It's purely *my* decision."

Witwer nodded, his expression still guileless. "Of course."

With an effort, Anderton cooled down a trifle. "I merely wanted to get things straight."

"From the start," Witwer agreed. "You're the boss. What you say goes." With every evidence of sincerity, he asked: "Would you care to show me the organization? I'd like to familiarize myself with the general routine as soon as possible."

As they walked along the busy, yellow-lit tiers of offices, Anderton said: "You're acquainted with the theory of precrime, of course. I presume we can take that for granted."

"I have the information publicly available," Witwer replied. "With the aid of your precog mutants, you've boldly and successfully abolished the post-crime punitive system of jails and fines. As we all realize, punishment was never much of a deterrent, and could scarcely have afforded comfort to a victim already dead."

They had come to the descent lift. As it carried them swiftly downward, Anderton said: "You've probably grasped the basic legalistic drawback to precrime methodology. We're taking in individuals who have broken no law."

"But they surely will," Witwer affirmed with conviction.

"Happily they *don't* — because we get them first, before they can commit an act of violence. So the commission of the crime itself is absolute metaphysics. We claim they're culpable. They, on the other hand, eternally claim they're innocent. And, in a sense, they *are* innocent."

The lift let them out, and they again paced down a yellow corridor. "In our society we have no major crimes," Anderton went on, "but we do have a detention camp full of would-be criminals."

Doors opened and closed, and they were in the analytical wing. Ahead of them rose impressive banks of equipment — the data-receptors, and the computing mechanisms that studied and restructured the incoming material. And beyond the machinery sat the three precogs, almost lost to view in the maze of wiring.

"There they are," Anderton said dryly. "What do you think of them?"

In the gloomy half-darkness the three idiots sat babbling. Every incoherent utterance, every random syllable, was analyzed, compared, reassembled in the form of visual symbols, transcribed on conventional punchcards, and ejected into various coded slots. All day long the idiots babbled, imprisoned in their special high-backed chairs, held in one rigid position by metal bands, and bundles of wiring, clamps. Their physical needs were taken care of automatically. They had no spiritual needs. Vegetable-like, they muttered and dozed and existed. Their minds were dull, confused, lost in shadows.

But not the shadows of today. The three gibbering, fumbling creatures, with their enlarged heads and wasted bodies, were contemplating the future. The analytical machinery was recording prophecies, and as the three precog idiots talked, the machinery carefully listened.

For the first time Witwer's face lost its breezy confidence. A sick, dismayed expression crept into his eyes, a mixture of shame and moral shock. "It's not — pleasant," he murmured. "I didn't realize they were so — " He groped in his mind for the right word, gesticulating. "So — deformed."

"Deformed and retarded," Anderton instantly agreed. "Especially the girl, there. Donna is forty-five years old. But she looks about ten. The talent absorbs everything; the esp-lobe shrivels the balance of the frontal area. But what do we care? We get their prophecies. They pass on what we need. They don't understand any of it, but *we* do."

Subdued, Witwer crossed the room to the machinery. From a slot he collected a stack of cards. "Are these names that have come up?" he asked.

"Obviously." Frowning, Anderton took the stack from him. "I haven't had a chance to examine them," he explained, impatiently concealing his annoyance.

Fascinated, Witwer watched the machinery pop a fresh card into the now empty slot. It was followed by a second — and a third. From the whirring disks came one card after another. "The precogs must see quite far into the future," Witwer exclaimed.

"They see a quite limited span," Anderton informed him. "One week or two ahead at the very most. Much of their data is worthless to us — simply not relevant to our line. We pass it on to the appropriate agencies. And they in turn trade data with us. Every important bureau has its cellar of treasured *monkeys.*"

"Monkeys?" Witwer stared at him uneasily. "Oh, yes, I understand. See no evil, speak no evil, et cetera. Very amusing."

"Very *apt.*" Automatically, Anderton collected the fresh cards which had been turned up by the spinning machinery. "Some of these names will be totally discarded. And most of the remainder record petty crimes: thefts, income tax evasion, assault, extortion. As I'm sure you know, Precrime has cut down felonies by ninety-nine and decimal point eight percent. We seldom get actual murder or treason. After all, the culprit knows we'll confine him in the detention camp a week before he gets a chance to commit the crime."

"When was the last time an actual murder was committed?" Witwer asked.

"Five years ago," Anderton said, pride in his voice.

"How did it happen?"

"The criminal escaped our teams. We had his name — in fact, we had all the details of the crime, including the victim's name. We knew the exact moment, the location of the planned act of violence. But in spite of us he was able to carry it out." Anderton shrugged. "After all, we can't get all of them." He riffled the cards. "But we do get most."

"One murder in five years." Witwer's confidence was returning. "Quite an impressive record ... something to be proud of."

Quietly Anderton said: "I *am* proud. Thirty years ago I worked out the theory — back in the days when the self-seekers were thinking in terms of quick raids on the stock market. I saw something legitimate ahead — something of tremendous social value."

He tossed the packet of cards to Wally Page, his subordinate in charge of the monkey block. "See which ones we want," he told him. "Use your own judgment."

As Page disappeared with the cards, Witwer said thoughtfully: "It's a big responsibility."

"Yes, it is," agreed Anderton. "If we let one criminal escape — as we did five years ago — we've got a human life on our conscience. We're solely responsible. If we slip up, somebody dies." Bitterly, he jerked three new cards from the slot. "It's a public trust."

"Are you ever tempted to — " Witwer hesitated. "I mean, some of the men you pick up must offer you plenty."

"It wouldn't do any good. A duplicate file of cards pops out at Army GHQ. It's check and balance. They can keep their eye on us as continuously as they wish." Anderton glanced briefly at the top card. "So even if we wanted to accept a — "

He broke off, his lips tightening.

"What's the matter?" Witwer asked curiously.

Carefully, Anderton folded up the top card and put it away in his pocket. "Nothing," he muttered. "Nothing at all."

The harshness in his voice brought a flush to Witwer's face. "You really don't like me," he observed.

"True," Anderton admitted. "I don't. But — "

He couldn't believe he disliked the young man that much. It didn't seem possible: it *wasn't* possible. Something was wrong. Dazed, he tried to steady his tumbling mind.

On the card was his name. Line one — an already accused future murderer! According to the coded punches, Precrime Commissioner John A. Anderton was going to kill a man — and within the next week.

With absolute, overwhelming conviction, he didn't believe it.

II

In the outer office, talking to Page, stood Anderton's slim and attractive young wife, Lisa. She was engaged in a sharp, animated discussion of policy, and barely glanced up as Witwer and her husband entered.

"Hello, darling," Anderton said.

Witwer remained silent. But his pale eyes flickered slightly as they rested on the brown-haired woman in her trim police uniform. Lisa was now an executive official of Precrime but once, Witwer knew, she had been Anderton's secretary.

Noticing the interest on Witwer's face Anderton paused and reflected. To plant the card in the machines would require an accomplice on the inside — someone who was closely connected with Precrime and had access to the analytical equipment. Lisa was an improbable element. But the possibility did exist.

Of course, the conspiracy could be large-scale and elaborate, involving far more than a "rigged" card inserted somewhere along the line. The original data itself might have been tampered with. Actually, there was no telling how far back the alteration went. A cold fear touched him as he began to see the possibilities. His original impulse — to tear open the machines and remove all the data — was uselessly primitive. Probably the tapes agreed with the card: He would only incriminate himself further.

He had approximately twenty-four hours. Then, the Army people would check over their cards and discover the discrepancy. They would find in their files a duplicate of the card he had appropriated. He had only one of two copies, which meant that the folded card in his pocket might just as well be lying on Page's desk in plain view of everyone.

From outside the building came the drone of police cars starting out on their routine round-ups. How many hours would elapse before one of them pulled up in front of *his* house?

"What's the matter, darling?" Lisa asked him uneasily. "You look as if you've just seen a ghost. Are you all right?"

"I'm fine," he assured her.

Lisa suddenly seemed to become aware of Ed Witwer's admiring scrutiny. "Is this gentleman your new co-worker, darling?" she asked.

Warily, Anderton introduced his new associate. Lisa smiled in friendly greeting. Did a covert awareness pass between them? He couldn't tell. God, he was beginning to suspect everybody — not only his wife and Witwer, but a dozen members of his staff.

"Are you from New York?" Lisa asked.

"No," Witwer replied. "I've lived most of my life in Chicago. I'm staying at a hotel — one of the big downtown hotels. Wait — I have the name written on a card somewhere."

While he self-consciously searched his pockets, Lisa suggested: "Perhaps you'd like to have dinner with us. We'll be working in close cooperation, and I really think we ought to get better acquainted."

Startled, Anderton backed off. What were the chances of his wife's friendliness being benign, accidental? Witwer would be present the balance of the evening, and would now have an excuse to trail along to Anderton's private residence. Profoundly disturbed, he turned impulsively, and moved toward the door.

"Where are you going?" Lisa asked, astonished.

"Back to the monkey block," he told her. "I want to check over some rather puzzling data tapes before the Army sees them." He was out in the corridor before she could think of a plausible reason for detaining him.

Rapidly, he made his way to the ramp at its far end. He was striding down the outside stairs toward the public sidewalk, when Lisa appeared breathlessly behind him.

"What on earth has come over you?" Catching hold of his arm, she moved quickly in front of him. "I *knew* you were leaving," she exclaimed, blocking his way. "What's wrong with you? Everybody thinks you're — " She checked herself. "I mean, you're acting so erratically."

People surged by them — the usual afternoon crowd. Ignoring them, Anderton pried his wife's fingers from his arm. "I'm getting out," he told her. "While there's still time."

"But — *why?*"

"I'm being framed — deliberately and maliciously. This creature is out to get my job. The Senate is getting at me *through* him."

Lisa gazed up at him, bewildered. "But he seems like such a nice young man."

"Nice as a water moccasin."

Lisa's dismay turned to disbelief. "I don't believe it. Darling, all this strain you've been under — " Smiling uncertainly, she faltered: "It's not really credible that Ed Witwer is trying to frame you. How could he, even if he wanted to? Surely Ed wouldn't — "

"Ed?"

"That's his name, isn't it?"

Her brown eyes flashed in startled, wildly incredulous protest. "Good heavens, you're suspicious of everybody. You actually believe I'm mixed up with it in some way, don't you?"

He considered. "I'm not sure."

She drew closer to him, her eyes accusing. "That's not true. You really believe it. Maybe you *ought* to go away for a few weeks. You desperately need a rest. All this tension and trauma, a younger man coming in. You're acting paranoiac. Can't you see that? People plotting against you. Tell me, do you have any actual proof?"

Anderton removed his wallet and took out the folded card. "Examine this carefully," he said, handing it to her.

The color drained out of her face, and she gave a little harsh, dry gasp.

"The set-up is fairly obvious," Anderton told her, as levelly as he could. "This will give Witwer a legal pretext to remove me right now. He won't have to wait until I resign." Grimly, he added: "They know I'm good for a few years yet."

"But — "

"It will end the check and balance system. Precrime will no longer be an independent agency. The Senate will control the police, and after that — " His lips tightened. "They'll absorb the Army too. Well, it's outwardly logical enough. *Of course* I feel hostility and resentment toward Witwer — *of course* I have a motive."

"Nobody likes to be replaced by a younger man, and find himself turned out to pasture. It's all really quite plausible — except that I haven't the remotest intention of killing Witwer. But I can't prove that. So what can I do?"

Mutely, her face very white, Lisa shook her head. "I — I don't know. Darling, if only — "

"Right now," Anderton said abruptly, "I'm going home to pack my things. That's about as far ahead as I can plan."

"You're really going to — to try to hide out?"

"I am. As far as the Centaurian-colony planets, if necessary. It's been done successfully before, and I have a twenty-four-hour start." He turned resolutely. "Go back inside. There's no point in your coming with me."

"Did you imagine I would?" Lisa asked huskily.

Startled, Anderton stared at her. "Wouldn't you?" Then with amazement, he murmured: "No, I can see you don't believe me. You still think I'm imagining all this." He jabbed savagely at the card. "Even with that evidence you still aren't convinced."

"No," Lisa agreed quickly, "I'm not. You didn't look at it closely enough, darling. Ed Witwer's name isn't on it."

Incredulous, Anderton took the card from her.

"Nobody says you're going to kill Ed Witwer," Lisa continued rapidly, in a thin, brittle voice. "The card *must* be genuine, understand? And it has nothing to do with Ed. He's not plotting against you and neither is anybody else."

Too confused to reply, Anderton stood studying the card. She was right. Ed Witwer was not listed as his victim. On line five, the machine had neatly stamped another name.

LEOPOLD KAPLAN

Numbly, he pocketed the card. He had never heard of the man in his life.

III

The house was cool and deserted, and almost immediately Anderton began making preparations for his journey. While he packed, frantic thoughts passed through his mind.

Possibly he was wrong about Witwer — but how could he be sure? In any event, the conspiracy against him was far more complex than he had realized. Witwer, in the over-all picture, might be merely an insignificant puppet animated by someone else — by some distant, indistinct figure only vaguely visible in the background.

It had been a mistake to show the card to Lisa. Undoubtedly, she would describe it in detail to Witwer. He'd never get off Earth, never have an opportunity to find out what life on a frontier planet might be like.

While he was thus preoccupied, a board creaked behind him. He turned from the bed, clutching a weather-stained winter sports jacket, to face the muzzle of a gray-blue A-pistol.

"It didn't take you long," he said, staring with bitterness at the tight-lipped, heavyset man in a brown overcoat who stood holding the gun in his gloved hand. "Didn't she even hesitate?"

The intruder's face registered no response. "I don't know what you're talking about," he said. "Come along with me."

Startled, Anderton laid down the sports jacket. "You're not from my agency? You're not a police officer?"

Protesting and astonished, he was hustled outside the house to a waiting limousine. Instantly three heavily armed men closed in behind him. The door slammed and the car shot off down the highway, away from the city. Impassive and remote, the faces around him jogged with the motion of the speeding vehicle as open fields, dark and somber, swept past.

Anderton was till trying futilely to grasp the implications of what had happened, when the car came to a rutted side road, turned off, and descended into a gloomy sub-surface garage. Someone shouted an order. The heavy metal lock grated shut and overhead lights blinked on. The driver turned off the car motor.

"You'll have reason to regret this," Anderton warned hoarsely, as they dragged him from the car. "Do you realize who I am?"

"We realize," the man in the brown overcoat said.

At gun-point, Anderton was marched upstairs, from the clammy silence of the garage into a deep-carpeted hallway. He was, apparently, in a luxurious private residence, set out in the war-devoured rural area. At the far end of the hallway he could make out a room — a book-lined study simply but tastefully furnished. In a circle of lamplight, his face partly in shadows, a man he had never met sat waiting for him.

As Anderton approached, the man nervously slipped a pair of rimless glasses in place, snapped the case shut, and moistened his dry lips. He was elderly, perhaps seventy or older, and under his arm was a slim silver cane. His body was thin, wiry, his attitude curiously rigid. What little hair he had was dusty brown — a carefully-smoothed sheen of neutral color above his pale, bony skull. Only his eyes seemed really alert.

"Is this Anderton?" he inquired querulously, turning to the man in the brown overcoat. "Where did you pick him up?"

"At his home," the other replied. "He was packing — as we expected."

The man at the desk shivered visibly. "Packing." He took off his glasses and jerkily returned them to their case. "Look here," he said bluntly to Anderton, "what's the matter with you? Are you hopelessly insane? How could you kill a man you've never met?"

The old man, Anderton suddenly realized, was Leopold Kaplan.

"First, I'll ask you a question," Anderton countered rapidly. "Do you realize what you've done? I'm Commissioner of Police. I can have you sent up for twenty years."

He was going to say more, but a sudden wonder cut him short.

"How did you find out?" he demanded. Involuntarily, his hand went to his pocket, where the folded card was hidden. "It won't be for another — "

"I wasn't notified through your agency," Kaplan broke in, with angry impatience. "The fact that you've never heard of me doesn't surprise me too much. Leopold Kaplan, General of the Army of the Federated Westbloc Alliance." Begrudgingly, he added. "Retired, since the end of the Anglo-Chinese War, and the abolishment of AFWA."

It made sense. Anderton had suspected that the Army processed its duplicate cards immediately, for its own protection. Relaxing somewhat, he demanded: "Well? You've got me here. What next?"

"Evidently," Kaplan said, "I'm not going to have you destroyed, or it would have shown up on one of those miserable little cards. I'm curious about you. It seemed incredible to me that a man of your stature could contemplate the cold-blooded murder of a total stranger. There must be something more here. Frankly, I'm puzzled. If it represented some kind of Police strategy — " He shrugged his thin shoulders. "Surely you wouldn't have permitted the duplicate card to reach us."

"Unless," one of his men suggested, "it's a deliberate plant."

Kaplan raised his bright, bird-like eyes and scrutinized Anderton. "What do you have to say?"

"That's exactly what it is," Anderton said, quick to see the advantage of stating frankly what he believed to be the simple truth. "The prediction on the card was deliberately fabricated by a clique inside the police agency. The card is prepared and I'm netted. I'm relieved of my authority automatically. My assistant steps in and claims he prevented the murder in the usual efficient Precrime manner. Needless to say, there is no murder or intent to murder."

"I agree with you that there will be no murder," Kaplan affirmed grimly. "You'll be in police custody. I intend to make certain of that."

Horrified, Anderton protested: "You're taking me back there? If I'm in custody I'll never be able to prove — "

"I don't care what you prove or don't prove," Kaplan interrupted. "All I'm interested in is having you out of the way." Frigidly, he added: "For my own protection."

"He was getting ready to leave," one of the men asserted.

"That's right," Anderton said, sweating. "As soon as they get hold of me I'll be confined in the detention camp. Witwer will take over — lock, stock and barrel." His face darkened. "And my wife. They're acting in concert, apparently."

For a moment Kaplan seemed to waver. "It's possible," he conceded, regarding Anderton steadily. Then he shook his head. "I can't take the chance. If this is a frame against you, I'm sorry. But it's simply not my affair." He smiled slightly. "However, I wish you luck." To the men he said: "Take him to the police building and turn him over to the highest authority." He mentioned the name of the acting commissioner, and waited for Anderton's reaction.

"Witwer!" Anderton echoed, incredulous.

Still smiling slightly, Kaplan turned and clicked on the console radio in the study. "Witwer has already assumed authority. Obviously, he's going to create quite an affair out of this."

There was a brief static hum, and then, abruptly, the radio blared out into the room — a noisy professional voice, reading a prepared announcement.

" ... all citizens are warned not to shelter or in any fashion aid or assist this dangerous marginal individual. The extraordinary circumstance of an escaped criminal at liberty and in a position to commit an act of violence is unique in modern times. All citizens are hereby notified that legal statutes still in force implicate any and all persons failing to cooperate fully with the police in their task of apprehending John Allison Anderton. To repeat: The Precrime Agency of the Federal Westbloc Government is in the process of locating and neutralizing its former Commissioner, John Allison Anderton, who, through the methodology of the precrime-system, is hereby declared a potential murderer and as such forfeits his rights to freedom and all its privileges."

"It didn't take him long," Anderton muttered, appalled. Kaplan snapped off the radio and the voice vanished.

"Lisa must have gone directly to him," Anderton speculated bitterly.

"Why should he wait?" Kaplan asked. "You made your intentions clear." He nodded to his men. "Take him back to town. I feel uneasy having him so close. In that respect I concur with Commissioner Witwer. I want him neutralized as soon as possible."

IV

Cold, light rain beat against the pavement, as the car moved through the dark streets of New York City toward the police building.

"You can see his point," one of the men said to Anderton. "If you were in his place you'd act just as decisively."

Sullen and resentful, Anderton stared straight ahead.

"Anyhow," the man went on, "you're just one of many. Thousands of people have gone to that detention camp. You won't be lonely. As a matter of fact, you may not want to leave."

Helplessly, Anderton watched pedestrians hurrying along the rain-swept sidewalks. He felt no strong emotion. He was aware only of an overpowering fatigue. Dully, he checked off the street numbers: they were getting near the police station.

"This Witwer seems to know how to take advantage of an opportunity," one of the men observed conversationally. "Did you ever meet him?"

"Briefly," Anderton answered.

"He wanted your job — so he framed you. Are you sure of that?"

Anderton grimaced. "Does it matter?"

"I was just curious." The man eyed him languidly. "So you're the ex-Commissioner of Police. People in the camp will be glad to see you coming. They'll remember you."

"No doubt," Anderton agreed.

"Witwer sure didn't waste any time. Kaplan's lucky — with an official like that in charge." The man looked at Anderton almost pleadingly. "You're really convinced it's a plot, eh?"

"Of course."

"You wouldn't harm a hair of Kaplan's head? For the first time in history, Precrime goes wrong? An innocent man is framed by one of those cards. Maybe there've been other innocent people — right?"

"It's quite possible," Anderton admitted listlessly.

"Maybe the whole system can break down. Sure, you're not going to commit a murder — and maybe none of them were. Is that why you told Kaplan you wanted to keep yourself outside? Were you hoping to prove the system wrong? I've got an open mind, if you want to talk about it."

Another man leaned over, and asked, "Just between the two of us, is there really anything to this plot stuff? Are you really being framed?"

Anderton sighed. At that point he wasn't certain, himself. Perhaps he was trapped in a closed, meaningless time-circle with no motive and no beginning. In fact, he was almost ready to concede that he was the victim of a weary, neurotic fantasy, spawned by growing insecurity. Without a fight, he was willing to give himself up. A vast weight of exhaustion lay upon him. He was struggling against the impossible — and all the cards were stacked against him.

The sharp squeal of tires roused him. Frantically, the driver struggled to control the car, tugging at the wheel and slamming on the brakes, as a massive bread truck loomed up from the fog and ran directly across the lane ahead. Had he gunned the motor instead he might have saved himself. But too late he realized his error. The car skidded, lurched, hesitated for a brief instant, and then smashed head on into the bread truck.

Under Anderton the seat lifted up and flung him face-forward against the door. Pain, sudden, intolerable, seemed to burst in his brain as he lay gasping and trying feebly to pull himself to his knees. Somewhere the crackle of fire echoed dismally, a patch of hissing brilliance winking in the swirls of mist making their way into the twisted hulk of the car.

Hands from outside the car reached for him. Slowly he became aware that he was being dragged through the rent that had been the door. A heavy seat cushion was shoved brusquely aside, and all at once he found himself on his feet, leaning heavily against a dark shape and being guided into the shadows of an alley a short distance from the car.

In the distance, police sirens wailed.

"You'll live," a voice grated in his ear, low and urgent. It was a voice he had never heard before, as unfamiliar and harsh as the rain beating into his face. "Can you hear what I'm saying?"

"Yes," Anderton acknowledged. He plucked aimlessly at the ripped sleeve of his shirt. A cut on his cheek was beginning to throb. Confused, he tried to orient himself. "You're not — "

"Stop talking and listen." The man was heavyset, almost fat. Now his big hands held Anderton propped against the wet brick wall of the building, out of the rain and the flickering light of the burning car. "We had to do it that way," he said. "It was the only alternative. We didn't have much time. We thought Kaplan would keep you at his place longer."

"Who are you?" Anderton managed.

The moist, rain-streaked face twisted into a humorless grin. "My name's Fleming. You'll see me again. We have about five seconds before the police get here. Then we're back where we started." A flat packet was stuffed into Anderton's hands. "That's enough loot to keep you going. And there's a full set of identification in there. We'll contact you from time to time." His grin increased and became a nervous chuckle. "Until you've proved your point."

Anderton blinked. "It is a frameup, then?"

"Of course." Sharply, the man swore. "You mean they got you to believe it, too?"

"I thought — " Anderton had trouble talking; one of his front teeth seemed to be loose. "Hostility toward Witwer ... replaced, my wife and a younger man, natural resentment.... "

"Don't kid yourself," the other said. "You know better than that. This whole business was worked out carefully. They had every phase of it under control. The card was set to pop the day Witwer appeared. They've already got the first part wrapped up. Witwer is Commissioner, and you're a hunted criminal."

"Who's behind it?"

"Your wife."

Anderton's head spun. "You're positive?"

The man laughed. "You bet your life." He glanced quickly around. "Here come the police. Take off down this alley. Grab a bus, get yourself into the slum section, rent a room and buy a stack of magazines to keep you busy. Get other clothes — You're smart enough to take care of yourself. Don't try to leave Earth. They've got all the intersystem transports screened. If you can keep low for the next seven days, you're made."

"Who are you?" Anderton demanded.

Fleming let go of him. Cautiously, he moved to the entrance of the alley and peered out. The first police car had come to rest on the damp pavement; its motor spinning tinnily, it crept suspiciously toward the smouldering ruin that had been Kaplan's car. Inside the wreck the squad of men were stirring feebly, beginning to creep painfully through the tangle of steel and plastic out into the cold rain.

"Consider us a protective society," Fleming said softly, his plump, expressionless face shining with moisture. "A sort of police force that watches the police. To see," he added, "that everything stays on an even keel."

His thick hand shot out. Stumbling, Anderton was knocked away from him, half-falling into the shadows and damp debris that littered the alley.

"Get going," Fleming told him sharply. "And don't discard that packet." As Anderton felt his way hesitantly toward the far exit of the alley, the man's last words drifted to him. "Study it carefully and you may still survive."

V

The identification cards described him as Ernest Temple, an unemployed electrician, drawing a weekly subsistence from the State of New York, with a wife and four children in Buffalo and less than a hundred dollars in assets. A sweat-stained green card gave him permission to travel and to maintain no fixed address. A man looking for work needed to travel. He might have to go a long way.

As he rode across town in the almost empty bus, Anderton studied the description of Ernest Temple. Obviously, the cards had been made out with him in mind, for all the measurements fitted. After a time he wondered about the fingerprints and the brain-wave pattern. They couldn't possibly stand comparison. The walletful of cards would get him past only the most cursory examinations.

But it was something. And with the ID cards came ten thousand dollars in bills. He pocketed the money and cards, then turned to the neatly-typed message in which they had been enclosed.

At first he could make no sense of it. For a long time he studied it, perplexed.

The existence of a majority logically implies
a corresponding minority.

The bus had entered the vast slum region, the tumbled miles of cheap hotels and broken-down tenements that had sprung up after the mass destruction of the war. It slowed to a stop, and Anderton got to his feet. A few passengers idly observed his cut cheek and damaged clothing. Ignoring them, he stepped down onto the rain-swept curb.

Beyond collecting the money due him, the hotel clerk was not interested. Anderton climbed the stairs to the second floor and entered the narrow, musty-smelling room that now belonged to him. Gratefully, he locked the door and pulled down the window shades. The room was small but clean. Bed, dresser, scenic calendar, chair, lamp, a radio with a slot for the insertion of quarters.

He dropped a quarter into it and threw himself heavily down on the bed. All main stations carried the police bulletin. It was novel, exciting, something unknown to the present generation. An escaped criminal! The public was avidly interested.

" ... this man has used the advantage of his high position to carry out an initial escape," the announcer was saying, with professional indignation. "Because of his high office he had access to the previewed data and the trust placed in him permitted him to evade the normal process of detection and re-location. During the period of his tenure he exercised his authority to send countless potentially guilty individuals to their proper confinement, thus sparing the lives of innocent victims. This man, John Allison Anderton, was instrumental in the original creation of the Precrime system, the prophylactic pre-detection of criminals through the ingenious use of mutant precogs, capable of previewing future events and transferring orally that data to analytical machinery. These three precogs, in their vital function. ... "

The voice faded out as he left the room and entered the tiny bathroom.

There, he stripped off his coat, and shirt, and ran hot water in the wash bowl. He began bathing the cut on his cheek. At the drugstore on the corner he had bought iodine and Band-aids, a razor, comb, toothbrush, and other small things he would need. The next morning he intended to find a second-hand clothing store and buy more suitable clothing. After all, he was now an unemployed electrician, not an accident-damaged Commissioner of Police.

In the other room the radio blared on. Only subconsciously aware of it, he stood in front of the cracked mirror, examining a broken tooth.

" ... the system of three precogs finds its genesis in the computers of the middle decades of this century. How are the results of an electronic computer checked? By feeding the data to a second computer of identical design. But two computers are not sufficient. If each computer arrived at a different answer it is impossible to tell *a priori* which is correct. The solution, based on a careful study of statistical method, is to utilize a third computer to check the results of the first two. In this manner, a so-called majority report is obtained. It can be assumed with fair probability that the agreement of two out of three computers indicates which of the alternative results is accurate. It would not be likely that two computers would arrive at identically incorrect solutions — "

Anderton dropped the towel he was clutching and raced into the other room. Trembling, he bent to catch the blaring words of the radio.

" ... unanimity of all three precogs is a hoped-for but seldom-achieved phenomenon, acting-Commissioner Witwer explains. It is much more common to obtain a collaborative majority report of two precogs, plus a minority report of some slight variation, usually with reference to time and place, from the third mutant. This is explained by the theory of *multiple-futures*. If only one time-path existed, precognitive information would be of no importance, since no possibility would exist, in possessing this information, of altering the future. In the Precrime Agency's work we must first of all assume — "

Frantically, Anderton paced around the tiny room. Majority report — only two of the precogs had concurred on the material underlying the card. That was the meaning of the message enclosed with the packet. The report of the third precog, the minority report, was somehow of importance.

Why?

His watch told him that it was after midnight. Page would be off duty. He wouldn't be back in the monkey block until the next afternoon. It was a slim chance, but worth taking. Maybe Page would cover for him, and maybe not. He would have to risk it.

He had to see the minority report.

VI

Between noon and one o'clock the rubbish-littered streets swarmed with people. He chose that time, the busiest part of the day, to make his call. Selecting a phonebooth in a patron-teeming super drugstore, he dialed the familiar police number and stood holding the cold receiver to his ear. Deliberately, he had selected the aud, not the vid line: in spite of his second-hand clothing and seedy, unshaven appearance, he might be recognized.

The receptionist was new to him. Cautiously, he gave Page's extension. If Witwer were removing the regular staff and putting in his satellites, he might find himself talking to a total stranger.

"Hello," Page's gruff voice came.

Relieved, Anderton glanced around. Nobody was paying any attention to him. The shoppers wandered among the merchandise, going about their daily routines. "Can you talk?" he asked. "Or are you tied up?"

There was a moment of silence. He could picture Page's mild face torn with uncertainty as he wildly tried to decide what to do. At last came halting words. "Why — are you calling here?"

Ignoring the question, Anderton said, "I didn't recognize the receptionist. New personnel?"

"Brand-new," Page agreed, in a thin, strangled voice. "Big turnovers, these days."

"So I hear." Tensely, Anderton asked, "How's your job? Still safe?"

"Wait a minute." The receiver was put down and the muffled sound of steps came in Anderton's ear. It was followed by the quick slam of a door being hastily shut. Page returned. "We can talk better now," he said hoarsely.

"How much better?"

"Not a great deal. Where are you?"

"Strolling through Central Park," Anderton said. "Enjoying the sunlight." For all he knew, Page had gone to make sure the line-tap was in place. Right now, an airborne police team was probably on its way. But he had to take the chance. "I'm in a new field," he said curtly. "I'm an electrician these days."

"Oh?" Page said, baffled.

"I thought maybe you had some work for me. If it can be arranged, I'd like to drop by and examine your basic computing equipment. Especially the data and analytical banks in the monkey block."

After a pause, Page said: "It — might be arranged. If it's really important."

"It is," Anderton assured him. "When would be best for you?"

"Well," Page said, struggling. "I'm having a repair team come in to look at the intercom equipment. The acting-Commissioner wants it improved, so he can operate quicker. You might trail along."

"I'll do that. About when?"

"Say four o'clock. Entrance B, level 6. I'll — meet you."

"Fine," Anderton agreed, already starting to hang up. "I hope you're still in charge, when I get there."

He hung up and rapidly left the booth. A moment later he was pushing through the dense pack of people crammed into the nearby cafeteria. Nobody would locate him there.

He had three and a half hours to wait. And it was going to seem a lot longer. It proved to be the longest wait of his life before he finally met Page as arranged.

The first thing Page said was: "You're out of your mind. Why in hell did you come back?"

"I'm not back for long." Tautly, Anderton prowled around the monkey block, systematically locking one door after another. "Don't let anybody in. I can't take chances."

"You should have quit when you were ahead." In an agony of apprehension, Page followed after him. "Witwer is making hay, hand over fist. He's got the whole country screaming for your blood."

Ignoring him, Anderton snapped open the main control bank of the analytical machinery. "Which of the three monkeys gave the minority report?"

"Don't question me — I'm getting out." On his way to the door Page halted briefly, pointed to the middle figure, and then disappeared. The door closed; Anderton was alone.

The middle one. He knew that one well. The dwarfed, hunched-over figure had sat buried in its wiring and relays for fifteen years. As Anderton approached, it didn't look up. With eyes glazed and blank, it contemplated a world that did not yet exist, blind to the physical reality that lay around it.

"Jerry" was twenty-four years old. Originally, he had been classified as a hydrocephalic idiot but when he reached the age of six the psych testers had identified the precog talent, buried under the layers of tissue corrosion. Placed in a government-operated training school, the latent talent had been cultivated. By the time he was nine the talent had advanced to a useful stage. "Jerry," however, remained in the aimless chaos of idiocy; the burgeoning faculty had absorbed the totality of his personality.

Squatting down, Anderton began disassembling the protective shields that guarded the tape-reels stored in the analytical machinery. Using schematics, he traced the leads back from the final stages of the integrated computers, to the point where "Jerry's" individual equipment branched off. Within minutes he was shakily lifting out two half-hour tapes: recent rejected data not fused with majority reports. Consulting the code chart, he selected the section of tape which referred to his particular card.

A tape scanner was mounted nearby. Holding his breath, he inserted the tape, activated the transport, and listened. It took only a second. From the first statement of the report it was clear what had happened. He had what he wanted; he could stop looking.

"Jerry's" vision was misphased. Because of the erratic nature of precognition, he was examining a time-area slightly different from that of his companions. For him, the report that Anderton would commit a murder was an event to be integrated along with everything else. That assertion — and Anderton's reaction — was one more piece of datum.

Obviously, "Jerry's" report superseded the majority report. Having been informed that he would commit a murder, Anderton would change his mind and not do so. The preview of the murder had cancelled out the murder; prophylaxis had occurred simply in his being informed. Already, a new time-path had been created. But "Jerry" was outvoted.

Trembling, Anderton rewound the tape and clicked on the recording head. At high speed he made a copy of the report, restored the original, and removed the duplicate from the transport. Here was the proof that the card was invalid: *obsolete*. All he had to do was show it to Witwer. . . .

His own stupidity amazed him. Undoubtedly, Witwer had seen the report; and in spite of it, had assumed the job of Commissioner, had kept the police teams out. Witwer didn't intend to back down; he wasn't concerned with Anderton's innocence.

What, then, could he do? Who else would be interested?

"You damn fool!" a voice behind him grated, wild with anxiety.

Quickly, he turned. His wife stood at one of the doors, in her police uniform, her eyes frantic with dismay. "Don't worry," he told her briefly, displaying the reel of tape. "I'm leaving."

Her face distorted, Lisa rushed frantically up to him. "Page said you were here, but I couldn't believe it. He shouldn't have let you in. He just doesn't understand what you are."

"What am I?" Anderton inquired caustically. "Before you answer, maybe you better listen to this tape."

"I don't want to listen to it! I just want you to get out of here! Ed Witwer knows somebody's down here. Page is trying to keep him occupied, but — " She broke off, her head turned stiffly to one side. "He's here now! He's going to force his way in."

"Haven't you got any influence? Be gracious and charming. He'll probably forget about me."

Lisa looked at him in bitter reproach. "There's a ship parked on the roof. If you want to get away. . . . " Her voice choked and for an instant she was silent. Then she said, "I'll be taking off in a minute or so. If you want to come — "

"I'll come," Anderton said. He had no other choice. He had secured his tape, his proof, but he hadn't worked out any method of leaving. Gladly, he hurried after the slim figure of his wife as she strode from the block, through a side door and down a supply corridor, her heels clicking loudly in the deserted gloom.

"It's a good fast ship," she told him over her shoulder. "It's emergency-fueled — ready to go. I was going to supervise some of the teams."

VII

Behind the wheel of the high-velocity police cruiser, Anderton outlined what the minority report tape contained. Lisa listened without comment, her face pinched and strained, her hands clasped tensely in her lap. Below the ship, the war-ravaged rural countryside spread out like a relief map, the vacant regions between cities crater-pitted and dotted with the ruins of farms and small industrial plants.

"I wonder," she said, when he had finished, "how many times this has happened before."

"A minority report? A great many times."

"I mean, one precog misphased. Using the report of the others as data — superseding them." Her eyes dark and serious, she added, "Perhaps a lot of the people in the camps are like you."

"No," Anderton insisted. But he was beginning to feel uneasy about it, too. "I was in a position to see the card, to get a look at the report. That's what did it."

"But — " Lisa gestured significantly. "Perhaps all of them would have reacted that way. We could have told them the truth."

"It would have been too great a risk," he answered stubbornly.

Lisa laughed sharply. "Risk? Chance? Uncertainty? With precogs around?"

Anderton concentrated on steering the fast little ship. "This is a unique case," he repeated. "And we have an immediate problem. We can tackle the theoretical aspects later on. I have to get this tape to the proper people — before your bright young friend demolishes it."

"You're taking it to Kaplan?"

"I certainly am." He tapped the reel of tape which lay on the seat between them. "He'll be interested. Proof that his life isn't in danger ought to be of vital concern to him."

From her purse, Lisa shakily got out her cigarette case. "And you think he'll help you."

"He may — or he may not. It's a chance worth taking."

"How did you manage to go underground so quickly?" Lisa asked. "A completely effective disguise is difficult to obtain."

"All it takes is money," he answered evasively.

As she smoked, Lisa pondered. "Probably Kaplan will protect you," she said. "He's quite powerful."

"I thought he was only a retired general."

"Technically — that's what he is. But Witwer got out the dossier on him. Kaplan heads an unusual kind of exclusive veterans' organization. It's actually a kind of club, with a few restricted members. High officers only — an international class from both sides of the war. Here in New York they maintain a great mansion of a house, three glossy-paper publications, and occasional TV coverage that costs them a small fortune."

"What are you trying to say?"

"Only this. You've convinced me that you're innocent. I mean, it's obvious that you *won't* commit a murder. But you must realize now that the original report, the majority report, *was not a fake*. Nobody falsified it. Ed Witwer didn't create it. There's no plot against you, and there never was. If you're going to accept this minority report as genuine you'll have to accept the majority one, also."

Reluctantly, he agreed. "I suppose so."

"Ed Witwer," Lisa continued, "is acting in complete good faith. He really believes you're a potential criminal — and why not? He's got the majority report sitting on his desk, but you have that card folded up in your pocket."

"I destroyed it," Anderton said, quietly.

Lisa leaned earnestly toward him. "Ed Witwer isn't motivated by any desire to get your job," she said. "He's motivated by the same desire that has always dominated you. He believes in Precrime. He wants the system to continue. I've talked to him and I'm convinced he's telling the truth."

Anderton asked, "Do you want me to take this reel to Witwer? If I do — he'll destroy it."

"Nonsense," Lisa retorted. "The originals have been in his hands from the start. He could have destroyed them any time he wished."

"That's true." Anderton conceded. "Quite possibly he didn't know."

"Of course he didn't. Look at it this way. If Kaplan gets hold of that tape, the police will be discredited. Can't you see why? It would prove that the majority report was an error. Ed Witwer is absolutely right. You have to be taken in — if Precrime is to survive. You're thinking of your own safety. But think, for a moment, about the system." Leaning over, she stubbed out her cigarette and fumbled in her purse for another. "Which means more to you — your own personal safety or the existence of the system?"

"My safety," Anderton answered, without hesitation.

"You're positive?"

"If the system can survive only by imprisoning innocent people, then it deserves to be destroyed. My personal safety is important because I'm a human being. And furthermore — "

From her purse, Lisa got out an incredibly tiny pistol. "I believe," she told him huskily, "that I have my finger on the firing release. I've never used a weapon like this before. But I'm willing to try."

After a pause, Anderton asked: "You want me to turn the ship around? Is that it?"

"Yes, back to the police building. I'm sorry. If you could put the good of the system above your own selfish — "

"Keep your sermon," Anderton told her. "I'll take the ship back. But I'm not going to listen to your defense of a code of behavior no intelligent man could subscribe to."

Lisa's lips pressed into a thin, bloodless line. Holding the pistol tightly, she sat facing him, her eyes fixed intently on him as he swung the ship in a broad arc. A few loose articles rattled from the glove compartment as the little craft turned on a radical slant, one wing rising majestically until it pointed straight up.

Both Anderton and his wife were supported by the constraining metal arms of their seats. But not so the third member of the party.

Out of the corner of his eye, Anderton saw a flash of motion. A sound came simultaneously, the clawing struggle of a large man as he abruptly lost his footing and plunged into the reinforced wall of the ship. What followed happened quickly. Fleming scrambled instantly to his feet, lurching and wary, one arm lashing out for the woman's pistol. Anderton was too startled to cry out. Lisa turned, saw the man — and screamed. Fleming knocked the gun from her hand, sending it clattering to the floor.

Grunting, Fleming shoved her aside and retrieved the gun. "Sorry," he gasped, straightening up as best he could. "I thought she might talk more. That's why I waited."

"You were here when — " Anderton began — and stopped. It was obvious that Fleming and his men had kept him under surveillance. The existence of Lisa's ship had been duly noted and factored in, and while Lisa had debated whether it would be wise to fly him to safety, Fleming had crept into the storage compartment of the ship.

"Perhaps," Fleming said, "you'd better give me that reel of tape." His moist, clumsy fingers groped for it. "You're right — Witwer would have melted it down to a puddle."

"Kaplan, too?" Anderton asked numbly, still dazed by the appearance of the man.

"Kaplan is working directly with Witwer. That's why his name showed on line five of the card. Which one of them is the actual boss, we can't tell. Possibly neither." Fleming tossed the tiny pistol away and got out his own heavy-duty military weapon. "You pulled a real flub in taking off with this woman. I told you she was back of the whole thing."

"I can't believe that," Anderton protested. "If she — "

"You've got no sense. This ship was warmed up by Witwer's order. They wanted to fly you out of the building so that we couldn't get to you. With you on your own, separated from us, you didn't stand a chance."

A strange look passed over Lisa's stricken features. "It's not true," she whispered. "Witwer never saw this ship. I was going to supervise — "

"You almost got away with it," Fleming interrupted inexorably. "We'll be lucky if a police patrol ship isn't hanging on us. There wasn't time to check." He squatted down as he spoke, directly behind the woman's chair. "The first thing is to get this woman out of the way. We'll have to drag you completely out of this area. Page tipped off Witwer on your new disguise, and you can be sure it has been widely broadcast."

Still crouching, Fleming seized hold of Lisa. Tossing his heavy gun to Anderton, he expertly tilted her chin up until her temple was shoved back against the seat. Lisa clawed frantically at him; a thin, terrified wail rose in her throat. Ignoring her, Fleming closed his great hands around her neck and began relentlessly to squeeze.

"No bullet wound," he explained, gasping. "She's going to fall out — natural accident. It happens all the time. But in this case, her neck will be broken *first*."

It seemed strange that Anderton waited so long. As it was, Fleming's thick fingers were cruelly embedded in the woman's pale flesh before he lifted the butt of the heavyduty pistol and brought it down on the back of Fleming's skull. The monstrous hands relaxed. Staggered, Fleming's head fell forward and he sagged against the wall of the ship. Trying feebly to collect himself, he began dragging his body upward. Anderton hit him again, this time above the left eye. He fell back, and lay still.

Struggling to breathe, Lisa remained for a moment huddled over, her body swaying back and forth. Then, gradually, the color crept back into her face.

"Can you take the controls?" Anderton asked, shaking her, his voice urgent.

"Yes, I think so." Almost mechanically she reached for the wheel. "I'll be all right. Don't worry about me."

"This pistol," Anderton said, "is Army ordnance issue. But it's not from the war. It's one of the useful new ones they've developed. I could be a long way off but there's just a chance — "

He climbed back to where Fleming lay spread out on the deck. Trying not to touch the man's head, he tore open his coat and rummaged in his pockets. A moment later Fleming's sweat-sodden wallet rested in his hands.

Tod Fleming, according to his identification, was an Army Major attached to the Internal Intelligence Department of Military Information. Among the various papers was a document signed by General Leopold Kaplan, stating that Fleming was under the special protection of his own group — the International Veterans' League.

Fleming and his men were operating under Kaplan's orders. The bread truck, the accident, had been deliberately rigged.

It meant that Kaplan had deliberately kept him out of police hands. The plan went back to the original contact in his home, when Kaplan's men had picked him up as he was packing. Incredulous, he realized what had really happened. Even then, they were making sure they got him before the police. From the start, it had been an elaborate strategy to make certain that Witwer would fail to arrest him.

"You were telling the truth," Anderton said to his wife, as he climbed back in the seat. "Can we get hold of Witwer?"

Mutely, she nodded. Indicating the communications circuit of the dashboard, she asked: "What — did you find?"

"Get Witwer for me. I want to talk to him as soon as I can. It's very urgent."

Jerkily, she dialed, got the closed-channel mechanical circuit, and raised police headquarters in New York. A visual panorama of petty police officials flashed by before a tiny replica of Ed Witwer's features appeared on the screen.

"Remember me?" Anderton asked him.

Witwer blanched. "Good God. What happened? Lisa, are you bringing him in?" Abruptly his eyes fastened on the gun in Anderton's hands. "Look," he said savagely, "don't do anything to her. Whatever you may think, she's not responsible."

"I've already found that out," Anderton answered. "Can you get a fix on us? We may need protection getting back."

"*Back!*" Witwer gazed at him unbelievingly. "You're coming in? You're giving yourself up?"

"I am, yes." Speaking rapidly, urgently, Anderton added, "There's something you must do immediately. Close off the monkey block. Make certain nobody gets it — Page or anyone else. *Especially Army people.*"

"Kaplan," the miniature image said.

"What about him?"

"He was here. He — he just left."

Anderton's heart stopped beating. "What was he doing?"

"Picking up data. Transcribing duplicates of our precog reports on you. He insisted he wanted them solely for his protection."

"Then he's already got it," Anderton said. "It's too late."

Alarmed, Witwer almost shouted: "Just what do you mean? What's happening?"

"I'll tell you," Anderton said heavily, "when I get back to my office."

VIII

Witwer met him on the roof on the police building. As the small ship came to rest, a cloud of escort ships dipped their fins and sped off. Anderton immediately approached the blond-haired young man.

"You've got what you wanted," he told him. "You can lock me up, and send me to the detention camp. But that won't be enough."

Witwer's blue eyes were pale with uncertainty. "I'm afraid I don't understand — "

"It's not my fault. I should never have left the police building. Where's Wally Page?"

"We've already clamped down on him," Witwer replied. "He won't give us any trouble."

Anderton's face was grim.

"You're holding him for the wrong reason," he said. "Letting me into the monkey block was no crime. But passing information to Army is. You've had an Army plant working here." He corrected himself, a little lamely, "I mean, I have."

"I've called back the order on you. Now the teams are looking for Kaplan."

"Any luck?"

"He left here in an Army truck. We followed him, but the truck got into a militarized Barracks. Now they've got a big wartime R-3 tank blocking the street. It would be civil war to move it aside."

Slowly, hesitantly, Lisa made her way from the ship. She was still pale and shaken and on her throat an ugly bruise was forming.

"What happened to you?" Witwer demanded. Then he caught sight of Fleming's inert form lying spread out inside. Facing Anderton squarely, he said: "Then you've finally stopped pretending this is some conspiracy of mine."

"I have."

"You don't think I'm — " He made a disgusted face. "*Plotting* to get your job."

"Sure you are. Everybody is guilty of that sort of thing. And I'm plotting to keep it. But this is something else — and you're not responsible."

"Why do you assert," Witwer inquired, "that it's too late to turn yourself in? My God, we'll put you in the camp. The week will pass and Kaplan will still be alive."

"He'll be alive, yes," Anderton conceded. "But he can prove he'd be just as alive if I were walking the streets. He has the information that proves the majority report obsolete. He can break the Precrime system." He finished, "Heads or tails, he wins — and we lose. The Army discredits us; their strategy paid off."

"But why are they risking so much? What exactly do they want?"

"After the Anglo-Chinese War, the Army lost out. It isn't what it was in the good old AFWA days. They ran the complete show, both military and domestic. And they did their own police work."

"Like Fleming," Lisa said faintly.

"After the war, the Westbloc was demilitarized. Officers like Kaplan were retired and discarded. Nobody likes that." Anderton grimaced. "I can sympathize with him. He's not the only one. But we couldn't keep on running things that way. We had to divide up the authority."

"You say Kaplan has won," Witwer said. "Isn't there anything we can do?"

"I'm not going to kill him. We know it and he knows it. Probably he'll come around and offer us some kind of deal. We'll continue to function, but the Senate will abolish our real pull. You wouldn't like that, would you?"

"I should say not," Witwer answered emphatically. "One of these days I'm going to be running this agency." He flushed. "Not immediately, of course."

Anderton's expression was somber. "It's too bad you publicized the majority report. If you had kept it quiet, we could cautiously draw it back in. But everybody's heard about it. We can't retract it now."

"I guess not," Witwer admitted awkwardly. "Maybe I — don't have this job down as neatly as I imagined."

"You will, in time. You'll be a good police officer. You believe in the status quo. But learn to take it easy." Anderton moved away from them. "I'm going to study the data tapes of the majority report. I want to find out exactly how I was supposed to kill Kaplan." Reflectively, he finished: "It might give me some ideas."

The data tapes of the precogs "Donna" and "Mike" were separately stored. Choosing the machinery responsible for the analysis of "Donna," he opened the protective shield and laid out the contents. As before, the code informed him which reels were relevant and in a moment he had the tape-transport mechanism in operation.

It was approximately what he had suspected. This was the material utilized by "Jerry" — the superseded time-path. In it Kaplan's Military Intelligence agents kidnapped Anderton as he drove home from work. Taken to Kaplan's villa, the organization GHQ of the International Veterans' League. Anderton was given an ultimatum: voluntarily disband the Precrime system or face open hostilities with Army.

In this discarded time-path, Anderton, as Police Commissioner, had turned to the Senate for support. No support was forthcoming. To avoid civil war, the Senate had ratified the dismemberment of the police system, and decreed a return to military law "to cope with the emergency." Taking a corps of fanatic police, Anderton had located Kaplan and shot him, along with other officials of the Veterans' League. Only Kaplan had died. The others had been patched up. And the coup had been successful.

This was "Donna." He rewound the tape and turned to the material previewed by "Mike." It would be identical; both precogs had combined to present a unified picture. "Mike" began as "Donna" had begun: Anderton had become aware of Kaplan's plot against the police. But something was wrong. Puzzled, he ran the tape back to the beginning. Incomprehensibly, it didn't jibe. Again he relayed the tape, listening intently.

The "Mike" report was quite different from the "Donna" report.

An hour later, he had finished his examination, put away the tapes, and left the monkey block. As soon as he emerged, Witwer asked. "What's the matter? I can see something's wrong."

"No," Anderton answered slowly, still deep in thought. "Not exactly wrong." A sound came to his ears. He walked vaguely over to the window and peered out.

The street was crammed with people. Moving down the center lane was a four-column line of uniformed troops. Rifles, helmets ... marching soldiers in their dingy wartime uniforms, carrying the cherished pennants of AFWA flapping in the cold afternoon wind.

"An Army rally," Witwer explained bleakly. "I was wrong. They're not going to make a deal with us. Why should they? Kaplan's going to make it public."

Anderton felt no surprise. "He's going to read the minority report?"

"Apparently. They're going to demand the Senate disband us, and take away our authority. They're going to claim we've been arresting innocent men — nocturnal police raids, that sort of thing. Rule by terror."

"You suppose the Senate will yield?"

Witwer hesitated. "I wouldn't want to guess."

"I'll guess," Anderton said. "They will. That business out there fits with what I learned downstairs. We've got ourselves boxed in and there's only one direction we can go. Whether we like it or not, we'll have to take it." His eyes had a steely glint.

Apprehensively, Witwer asked: "What is it?"

"Once I say it, you'll wonder why you didn't invent it. Very obviously, I'm going to have to fulfill the publicized report. I'm going to have to kill Kaplan. That's the only way we can keep them from discrediting us."

"But," Witwer said, astonished, "the majority report has been superseded."

"I can do it," Anderton informed him, "but it's going to cost. You're familiar with the statutes governing first-degree murder?"

"Life imprisonment."

"At least. Probably, you could pull a few wires and get it commuted to exile. I could be sent to one of the colony planets, the good old frontier."

"Would you — prefer that?"

"Hell, no," Anderton said heartily. "But it would be the lesser of the two evils. And it's got to be done."

"I don't see how you can kill Kaplan."

Anderton got out the heavy-duty military weapon Fleming had tossed to him. "I'll use this."

"They won't stop you?"

"Why should they? They've got that minority report that says I've changed my mind."

"Then the minority report is incorrect?"

"No," Anderton said, "it's absolutely correct. But I'm going to murder Kaplan anyhow."

IX

He had never killed a man. He had never even seen a man killed. And he had been Police Commissioner for thirty years. For this generation, deliberate murder had died out. It simply didn't happen.

A police car carried him to within a block of the Army rally. There, in the shadows of the back seat, he painstakingly examined the pistol Fleming had provided him. It seemed to be intact. Actually, there was no doubt of the outcome. He was absolutely certain of what would happen within the next half hour. Putting the pistol back together, he opened the door of the parked car and stepped warily out.

Nobody paid the slightest attention to him. Surging masses of people pushed eagerly forward, trying to get within hearing distance of the rally. Army uniforms predominated and at the perimeter of the cleared area, a line of tanks and major weapons was displayed — formidable armament still in production.

Army had erected a metal speaker's stand and ascending steps. Behind the stand hung the vast AFWA banner, emblem of the combined powers that had fought in the war. By a curious corrosion of time, the AFWA Veterans' League included officers from the wartime enemy. But a general was a general and fine distinctions had faded over the years.

Occupying the first rows of seats sat the high brass of the AFWA command. Behind them came junior commissioned officers. Regimental banners swirled in a variety of colors and symbols. In fact, the occasion had taken on the aspect of a festive pageant. On the raised stand itself sat stern-faced dignitaries of the Veterans' League, all of them tense with expectancy. At the extreme edges, almost unnoticed, waited a few police units, ostensibly to keep order. Actually, they were informants making observations. If order were kept, the Army would maintain it.

The late-afternoon wind carried the muffled booming of many people packed tightly together. As Anderton made his way through the dense mob he was engulfed by the solid presence of humanity. An eager sense of anticipation held everybody rigid. The crowd seemed to sense that something spectacular was on the way. With difficulty, Anderton forced his way past the rows of seats and over to the tight knot of Army officials at the edge of the platform.

Kaplan was among them. But he was now General Kaplan.

The vest, the gold pocket watch, the cane, the conservative business suit — all were gone. For this event, Kaplan had got his old uniform from its mothballs. Straight and impressive, he stood surrounded by what had been his general staff. He wore his service bars, his medals, his boots, his decorative short-sword, and his visored cap. It was amazing how transformed a bald man became under the stark potency of an officer's peaked and visored cap.

Noticing Anderton, General Kaplan broke away from the group and strode to where the younger man was standing. The expression on his thin, mobile countenance showed how incredulously glad he was to see the Commissioner of Police.

"This is a surprise," he informed Anderton, holding out his small gray-gloved hand. "It was my impression you had been taken in by the acting Commissioner."

"I'm still out," Anderton answered shortly, shaking hands. "After all, Witwer has that same reel of tape." He indicated the package Kaplan clutched in his steely fingers and met the man's gaze confidently.

In spite of his nervousness, General Kaplan was in good humor. "This is a great occasion for the Army," he revealed. "You'll be glad to hear I'm going to give the public a full account of the spurious charge brought against you."

"Fine," Anderton answered noncommittally.

"It will be made clear that you were unjustly accused." General Kaplan was trying to discover what Anderton knew. "Did Fleming have an opportunity to acquaint you with the situation?"

"To some degree," Anderton replied. "You're going to read only the minority report? That's all you've got there?"

"I'm going to compare it to the majority report." General Kaplan signalled an aide and a leather briefcase was produced. "Everything is here — all the evidence we need," he said. "You don't mind being an example, do you? Your case symbolizes the unjust arrests of countless individuals." Stiffly, General Kaplan examined his wristwatch. "I must begin. Will you join me on the platform?"

"Why?"

Coldly, but with a kind of repressed vehemence, General Kaplan said: "So they can see the living proof. You and I together — the killer and his victim. Standing side by side, exposing the whole sinister fraud which the police have been operating."

"Gladly," Anderton agreed. "What are we waiting for?"

Disconcerted, General Kaplan moved toward the platform. Again, he glanced uneasily at Anderton, as if visibly wondering why he had appeared and what he really knew. His uncertainty grew as Anderton willingly mounted the steps of the platform and found himself a seat directly beside the speaker's podium.

"You fully comprehend what I'm going to be saying?" General Kaplan demanded. "The exposure will have considerable repercussions. It may cause the Senate to reconsider the basic validity of the Precrime system."

"I understand," Anderton answered, arms folded. "Let's go."

A hush had descended on the crowd. But there was a restless, eager stirring when General Kaplan obtained the briefcase and began arranging his material in front of him.

"The man sitting at my side," he began, in a clean, clipped voice, "is familiar to you all. You may be surprised to see him, for until recently he was described by the police as a dangerous killer."

The eyes of the crowd focused on Anderton. Avidly, they peered at the only potential killer they had ever been privileged to see at close range.

"Within the last few hours, however," General Kaplan continued, "the police order for his arrest has been cancelled; because former Commissioner Anderton voluntarily gave himself up? No, that is not strictly accurate. He is sitting here. He has not given himself up, but the police are no longer interested in him. John Allison Anderton is innocent of any crime in the past, present, and future. The allegations against him were patent frauds, diabolical distortions of a contaminated penal system based on a false premise — a vast, impersonal engine of destruction grinding men and women to their doom."

Fascinated, the crowd glanced from Kaplan to Anderton. Everyone was familiar with the basic situation.

"Many men have been seized and imprisoned under the so-called prophylactic Precrime structure," General Kaplan continued, his voice gaining feeling and strength. "Accused not of crimes they have committed, *but of crimes they will commit*. It is asserted that these men, if allowed to remain free, will at some future time commit felonies."

"But there can be no valid knowledge about the future. As soon as precognitive information is obtained, *it cancels itself out*. The assertion that this man will commit a future crime is paradoxical. The very act of possessing this data renders it spurious. In every case, without exception, the report of the three police precogs has invalidated their own data. If no arrests had been made, there would still have been no crimes committed."

Anderton listened idly, only half-hearing the words. The crowd, however, listened with great interest. General Kaplan was now gathering up a summary made from the minority report. He explained what it was and how it had come into existence.

From his coat pocket, Anderton slipped out his gun and held it in his lap. Already, Kaplan was laying aside the minority report, the precognitive material obtained from "Jerry." His lean, bony fingers groped for the summary of first, "Donna," and after that, "Mike."

"This was the original majority report," he explained. "The assertion, made by the first two precogs, that Anderton would commit a murder. Now here is the automatically invalidated material. I shall read it to you." He whipped out his rimless glasses, fitted them to his nose, and started slowly to read.

A queer expression appeared on his face. He halted, stammered, and abruptly broke off. The papers fluttered from his hands. Like a cornered animal, he spun, crouched, and dashed from the speaker's stand.

For an instant his distorted face flashed past Anderton. On his feet now, Anderton raised the gun, stepped quickly forward, and fired. Tangled up in the rows of feet projecting from the chairs that filled the platform, Kaplan gave a single shrill shriek of agony and fright. Like a ruined bird, he tumbled, fluttering and flailing, from the platform to the ground below. Anderton stepped to the railing, but it was already over.

Kaplan, as the majority report had asserted, was dead. His thin chest was a smoking cavity of darkness, crumbling ash that broke loose as the body lay twitching.

Sickened, Anderton turned away, and moved quickly between the rising figures of stunned Army officers. The gun, which he still held, guaranteed that he would not be interfered with. He leaped from the platform and edged into the chaotic mass of people at its base. Stricken, horrified, they struggled to see what had happened. The incident, occurring before their very eyes, was incomprehensible. It would take time for acceptance to replace blind terror.

At the periphery of the crowd, Anderton was seized by the waiting police. "You're lucky to get out," one of them whispered to him as the car crept cautiously ahead.

"I guess I am," Anderton replied remotely. He settled back and tried to compose himself. He was trembling and dizzy. Abruptly, he leaned forward and was violently sick.

"The poor devil," one the cops murmured sympathetically.

Through the swirls of misery and nausea, Anderton was unable to tell whether the cop was referring to Kaplan or to himself.

X

Four burly policemen assisted Lisa and John Anderton in the packing and loading of their possessions. In fifty years, the ex-Commissioner of Police had accumulated a vast collection of material goods. Somber and pensive, he stood watching the procession of crates on their way to the waiting trucks.

By truck they would go directly to the field — and from there to Centaurus X by inter-system transport. A long trip for an old man. But he wouldn't have to make it back.

"There goes the second from the last crate," Lisa declared, absorbed and preoccupied by the task. In sweater and slacks, she roamed through the barren rooms, checking on last-minute details. "I suppose we won't be able to use these new atronic appliances. They're still using electricity on Centten."

"I hope you don't care too much," Anderton said.

"We'll get used to it," Lisa replied, and gave him a fleeting smile. "Won't we?"

"I hope so. You're positive you'll have no regrets. If I thought — "

"No regrets," Lisa assured him. "Now suppose you help me with this crate."

As they boarded the lead truck, Witwer drove up in a patrol car. He leaped out and hurried up to them, his face looking strangely haggard. "Before you take off," he said to Anderton, "you'll have to give me a break-down on the situation with the precogs. I'm getting inquiries from the Senate. They want to find out if the middle report, the retraction, was an error — or what." Confusedly, he finished: "I still can't explain it. The minority report was wrong, wasn't it?"

"Which minority report?" Anderton inquired, amused.

Witwer blinked. "Then that *is* it. I might have known."

Seated in the cabin of the truck, Anderton got out his pipe and shook tobacco into it. With Lisa's lighter he ignited the tobacco and began operations. Lisa had gone back to the house, wanting to be sure nothing vital had been overlooked.

"There were three minority reports," he told Witwer, enjoying the young man's confusion. Someday, Witwer would learn not to wade into situations he didn't fully understand. Satisfaction was Anderton's final emotion. Old and worn-out as he was, he had been the only one to grasp the real nature of the problem.

"The three reports were consecutive," he explained. "The first was 'Donna.' In that time-path, Kaplan told me of the plot, and I promptly murdered him. 'Jerry,' phased slightly ahead of 'Donna,' used her report as data. He factored in my knowledge of the report. In that, the second time-path, all I wanted to do was to keep my job. It wasn't Kaplan I wanted to kill. It was my own position and life I was interested in."

"And 'Mike' was the third report? That came *after* the minority report?" Witwer corrected himself. "I mean, it came last?"

" 'Mike' was the last of the three, yes. Faced with the knowledge of the first report, I had decided *not* to kill Kaplan. That produced report two. But faced with *that* report, I changed my mind back. Report two, situation two, was the situation Kaplan wanted to create. It was to the advantage of the police to recreate position one. And by that time I was thinking of the police. I had figured out what Kaplan was doing. The third report invalidated the second one in the same way the second one invalidated the first. That brought us back where we started from."

Lisa came over, breathless and gasping. "Let's go — we're all finished here." Lithe and agile, she ascended the metal rungs of the truck and squeezed in beside her husband and the driver. The latter obediently started up his truck and the others followed.

"Each report was different," Anderton concluded. "Each was unique. But two of them agreed on one point. If left free, *I would kill Kaplan*. That created the illusion of a majority report. Actually, that's all it was — an illusion. 'Donna' and 'Mike' previewed the same event — but in two totally different time-paths, occurring under totally different situations. 'Donna' and 'Jerry,' the so-called minority report and half of the majority report, were incorrect. Of the three, 'Mike' was correct — since no report came after his, to invalidate him. That sums it up."

Anxiously, Witwer trotted along beside the truck, his smooth, blond face creased with worry. "Will it happen again? Should we overhaul the set-up?"

"It can happen in only one circumstance," Anderton said. "My case was unique, since I had access to the data. It *could* happen again — but only to the next Police Commissioner. So watch your step." Briefly, he grinned, deriving no inconsiderable comfort from Witwer's strained expression. Beside him, Lisa's red lips twitched and her hand reached out and closed over his.

"Better keep your eyes open," he informed young Witwer. "It might happen to you at any time."

RECALL MECHANISM

THE ANALYST SAID: "I'm Humphrys, the man you came to see." There were fear and hostility on the patient's face, so Humphrys said: "I could tell a joke about analysts. Would that make you feel better? Or I could remind you that the National Health Trust is paying my fee; it's not going to cost you a cent. Or I could cite the case of Psychoanalyst Y, who committed suicide last year because of overburdening anxiety resulting from a fraudulently filled out income tax."

Grudgingly, the patient smiled. "I heard about that. So psychologists are fallible." He got to his feet and held out his hand. "My name is Paul Sharp. My secretary made the arrangements with you. I have a little problem, nothing important, but I'd like to clear it up."

The expression on his face showed that it was no small problem, and that, if he didn't clear it up, it would probably destroy him.

"Come inside," Humphrys said genially, opening the door to his office, "so we can both sit down."

Sinking down in a soft easy chair, Sharp stretched his legs out in front of him. "No couch," he observed.

"The couch vanished back around 1980," Humphrys said. "Post-war analysts feel enough confidence to face their patients on an equal level." He offered a pack of cigarettes to Sharp and then lit up himself. "Your secretary gave me no details; she just said you wanted a conference."

Sharp said: "I can talk frankly?"

"I'm bonded," Humphrys said, with pride. "If any of the material you tell me gets into the hands of security organizations, I forfeit approximately ten thousand dollars in Westbloc silver — hard cash, not paper stuff."

"That's good enough for me," Sharp said, and began. "I'm an economist,

working for the Department of Agriculture — the Division of War Destruction Salvage. I poke around H-bomb craters seeing what's worth rebuilding."
He corrected himself. "Actually, I analyze reports on H-bomb craters and
make recommendations. It was my recommendation to reclaim the farm lands
around Sacramento and the industrial ring here at Los Angeles."

In spite of himself, Humphrys was impressed. Here was a man in the
policy-planning level of the Government. It gave him an odd feeling to realize
that Sharp, like any other anxiety-ridden citizen, had come to the Psych Front
for therapy.

"My sister-in-law got a nice advantage from the Sacramento reclamation," Humphrys commented. "She had a small walnut orchard up there. The
Government hauled off the ash, rebuilt the house and outbuildings, even
staked her to a few dozen new trees. Except for her leg injury, she's as well off
as before the war."

"We're pleased with our Sacramento project," Sharp said. He had begun
to perspire; his smooth, pale forehead was streaked, and his hands, as he held
his cigarette, shook. "Of course, I have a personal interest in Northern California. I was born there myself, up around Petaluma, where they used to turn
out hens' eggs by the million ... " His voice trailed off huskily. "Humphrys,"
he muttered, "what am I going to do?"

"First," Humphrys said, "give me more information."

"I — " Sharp grinned inanely. "I have some kind of hallucination. I've
had it for years, but it's getting worse. I've tried to shake it, but — " he
gestured — "it comes back, stronger, bigger, more often."

Beside Humphrys' desk the vid and aud recorders were scanning covertly.
"Tell me what the hallucination is," he instructed. "Then maybe I can tell you
why you have it."

He was tired. In the privacy of his living room, he sat dully examining a
series of reports on carrot mutation. A variety, externally indistinguishable
from the norm, was sending people in Oregon and Mississippi to the hospital
with convulsions, fever and partial blindness. Why Oregon and Mississippi?
Here with the report were photographs of the feral mutation; it *did* look like an
ordinary carrot. And with the report came an exhaustive analysis of the toxic
agent and recommendation for a neutralizing antidote.

Sharp wearily tossed the report aside and selected the next in order.

According to the second report, the notorious Detroit rat had shown up in
St. Louis and Chicago, infesting the industrial and agricultural settlements
replacing the destroyed cities. The Detroit rat — he had seen one once. That
was three years ago; coming home one night, he had unlocked the door and
seen, in the darkness, something scuttle away to safety. Arming himself with a
hammer, he had pushed furniture around until he found it. The rat, huge and

gray, had been in the process of building itself a wall-to-wall web. As it leaped up, he killed it with the hammer. A rat that spun webs ...

He called an official exterminator and reported its presence.

A Special Talents Agency had been set up by the Government to utilize parabilities of wartime mutants evolved from the various radiation-saturated areas. But, he reflected, the Agency was equipped to handle only human mutants and their telepathic, precog, parakinetic and related abilities. There should have been a Special Talents Agency for vegetables and rodents, too.

From behind his chair came a stealthy sound. Turning quickly, Sharp found himself facing a tall, thin man wearing a drab raincoat and smoking a cigar.

"Did I scare you?" Giller asked, and snickered. "Take it easy, Paul. You look as if you're going to pass out."

"I was working," Sharp said defensively, partially recovering his equilibrium.

"So I see," said Giller.

"And thinking about rats." Sharp pushed his work to one side. "How'd you get in?"

"Your door was unlocked." Giller removed his raincoat and tossed it on the couch. "That's right—you killed a Detroit. Right here in this room." He gazed around the neat, unostentatious living room. "Are those things fatal?"

"Depends where they get you." Going into the kitchen, Sharp found two beers in the refrigerator. As he poured, he said: "They shouldn't waste grain making this stuff ... but as long as they do, it's a shame not to drink it."

Giller accepted his beer greedily. "Must be nice to be a big wheel and have luxuries like this." His small, dark eyes roved speculatively around the kitchen. "Your own stove, and your own refrigerator." Smacking his lips, he added: "And beer. I haven't had a beer since last August."

"You'll live," Sharp said, without compassion. "Is this a business call? If so, get to the point; I've got plenty of work to do."

Giller said: "I just wanted to say hello to a fellow Petaluman."

Wincing, Sharp answered: "It sounds like some sort of synthetic fuel."

Giller wasn't amused. "Are you ashamed to have come from the very section that was once — "

"I know. The egg-laying capital of the universe. Sometimes I wonder — how many chicken feathers do you suppose were drifting around, the day the first H-bomb hit our town?"

"Billions," Giller said morosely. "And some of them were mine. My chickens, I mean. Your family had a farm, didn't they?"

"No," Sharp said, refusing to be identified with Giller. "My family operated a drug store facing on Highway 101. A block from the park, near the sporting goods shop." And, he added under his breath: You can go to hell.

Because I'm not going to change my mind. You can camp on my doorstep the rest of your life and it still won't do any good. Petaluma isn't that important. And anyhow, the chickens are dead.

"How's the Sac rebuild coming?" Giller inquired.

"Fine."

"Plenty of those walnuts again?"

"Walnuts coming out of people's ears."

"Mice getting in the shell heaps?"

"Thousands of them," Sharp sipped his beer; it was good quality, probably as good as pre-war. He wouldn't know, because in 1961, the year the war broke out, he had been only six years old. But the beer tasted the way he remembered the old days: opulent and carefree and satisfying.

"We figure," Giller said hoarsely, an avid gleam in his face, "that the Petaluma-Sonoma area can be built up again for about seven billion Westbloc. That's nothing compared to what you've been doling out."

"And the Petaluma-Sonoma area is nothing compared with the areas we've been rebuilding," Sharp said. "You think we need eggs and wine? What we need is machinery. It's Chicago and Pittsburgh and Los Angeles and St. Louis and — "

"You've forgotten," Giller droned on, "that you're a Petaluman. You're turning your back on your origin — and on your duty."

"Duty! You suppose the Government hired me to be a lobbyist for one trivial farm area?" Sharp flushed with outrage. "As far as I'm concerned — "

"We're your people," Giller said inflexibly. "And your people come first."

When he had got rid of the man, Sharp stood for a time in the night darkness, gazing down the road after Giller's receding car. Well, he said to himself, there goes the way of the world — me first and to hell with everybody else.

Sighing, he turned and made his way up the path toward the front porch of his house. Lights gleamed friendlily in the window. Shivering, he put his hand out and groped for the railing.

And then, as he clumsily mounted the stairs, the terrible thing happened.

With a rush, the lights of the window winked out. The porch railing dissolved under his fingers. In his ears a shrill screaming whine rose up and deafened him. He was falling. Struggling frantically, he tried to get hold of something, but there was only empty darkness around him, no substance, no reality, only the depth beneath him and the din of his own terrified shrieks.

"Help!" he shouted, and the sound beat futilely back at him. "I'm falling!"

And then, gasping, he was outstretched on the damp lawn, clutching handfuls of grass and dirt. Two feet from the porch — he had missed the first step in the darkness and had slipped and fallen. An ordinary event: the window lights had been blocked by the concrete railing. The whole thing had happened in a split second and he had fallen only the length of his own body. There was blood on his forehead; he had cut himself as he struck.

Silly. A childish, infuriating event.

Shakily, he climbed to his feet and mounted the steps. Inside the house, he stood leaning against the wall, shuddering and panting. Gradually the fear faded out and rationality returned.

Why was he so afraid of falling?

Something had to be done. This was worse than ever before, even worse than the time he had stumbled coming out of the elevator at the office — and had instantly been reduced to screaming terror in front of a lobbyful of people.

What would happen to him if he *really* fell? If, for example, he were to step off one of the overhead ramps connecting the major Los Angeles office buildings? The fall would be stopped by safety screens; no physical harm was ever done, though people fell all the time. But for him — the psychological shock might be fatal. *Would* be fatal; to his mind, at least.

He made a mental note: no more going out on the ramps. Under no circumstances. He had been avoiding them for years, but from now on, ramps were in the same class as air travel. Since 1982 he hadn't left the surface of the planet. And, in the last few years, he seldom visited offices more than ten flights up.

But if he stopped using the ramps, how was he going to get into his own research files? The file room was accessibly only by ramp: the narrow metallic path leading up from the office area.

Perspiring, terrified, he sank down on the couch and sat huddled over, wondering how he was going to keep his job, do his work.

And how he was going to stay alive.

Humphrys waited, but his patient seemed to have finished.

"Does it make you feel any better," Humphrys asked, "to know that fear of falling is a common phobia?"

"No," Sharp answered.

"I guess there's no reason why it should. You say it's shown up before? When was the first time?"

"When I was eight. The war had been going on two years. I was on the surface, examining my vegetable garden." Sharp smiled weakly. "Even when I was a kid, I grew things. The San Francisco network picked up exhaust trails of a Soviet missile and all the warning towers went off like Roman candles. I was almost on top of the shelter. I raced to it, lifted the lid and started down the stairs. At the bottom were my mother and father. They yelled for me to hurry. I started to run down the stairs."

"And fell?" Humphrys asked expectantly.

"I didn't fall; I suddenly got afraid. I couldn't go any farther; I just stood there. And they were yelling up at me. They wanted to get the bottom plate screwed in place. And they couldn't until I was down."

With a touch of aversion, Humphrys acknowledged: "I remember those old two-stage shelters. I wonder how many people got shut between the lid and the bottom plate." He eyed his patient. "As a child, had you heard of that happening? People being trapped on the stairs, not able to get back up, not able to get down ... "

"I wasn't scared of being trapped! I was scared of falling — afraid I'd pitch head-forward off the steps." Sharp licked his dry lips. "Well, so I turned around — " His body shuddered. "I went back up and outside."

"During the attack?"

"They shot down the missile. But I spent the alert tending my vegetables. Afterward, my family beat me nearly unconscious."

Humphrys' mind formed the words: origin of guilt.

"The next time," Sharp continued, "was when I was fourteen. The war had been over a few months. We started back to see what was left of our town. Nothing was left, only a crater of radioactive slag several hundred feet deep. Work teams were creeping down into the crater. I stood on the edge watching them. The fear came." He put out his cigarette and sat waiting until the analyst found him another. "I left the area after that. Every night I dreamed about that crater, that big dead mouth. I hitched a ride on a military truck and rode to San Francisco."

"When was the next time?" asked Humphrys.

Irritably, Sharp said: "Then it happened all the time, every time I was up high, every time I had to walk up or down a flight of steps — any situation where I was high and might fall. But to be afraid to walk up the steps of my own house — " He broke off temporarily. "I can't walk up three steps," he said wretchedly. "Three concrete steps."

"Any particular bad episodes, outside of those you've mentioned?"

"I was in love with a pretty brown-haired girl who lived on the top floor of the Atcheson Apartments. Probably she still lives there; I wouldn't know. I got five or six floors up and then — I told her good night and came back down." Ironically, he said: "She must have thought I was crazy."

"Others?" Humphrys asked, mentally noting the appearance of the sexual element.

"One time I couldn't accept a job because it involved travel by air. It had to do with inspecting agricultural projects."

Humphrys said: "In the old days, analysts looked for the origin of a phobia. Now we ask: *what does it do?* Usually it gets the individual out of situations he unconsciously dislikes."

A slow, disgusted flush appeared on Sharp's face. "Can't you do better than that?"

Disconcerted, Humphrys murmured: "I don't say I agree with the theory or that it's necessarily true in your case. I'll say this much though: it's not falling you're afraid of. It's something that falling reminds you of. With luck we ought to be able to dig up the prototype experience — what they used to call the original traumatic incident." Getting to his feet, he began to drag over a stemmed tower of electronic mirrors. "My lamp," he explained. "It'll melt the barriers."

Sharp regarded the lamp with apprehension. "Look," he muttered nervously, "I don't want my mind reconstructed. I may be a neurotic, but I take pride in my personality."

"This won't affect your personality." Bending down, Humphrys plugged in the lamp. "It will bring up material not accessible to your rational center. I'm going to trace your life-track back to the incident at which you were done great harm — and find out what you're *really* afraid of."

Black shapes drifted around him. Sharp screamed and struggled wildly, trying to pry loose the fingers closing over his arms and legs. Something smashed against his face. Coughing, he slumped forward, dribbling blood and saliva and bits of broken teeth. For an instant, blinding light flashed; he was being scrutinized.

"Is he dead?" a voice demanded.

"Not yet." A foot poked experimentally into Sharp's side. Dimly, in his half-consciousness, he could hear ribs cracking. "Almost, though."

"Can you hear me, Sharp?" a voice rasped, close to his ear.

He didn't respond. He lay trying not to die, trying not to associate himself with the cracked and broken thing that had been his body.

"You probably imagine," the voice said, familiar, intimate, "that I'm going to say you've got one last chance. But you don't, Sharp. Your chance is gone. I'm telling you what we're going to do with you."

Gasping, he tried not to hear. And, futilely, he tried not to feel what they were systematically doing to him.

"All right," the familiar voice said finally, when it had been done. "Now throw him out."

What remained of Paul Sharp was lugged to a circular hatch. The nebulous outline of darkness rose up around him and then — hideously — he was pitched into it. Down he fell, but this time he didn't scream.

No physical apparatus remained with which to scream.

Snapping the lamp off, Humphrys bent over and methodically roused the slumped figure.

"Sharp!" he ordered loudly. "Wake up! Come out of it!"

The man groaned, blinked his eyes, stirred. Over his face settled a glaze of pure, unmitigated torment.

"God," he whispered, eyes blank, body limp with suffering. "They — "

"You're back here," Humphrys said, shaken by what had been dredged up. "There's nothing to worry about; you're absolutely safe. It's over with — happened years ago."

"Over," Sharp murmured pathetically.

"You're back in the present. Understand?"

"Yes," Sharp muttered. "But — what was it? They pushed me out — through and into something. And I went on down." He trembled violently. "I fell."

"You fell through a hatch," Humphrys told him calmly. "You were beaten up and badly injured — fatally, they assumed. But you *did* survive. You are alive. You got out of it."

"Why did they do it?" Sharp asked brokenly. His face, sagging and gray, twitched with despair. "Help me, Humphrys ... "

"Consciously, you don't remember when it happened?"

"No."

"Do you remember where?"

"No." Sharp's face jerked spasmodically. "They tried to kill me — they *did* kill me!" Struggling upright, he protested: "Nothing like that happened to me. I'd remember if it had. It's a false memory — my mind's been tampered with!"

"It's been repressed," Humphrys said firmly, "deeply buried because of the pain and shock. A form of amnesia — it's been filtering indirectly up in the form of your phobia. But now that you recall it consciously — "

"Do I have to go back?" Sharp's voice rose hysterically. "Do I have to get under that damn lamp again?"

"It's got to come out on a conscious level," Humphrys told him, "but not all at once. You've had your limit for today."

Sagging with relief, Sharp settled back in the chair. "Thanks," he said weakly. Touching his face, his body, he whispered: "I've been carrying that in my mind all these years. Corroding, eating away — "

"There should be some diminution of the phobia," the analyst told him, "as you grapple with the incident itself. We've made progress; we now have some idea of the real fear. It involves bodily injury at the hands of professional criminals. Ex-soldiers in the early post-war years ... gangs of bandits. I remember."

A measure of confidence returned to Sharp. "It isn't hard to understand a falling fear, under the circumstances. Considering what happened to me ... " Shakily, he started to his feet.

And screamed shrilly.

"What is it?" Humphrys demanded, hastily coming over and grabbing hold of his arm. Sharp leaped violently away, staggered, and collapsed inertly in the chair. "What happened?"

Face working, Sharp managed: "I can't get up."

"What?"

"I can't stand up." Imploringly, he gazed up at the analyst, stricken and terrified. "I'm — afraid I'll fall. Doctor, now I can't even get to my feet."

For an interval neither man spoke. Finally, his eyes on the floor, Sharp whispered: "The reason I came to you, Humphrys, is because your office is on the ground floor. That's a laugh, isn't it? I couldn't go any higher."

"We're going to have to turn the lamp back on you," Humphrys said.

"I realize it. I'm scared." Gripping the arms of the chair, he continued: "Go ahead. What else can we do? I can't leave here. Humphrys, this thing is going to kill me."

"No, it isn't." Humphrys got the lamp into position. "We'll get you out of this. Try to relax; try to think of nothing in particular." Clicking the mechanism on, he said softly: "This time I don't want the traumatic incident itself. I want the envelope of experience that surrounds it. I want the broader segment of which it's a part."

Paul Sharp walked quietly through the snow. His breath, in front of him, billowed outward and formed a sparkling cloud of white. To his left lay the jagged ruins of what had been buildings. The ruins, covered with snow, seemed almost lovely. For a moment he paused, entranced.

"Interesting," a member of his research team observed, coming up. "Could be anything — absolutely anything — under there."

"It's beautiful, in a way," Sharp commented.

"See that spire?" The young man pointed with one heavily gloved finger; he still wore his lead-shielded suit. He and his group had been poking around the still-contaminated crater. Their boring bars were lined up in an orderly row. "That was a church," he informed Sharp. "A nice one, by the looks of it. And over there — " he indicated an indiscriminate jumble of ruin — "that was the main civic center."

"The city wasn't directly hit, was it?" Sharp asked.

"It was bracketed. Come on down and see what we've run into. The crater to our right — "

"No, thanks," Sharp said, pulling back with intense aversion. "I'll let you do the crawling around."

The youthful expert glanced curiously at Sharp, then forgot the matter. "Unless we run into something unexpected, we should be able to start reclamation within a week. The first step, of course, is to clear off the slag-layer. It's fairly well cracked — a lot of plant growth has perforated it, and natural decay has reduced a great deal of it to semi-organic ash."

"Fine," Sharp said, with satisfaction. "I'll be glad to see something here again, after all these years."

The expert asked: "What was it like before the war? I never saw that; I was born after the destruction began."

"Well," Sharp said, surveying the fields of snow, "this was a thriving agricultural center. They grew grapefruit here. Arizona grapefruit. The Roosevelt Dam was along this way."

"Yes," the expert said, nodding. "We located the remnants of it."

"Cotton was grown here. So was lettuce, alfalfa, grapes, olives, apricots — the thing I remember most, the time I came through Phoenix with my family, was the eucalyptus trees."

"We won't have all that back," the expert said regretfully. "What the heck — eucalyptus? I never heard of that."

"There aren't any left in the United States," Sharp said. "You'd have to go to Australia."

Listening, Humphrys jotted down a notation. "Okay," he said aloud, switching off the lamp. "Come back, Sharp."

With a grunt, Paul Sharp blinked and opened his eyes. "What — " Struggling up, he yawned, stretched, peered blankly around the office. "Something about reclamation. I was supervising a team of recon men. A young kid."

"When did you reclaim Phoenix?" Humphrys asked. "That seems to be included in the vital time-space segment."

Sharp frowned. "We never reclaimed Phoenix. That's still projected. We hope to get at it sometime in the next year."

"Are you positive?"

"Naturally. That's my job."

"I'm going to have to send you back," Humphrys said, already reaching for the lamp.

"What happened?"

The lamp came on. "Relax," Humphrys instructed briskly, a trifle too briskly for a man supposed to know exactly what he was doing. Forcing himself to slow down, he said carefully: "I want your perspective to broaden. Take in an earlier incident, one preceding the Phoenix reclamation."

In an inexpensive cafeteria in the business district, two men sat facing each other across a table.

"I'm sorry," Paul Sharp said, with impatience. "I've got to get back to my work." Picking up his cup of ersatz coffee, he gulped the contents down.

The tall, thin man carefully pushed away his empty dishes and, leaning back, lit a cigar.

"For two years," Giller said bluntly, "you've been giving us the runaround. Frankly, I'm a little tired of it."

"Runaround?" Sharp had started to rise. "I don't get your drift."

"You're going to reclaim an agricultural area — you're going to tackle Phoenix. So don't tell me you're sticking to industrial. How long do you imagine those people are going to keep on living? Unless you reclaim their farms and lands — "

"What people?"

Harshly, Giller said: "The people living at Petaluma. Camped around the craters."

With vague dismay, Sharp murmured: "I didn't realize there was anybody living there. I thought you all headed for the nearest reclaimed regions, San Francisco and Sacramento."

"You never read the petitions we presented," Giller said softly.

Sharp colored. "No, as a matter of fact. Why should I? If there're people camping in the slag, it doesn't alter the basic situation; you should leave, get out of there. That area is through." He added: "I got out."

Very quietly, Giller said: "You would have stuck around if you'd farmed there. If your family had farmed there for over a century. It's different from running a drug store. Drug stores are the same everywhere in the world."

"So are farms."

"No," Giller said dispassionately. "Your land, your family's land, has a unique feeling. We'll keep on camping there until we're dead or until you decide to reclaim." Mechanically collecting the checks, he finished: "I'm sorry for you, Paul. You never had roots like we have. And I'm sorry you can't be made to understand." As he reached into his coat for his wallet, he asked: "When can you fly out there?"

"Fly!" Sharp echoed, shuddering. "I'm not flying anywhere."

"You've got to see the town again. You can't decide without having seen those people, seen how they're living."

"No," Sharp said emphatically. "I'm not flying out there. I can decide on the basis of reports."

Giller considered. "You'll come," he declared.

"Over my dead body!"

Giller nodded. "Maybe so. But you're going to come. You can't let us die without looking at us. You've got to have the courage to see what it is you're doing." He got out a pocket calendar and scratched a mark by one of the dates. Tossing it across the table to Sharp, he informed him: "We'll come by your office and pick you up. We have the plane we flew down here. It's mine. It's a sweet ship."

Trembling, Sharp examined the calendar. And, standing over his mumbling, supine patient, so did Humphrys.

He had been right. Sharp's traumatic incident, the repressed material, didn't lie in the past.

Sharp was suffering from a phobia based on an event six months in the future.

"Can you get up?" Humphrys inquired.

In the chair, Paul Sharp stirred feebly. "I — " he began, and then sank into silence.

"No more for a while," Humphrys told him reassuringly. "You've had enough. But I wanted to get you away from the trauma itself."

"I feel better now."

"Try to stand." Humphrys approached and stood waiting, as the man crept unsteadily to his feet.

"Yes," Sharp breathed. "It has receded. What was that last? I was in a cafe or something. With Giller."

From his desk Humphrys got a prescription pad. "I'm going to write you out a little comfort. Some round white pills to take every four hours." He scribbled and then handed the slip to his patient. "So you will relax. It'll take away some of the tension."

"Thanks," Sharp said, in a weak, almost inaudible voice. Presently, he asked: "A lot of material came up, didn't it?"

"It certainly did," Humphrys admitted tightly.

There was nothing he could do for Paul Sharp. The man was very close to death now — in six short months, Giller would go to work on him. And it was too bad, because Sharp was a nice guy, a nice, conscientious, hard-working bureaucrat who was only trying to do his job as he saw it.

"What do you think?" Sharp asked pathetically. "Can you help me?"

"I'll — try," Humphrys answered, not able to look directly at him. "But it goes very deep."

"It's been a long time growing," Sharp admitted humbly. Standing by the chair, he seemed small and forlorn; not an important official but only one isolated, unprotected individual. "I'd sure appreciate your help. If this phobia keeps up, no telling where it'll end."

Humphrys asked suddenly, "Would you consider changing your mind and granting Giller's demands?"

"I can't," Sharp said. "It's bad policy. I'm opposed to special pleading, and that's what it is."

"Even if you come from the area? Even if the people are friends and former neighbors of yours?"

"It's my job," Sharp said. "I have to do it without regard for my feelings or anybody else's"

"You're not a bad fellow," Humphrys said involuntarily. "I'm sorry — " He broke off.

"Sorry what?" Sharp moved mechanically toward the exit door. "I've taken enough of your time. I realize how busy you analysts are. When shall I come back. *Can* I come back?"

"Tomorrow." Humphrys guided him outside and into the corridor. "About this same time, if it's convenient."

"Thanks a lot," Sharp said, with relief. "I really appreciate it."

*   *   *

As soon as he was alone in his office, Humphrys closed the door and strode back to his desk. Reaching down, he grabbed the telephone and unsteadily dialed.

"Give me somebody on your medical staff," he ordered curtly when he had been connected with the Special Talents Agency.

"This is Kirby," a professional-sounding voice came presently. "Medical research."

Humphrys briefly identified himself. "I have a patient here," he said, "who seems to be a latent precog."

Kirby was interested. "What area does he come from?"

"Petaluma. Sonoma County, north of San Francisco Bay. It's east of — "

"We're familiar with the area. A number of precogs have showed up there. That's been a gold mine for us."

"Then I was right," Humphrys said.

"What's the date of the patient's birth?"

"He was six years old when the war began."

"Well," Kirby said, disappointed, "then he didn't really get enough of a dose. He'll never develop a full precog talent, such as we work with here."

"In other words, you won't help?"

"Latents — people with a touch of it — outnumber the real carriers. We don't have time to fool with them. You'll probably run into dozens like your patient, if you stir around. When it's imperfect, the talent isn't valuable; it's going to be a nuisance for the man, probably nothing else."

"Yes, it's a nuisance," Humphrys agreed caustically. "The man is only months away from a violent death. Since he was a child, he's been getting advanced phobic warnings. As the event gets closer, the reactions intensify."

"He's not conscious of the future material?"

"It operates strictly on a sub-rational level."

"Under the circumstances," Kirby said thoughtfully, "maybe it's just as well. These things appear to be fixed. If he knew about it, he still couldn't change it."

Dr. Charles Bamberg, consulting psychiatrist, was just leaving his office when he noticed a man sitting in the waiting room.

Odd, Bamberg thought. I have no patients left for today.

Opening the door, he stepped into the waiting room. "Did you wish to see me?"

The man sitting on the chair was tall and thin. He wore a wrinkled tan raincoat, and, as Bamberg appeared, he began tensely stubbing out a cigar.

"Yes," he said, getting clumsily to his feet.

"Do you have an appointment?"

"No appointment." The man gazed at him in appeal. "I picked you — "
He laughed with confusion. "Well, you're on the top floor."

"The top floor?" Bamberg was intrigued. "What's that got to do with it?"

"I — well, Doc, I feel much more comfortable when I'm up high."

"I see," Bamberg said. A compulsion, he thought to himself. Fascinating.
"And," he said aloud, "when you're up high, how do you feel? Better?"

"Not better," the man answered. "Can I come in? Do you have a second to
spare me?"

Bamberg looked at his watch. "All right," he agreed, admitting the man.
"Sit down and tell me about it."

Gratefully, Giller seated himself. "It interferes with my life," he said rapidly, jerkily. "Every time I see a flight of stairs, I have an irresistible compulsion to go up it. And plane flight — I'm always flying around. I have my own
ship; I can't afford it, but I've got to have it."

"I see," Bamberg said. "Well," he continued genially, "that's not really so
bad. After all, it isn't exactly a fatal compulsion."

Helplessly, Giller replied: "When I'm up there — " He swallowed
wretchedly, his dark eyes gleaming. "Doctor, when I'm up high, in an office
building, or in my plane — I feel another compulsion."

"What is it?"

"I — " Giller shuddered. "I have an irresistible urge to push people."

"To push people?"

"Toward windows. Out." Giller made a gesture. "What am I going to do,
Doc? I'm afraid I'll kill somebody. There was a little shrimp of a guy I pushed
once — and one day a girl was standing ahead of me on an escalator — I
shoved her. She was injured."

"I see," Bamberg said, nodding. Repressed hostility, he thought to himself. Interwoven with sex. Not unusual.

He reached for his lamp.

THE UNRECONSTRUCTED M

I

THE MACHINE was a foot wide and two feet long; it looked like an oversized box of crackers. Silently, with great caution, it climbed the side of a concrete building; it had lowered two rubberized rollers and was now beginning the first phase of its job.

From its rear, a flake of blue enamel was exuded. The machine pressed the flake firmly against the rough concrete and then continued on. Its upward path carried it from vertical concrete to vertical steel: it had reached a window. The machine paused and produced a microscopic fragment of cloth fabric. The cloth, with great care, was embedded in the fitting of the steel window frame.

In the chill darkness, the machine was virtually invisible. The glow of a distant tangle of traffic briefly touched it, illuminated its polished hull, and departed. The machine resumed its work.

It projected a plastic pseudopodium and incinerated the pane of window glass. There was no response from within the gloomy apartment: nobody was home. The machine, now dulled with particles of glass-dust, crept over the steel frame and raised an inquisitive receptor.

While it received, it exerted precisely two hundred pounds pressure on the steel window frame; the frame obediently bent. Satisfied, the machine descended the inside of the wall to the moderately thick carpet. There it began the second phase of its job.

One single human hair — follicle and speck of scalp included — was deposited on the hardwood floor by the lamp. Not far from the piano, two dried grains of tobacco were ceremoniously laid out. The machine waited an interval of ten seconds and then, as an internal section of magnetic tape clicked into place, it suddenly said, "Ugh! Damn it … "

Curiously, its voice was husky and masculine.

The machine made its way to the closet door, which was locked. Climbing the wood surface, the machine reached the lock mechanism, and, inserting a thin section of itself, caressed the tumblers back. Behind the row of coats was a small mound of batteries and wires: a self-powered video recorder. The machine destroyed the reservoir of film — which was vital — and then, as it left the closet, expelled a drop of blood on the jagged tangle that had been the lens-scanner. The drop of blood was even more vital.

While the machine was pressing the artificial outline of a heel mark into the greasy film that covered the flooring of the closet, a sharp sound came from the hallway. The machine ceased its work and became rigid. A moment later a small, middle-aged man entered the apartment, coat over one arm, briefcase in the other.

"Good God," he said, stopping instantly as he saw the machine. "What are you?"

The machine lifted the nozzle of its front section and shot an explosive pellet at the man's half-bald head. The pellet traveled into the skull and detonated. Still clutching his coat and briefcase, bewildered expression on his face, the man collapsed to the rug. His glasses, broken, lay twisted beside his ear. His body stirred a little, twitched, and then was satisfactorily quiet.

Only two steps remained to the job, now that the main part was done. The machine deposited a bit of burnt match in one of the spotless ashtrays resting on the mantel, and entered the kitchen to search for a water glass. It was starting up the side of the sink when the noise of human voices startled it.

"This is the apartment," a voice said, clear and close.

"Get ready — he ought to still be here." Another voice, a man's voice, like the first. The hall door was pushed open and two individuals in heavy overcoats sprinted purposefully into the apartment. At their approach, the machine dropped to the kitchen floor, the water glass forgotten. Something had gone wrong. Its rectangular outline flowed and wavered; pulling itself into an upright package it fused its shape into that of a conventional TV unit.

It was holding that emergency form when one of the men — tall, red-haired — peered briefly into the kitchen.

"Nobody in here," the man declared, and hurried on.

"The window," his companion said, panting. Two more figures entered the apartment, an entire crew. "The glass is gone — missing. He got in that way."

"But he's gone." The red-haired man reappeared at the kitchen door; he snapped on the light and entered, a gun visible in his hand. "Strange ... we got here right away, as soon as we picked up the rattle." Suspiciously, he examined his wristwatch. "Rosenburg's been dead only a few seconds ... how could he have got out again so fast?"

Standing in the street entrance, Edward Ackers listened to the voice. During the last half hour the voice had taken on a carping, nagging whine; sinking almost to inaudibility, it plodded along, mechanically turning out its message of complaint.

"You're tired," Ackers said. "Go home. Take a hot bath."

"No," the voice said, interrupting its tirade. The locus of the voice was a large illuminated blob on the dark sidewalk, a few yards to Acker's right. The revolving neon sign read:

BANISH IT!

Thirty times — he had counted — within the last few minutes the sign had captured a passerby and the man in the booth had begun his harangue. Beyond the booth were several theaters and restaurants: the booth was well-situated.

But it wasn't for the crowd that the booth had been erected. It was for Ackers and the offices behind him; the tirade was aimed directly at the Interior Department. The nagging racket had gone on so many months that Ackers was scarcely aware of it. Rain on the roof. Traffic noises. He yawned, folded his arms, and waited.

"Banish it," the voice complained peevishly. "Come on, Ackers. Say something; do something."

"I'm waiting," Ackers said complacently.

A group of middle-class citizens passed the booth and were handed leaflets. The citizens scattered the leaflets after them, and Ackers laughed.

"Don't laugh," the voice muttered. "It's not funny; it costs us money to print those."

"Your personal money?" Ackers inquired.

"Partly." Garth was lonely, tonight. "What are you waiting for? What's happened? I saw a police team leave your roof a few minutes ago ... ?

"We may take in somebody," Ackers said, "there's been a killing."

Down the dark sidewalk the man stirred in his dreary propaganda booth. "Oh?" Harvey Garth's voice came. He leaned forward and the two looked directly at each other: Ackers, carefully-groomed, well-fed, wearing a respectable overcoat ... Garth, a thin man, much younger, with a lean, hungry face composed mostly of nose and forehead.

"So you see," Ackers told him, "we do need the system. Don't be utopian."

"A man is murdered; and you rectify the moral imbalance by killing the killer." Garth's protesting voice rose in a bleak spasm. "Banish it! Banish the system that condemns men to certain extinction!"

"Get you leaflets here," Ackers parodied dryly. "And your slogans. Either or both. What would you suggest in place of the system?"

Garth's voice was proud with conviction. "Education."

Amused, Ackers asked: "Is that all? You think that would stop anti-social activity? Criminals just don't — *know* better?"

"And psychotherapy, of course." His projected face bony and intense, Garth peered out of his booth like an aroused turtle. "They're sick ... that's why they commit crimes, healthy men don't commit crimes. And you compound it; you create a sick society of punitive cruelty." He waggled an accusing finger. "You're the real culprit, you and the whole Interior Department. You and the whole Banishment System."

Again and again the neon sign blinked BANISH IT! Meaning, of course, the system of compulsory ostracism for felons, the machinery that projected a condemned human being into some random backwater region of the sidereal universe, into some remote and out-of-the-way corner where he would be of no harm.

"No harm to us, anyhow," Ackers mused aloud.

Garth spoke the familiar argument. "Yes, but what about the local inhabitants?"

Too bad about the local inhabitants. Anyhow, the banished victim spent his energy and time trying to find a way back to the Sol System. If he got back before old age caught up with him he was readmitted by society. Quite a challenge ... especially to some cosmopolite who had never set foot outside Greater New York. There were — probably — many involuntary expatriates cutting grain in odd fields with primitive sickles. The remote sections of the universe seemed composed mostly of dank rural cultures, isolated agrarian enclaves typified by small-time bartering of fruit and vegetables and handmade artifacts.

"Did you know," Ackers said, "that in the Age of Monarchs, a pickpocket was usually hanged?"

"Banish it," Garth continued monotonously, sinking back into his booth. The sign revolved; leaflets were passed out. And Ackers impatiently watched the late-evening street for sign of the hospital truck.

He knew Heimie Rosenburg. A sweeter little guy there never was ... although Heimie had been mixed up in one of the sprawling slave combines that illegally transported settlers to outsystem fertile planets. Between them, the two largest slavers had settled virtually the entire Sirius System. Four out of six emigrants were hustled out in carriers registered as "freighters." It was hard to picture gentle little Heimie Rosenburg as a business agent for Tirol Enterprises, but there it was.

As he waited, Ackers conjectured on Heimie's murder. Probably one element of the incessant subterranean war going on between Paul Tirol and his major rival. David Lantano was a brilliant and energetic newcomer ... but murder was anybody's game. It all depended on how it was done; it could be commercial hack or the purest art.

"Here comes something," Garth's voice sounded, carried to his inner ear by the delicate output transformers of the booth's equipment. "Looks like a freezer."

It was; the hospital truck had arrived. Ackers stepped forward as the truck halted and the back was let down.

"How soon did you get there?" he asked the cop who jumped heavily to the pavement.

"Right away," the cop answered, "but no sign of the killer. I don't think we're going to get Heimie back ... they got him dead-center, right in the cerebellum. Expert work, no amateur stuff."

Disappointed, Ackers clambered into the hospital truck to inspect for himself.

Very tiny and still, Heimie Rosenburg lay on his back, arms at his sides, gazing sightlessly up at the roof of the truck. On his face remained the expression of bewildered wonder. Somebody — one of the cops — had placed his bent glasses in his clenched hand. In falling he had cut his cheek. The destroyed portion of his skull was covered by a moist plastic web.

"Who's back at the apartment?" Ackers asked presently.

"The rest of my crew," the cop answered. "And an independent researcher. Leroy Beam."

"Him," Ackers said, with aversion. "How is it he showed up?"

"Caught the rattle, too, happened to be passing with his rig. Poor Heimie had an awful big booster on that rattle ... I'm surprised it wasn't picked up here at the main offices."

"They say Heimie had a high anxiety level," Ackers said. "Bugs all over his apartment. You're starting to collect evidence?"

"The teams are moving in," the cop said. "We should begin getting specifications in half an hour. The killer knocked out the vid bug set up in the closet. But — " He grinned. "He cut himself breaking the circuit. A drop of blood, right on the wiring; it looks promising."

At the apartment, Leroy Beam watched the Interior police begin their analysis. They worked smoothly and thoroughly, but Beam was dissatisfied.

His original impression remained: he was suspicious. Nobody could have gotten away so quickly. Heimie had died, and his death — the cessation of his neural pattern — had triggered off an automatic squawk. A rattle didn't particularly protect its owner, but its existence ensured (or usually ensured) detection of the murderer. Why had it failed Heimie?

Prowling moodily, Leroy Beam entered the kitchen for the second time. There, on the floor by the sink, was a small portable TV unit, the kind popular with the sporting set: a gaudy little packet of plastic and knobs and multi-tinted lenses.

"Why this?" Beam asked, as one of the cops plodded past him. "This TV unit sitting here on the kitchen floor. It's out of place."

The cop ignored him. In the living room, elaborate police detection equipment was scraping the various surfaces inch by inch. In the half hour since Heimie's death, a number of specifications had been logged. First, the drop of blood on the damaged vid wiring. Second, a hazy heel mark where the murderer had stepped. Third, a bit of burnt match in the ashtray. More were expected; the analysis had only begun.

It usually took nine specifications to delineate the single individual.

Leroy Beam glanced cautiously around him. None of the cops was watching, so he bent down and picked up the TV unit; it felt ordinary. He clicked the *on* switch and waited. Nothing happened; no image formed. Strange.

He was holding it upside down, trying to see the inner chassis, when Edward Ackers from Interior entered the apartment. Quickly, Beam stuffed the TV unit into the pocket of his heavy overcoat.

"What are you doing here?" Ackers said.

"Seeking," Beam answered, wondering if Ackers noticed his tubby bulge. "I'm in business, too."

"Did you know Heimie?"

"By reputation," Beam answered vaguely. "Tied in with Tirol's combine, I hear; some sort of front man. Had an office on Fifth Avenue."

"Swank place, like the rest of those Fifth Avenue feather merchants." Ackers went on into the living room to watch detectives gather up evidence.

There was a vast nearsightedness to the wedge grinding ponderously across the carpet. It was scrutinizing at a microscopic level, and its field was sharply curtailed. As fast as material was obtained, it was relayed to the Interior offices, to the aggregate file banks where the civil population was represented by a series of punch cards, cross-indexed infinitely.

Lifting the telephone, Ackers called his wife. "I won't be home," he told her. "Business."

A lag and then Ellen responded. "Oh?" she said distantly. "Well, thanks for letting me know."

Over in the corner, two members of the police crew were delightedly examining a new discovery, valid enough to be a specification. "I'll call you again," he said hurriedly to Ellen, "before I leave. Goodbye."

"Goodbye," Ellen said curtly, and managed to hang up before he did.

The new discovery was the undamaged aud bug, which was mounted under the floor lamp. A continuous magnetic tape — still in motion — gleamed amiably; the murder episode had been recorded sound-wise in its entirety.

"Everything," a cop said gleefully to Ackers. "It was going before Heimie got home."

"You played it back?"

"A portion. There's a couple words spoken by the murderer, should be enough."

Ackers got in touch with Interior. "Have the specifications on the Rosenburg case been fed, yet?"

"Just the first," the attendant answered. "The file discriminates the usual massive category — about six billion names."

Ten minutes later the second specification was fed to the files. Persons with type O blood, with size 11½ shoes, numbered slightly over a billion. The third specification brought in the element of smoker-nonsmoker. That dropped the number to less than a billion, but not much less. Most adults smoked.

"The aud tape will drop it fast," Leroy Beam commented, standing beside Ackers, his arms folded to conceal his bulging coat. "Ought to be able to get age, at least."

The aud tape, analyzed, gave thirty to forty years as the conjectured age. And — timbre analysis — a man of perhaps two hundred pounds. A little later the bent steel window frame was examined, and the warp noted. It jibed with the specification of the aud tape. There were now six specifications, including that of sex (male). The number of persons in the in-group was falling rapidly.

"It won't be long," Ackers said genially. "And if he tacked one of those little buckets to the building side, we'll have a paint scrape."

Beam said: "I'm leaving. Good luck."

"Stick around."

"Sorry." Beam moved toward the hall door. "This is yours, not mine. I've got my own business to attend to ... I'm doing researchfor a hot-shot nonferrous mining concern."

Ackers eyed his coat. "Are you pregnant?"

"Not that I know of," Beam said, coloring. "I've led a good clean life." Awkwardly, he patted his coat. "You mean this?"

By the window, one of the police gave a triumphant yap. The two bits of pipe tobacco had been discovered: a refinement for the third specification. "Excellent," Ackers said, turning away from Beam and momentarily forgetting him.

Beam left.

Very shortly he was driving across town toward his own labs, the small and independent research outfit that he headed, unsupported by a government grant. Resting on the seat beside him was the portable TV unit; it was still silent.

"First of all," Beam's gowned technician declared, "it has a power supply approximately seventy times that of a portable TV pack. We picked up the Gamma radiation." He displayed the usual detector. "So you're right, it's not a TV set."

Gingerly, Beam lifted the small unit from the lab bench. Five hours had passed, and still he knew nothing about it. Taking firm hold of the back he pulled with all his strength. The back refused to come off. It wasn't stuck: there were no seams. The back was not a back; it only looked like a back.

"Then what is it?" he asked.

"Could be lots of things," the technician said noncommittally; he had been roused from the privacy of his home, and it was now two-thirty in the morning. "Could be some sort of scanning equipment. A bomb. A weapon. Any kind of gadget."

Laboriously, Beam felt the unit all over, searching for a flaw in the surface. "It's uniform," he murmured. "A single surface."

"You bet. The breaks are false — it's a poured substance. And," the technician added, "it's hard. I tried to chip off a representative sample but — " He gestured. "No results."

"Guaranteed not to shatter when dropped," Beam said absently. "New extra-tough plastic." He shook the unit energetically; the muted noise of metal parts in motion reached his ear. "It's full of guts."

"We'll get it open," the technician promised, "but not tonight."

Beam replaced the unit on the bench. He could, with bad luck, work days on this one item — to discover, after all, that it had nothing to do with the murder of Heimie Rosenburg. On the other hand …

"Drill me a hole in it," he instructed. "So we can see it."

His technician protested: "I drilled; the drill broke. I've sent out for an improved density. This substance is imported; somebody hooked it from a white dwarf system. It was conceived under stupendous pressure."

"You're stalling," Beam said, irritated. "That's how they talk in the advertising media."

The technician shrugged. "Anyhow, it's extra hard. A naturally-evolved element, or an artificially-processed product from somebody's labs. Who has funds to develop a metal like this?"

"One of the big slavers," Beam said. "That's where the wealth winds up. And they hop around to various systems … they'd have access to raw materials. Special ores."

"Can't I go home?" the technician asked. "What's so important about this?"

"This device either killed or helped kill Heimie Rosenburg. We'll sit here, you and I, until we get it open." Beam seated himself and began examining the check sheet showing which tests had been applied. "Sooner or later it'll fly open like a clam — if you can remember that far back."

Behind them, a warning bell sounded.

"Somebody in the anteroom," Beam said, surprised and wary. "At two-thirty?" He got up and made his way down the dark hall to the front of the building. Probably it was Ackers. His conscience stirred guiltily: somebody had logged the absence of the TV unit.

But it was not Ackers.

Waiting humbly in the cold, deserted anteroom was Paul Tirol; with him was an attractive young woman unknown to Beam. Tirol's wrinkled face broke into smiles, and he extended a hearty hand. "Beam," he said. They shook. "Your front door said you were down here. Still working?"

Guardedly, wondering who the woman was and what Tirol wanted, Beam said: "Catching up on some slipshod errors. Whole firm's going broke."

Tirol laughed indulgently. "Always a japer." His deep-set eyes darted; Tirol was a powerfully-built person, older than most, with a somber, intensely-creased face. "Have room for a few contracts? I thought I might slip a few jobs your way ... if you're open."

"I'm always open," Beam countered, blocking Tirol's view of the lab proper. The door, anyhow, had slid itself shut. Tirol had been Heimie's boss ... he no doubt felt entitled to all extant information on the murder. Who did it? When? How? Why? But that didn't explain why he was *here*.

"Terrible thing," Tirol said crudely. He made no move to introduce the woman; she had retired to the couch to light a cigarette. She was slender, with mahogany-colored hair; she wore a blue coat, and a kerchief tied around her head.

"Yes," Beam agreed. "Terrible."

"You were there, I understand."

That explained some of it. "Well," Beam conceded, "I showed up."

"But you didn't actually see it?"

"No," Beam admitted, "nobody saw it. Interior is collecting specification material. They should have it down to one card before morning."

Visibly, Tirol relaxed. "I'm glad of that. I'd hate to see the vicious criminal escape. Banishment's too good for him. He ought to be gassed."

"Barbarism," Beam murmured dryly. "The days of the gas chamber. Medieval."

Tirol peered past him. "You're working on — " Now he was overtly beginning to pry. "Come now, Leroy. Heimie Rosenburg — God bless his soul — was killed tonight and tonight I find you burning the midnight oil. You can talk openly with me; you've got something relevant to his death, haven't you?"

"That's Ackers you're thinking of."

Tirol chuckled. "Can I take a look?"

"Not until you start paying me; I'm not on your books yet."

In a strained, unnatural voice, Tirol bleated: "I want it."

Puzzled, Beam said: "You want what?"

With a grotesque shudder, Tirol blundered forward, shoved Beam aside, and groped for the door. The door flew open and Tirol started noisily down the dark corridor, feeling his way by instinct toward the research labs.

"Hey!" Beam shouted, outraged. He sprinted after the older man, reached the inner door, and prepared to fight it out. He was shaking, partly with amazement, partly with anger. "What the hell?" he demanded breathlessly. "You don't own me!"

Behind him the door mysteriously gave way. Foolishly, he sprawled backward, half-falling into the lab. There, stricken with helpless paralysis, was his technician. And, coming across the floor of the lab was something small and metallic. It looked like an oversized box of crackers, and it was going lickety-split toward Tirol. The object — metal and gleaming — hopped up into Tirol's arms, and the old man turned and lumbered back up the hall to the anteroom.

"What was it?" the technician said, coming to life.

Ignoring him, Beam hurried after Tirol. "He's got it!" he yelled futilely.

"It — " the technician mumbled. "It was the TV set. And it *ran.*"

II

The file banks at Interior were in agitated flux.

The process of creating a more and more restricted category was tedious, and it took time. Most of the Interior staff had gone home to bed; it was almost three in the morning, and the corridors and offices were deserted. A few mechanical cleaning devices crept here and there in the darkness. The sole source of life was the study chamber of the file banks. Edward Ackers sat patiently waiting for the results, waiting for specifications to come in, and for the file machinery to process them.

To his right a few Interior police played a benign lottery and waited stoically to be sent out for the pick-up. The lines of communication to Heimie Rosenburg's apartment buzzed ceaselessly. Down the street, along the bleak sidewalk, Harvey Garth was still at his propaganda booth, still flashing his BANISH IT! sign and muttering in people's ears. There were virtually no passersby, now, but Garth went on. He was tireless; he never gave up.

"Psychopath," Ackers said resentfully. Even where he sat, six floors up, the tinny, carping voice reached his middle ear.

"Take him in," one of the game-playing cops suggested. The game, intricate and devious, was a version of a Centaurian III practice. "We can revoke his vendor's license."

Ackers had, when there was nothing else to do, concocted and refined an indictment of Garth, a sort of lay analysis of the man's mental aberrations. He enjoyed playing the psychoanalytic game; it gave him a sense of power.

> Garth, Harvey
> Prominent compulsive syndrome. Has assumed role of
> ideological anarchist, opposing legal and social system.
> No rational expression, only repetition of key words and
> phrases. Idée fixe is *Banish the banishment system.*
> Cause dominates life. Rigid fanatic, probably of manic
> type, since ...

Ackers let the sentence go, since he didn't really know what the structure of the manic type was. Anyhow, the analysis was excellent, and someday it would be resting in an official slot instead of merely drifting through his mind. And, when that happened, the annoying voice would conclude.

"Big turmoil," Garth droned. "Banishment system in vast upheaval ... crisis moment has arrived."

"Why crisis?" Ackers asked aloud.

Down below on the pavement Garth responded. "All your machines are humming. Grand excitement reigns. Somebody's head will be in the basket before sun-up." His voice trailed off in a weary blur. "Intrigue and murder. Corpses ... the police scurry and a beautiful woman lurks."

To his analysis Ackers added an amplifying clause.

> ... Garth's talents are warped by his compulsive sense
> of *mission*. Having designed an ingenious communica-
> tion device he sees only its propaganda possibility.
> Whereas Garth's voice-ear mechanism could be put to
> work for All Humanity.

That pleased him. Ackers got up and wandered over to the attendant operating the file. "How's it coming?" he asked.

"Here's the situation," the attendant said. There was a line of gray stubble smeared over his chin, and he was bleary-eyed. "We're gradually paring it down."

Ackers, as he resumed his seat, wished he were back in the days of the almighty fingerprint. But a print hadn't shown up in months; a thousand techniques existed for print-removal and print alteration. There was no single specification capable, in itself, of delineating the individual. A composite was needed, a gestalt of the assembled data.

> 1) blood sample (type O) 6,139,481,601
> 2) shoe size (11½) 1,268,303,431
> 3) smoker 791,992,386
> 3a) smoker (pipe) 52,774,853
> 4) sex (male) 26,449,094
> 5) age (30–40 years) 9,221,397
> 6) weight (200 lbs) 488,290
> 7) fabric of clothing 17,459
> 8) hair variety 866
> 9) ownership of utilized weapon 40

A vivid picture was emerging from the data. Ackers could see him clearly. The man was practically standing there, in front of his desk. A fairly young man, somewhat heavy, a man who smoked a pipe and wore an extremely expensive tweed suit. An individual created by nine specifications; no tenth had been listed because no more data of specification level had been found.

Now, according to the report, the apartment had been thoroughly searched. The detection equipment was going outdoors.

"One more should do it," Ackers said, returning the report to the attendant. He wondered if it would come in and how long it would take.

To waste time he telephoned his wife, but instead of getting Ellen he got the automatic response circuit. "Yes, sir," it told him. "Mrs. Ackers has retired for the night. You may state a thirty-second message which will be transcribed for her attention tomorrow morning. Thank you."

Ackers raged at the mechanism futilely and then hung up. He wondered if Ellen were really in bed; maybe she had, as often before, slipped out. But, after all, it was almost three o'clock in the morning. Any sane person would be asleep: only he and Garth were still at their little stations, performing their vital duties.

What had Garth meant by a *"beautiful woman"*?

"Mr. Ackers," the attendant said, "there's a tenth specification coming in over the wires."

Hopefully, Ackers gazed up at the file bank. He could see nothing, of course; the actual mechanism occupied the underground levels of the building, and all that existed here was the input receptors and throw-out slots. But just looking at the machinery was in itself comforting. At this moment the bank was accepting the tenth piece of material. In a moment he would know how many citizens fell into the ten categories . . . he would know if already he had a group small enough to be sorted one by one.

"Here it is," the attendant said, pushing the report to him.

Type of utilized vehicle (color) 7

"My God," Ackers said mildly. "That's low enough. Seven persons — we can go to work."

"You want the seven cards popped?"

"Pop them," Ackers said.

A moment later, the throw-out slot deposited seven neat white cards in the tray. The attendant passed them to Ackers and he quickly riffled them. The next step was personal motive and proximity: items that had to be gotten from the suspects themselves.

Of the seven names six meant nothing to him. Two lived on Venus, one in the Centaurus System, one was somewhere in Sirius, one was in the hospital, and one lived in the Soviet Union. The seventh, however, lived within a few miles, on the outskirts of New York.

LANTANO, DAVID

That clinched it. The gestalt, in Ackers' mind, locked clearly in place; the image hardened to reality. He had half expected, even prayed to see Lantano's card brought up.

"Here's your pick-up," he said shakily to the game-playing cops. "Better get as large a team together as possible, this one won't be easy." Momentously, he added: "Maybe I'd better come along."

Beam reached the anteroom of his lab as the ancient figure of Paul Tirol disappeared out the street door and onto the dark sidewalk. The young woman, trotting ahead of him, had climbed into a parked car and started it forward; as Tirol emerged, she swept him up and at once departed.

Panting, Beam stood impotently collecting himself on the deserted pavement. The ersatz TV unit was gone; now he had nothing. Aimlessly, he began to run down the street. His heels echoed loudly in the cold silence. No sign of them; no sign of anything.

"I'll be damned," he said, with almost religious awe. The unit — a robot device of obvious complexity — clearly belonged to Paul Tirol; as soon as it had identified his presence it had sprinted gladly to him. For ... protection?

It had killed Heimie; and it belonged to Tirol. So, by a novel and indirect method, Tirol had murdered his employee, his Fifth Avenue front man. At a rough guess, such a highly-organized robot would cost in the neighborhood of a hundred thousand dollars.

A lot of money, considering that murder was the easiest of criminal acts. Why not hire an itinerant goon with a crowbar?

Beam started slowly back toward his lab. Then, abruptly, he changed his mind and turned in the direction of the business area. When a free-wheeling cab came by, he hailed it and clambered in.

"Where to, sport?" the starter at cab relay asked. City cabs were guided by remote control from one central source.

He gave the name of a specific bar. Settling back against the seat he pondered. Anybody could commit a murder; an expensive, complicated machine wasn't necessary.

The machine had been built to do something else. The murder of Heimie Rosenburg was incidental.

Against the nocturnal skyline, a huge stone residence loomed. Ackers inspected it from a distance. There were no lights burning; everything was locked up tight. Spread out before the house was an acre of grass. David Lantano was probably the last person on Earth to own an acre of grass outright; it was less expensive to buy an entire planet in some other system.

"Let's go," Ackers commanded; disgusted by such opulence, he deliberately trampled through a bed of roses on his way up the wide porch steps. Behind him flowed the team of shock-police.

"Gosh," Lantano rumbled, when he had been roused from his bed. He was a kindly-looking, rather youthful fat man, wearing now an abundant silk dressing robe. He would have seemed more in place as director of a boys' summer camp;

there was an expression of perpetual good humor on his soft, sagging face. "What's wrong, officer?"

Ackers loathed being called officer. "You're under arrest," he stated.

"Me?" Lantano echoed feebly. "Hey, officer, I've got lawyers to take care of these things." He yawned voluminously. "Care for some coffee?" Stupidly, he began puttering around his front room, fixing a pot.

It had been years since Ackers had splurged and bought himself a cup of coffee. With Terran land covered by dense industrial and residential installations there was no room for crops, and coffee had refused to "take" in any other system. Lantano probably grew his somewhere on an illicit plantation in South America — the pickers probably believed they had been transported to some remote colony.

"No thanks," Ackers said. "Let's get going."

Still dazed, Lantano plopped himself down in an easy chair and regarded Ackers with alarm. "You're serious." Gradually his expression faded; he seemed to be drifting back to sleep. "Who?" he murmured distantly.

"Heimie Rosenburg."

"No kidding." Lantano shook his head listlessly. "I always wanted him in my company. Heimie's got real charm. Had, I mean."

It made Ackers nervous to remain here in the vast lush mansion. The coffee was heating, and the smell of it tickled his nose. And, heaven forbid — there on the table was a basket of *apricots*.

"Peaches," Lantano corrected, noticing his fixed stare. "Help yourself."

"Where — did you get them?"

Lantano shrugged. "Synthetic dome. Hydroponics. I forget where ... I don't have a technical mind."

"You know what the fine is for possessing natural fruit?"

"Look," Lantano said earnestly, clasping his mushy hands together. "Give me the details on this affair, and I'll prove to you I had nothing to do with it. Come on, officer."

"Ackers," Ackers said.

"Okay, Ackers. I thought I recognized you, but I wasn't sure; didn't want to make a fool of myself. When was Heimie killed?"

Grudgingly, Ackers gave him the pertinent information.

For a time Lantano was silent. Then, slowly, gravely, he said: "You better look at those seven cards again. One of those fellows isn't in the Sirius System ... he's back here."

Ackers calculated the chances of successfully banishing a man of David Lantano's importance. His organization — Interplay Export — had fingers all over the galaxy; there'd be search crews going out like bees. But nobody went out banishment distance. The condemned, temporarily ionized, rendered in terms of charged particles of energy, radiated outward at the velocity of light. This was an experimental technique that had failed; it worked only one way.

"Consider," Lantano said thoughtfully. "If I *was* going to kill Heimie — *would I do it myself?* You're not being logical, Ackers. I'd send somebody." He pointed a fleshy finger at Ackers. "You imagine I'd risk my own life? I know you pick up everybody ... you usually turn up enough specifications."

"We have ten on you," Ackers said briskly.

"So you're going to banish me?"

"If you're guilty, you'll have to face banishment like anyone else. Your particular prestige has no bearing."

Nettled, Ackers added, "Obviously, you'll be released. You'll have plenty of opportunity to prove your innocence; you can question each of the ten specifications in turn."

He started to go on and describe the general process of court procedure employed in the twenty-first century, but something made him pause. David Lantano and his chair seemed to be gradually sinking into the floor. Was it an illusion? Blinking, Ackers rubbed his eyes and peered. At the same time, one of the policemen yelped a warning of dismay; Lantano was quietly leaving them.

"Come back!" Ackers demanded; he leaped forward and grabbed hold of the chair. Hurriedly, one of his men shorted out the power supply of the building; the chair ceased descending and groaned to a halt. Only Lantano's head was visible above the floor level. He was almost entirely submerged in a concealed escape shaft.

"What seedy, useless — " Ackers began.

"I know," Lantano admitted, making no move to drag himself up. He seemed resigned; his mind was again off in clouds of contemplation. "I hope we can clear all this up. Evidently I'm being framed. Tirol got somebody who looks like me, somebody to go in and murder Heimie."

Ackers and the police crew helped him up from his depressed chair. He gave no resistance; he was too deep in his brooding.

The cab let Leroy Beam off in front of the bar. To his right, in the next block, was the Interior Building ... and, on the sidewalk, the opaque blob that was Harvey Garth's propaganda booth.

Entering the bar, Beam found a table in the back and seated himself. Already he could pick up the faint, distorted murmur of Garth's reflections. Garth, speaking to himself in a directionless blur, was not yet aware of him.

"Banish it," Garth was saying. "Banish all of them. Bunch of crooks and thieves." Garth, in the miasma of his booth, was rambling vitriolically.

"What's going on?" Beam asked. "What's the latest?"

Garth's monologue broke off as he focussed his attention on Beam. "You in there? In the bar?"

"I want to find out about Heimie's death."

"Yes," Garth said. "He's dead; the files are moving, kicking out cards."

"When I left Heimie's apartment," Beam said, "they had turned up six specifications." He punched a button on the drink selector and dropped in a token.

"That must have been earlier," Garth said; "they've got more."

"How many?"

"Ten in all."

Ten. That was usually enough. And all ten of them laid out by a robot device ... a little procession of hints strewn along its path: between the concrete side of the building and the dead body of Heimie Rosenburg.

"That's lucky," he said speculatively. "Helps out Ackers."

"Since you're paying me," Garth said, "I'll tell you the rest. They've already gone out on their pick-up: Ackers went along."

Then the device had been successful. Up to a point, at least. He was sure of one thing: the device should have been out of the apartment. Tirol hadn't known about Heimie's death rattle; Heimie had been wise enough to do the installation privately.

Had the rattle not brought persons into the apartment, the device would have scuttled out and returned to Tirol. Then, no doubt, Tirol would have detonated it. Nothing would remain to indicate that a machine could lay down a trail of synthetic clues: blood type, fabric, pipe tobacco, hair ... all the rest, and all spurious.

"Who's the pick-up on?" Beam asked.

"David Lantano."

Beam winced. "Naturally. That's what the whole thing's about; he's being framed!"

Garth was indifferent; he was a hired employee, stationed by the pool of independent researchers to siphon information from the Interior Department. He had no actual interest in politics; his *Banish It!* was sheer window-dressing.

"I know it's a frame," Beam said, "and so does Lantano. But neither of us can prove it ... unless Lantano has an absolutely airtight alibi."

"Banish it," Garth murmured, reverting to his routine. A small group of late-retiring citizens had strolled past his booth, and he was masking his conversation with Beam. The conversation, directed to the one listener, was inaudible to everyone else; but it was better not to take risks. Sometimes, very close to the booth, there was an audible feedback of the signal.

Hunched over his drink, Leroy Beam contemplated the various items he could try. He could inform Lantano's organization, which existed relatively intact ... but the result would be epic civil war. And, in addition, he didn't really care if Lantano was framed; it was all the same to him. Sooner or later one of the big slavers had to absorb the other: cartel is the natural conclusion of big business. With Lantano gone, Tirol would painlessly swallow his organization; everybody would be working at his desk as always.

On the other hand, there might someday be a device — now half-completed in Tirol's basement — that left a trail of *Leroy Beam* clues. Once the idea caught on, there was no particular end.

"And I had the damn thing," he said fruitlessly. "I hammered on it for five hours. It was a TV unit, then, but it was still the device that killed Heimie."

"You're positive it's gone?"

"It's not only gone — it's out of existence. Unless she wrecked the car driving Tirol home."

"She?" Garth asked.

"The woman." Beam pondered. "She saw it. Or she knew about it; she was with him." But, unfortunately, he had no idea who the woman might be.

"What'd she look like?" Garth asked.

"Tall, mahogany hair. Very nervous mouth."

"I didn't realize she was working with him openly. They must have really needed the device." Garth added: "You didn't identify her? I guess there's no reason why you should; she's kept out of sight."

"Who is she?"

"That's Ellen Ackers."

Beam laughed sharply. "And she's driving Paul Tirol around?"

"She's — well, she's driving Tirol around, yes. You can put it that way."

"How long?"

"I thought you were in on it. She and Ackers split up; that was last year. But he wouldn't let her leave; he wouldn't give her a divorce. Afraid of the publicity. Very important to keep up respectability ... keep the shirt fully stuffed."

"He knows about Paul Tirol and her?"

"Of course not. He knows she's — spiritually hooked up. But he doesn't care ... as long as she keeps it quiet. It's his position he's thinking about."

"If Ackers found out," Beam murmured. "If he saw the link between his wife and Tirol ... he'd ignore his ten interoffice memos. He'd *want* to haul in Tirol. The hell with the evidence; he could always collect that later." Beam pushed away his drink; the glass was empty anyhow. "Where is Ackers?"

"I told you. Out at Lantano's place, picking him up."

"He'd come back here? He wouldn't go home?"

"Naturally he'd come back here." Garth was silent a moment. "I see a couple of Interior vans turning into the garage ramp. That's probably the pick-up crew returning."

Beam waited tensely. "Is Ackers along?"

"Yes, he's there. *Banish It!*" Garth's voice rose in stentorian frenzy. *"Banish the system of Banishment! Root out the crooks and pirates!"*

Sliding to his feet, Beam left the bar.

A dull light showed in the rear of Edward Ackers' apartment: probably the kitchen light. The front door was locked. Standing in the carpeted hallway, Beam skillfully tilted with the door mechanism. It was geared to respond to specific neural patterns: those of its owners and a limited circle of friends. For him there was no activity.

Kneeling down, Beam switched on a pocket oscillator and started sine wave emission. Gradually, he increased the frequency. At perhaps 150,000 cps the lock guiltily clicked; that was all he needed. Switching the oscillator off, he rummaged through his supply of skeleton patterns until he located the closet cylinder. Slipped into the turret of the oscillator, the cylinder emitted a synthetic neural pattern close enough to the real thing to affect the lock.

The door swung open. Beam entered.

In half-darkness the living room seemed modest and tasteful. Ellen Ackers was an adequate housekeeper. Beam listened. Was she home at all? And if so, where? Awake? Asleep?

He peeped into the bedroom. There was the bed, but nobody was in it.

If she wasn't here she was at Tirol's. But he didn't intend to follow her; this was as far as he cared to risk.

He inspected the dining room. Empty. The kitchen was empty, too. Next came an upholstered general-purpose rumpus room; on one side was a gaudy bar and on the other a wall-to-wall couch. Tossed on the couch was a woman's coat, purse, gloves. Familiar clothes: Ellen Ackers had worn them. So she had come here after leaving his research lab.

The only room left was the bathroom. He fumbled with the knob; it was locked from the inside. There was no sound, but somebody was on the other side of the door. He could sense her in there.

"Ellen," he said, against the panelling. "Mrs. Ellen Ackers; is that you?"

No answer. He could sense her not making any sound at all: a stifled, frantic silence.

While he was kneeling down, fooling with his pocketful of magnetic lock-pullers, an explosive pellet burst through the door at head level and splattered into the plaster of the wall beyond.

Instantly the door flew open; there stood Ellen Ackers, her face distorted with fright. One of her husband's government pistols was clenched in her small, bony hand. She was less than a foot from him. Without getting up, Beam grabbed her wrist; she fired over his head, and then the two of them deteriorated into harsh, labored breathing.

"Come on," Beam managed finally. The nozzle of the gun was literally brushing the top of his head. To kill him, she would have to pull the pistol back against her. But he didn't let her; he kept hold of her wrist until finally, reluctantly, she dropped the gun. It clattered to the floor and he got stiffly up.

"You were sitting down," she whispered, in a stricken, accusing voice.

"Kneeling down: picking the lock. I'm glad you aimed for my brain." He picked up the gun and succeeded in getting it into his overcoat pocket; his hands were shaking.

Ellen Ackers gazed at him starkly; her eyes were huge and dark, and her face was an ugly white. Her skin had a dead cast, as if it were artificial, totally dry, thoroughly sifted with talc. She seemed on the verge of hysteria; a harsh, muffled shudder struggled up inside her, lodging finally in her throat. She tried to speak but only a rasping noise came out.

"Gee, lady," Beam said, embarrassed. "Come in the kitchen and sit down."

She stared at him as if he had said something incredible or obscene or miraculous; he wasn't sure which.

"Come on." He tried to take hold of her arm but she jerked frantically away. She had on a simple green suit, and in it she looked very nice; a little too thin and terribly tense, but still attractive. She had on expensive earrings, an imported stone that seemed always in motion ... but otherwise her outfit was austere.

"You — were the man at the lab," she managed, in a brittle, choked voice.

"I'm Leroy Beam. An independent." Awkwardly guiding her, he led her into the kitchen and seated her at the table. She folded her hands in front of her and studied them fixedly; the bleak boniness of her face seemed to be increasing rather than receding. He felt uneasy.

"Are you all right?" he asked.

She nodded.

"Cup of coffee?" He began searching the cupboards for a bottle of Venusian-grown coffee substitute. While he was looking, Ellen Ackers said tautly: "You better go in there. In the bathroom. I don't think he's dead, but he might be."

Beam raced into the bathroom. Behind the plastic shower curtain was an opaque shape. It was Paul Tirol, lying wadded up in the tub, fully clothed. He was not dead but he had been struck behind the left ear and his scalp was leaking a slow, steady trickle of blood. Beam took his pulse, listened to his breathing, and then straightened up.

At the doorway Ellen Ackers materialized, still pale with fright. "Is he? Did I kill him?"

"He's fine."

Visibly, she relaxed. "Thank God. It happened so fast — he stepped ahead of me to take the *M* inside his place, and then I did it. I hit him as lightly as I could. He was so interested in it ... he forgot about me." Words spilled from her, quick, jerky sentences, punctuated by rigid tremors of her hands. "I lugged him back in the car and drove here; it was all I could think of."

"What are you in this for?"

Her hysteria rose in a spasm of convulsive muscle-twitching. "It was all planned — I had *everything* worked out. As soon as I got hold of it I was going to — " She broke off.

"Blackmail Tirol?" he asked, fascinated.

She smiled weakly. "No, not Paul. It was Paul who gave me the idea ... it was his first idea, when his researchers showed him the thing. The — *unreconstructed*

M, he calls it. *M* stands for machine. He means it can't be educated, morally corrected."

Incredulous, Beam said: "You were going to blackmail your husband."

Ellen Ackers nodded. "So he'd let me leave."

Suddenly Beam felt sincere respect for her. "My God — the rattle. Heimie didn't arrange that; *you* did. So the device would be trapped in the apartment."

"Yes," she agreed. "I was going to pick it up. But Paul showed up with other ideas; he wanted it, too."

"What went haywire? You have it, don't you?"

Silently she indicated the linen closet. "I stuffed it away when I heard you."

Beam opened the linen closet. Resting primly on the neatly-folded towels was a small, familiar, portable TV unit.

"It's reverted," Ellen said, from behind him, in an utterly defeated monotone. "As soon as I hit Paul it changed. For half an hour I've been trying to get it to shift. It won't. It'll stay that way forever."

III

Beam went to the telephone and called a doctor. In the bathroom, Tirol groaned and feebly thrashed his arms. He was beginning to return to consciousness.

"Was that necessary?" Ellen Ackers demanded. "The doctor — did you have to call?"

Beam ignored her. Bending, he lifted the portable TV unit and held it in his hands; he felt its weight move up his arms like a slow, leaden fatigue. The ultimate adversary, he thought; too stupid to be defeated. It was worse than an animal. It was a rock, solid and dense, lacking all qualities. Except, he thought, the quality of determination. It was determined to persist, to survive; a rock with will. He felt as if he were holding up the universe, and he put the unreconstructed M down.

From behind him Ellen said: "It drives you crazy." Her voice had regained tone. She lit a cigarette with a silver cigarette lighter and then shoved her hands in the pockets of her suit.

"Yes," he said.

"There's nothing you can do, is there? You tried to get it open before. They'll patch Paul up, and he'll go back to his place, and Lantano will be banished — " She took a deep shuddering breath. "And the Interior Department will go on as always."

"Yes," he said. Still kneeling, he surveyed the M. Now, with what he knew, he did not waste time struggling with it. He considered it impassively; he did not even bother to touch it.

In the bathroom, Paul Tirol was trying to crawl from the tub. He slipped back, cursed and moaned, and started his laborious ascent once again.

"Ellen?" his voice quavered, a dim and distorted sound, like dry wires rubbing.

"Take it easy," she said between her teeth; not moving she stood smoking rapidly on her cigarette.

"Help me, Ellen," Tirol muttered. "Something happened to me ... I don't remember what. Something hit me."

"He'll remember," Ellen said.

Beam said: "I can take this thing to Ackers as it is. You can tell him what it's for — what it did. That ought to be enough; he won't go through with Lantano."

But he didn't believe it, either. Ackers would have to admit a mistake, a basic mistake, and if he had been wrong to pick up Lantano, he was ruined. And so, in a sense, was the whole system of delineation. It could be fooled; it had been fooled. Ackers was rigid, and he would go right on in a straight line: the hell with Lantano. The hell with abstract justice. Better to preserve cultural continuity and keep society running on an even keel.

"Tirol's equipment," Beam said. "Do you know where it is?"

She shrugged wildly. "What equipment?"

"This thing — " he jabbed at the M — "was made somewhere."

"Not here, Tirol didn't make it."

"All right," he said reasonably. They had perhaps six minutes more before the doctor and the emergency medical carrier arrived on rooftop. "Who did make it?"

"The alloy was developed on Bellatrix." She spoke jerkily, word by word. "The rind ... forms a skin on the outside, a bubble that gets sucked in and out of a reservoir. That's its rind, the TV shape. It sucks it back and becomes the M; it's ready to act."

"What made it?" he repeated.

"A Bellatrix machine tool syndicate ... a subsidiary of Tirol's organization. They're made to be watchdogs. The big plantations on outplanets use them; they patrol. They get poachers."

Beam said: "Then originally they're not set for one person."

"No."

"Then *who* set this for Heimie? Not a machine tool syndicate."

"That was done here."

He straightened up and lifted the portable TV unit. "Let's go. Take me there, where Tirol had it altered."

For a moment the woman did not respond. Grabbing her arm he hustled her to the door. She gasped and stared at him mutely.

"Come on," he said, pushing her out into the hall. The portable TV unit bumped against the door as he shut it; he held the unit tight and followed after Ellen Ackers.

The town was slatternly and run-down, a few retail stores, fuel station, bars and dance halls. It was two hours' flight from Greater New York and it was called Olum.

"Turn right," Ellen said listlessly. She gazed out at the neon signs and rested her arm on the window sill of the ship.

They flew above warehouses and deserted streets. Lights were few. At an intersection Ellen nodded and he set the ship down on a roof.

Below them was a sagging, fly-specked wooden frame store. A peeling sign was propped up in the window: FULTON BROTHERS LOCKSMITHS. With the sign were doorknobs, locks, keys, saws, and spring-wound alarm clocks. Somewhere in the interior of the store a yellow night light burned fitfully.

"This way," Ellen said. She stepped from the ship and made her way down a flight of rickety wooden stairs. Beam laid the portable TV unit on the floor of the ship, locked the doors, and then followed after the woman. Holding onto the railing, he descended to a back porch on which were trash cans and a pile of sodden newspapers tied with string. Ellen was unlocking a door and feeling her way inside.

First he found himself in a musty, cramped storeroom. Pipe and rolls of wire and sheets of metal were heaped everywhere; it was like a junkyard. Next came a narrow corridor and then he was standing in the entrance of a workshop. Ellen reached overhead and groped to find the hanging string of a light. The light clicked on. To the right was a long and littered workbench with a hand grinder at one end, a vise, a keyhole saw; two wooden stools were before the bench and half-assembled machinery was stacked on the floor in no apparent order. The workshop was chaotic, dusty, and archaic. On the wall was a threadbare blue coat hung from a nail: the workcoat of a machinist.

"Here," Ellen said, with bitterness. "This is where Paul had it brought. This outfit is owned by the Tirol organization; this whole slum is part of their holdings."

Beam walked to the bench. "To have altered it," he said, "Tirol must have had a plate of Heimie's neural pattern." He overturned a heap of glass jars; screws and washers poured onto the pitted surface of the bench.

"He got it from Heimie's door," Ellen said. "He had Heimie's lock analyzed and Heimie's pattern inferred from the setting of the tumblers."

"And he had the M opened?"

"There's an old mechanic," Ellen said. "A little dried-up old man; he runs this shop. Patrick Fulton. He installed the bias on the M."

"A bias," Beam said, nodding.

"A bias against killing people. Heimie was the exception, for everybody else it took its protective form. Out in the wilds they would have set it for something else, not a TV unit." She laughed, a sudden ripple close to hysteria. "Yes, that would have looked odd, it sitting out in a forest somewhere, a TV unit. They would have made it into a rock or a stick."

"A rock," Beam said. He could imagine it. The M waiting, covered with moss, waiting for months, years, and then weathered and corroded, finally picking up the presence of a human being. Then the M ceasing to be a rock, becoming, in a quick blur of motion, a box one foot wide and two feet long. An oversized cracker box that started forward —

But there was something missing. "The fakery," he said. "Emitting flakes of paint and hair and tobacco. How did that come in?"

In a brittle voice Ellen said: "The landowner murdered the poacher, and he was culpable in the eyes of the law. So the M left clues. Claw marks. Animal blood. Animal hair."

"God," he said, revolted. "Killed by an animal."

"A bear, a wildcat — whatever was indigenous, it varied. The predator of the region, a natural death." With her toe she touched a cardboard carton under the workbench. "It's in there, it used to be, anyhow. The neural plate, the transmitter, the discarded parts of the M, the schematics."

The carton had been a shipping container for power packs. Now the packs were gone, and in their place was a carefully-wrapped inner box, sealed against moisture and insect infestation. Beam tore away the metal foil and saw that he had found what he wanted. He gingerly carried the contents out and spread them on the workbench among the soldering irons and drills.

"It's all there," Ellen said, without emotion.

"Maybe," he said, "I can leave you out of this. I can take this and the TV unit to Ackers and try it without your testimony."

"Sure," she said wearily.

"What are you going to do?"

"Well," she said, "I can't go back to Paul, so I guess there's not much I can do."

"The blackmail bit was a mistake," he said.

Her eyes glowed. "Okay."

"If he releases Lantano," Beam said, "he'll be asked to resign. Then he'll probably give you your divorce, it won't be important to him one way or another."

"I — " she began. And then she stopped. Her face seemed to fade, as if the color and texture of her flesh was vanishing from within. She lifted one hand and half-turned, her mouth open and the sentence still unfinished.

Beam, reaching, slapped the overhead light out; the workroom winked into darkness. He had heard it too, had heard it at the same time as Ellen Ackers. The rickety outside porch had creaked and now the slow, ponderous motion was past the storeroom and into the hall.

A heavy man, he thought. A slow-moving man, sleepy, making his way step by step, his eyes almost shut, his great body sagging beneath his suit. Beneath, he thought, his expensive tweed suit. In the darkness the man's shape was looming; Beam could not see it but he could sense it there, filling up the doorway as it halted. Boards creaked under its weight. In a daze he wondered if Ackers already knew, if his order had already been rescinded. Or had the man got out on his own, worked through his own organization?

The man, starting forward again, spoke in a deep, husky voice. "Ugh," Lantano said. "Damn it."

Ellen began to shriek. Beam still did not realize what it was; he was still fumbling for the light and wondering stupidly why it did not come on. He had smashed the bulb, he realized. He lit a match; the match went out and he grabbed for Ellen Ackers' cigarette lighter. It was in her purse, and it took him an agonized second to get it out.

The unreconstructed M was approaching them slowly, one receptor stalk extended. Again it halted, swiveled to the left until it was facing the workbench. It was not now in the shape of a portable TV unit; it had retaken its cracker-box shape.

"The plate," Ellen Ackers whispered. "It responded to the plate."

The M had been roused by Heimie Rosenburg's looking for it. But Beam still felt the presence of David Lantano. The big man was still here in the room; the sense of heaviness, the proximity of weight and ponderousness had arrived with the machine, as it moved, sketching Lantano's existence. As he fixedly watched, the machine produced a fragment of cloth fabric and pressed it into a nearby heap of grid-mesh. Other elements, blood and tobacco and hair, were being produced, but they were too small for him to see. The machine pressed a heel mark into the dust of the floor and then projected a nozzle from its anterior section.

Her arm over her eyes, Ellen Ackers ran away. But the machine was not interested in her; revolving in the direction of the workbench it raised itself and fired. An explosive pellet, released by the nozzle, traveled across the workbench and entered the debris heaped across the bench. The pellet detonated; bits of wire and nails showered in particles.

Heimie's dead, Beam thought, and went on watching. The machine was searching for the plate, trying to locate and destroy the synthetic neural emission. It swiveled, lowered its nozzle hesitantly, and then fired again. Behind the workbench, the wall burst and settled into itself.

Beam, holding the cigarette lighter, walked toward the M. A receptor stalk waved toward him and the machine retreated. Its lines wavered, flowed, and then painfully reformed. For an interval, the device struggled with itself; then, reluctantly, the portable TV unit again became visible. From the machine a high-pitched whine emerged, an anguished squeal. Conflicting stimuli were present; the machine was unable to make a decision.

The machine was developing a situation neurosis and the ambivalence of its response was destroying it. In a way its anguish had a human quality, but he could not feel sorry for it. It was a mechanical contraption trying to assume a posture of disguise and attack at the same time; the breakdown was one of relays and tubes, not of a living brain. And it had been a living brain into which it had fired its original pellet. Heimie Rosenburg was dead, and there were no more like him and no possibility that more could be assembled. He went over to the machine and nudged it onto its back with his foot.

The machine whirred snake-like and spun away. "Ugh, damn it!" it said. It showered bits of tobacco as it rolled off; drops of blood and flakes of blue enamel fell from it as it disappeared into the corridor. Beam could hear it moving about, bumping into the walls like a blind, damaged organism. After a moment he followed after it.

In the corridor, the machine was traveling in a slow circle. It was erecting around itself a wall of particles: cloth and hairs and burnt matches and bits of tobacco, the mass cemented together with blood.

"Ugh, damn it," the machine said in its heavy masculine voice. It went on working, and Beam returned to the other room.

"Where's a phone?" he said to Ellen Ackers.

She stared at him vacantly.

"It won't hurt you," he said. He felt dull and worn-out. "It's in a closed cycle. It'll go on until it runs down."

"It went crazy," she said. She shuddered.

"No," he said. "Regression. It's trying to hide."

From the corridor the machine said, "Ugh. Damn it." Beam found the phone and called Edward Ackers.

Banishment for Paul Tirol meant first a procession of bands of darkness and then a protracted, infuriating interval in which empty matter drifted randomly around him, arranging itself into first one pattern and then another.

The period between the time Ellen Ackers attacked him and the time banishment sentence had been pronounced was vague and dim in his mind. Like the present shadows, it was hard to pin down.

He had — he thought — awakened in Ackers' apartment. Yes, that was it; and Leroy Beam was there, too. A sort of transcendental Leroy Beam who hovered robustly around, arranging everybody in configurations of his choice. A doctor had come. And finally Edward Ackers had shown up to face his wife and the situation.

Bandaged, and on his way into Interior, he had caught a glimpse of a man going out. The ponderous, bulbous shape of David Lantano, on his way home to his luxurious stone mansion and acre of grass.

At sight of him Tirol had felt a goad of fear. Lantano hadn't even noticed him; an acutely thoughtful expression on his face, Lantano padded into a waiting car and departed.

"You have one thousand dollars," Edward Ackers was saying wearily, during the final phase. Distorted, Ackers' face bloomed again in the drifting shadows around Tirol, an image of the man's last appearance. Ackers, too, was ruined, but in a different way. "The law supplies you with one thousand dollars to meet your immediate needs, also you'll find a pocket dictionary of representative out-system dialects."

Ionization itself was painless. He had no memory of it; only a blank space darker than the blurred images on either side.

"You hate me," he had declared accusingly, his last words to Ackers. "I destroyed you. But ... it wasn't you." He had been confused. "Lantano. Maneuvered but not. How? You did ... "

But Lantano had had nothing to do with it. Lantano had shambled off home, a withdrawn spectator throughout. The hell with Lantano. The hell with Ackers and Leroy Beam and — reluctantly — the hell with Mrs. Ellen Ackers.

"Wow," Tirol babbled, as his drifting body finally collected physical shape. "We had a lot of good times ... didn't we, Ellen?"

And then a roaring hot field of sunlight was radiating down on him. Stupefied, he sat slumped over, limp and passive. Yellow, scalding sunlight ... everywhere. Nothing but the dancing heat of it, blinding him, cowing him into submission.

He was sprawled in the middle of a yellow clay road. To his right was a baking, drying field of corn wilted in the midday heat. A pair of large, disreputable-looking birds wheeled silently overhead. A long way off was a line of blunted hills: ragged troughs and peaks that seemed nothing more than heaps of dust. At their base was a meager lump of man-made buildings.

At least he *hoped* they were man-made.

As he climbed shakily to his feet, a feeble noise drifted to his ears. Coming down the hot, dirty road was a car of some sort. Apprehensive and cautious, Tirol walked to meet it.

The driver was human, a thin, almost emaciated youth with pebbled black skin and a heavy mass of weed-colored hair. He wore a stained canvas shirt and overalls. A bent, unlit cigarette hung from his lower lip. The car was a combustion-driven model and had rolled out of the twentieth century; battered and twisted, it rattled to a halt as the driver critically inspected Tirol. From the car's radio yammered a torrent of tinny dance music.

"You a tax collector?" the driver asked.

"Certainly not," Tirol said, knowing the bucolic hostility toward tax collectors. But — he floundered. He couldn't confess that he was a banished criminal from Earth; that was an invitation to be massacred, usually in some picturesque way. "I'm an inspector," he announced, "Department of Health."

Satisfied, the driver nodded. "Lots of scuttly cutbeetle, these days. You fellows got a spray, yet? Losing one crop after another."

Tirol gratefully climbed into the car. "I didn't realize the sun was so hot," he murmured.

"You've got an accent," the youth observed, starting up the engine. "Where you from?"

"Speech impediment," Tirol said cagily. "How long before we reach town?"

"Oh, maybe an hour," the youth answered, as the car wandered lazily forward.

Tirol was afraid to ask the name of the planet. It would give him away. But he was consumed with the need to know. He might be two star-systems away or two million; he might be a month out of Earth or seventy years. Naturally, he had to get back; he had no intention of becoming a sharecropper on some backwater colony planet.

"Pretty swip," the youth said, indicating the torrent of noxious jazz pouring from the car radio. "That's Calamine Freddy and his Woolybear Creole Original Band. Know that tune?"

"No," Tirol muttered. The sun and dryness and heat made his head ache, and he wished to God he knew where he was.

The town was miserably tiny. The houses were dilapidated; the streets were dirt. A kind of domestic chicken roamed here and there, pecking in the rubbish. Under a porch a bluish quasi-dog lay sleeping. Perspiring and unhappy, Paul Tirol entered the bus station and located a schedule. A series of meaningless entries flashed by: names of towns. The name of the planet, of course, was not listed.

"What's the fare to the nearest port?" he asked the indolent official behind the ticket window.

The official considered. "Depends on what sort of port you want. Where you planning to go?"

"Toward Center," Tirol said. "Center" was the term used in out-systems for the Sol Group.

Dispassionately, the official shook his head. "No inter-system port around here."

Tirol was baffled. Evidently, he wasn't on the hub planet of this particular system. "Well," he said, "then the nearest interplan port."

The official consulted a vast reference book. "You want to go to which system-member?"

"Whichever one has the inter-system port," Tirol said patiently. He would leave from there.

"That would be Venus."

Astonished, Tirol said: "Then this system — " He broke off, chagrined, as he remembered. It was the parochial custom in many out-systems, especially those a long way out, to name their member planets after the original nine. This one was probably called "Mars" or "Jupiter" or "Earth," depending on its position in the group. "Fine," Tirol finished. "One-way ticket to — Venus."

Venus, or what passed for Venus, was a dismal orb no larger than an asteroid.

A bleak cloud of metallic haze hung over it, obscuring the sun. Except for mining and smelting operations the planet was deserted. A few dreary shacks dotted the barren countryside. A perpetual wind blew, scattering debris and trash.

But the inter-system port was here, the field which linked the planet to its nearest star-neighbor and, ultimately, with the balance of the universe. At the moment a giant freighter was taking ore.

Tirol entered the ticket office. Spreading out most of his remaining money he said: "I want a one-way ticket taking me toward Center. As far as I can go."

The clerk calculated. "You care what class?"

"No," he said, mopping his forehead.

"How fast?"

"No."

The clerk said: "That'll carry you as far as the Betelgeuse System."

"Good enough," Tirol said, wondering what he did then. But at least he could contact his organization from there; he was already back in the charted universe. But now he was almost broke. He felt a prickle of icy fear, despite the heat.

The hub planet of the Betelgeuse System was called Plantagenet III. It was a thriving junction for passenger carriers transporting settlers to undeveloped colony planets. As soon as Tirol's ship landed he hurried across the field to the taxi stand.

"Take me to Tirol Enterprises," he instructed, praying there was an outlet here. There had to be, but it might be operating under a front name. Years ago he lost track of the particulars of his sprawling empire.

"Tirol Enterprises," the cab driver repeated thoughtfully. "Nope, no such outfit, mister."

Stunned, Tirol said: "Who does the slaving around here?"

The driver eyed him. He was a wizened, dried-up little man with glasses; he peered turtle-wise, without compassion. "Well," he said, "I've been told you can get carried out-system without papers. There's a shipping contractor ... called — " He reflected. Tirol, trembling, handed him a last bill.

"The Reliable Export-Import," the driver said.

That was one of Lantano's fronts. In horror Tirol said: "And that's it?"

The driver nodded.

Dazed, Tirol moved away from the cab. The buildings of the field danced around him; he settled down on a bench to catch his breath. Under his coat his heart pounded unevenly. He tried to breathe, but his breath caught painfully in his throat. The bruise on his head where Ellen Ackers had hit him began to throb. It was true, and he was gradually beginning to understand and believe it. He was not going to get to Earth; he was going to spend the rest of his life here on this rural world, cut off from his organization and everything he had built up over the years.

And, he realized, as he sat struggling to breathe, the rest of his life was not going to be very long.

He thought about Heimie Rosenburg.

"Betrayed," he said, and coughed wrackingly. "You betrayed me. You hear that? Because of you I'm here. It's your fault; I never should have hired you."

He thought about Ellen Ackers. "You too," he gasped, coughing. Sitting on the bench he alternately coughed and gasped and thought about the people who had betrayed him. There were hundreds of them.

The living room of David Lantano's house was furnished in exquisite taste. Priceless late nineteenth century Blue Willow dishes lined the walls in a rack of wrought iron. At his antique yellow plastic and chrome table, David Lantano was eating dinner, and the spread of food amazed Beam even more than the house.

Lantano was in good humor and he ate with enthusiasm. His linen napkin was tucked under his chin and once, as he sipped coffee, he dribbled and belched. His brief period of confinement was over; he ate to make up for the ordeal.

He had been informed, first by his own apparatus and now by Beam, that banishment had successfully carried Tirol past the point of return. Tirol would not be coming back and for that Lantano was thankful. He felt expansive toward Beam; he wished Beam would have something to eat.

Moodily, Beam said: "It's nice here."

"You could have something like this," Lantano said.

On the wall hung a framed folio of ancient paper protected by helium-filled glass. It was the first printing of a poem of Ogden Nash, a collector's item that should have been in a museum. It aroused in Beam a mixed feeling of longing and aversion.

"Yes," Beam said. "I could have this." This, he thought, or Ellen Ackers or the job at Interior or perhaps all three at once. Edward Ackers had been retired on pension and he had given his wife a divorce. Lantano was out of jeopardy. Tirol had been banished. He wondered what he did want.

"You could go a long way," Lantano said sleepily.

"As far as Paul Tirol?"

Lantano chuckled and yawned.

"I wonder if he left any family," Beam said. "Any children." He was thinking about Heimie.

Lantano reached across the table toward the bowl of fruit. He selected a peach and carefully brushed it against the sleeve of his robe. "Try a peach," he said.

"No thanks," Beam said irritably.

Lantano examined the peach but he did not eat it. The peach was made of wax; the fruit in the bowl was imitation. He was not really as rich as he pretended, and many of the artifacts about the living room were fakes. Each time he offered fruit to a visitor he took a calculated risk. Returning the peach to the bowl he leaned back in his chair and sipped his coffee.

If Beam did not have plans, at least *he* had, and with Tirol gone the plans had a better than even chance of working out. He felt peaceful. Someday, he thought, and not too far off, the fruit in the bowl would be real.

EXPLORERS WE

"GOLLY," PARKHURST GASPED, his red face tingling with excitement. "Come here, you guys. Look!"

They crowded around the viewscreen.

"There she is," Barton said. His heart beat strangely. "She sure looks good."

"Damn right she looks good," Leon agreed. He trembled. "Say — I can make out New York."

"The hell you can."

"I can! The gray. By the water."

"That's not even the United States. We're looking at it upside down. That's Siam."

The ship hurtled through space, meteoroid shields shrieking. Below it, the blue-green globe swelled. Clouds drifted around it, hiding the continents and oceans.

"I never expected to see her again," Merriweather said. "I thought sure as hell we were stuck up there." His face twisted. "Mars. That damned red waste. Sun and flies and ruins."

"Barton knows how to repair jets," Captain Stone said. "You can thank *him*."

"You know what I'm going to do, first thing I'm back?" Parkhurst yelled. "What?"

"Go to Coney Island."

"Why?"

"People. I want to see people again. Lots of them. Dumb, sweaty, noisy. Ice cream and water. The ocean. Beer bottles, milk cartons, paper napkins — "

"And gals," Vecchi said, eyes shining. "Long time, six months. I'll go with you. We'll sit on the beach and watch the gals."

"I wonder what kind of bathing suits they got now," Barton said.

"Maybe they don't wear any!" Parkhurst cried.

"Hey!" Merriweather shouted. "I'm going to see my wife again." He was suddenly dazed. His voice sank to a whisper. "My wife."

"I got a wife, too," Stone said. He grinned. "But I been married a long time." Then he thought of Pat and Jean. A stabbing ache choked his windpipe. "I bet they have grown."

"Grown?"

"My kids," Stone said huskily.

They looked at each other, six men, ragged, bearded, eyes bright and feverish.

"How long?" Vecchi whispered.

"An hour," Stone said. "We'll be down in an hour."

The ship struck with a crash that threw them on their faces. It leaped and bucked, brake jets screaming, tearing through rocks and soil. It came to rest, nose buried in a hillside.

Silence.

Parkhurst got unsteadily to his feet. He caught hold of the safety rail. Blood dripped down his face from a cut over his eye.

"We're down," he said.

Barton stirred. He groaned, forced himself up on his knees. Parkhurst helped him. "Thanks. Are we ... "

"We're down. We're back."

The jets were off. The roaring had ceased ... there was only the faint trickle of wall fluids leaking out on the ground.

The ship was a mess. The hull was cracked in three places. It billowed in, bent and twisted. Papers and ruined instruments were strewn everywhere.

Vecchi and Stone got slowly up. "Everything all right?" Stone muttered, feeling his arm.

"Give me a hand," Leon said. "My damn ankle's twisted or something."

They got him up. Merriweather was unconscious. They revived him and got him to his feet.

"We're down," Parkhurst repeated, as if he couldn't believe it. "This is Earth. We're back — alive!"

"I hope the specimens are all right," Leon said.

"The hell with the specimens!" Vecchi shouted excitedly. He worked the port bolts frantically, unscrewing the heavy hatch lock. "Let's get out and walk around."

"Where are we?" Barton asked Captain Stone.

"South of San Francisco. On the peninsula."

"San Francisco! Hey — we can ride the cable cars!" Parkhurst helped Vecchi unscrew the hatch. "San Francisco. I was through Frisco once. They got a big park. Golden Gate Park. We can go to the funhouse."

The hatch opened, swinging wide. Talk ceased abruptly. The men peered out, blinking in the white-hot sunlight.

A green field stretched down and away from them. Hills rose in the distance, sharp in the crystal air. Along a highway below, a few cars moved, tiny dots, the sun glinting on them. Telephone poles.

"What's that sound?" Stone said, listening intently.

"A train."

It was coming along the distant track, black smoke pouring from its stack. A faint wind moved across the field, stirring the grass. Over to the right lay a town. Houses and trees. A theater marquee. A Standard gas station. Roadside stands. A motel.

"Think anybody saw us?" Leon asked.

"Must have."

"Sure heard us," Parkhurst said. "We made a noise like God's indigestion when we hit."

Vecchi stepped out onto the field. He swayed wildly, arms outstretched. "I'm falling!"

Stone laughed. "You'll get used to it. We've been in space too long. Come on." He leaped down. "Let's start walking."

"Toward the town." Parkhurst fell in beside him. "Maybe they'll give us free eats ... Hell — champagne!" His chest swelled under his tattered uniform. "Returning heroes. Keys to the town. A parade. Military band. Floats with dames."

"Dames," Leon grunted. "You're obsessed."

"Sure." Parkhurst strode across the field, the others trailing after him. "Hurry up!"

"Look," Stone said to Leon. "Somebody over there. Watching us."

"Kids," Barton said. "A bunch of kids." He laughed excitedly. "Let's go say hello."

They headed toward the kids, wading through the moist grass on the rich earth.

"Must be spring," Leon said. "The air smells like spring." He took a deep breath. "And the grass."

Stone computed. "It's April ninth."

They hurried. The kids stood watching them, silent and unmoving.

"Hey!" Parkhurst shouted. "We're back!"

"What town is this?" Barton shouted.

The kids stared at them, eyes wide.

"What's wrong?" Leon muttered.

"Our beards. We look pretty bad." Stone cupped his hands. "Don't be scared! We're back from Mars. The rocket flight. Two years ago — remember? A year ago last October."

The kids stared, white-faced. Suddenly they turned and fled. They ran frantically toward the town.

The six men watched them go.

"What the hell," Parkhurst muttered, dazed. "What's the matter?"

"Our beards," Stone repeated uneasily.

"Something's wrong," Barton said, shakily. He began to tremble. "There's something terribly wrong."

"Can it!" Leon snapped. "It's our beards." He ripped a piece of his shirt savagely away. "We're dirty. Filthy tramps. Come on." He started after the children, toward the town. "Let's go. They probably got a special car on the way here. We'll meet them."

Stone and Barton glanced at each other. They followed Leon slowly. The others fell in behind.

Silent, uneasy, the six bearded men made their way across the field toward the town.

A youth on a bicycle fled at their approach. Some railroad workers, repairing the train track, threw down their shovels and ran, yelling.

Numbly, the six men watched them go.

"What is it?" Parkhurst muttered.

They crossed the track. The town lay on the other side. They entered a huge grove of eucalyptus trees.

"Burlingame," Leon said, reading a sign. They looked down a street. Hotels and cafes. Parked cars. Gas stations. Dime stores. A small suburban town, shoppers on the sidewalks. Cars moving slowly.

They emerged from the trees. Across the street a filling station attendant looked up —

And froze.

After a moment, he dropped the hose he held and ran down the main street, shouting shrill warnings.

Cars stopped. Drivers leaped out and ran. Men and women poured out of stores, scattering wildly. They surged away, retreating in frantic haste.

In a moment the street was deserted.

"Good God." Stone advanced, bewildered. "What — " He crossed onto the street. No one was in sight.

The six men walked down the main street, dazed and silent. Nothing stirred. Everyone had fled. A siren wailed, rising and falling. Down a side street a car backed quickly away.

In an upstairs window Barton saw a pale, frightened face. Then the shade was jerked down.

"I don't understand," Vecchi muttered.

"Have they gone nuts?" Merriweather asked.

Stone said nothing. His mind was blank. Numb. He felt tired. He sat down on the curb and rested, getting his breath. The others stood around him.

"My ankle," Leon said. He leaned against a stop sign, lips twisting with pain. "Hurts like hell."

"Captain," Barton said. "What's the matter with them?"

"I don't know," Stone said. He felt in his ragged pocket for a cigarette. Across the street was a deserted cafe. The people had run out of it. Food was still on the counter. A hamburger was scorching on the skillet, coffee was boiling in a glass pot on the burner.

On the sidewalk lay groceries spilling out from bags dropped by terrorized shoppers. The motor of a deserted parked car purred to itself.

"Well?" Leon said. "What'll we do?"

"I don't know."

"We can't just — "

"I don't know!" Stone got to his feet. He walked over and entered the cafe. They watched him sit down at the counter.

"What's he doing?" Vecchi asked.

"I don't know." Parkhurst followed Stone into the cafe. "What are you doing?"

"I'm waiting to be served."

Parkhurst plucked awkwardly at Stone's shoulder. "Come on, Captain. There's nobody here. They all left."

Stone said nothing. He sat at the counter, his face vacant. Waiting passively to be served.

Parkhurst went back out. "What the hell has happened?" he asked Barton. "What's wrong with them all?"

A spotted dog came nosing around. It passed them, stiff and alert, sniffing suspiciously. It trotted off down a side street.

"Faces," Barton said.

"Faces?"

"They're watching us. Up there." Barton gestured toward a building. "Hiding. *Why*? Why are they hiding from us?"

Suddenly Merriweather stiffened. "Something's coming."

They turned eagerly.

Down the street two black sedans turned the corner, headed toward them.

"Thank God," Leon muttered. He leaned against the wall of a building. "Here they are."

The two sedans pulled to a stop at the curb. The doors opened. Men spilled out, surrounded them silently. Well-dressed. Ties and hats and long gray coats.

"I'm Scanlan," one said. "FBI." An older man with iron-gray hair. His voice was clipped and frigid. He studied the five of them intently. "Where's the other?"

"Captain Stone? In there." Barton pointed to the cafe.

"Get him out here."

Barton went into the cafe. "Captain, they're outside. Come on."

Stone came along with him, back to the curb. "Who are they, Barton?" he asked haltingly.

"Six," Scanlan said, nodding. He waved to his men. "Okay. This is all."

The FBI men moved in, crowding them back toward the brick front of the cafe.

"Wait!" Barton cried thickly. His head spun. "What — what's happening?

"What is it?" Parkhurst demanded deprecatorily. Tears rolled down his face, streaking his cheeks. "Will you tell us, for God's sake — "

The FBI men had weapons. They got them out. Vecchi backed away, his hands up. "Please!" he wailed. "What have we done? What's happening?"

Sudden hope flickered in Leon's breast. "They don't know who we are. They think we're Commies." He addressed Scanlan. "We're the Earth-Mars Expedition. My name is Leon. Remember? A year ago last October. We're *back*. We're back from Mars." His voice trailed off. The weapons were coming up. Nozzles — hoses and tanks.

"We're back!" Merriweather croaked. "We're the Earth-Mars Expedition, come back!"

Scanlan's face was expressionless. "That sounds fine," he said coldly. "Only, the ship crashed and blew up when it reached Mars. None of the crew survived. We know because we sent up a robot scavenger team and brought back the corpses — six of them."

The FBI men fired. Blazing napalm sprayed toward the six bearded figures. They retreated, and then the flames touched them. The FBI men saw the figures ignite, and then the sight was cut off. They could no longer see the six figures thrashing about, but they could hear them. It was not something they enjoyed hearing, but they remained, waiting and watching.

Scanlan kicked at the charred fragments with his foot. "Not easy to be sure," he said. "Possibly only five here ... but I didn't see any of them get away. They didn't have time." At the pressure of his foot, a section of ash broke away; it fell into particles that still steamed and bubbled.

His companion Wilks stared down. New at this, he could not quite believe what he had seen the napalm do. "I — " he said. "Maybe I'll go back to the car," he muttered, starting off away from Scanlan.

"It's not over positively," Scanlan said, and then he saw the younger man's face. "Yes," he said, "you go sit down."

People were beginning to filter out onto the sidewalks. Peeping anxiously from doorways and windows.

"They got 'em!" a boy shouted excitedly. "They got the outer space spies!"

Cameramen snapped pictures. Curious people appeared on all sides, faces pale, eyes popping. Gaping down in wonder at the indiscriminate mass of charred ash.

His hands shaking, Wilks crept back into the car and shut the door after him. The radio buzzed, and he turned it off, not wanting to hear anything from it or say anything to it. At the doorway of the cafe, the gray-coated Bureau men remained, conferring with Scanlan. Presently a number of them started off at a trot, around the side of the cafe and up the alley. Wilks watched them go. What a nightmare, he thought.

Coming over, Scanlan leaned down and put his head into the car. "Feel better?"

"Some." Presently he asked, "What's this — the twenty-second time?"

Scanlan said, "Twenty-first. Every couple of months ... the same names, same men. I won't tell you that you'll get used to it. But at least it won't surprise you."

"I don't see any difference between them and us," Wilks said, speaking distinctly. "It was like burning up six human beings."

"No," Scanlan said. He opened the car door and got into the back seat, behind Wilks. "They only looked like six human beings. That's the whole point. They want to. They intend to. You know that Barton, Stone, and Leon — "

"I know," he said. "Somebody or something that lives somewhere out there saw their ship go down, saw them die, and investigated. Before we got there. And got enough to go on, enough to give them what they needed. But — " He gestured. "Isn't there anything else we can do with them?"

Scanlan said, "We don't know enough about them. Only this — sending in of imitations, again and again. Trying to sneak them past us." His face became rigid, despairing. "Are they crazy? Maybe they're so different no contact's possible. Do they think we're all named Leon and Merriweather and Parkhurst and Stone? That's the part that personally gets me down ... Or maybe that's our chance, the fact that they don't understand we're individuals. Figure how much worse if sometime they made up a — whatever it is ... a spore ... a seed. But not like one of those poor miserable six who died on Mars — something we wouldn't know was an imitation ... "

"They have to have a model," Wilks said.

One of the Bureau men waved, and Scanlan scrambled out of the car. He came back in a moment to Wilks. "They say there're only five," he said. "One got away; they think they saw him. He's crippled and not moving fast. The rest of us are going after him — you stay here, keep your eyes open." He strode off up the alley with the other Bureau men.

Wilks lit a cigarette and sat with his head resting on his arm. Mimicry ... everybody terrified. But —

Had anybody really tried to make contact?

Two policemen appeared, herding people back out of the way. A third black Dodge, loaded with Bureau men, moved along at the curb, stopped, and the men got out.

One of the Bureau men, whom he did not recognize, approached the car. "Don't you have your radio on?"

"No," Wilks said. He snapped it back on.

"If you see one, do you know how to kill it?"

"Yes," he said.

The Bureau man went on to join his group.

If it was up to me, Wilks asked himself, what would I do? Try to find out what they want? Anything that looks so human, behaves in such a human way, must *feel* human ... and if they — whatever they are — feel human, might they not become human, in time?

At the edge of the crowd of people, an individual shape detached itself and moved toward him. Uncertainly, the shape halted, shook its head, staggered and caught itself, and then assumed a stance like that of the people near it. Wilks recognized it because he had been trained to, over a period of months. It had gotten different clothes, a pair of slacks, a shirt, but it had buttoned the shirt wrong, and one of its feet was bare. Evidently it did not understand the shoes. Or, he thought, maybe it was too dazed and injured.

As it approached him, Wilks raised his pistol and took aim at its stomach. They had been taught to fire there; he had fired, on the practice range, at chart after chart. Right in the midsection ... bisect it, like a bug.

On its face the expression of suffering and bewilderment deepened as it saw him prepare to fire. It halted, facing him, making no move to escape. Now Wilks realized that it had been severely burned; probably it would not survive in any case.

"I have to," he said.

It stared at him, and then it opened its mouth and started to say something. He fired.

Before it could speak, it had died. Wilks got out as it pitched over and lay beside the car.

I did wrong, he thought to himself as he stood looking down at it. I shot it because I was afraid. But I had to. Even if it was wrong. It came here to infiltrate us, imitating us so we won't recognize it. That's what we're told — we have to believe that they are plotting against us, are inhuman, and will never be more than that.

Thank God, he thought. It's over.

And then he remembered it wasn't ...

*   *   *

It was a warm summer day, late in July.

The ship landed with a roar, dug across a plowed field, tore through a fence, a shed, and came finally to rest in a gully.

Silence.

Parkhurst got shakily to his feet. He caught hold of the safety rail. His shoulder hurt. He shook his head, dazed.

"We're down," he said. His voice rose with awe and excitement. "We're down!"

"Help me up," Captain Stone gasped. Barton gave him a hand.

Leon sat wiping a trickle of blood from his neck. The interior of the ship was a shambles. Most of the equipment was smashed and strewn about.

Vecchi made his way unsteadily to the hatch. With trembling fingers, he began to unscrew the heavy bolts.

"Well," Barton said, "we're back."

"I can hardly believe it," Merriweather murmured. The hatch came loose and they swung it quickly aside. "It doesn't seem possible. Good old Earth."

"Hey, listen," Leon gasped, as he clambered down to the ground. "Somebody get the camera."

"That's ridiculous," Barton said, laughing.

"Get it!" Stone yelled.

"Yes, get it," Merriweather said. "Like we planned, if we ever got back. A historic record, for the schoolbooks."

Vecchi rummaged around among the debris. "It's sort of banged up," he said. He held up the dented camera.

"Maybe it'll work anyhow," Parkhurst said, panting with exertion as he followed Leon outside. "How're we going to take all six of us? Somebody has to snap the shutter."

"I'll set it for time," Stone said, taking the camera and adjusting the knobs. "Everybody line up." He pushed a button, and joined the others.

The six bearded, tattered men stood by their smashed ship, as the camera ticked. They gazed across the green countryside, awed and suddenly silent. They glanced at each other, eyes bright.

"We're back!" Stone shouted. "We're back!"

WAR GAME

IN HIS OFFICE at the Terran Import Bureau of Standards, the tall man gathered up the morning's memos from their wire basket, and, seating himself at his desk, arranged them for reading. He put on his iris lenses, lit a cigarette.

"Good morning," the first memo said in its tinny, chattery voice, as Wiseman ran his thumb along the line of pasted tape. Staring off through the open window at the parking lot, he listened to it idly. "Say, look, what's wrong with you people down there? We sent that lot of" — a pause as the speaker, the sales manager of a chain of New York department stores, found his records — "those Ganymedean toys. You realize we have to get them approved in time for the autumn buying plan, so we can get them stocked for Christmas." Grumbling, the sales manager concluded, "War games are going to be an important item again this year. We intend to buy big."

Wiseman ran his thumb down to the speaker's name and title.

"Joe Hauck," the memo-voice chattered. "Appeley's Children's."

To himself, Wiseman said, "Ah." He put down the memo, got a blank and prepared to replay. And then he said, half-aloud, "Yes, what about that lot of Ganymedean toys?"

It seemed like a long time that the testing labs had been on them. At least two weeks.

Of course, any Ganymedean products got special attention these days; the Moons had, during the last year, gotten beyond their usual state of economic greed and had begun — according to intelligence circles — mulling overt military action against competitive interest, of which the Inner Three planets could be called the foremost element. But so far nothing had shown up. Exports remained of adequate quality, with no special jokers, no toxic paint to be licked off, no capsules of bacteria.

157

And yet. . . .

Any group of people as inventive as the Ganymedeans could be expected to show creativity in whatever field they entered. Subversion would be tackled like any other venture — with imagination and a flair for wit.

Wiseman got to his feet and left his office, in the direction of the separate building in which the testing labs operated.

Surrounded by half-disassembled consumers' products, Pinario looked up to see his boss, Leon Wiseman, shutting the final door of the lab.

"I'm glad you came down," Pinario said, although actually he was stalling; he knew that he was at least five days behind in his work, and this session was going to mean trouble. "Better put on a prophylaxis suit — don't want to take risks." He spoke pleasantly, but Wiseman's expression remained dour.

"I'm here about those inner-citadel-storming shock troops at six dollars a set," Wiseman said, strolling among the stacks of many-sized unopened products waiting to be tested and released.

"Oh, that set of Ganymedean toy soldiers," Pinario said with relief. His conscience was clear on that item; every tester in the labs knew the special instructions handed down by the Cheyenne Government on the Dangers of Contamination from Culture Particles Hostile to Innocent Urban Populations, a typically muddy ukase from officialdom. He could always — legitimately — fall back and cite the number of that directive. "I've got them off by themselves," he said, walking over to accompany Wiseman, "due to the special danger involved."

"Let's have a look," Wiseman said. "Do you believe there's anything in this caution, or is it more paranoia about 'alien milieux'?"

Pinario said, "It's justified, especially where children's artifacts are concerned."

A few hand-signals, and a slab of wall exposed a side room.

Propped up in the center was a sight that caused Wiseman to halt. A plastic life-size dummy of a child, perhaps five years in appearance, wearing ordinary clothes, sat surrounded by toys. At this moment, the dummy was saying, "I'm tired of that. Do something else." It paused a short time, and then repeated, "I'm tired of that. Do something else."

The toys on the floor, triggered to respond to oral instructions, gave up their various occupations, and started afresh.

"It saves on labor costs," Pinario explained. "This is a crop of junk that's got an entire repertoire to go through, before the buyer has his money's worth. If we stuck around to keep them active, we'd be in here all the time."

Directly before the dummy was the group of Ganymedean soldiers, plus the citadel which they had been built to storm. They had been sneaking up on it in an elaborate pattern, but, at the dummy's utterance, they had halted. Now they were regrouping.

"You're getting this all on tape?" Wiseman asked.

"Oh, yes," Pinario said.

The model soldiers stood approximately six inches high, made from the almost indestructible thermoplastic compounds that the Ganymedean manufacturers were famous for. Their uniforms were synthetic, a hodgepodge of various military costumes from the Moons and nearby planets. The citadel itself, a block of ominous dark metal-like stuff, resembled a legendary fort; peepholes dotted its upper surfaces, a drawbridge had been drawn up out of sight, and from the top turret a gaudy flag waved.

With a whistling pop, the citadel fired a projectile at its attackers. The projectile exploded in a cloud of harmless smoke and noise, among a cluster of soldiers.

"It fights back," Wiseman observed.

"But ultimately it loses," Pinario said. "It has to. Psychologically speaking, it symbolizes the external reality. The dozen soldiers, of course, represent to the child his own efforts to cope. By participating in the storming of the citadel, the child undergoes a sense of adequacy in dealing with the harsh world. Eventually he prevails, but only after a painstaking period of effort and patience." He added, "Anyhow, that's what the instruction booklet says." He handed Wiseman the booklet.

Glancing over the booklet, Wiseman asked, "And their pattern of assault varies each time?"

"We've had it running for eight days now. The same pattern hasn't cropped up twice. Well, you've got quite a few units involved."

The soldiers were sneaking around, gradually nearing the citadel. On the walls, a number of monitoring devices appeared and began tracking the soldiers. Utilizing other toys being tested, the soldiers concealed themselves.

"They can incorporate accidental configurations of terrain," Pinario explained. "They're object-tropic; when they see, for example, a dollhouse here for testing, they climb into it like mice. They'll be all through it." To prove his point, he picked up a large toy spaceship manufactured by a Uranian company; shaking it, he spilled two soldiers from it.

"How many times do they take the citadel," Wiseman asked, "on a percentage basis?"

"So far, they've been successful one out of nine tries. There's an adjustment in the back of the citadel. You can set it for a higher yield of successful tries."

He threaded a path through the advancing soldiers; Wiseman accompanied him, and they bent down to inspect the citadel.

"This is actually the power supply," Pinario said. "Cunning. Also, the instructions to the soldiers emanate from it. High-frequency transmission, from a shot-box."

Opening the back of the citadel, he showed his boss the container of shot.

Each shot was an instruction iota. For an assault pattern, the shot were tossed up, vibrated, allowed to settle in a new sequence. Randomness was thereby achieved. But since there was a finite number of shot, there had to be a finite number of patterns.

"We're trying them all," Pinario said.

"And there's no way to speed it up?"

"It'll just have to take time. It may run through a thousand patterns and then — "

"The next one," Wiseman finished, "may have them make a ninety-degree turn and start firing at the nearest human being."

Pinario said somberly, "Or worse. There're a good deal of ergs in that power pack. It's made to put out for five years. But if it all went into something simultaneously — "

"Keep testing," Wiseman said.

They looked at each other and then at the citadel. The soldiers had by now almost reached it. Suddenly one wall of the citadel flapped down, a gun-muzzle appeared, and the soldiers had been flattened.

"I never saw that before," Pinario murmured.

For a moment nothing stirred. And then the lab's child-dummy, seated among its toys, said, "I'm tired of that. Do something else."

With a tremor of uneasiness, the two men watched the soldiers pick themselves up and regroup.

Two days later, Wiseman's superior, a heavy-set, short, angry man with popping eyes, appeared in his office. "Listen," Fowler said, "you get those damn toys out of testing. I'll give you until tomorrow." He started back out, but Wiseman stopped him.

"This is too serious," he said. "Come down to the lab and I'll show you."

Arguing all the way, Fowler accompanied him to the lab. "You have no concept of the capital some of these firms have invested in this stuff!" he was saying as they entered. "For every product you've got represented here, there's a ship or a warehouse full on Luna, waiting for official clearance so it can come in!"

Pinario was nowhere in sight. So Wiseman used his key, by-passing the hand-signals that opened up the testing room.

There, surrounded by toys, sat the dummy that the lab men had built. Around it the numerous toys went through their cycles. The racket made Fowler wince.

"This is the item in particular," Wiseman said, bending down by the citadel. A soldier was in the process of squirming on his belly toward it. "As you can see, there are a dozen soldiers. Given that many, and the energy available to them, plus the complex instruction data — "

Fowler interrupted, "I see only eleven."

"One's probably hiding," Wiseman said.

From behind them, a voice said, "No, he's right." Pinario, a rigid expression on his face, appeared. "I've been having a search made. One is gone."

The three men were silent.

"Maybe the citadel destroyed him," Wiseman finally suggested.

Pinario said, "There's a law of matter dealing with that. If it 'destroyed' him — *what did it do with the remains?*"

"Possibly converted him into energy," Fowler said, examining the citadel and the remaining soldiers.

"We did something ingenious," Pinario said, "when we realized that a soldier was gone. We weighed the remaining eleven plus the citadel. Their combined weight is exactly equal to that of the original set — the original dozen soldiers and the citadel. So he's in there somewhere." He pointed at the citadel, which at the moment was pinpointing the soldiers advancing toward it.

Studying the citadel, Wiseman had a deep intuitive feeling. It had changed. It was, in some manner, different.

"Run your tapes," Wiseman said.

"What?" asked Pinario, and then he flushed. "Of course." Going to the child-dummy, he shut it off, opened it, and removed the drum of video recording tape. Shakily, he carried it to the projector.

They sat watching the recording sequences flash by: one assault after another, until the three of them were bleary-eyed. The soldiers advanced, retreated, were fired on, picked themselves up, advanced again . . .

"Stop the transport," Wiseman said suddenly.

The last sequence was re-run.

A soldier moved steadily toward the base of the citadel. A missile, fired at him, exploded and for a time obscured him. Meanwhile, the other eleven soldiers scurried in a wild attempt to mount the walls. The soldier emerged from the cloud of dust and continued. He reached the wall. A section slid back.

The soldier, blending with the dingy wall of the citadel, used the end of his rifle as a screwdriver to remove his head, then one arm, then both legs. The disassembled pieces were passed into the aperture of the citadel. When only the arm and rifle remained, that, too, crawled into the citadel, worming blindly, and vanished. The aperture slid out of existence.

After a long time, Fowler said in a hoarse voice, "The presumption by the parent would be that the child had lost or destroyed one of the soldiers. Gradually the set would dwindle — with the child getting the blame."

Pinario said, "What do you recommend?"

"Keep it in action," Fowler said, with a nod from Wiseman. "Let it work out its cycle. But don't leave it alone."

"I'll have somebody in the room with it from now on," Pinario agreed.

"Better yet, stay with it yourself," Fowler said.

To himself, Wiseman thought: *Maybe we all better stay with it. At least two of us, Pinario and myself.*

I wonder what it did with the pieces, he thought.

What did it make?

By the end of the week, the citadel had absorbed four more of the soldiers.

Watching it through a monitor, Wiseman could see in it no visible change. Naturally. The growth would be strictly internal, down out of sight.

On and on the eternal assaults, the soldiers wriggling up, the citadel firing in defense. Meanwhile, he had before him a new series of Ganymedean products. More recent children's toys to be inspected.

"Now what?" he asked himself.

The first was an apparently simple item: a cowboy costume from the ancient American West. At least, so it was described. But he paid only cursory attention to the brochure: the hell with what the Ganymedeans had to say about it.

Opening the box, he laid out the costume. The fabric had a gray, amorphous quality. *What a miserably bad job,* he thought. It only vaguely resembled a cowboy suit; the lines seemed unformed, hesitant. And the material stretched out of shape as he handled it. He found that he had pulled an entire section of it into a pocket that hung down.

"I don't get it," he said to Pinario. "This won't sell."

"Put it on," Pinario said. "You'll see."

With effort, Wiseman managed to squeeze himself into the suit. "Is it safe?" he asked.

"Yes," Pinario said. "I had it on earlier. This is a more benign idea. But it could be effective. To start it into action, you fantasize."

"Along what lines?"

"Any lines."

The suit made Wiseman think of cowboys, and so he imagined to himself that he was back at the ranch, trudging along the gravel road by the field in which black-faced sheep munched hay with that odd, rapid grinding motion of their lower jaws. He had stopped at the fence — barbed wire and occasional upright posts — and watched the sheep. Then, without warning, the sheep lined up and headed off, in the direction of a shaded hillside beyond his range of vision.

He saw trees, cypress growing against the skyline. A chicken hawk, far up, flapped its wings in a pumping action ... *as if,* he thought, *it's filling itself with more air, to rise higher.* The hawk glided energetically off, then sailed at a leisurely pace. Wiseman looked for a sign of its prey. Nothing but the dry mid-summer fields munched flat by the sheep. Frequent grasshoppers. And, on the road itself, a toad. The toad had burrowed into the loose dirt; only its top part was visible.

As he bent down, trying to get up enough courage to touch the warty top of the toad's head, a man's voice said nearby him, "How do you like it?"

"Fine," Wiseman said. He took a deep breath of the dry grass smell; he filled his lungs. "Hey, how do you tell a female toad from a male toad? By the spots, or what?"

"Why?" asked the man, standing behind him slightly out of sight.

"I've got a toad here."

"Just for the record," the man said, "can I ask you a couple of questions?"

"Sure," Wiseman said.

"How old are you?"

That was easy. "Ten years and four months," he said, with pride.

"Where exactly are you, at this moment?"

"Out in the country, Mr. Gaylord's ranch, where my dad takes me and my mother every weekend when we can."

"Turn around and look at me," the man said. "And tell me if you know me."

With reluctance, he turned from the half-buried toad to look. He saw an adult with a thin face and a long, somewhat irregular nose. "You're the man who delivers the butane gas," he said. "For the butane company." He glanced around, and sure enough, there was the truck, parked by the butane gate. "My dad says butane is expensive, but there's no other — "

The man broke in, "Just for the sake of curiosity, what's the name of the butane company?"

"It's right on the truck," Wiseman said, reading the large painted letters. "Pinario Butane Distributors, Petaluma, California. You're Mr. Pinario."

"Would you be willing to swear that you're ten years old, standing in a field near Petaluma, California?" Mr. Pinario asked.

"Sure." He could see, beyond the field, a range of wooded hills. Now he wanted to investigate them; he was tired of standing around gabbing. "I'll see you," he said, starting off. "I have to go get some hiking done."

He started running, away from Pinario, down the gravel road. Grasshoppers leaped away, ahead of him. Gasping, he ran faster and faster.

"Leon!" Mr. Pinario called after him. "You might as well give up! Stop running!"

"I've got business in those hills," Wiseman panted, still jogging along. Suddenly something struck him full force; he sprawled on his hands, tried to get back up. In the dry midday air, something shimmered; he felt fear and pulled away from it. A shape formed, a flat wall . . .

"You won't get to those hills," Mr. Pinario said, from behind him. "Better stay in roughly one place. Otherwise you collide with things."

Wiseman's hands were damp with blood; he had cut himself falling. In bewilderment, he stared down at the blood. . . .

Pinario helped him out of the cowboy suit, saying, "It's as unwholesome a toy as you could want. A short period with it on, and the child would be unable to face contemporary reality. Look at you."

Standing with difficulty, Wiseman inspected the suit; Pinario had forcibly taken it from him.

"Not bad," he said in a trembling voice. "It obviously stimulates the withdrawal tendencies already present. I know I've always had a latent retreat fantasy toward my childhood. That particular period, when we lived in the country."

"Notice how you incorporated real elements into it," Pinario said, "to keep the fantasy going as long as possible. If you'd had time, you would have figured a way of incorporating the lab wall into it, possibly as the side of a barn."

Wiseman admitted, "I — already had started to see the old dairy building, where the farmers brought their market milk."

"In time," Pinario said, "it would have been next to impossible to get you out of it."

To himself, Wiseman thought, *If it could do that to an adult, just imagine the effect on a child.*

"That other thing you have there," Pinario said, "that game, it's a screwball notion. You feel like looking at it now? It can wait."

"I'm okay," Wiseman said. He picked up the third item and began to open it.

"A lot like the old game of Monopoly," Pinario said. "It's called Syndrome."

The game consisted of a board, plus play money, dice, pieces to represent the players. And stock certificates.

"You acquire stock," Pinario said, "same as in all this kind, obviously." He didn't even bother to look at the instructions. "Let's get Fowler down here and play a hand; it takes at least three."

Shortly, they had the Division Director with them. The three men seated themselves at a table, the game of Syndrome in the center.

"Each player starts out equal with the others," Pinario explained, "same as all this type, and during the play, their statuses change according to the worth of the stock they acquire in various economic syndromes."

The syndromes were represented by small, bright plastic objects, much like the archaic hotels and houses of Monopoly.

They threw the dice, moved their counters along the board, bid for and acquired property, paid fines, collected fines, went to the "decontamination chamber" for a period. Meanwhile, behind them, the seven model soldiers crept up on the citadel again and again.

"I'm tired of that," the child-dummy said. "Do something else."

The soldiers regrouped. Once more they started out, getting nearer and nearer the citadel.

Restless and irritable, Wiseman said, "I wonder how long that damn thing has to go on before we find out what it's for."

"No telling." Pinario eyed a purple-and-gold share of stock that Fowler had acquired. "I can use that," he said. "That's a heavy uranium mine stock on Pluto. What do you want for it?"

"Valuable property," Fowler murmured, consulting his other stocks. "I might make a trade, though."

How can I concentrate on a game, Wiseman asked himself, *when that thing is getting closer and nearer to — God knows what? To whatever it was built to reach. Its critical mass,* he thought.

"Just a second," he said in a slow, careful voice. He put down his hand of stocks. "Could that citadel be a pile?"

"Pile of what?" Fowler asked, concerned with his hand.

Wiseman said loudly, "Forget this game."

"An interesting idea," Pinario said, also putting down his hand. "It's constructing itself into an atomic bomb, piece by piece. Adding until — " He broke off. "No, we thought of that. There're no heavy elements present in it. It's simply a five-year battery, plus a number of small machines controlled by instructions broadcast from the battery itself. You can't make an atomic pile out of that."

"In my opinion," Wiseman said, "we'd be safer getting it out of here." His experience with the cowboy suit had given him a great deal more respect for the Ganymedean artificers. And if the suit was the benign one ...

Fowler, looking past his shoulder, said, "There are only six soldiers now."

Both Wiseman and Pinario got up instantly. Fowler was right. Only half of the set of soldiers remained. One more had reached the citadel and been incorporated.

"Let's get a bomb expert from the Military Services in here," Wiseman said, "and let him check it. This is out of our department." He turned to his boss, Fowler. "Don't you agree?"

Fowler said, "Let's finish this game first."

"Why?"

"Because we want to be certain about it," Fowler said. But his rapt interest showed that he had gotten emotionally involved and wanted to play to the end of the game. "What will you give me for this share of Pluto stock? I'm open to offers."

He and Pinario negotiated a trade. The game continued for another hour. At last, all three of them could see that Fowler was gaining control of the various stocks. He had five mining syndromes, plus two plastics firms, an algae monopoly, and all seven of the retail trading syndromes. Due to his control of the stock, he had, as a byproduct, gotten most of the money.

"I'm out," Pinario said. All he had left were minor shares which controlled nothing. "Anybody want to buy these?"

With his last remaining money, Wiseman bid for the shares. He got them and resumed playing, this time against Fowler alone.

"It's clear that this game is a replica of typical interculture economic ventures," Wiseman said. "The retail trading syndromes are obviously Ganymedean holdings."

A flicker of excitement stirred in him; he had gotten a couple of good throws with the dice and was in a position to add a share to his meager holdings. "Children playing this would acquire a healthy attitude toward economic realities. It would prepare them for the adult world."

But a few minutes later, he landed on an enormous tract of Fowler holdings, and the fine wiped out his resources. He had to give up two shares of stock; the end was in sight.

Pinario, watching the soldiers advance toward the citadel, said, "You know, Leon, I'm inclined to agree with you. This thing may be one terminal of a bomb. A receiving station of some kind. When it's completely wired up, it might bring in a surge of power transmitted from Ganymede."

"Is such a thing possible?" Fowler asked, stacking his play money into different denominations

"Who knows what they can do?" Pinario said, wandering around with his hands in his pockets. "Are you almost finished playing?"

"Just about," Wiseman said.

"The reason I say that," Pinario said, "is that now there're only five soldiers. It's speeding up. It took a week for the first one, and only an hour for the seventh. I wouldn't be surprised if the rest go within the next two hours, all five of them."

"We're finished," Fowler said. He had acquired the last share of stock and the last dollar.

Wiseman arose from the table, leaving Fowler. "I'll call Military Services to check the citadel. About this game, though, it's nothing but a steal from our Terran game Monopoly."

"Possibly they don't realize that we have the game already," Fowler said, "under another name."

A stamp of admissibility was placed on the game of Syndrome and the importer was informed. In his office, Wiseman called Military Services and told them what he wanted.

"A bomb expert will be right over," the unhurried voice at the other end of the line said. "Probably you should leave the object alone until he arrives."

Feeling somewhat useless, Wiseman thanked the clerk and hung up. They had failed to dope out the soldiers-and-citadel war game; now it was out of their hands.

* * *

The bomb expert was a young man, with close-cropped hair, who smiled friendlily at them as he set down his equipment. He wore ordinary coveralls, with no protective devices.

"My first advice," he said, after he had looked the citadel over, "is to disconnect the leads from the battery. Or, if you want, we can let the cycle finish out, and then disconnect the leads before any reaction takes place. In other words, allow the last mobile elements to enter the citadel. Then, as soon as they're inside, we disconnect the leads and open her up and see what's been taking place."

"Is it safe?" Wiseman asked.

"I think so," the bomb expert said. "I don't detect any sign of radioactivity in it." He seated himself on the floor, by the rear of the citadel, with a pair of cutting pliers in his hand.

Now only three soldiers remained.

"It shouldn't be long," the young man said cheerfully.

Fifteen minutes later, one of the three soldiers crept up to the base of the citadel, removed his head, arm, legs, body, and disappeared piecemeal into the opening provided for him.

"That leaves two," Fowler said.

Ten minutes later, one of the two remaining soldiers followed the one ahead of him.

The four men looked at each other. "This is almost it," Pinario said huskily.

The last remaining soldier wove his way toward the citadel. Guns within the citadel fired at him, but he continued to make progress.

"Statistically speaking," Wiseman said aloud, to break some of the tension, "it should take longer each time, because there are fewer men for it to concentrate on. It should have started out fast, then got more infrequent until finally this last soldier should put in at least a month trying to — "

"Pipe down," the young bomb expert said in a quiet, reasonable voice. "If you don't mind."

The last of the twelve soldiers reached the base of the citadel. Like those before him, he began to dissemble himself.

"Get those pliers ready," Pinario grated.

The parts of the soldier traveled into the citadel. The opening began to close. From within, a humming became audible, a rising pitch of activity.

"Now, for God's sake!" Fowler cried.

The young bomb expert reached down his pliers and cut into the positive lead of the battery. A spark flashed from the pliers and the young bomb expert jumped reflexively; the pliers flew from his hands and skidded across the floor. "Jeez!" he said. "I must have been grounded." Groggily, he groped about for the pliers.

"You were touching the frame of the thing," Pinario said excitedly. He grabbed the pliers himself and crouched down, fumbling for the lead. "Maybe if I wrap a handkerchief around it," he muttered, withdrawing the pliers and fishing in his pocket for a handkerchief. "Anybody got anything I can wrap around this? I don't want to get knocked flat. No telling how many — "

"Give it to me," Wiseman demanded, snatching the pliers from him. He shoved Pinario aside and closed the jaws of the pliers about the lead.

Fowler said calmly, "Too late."

Wiseman hardly heard his superior's voice; he heard the constant tone within his head, and he put up his hands to his ears, futilely trying to shut it out. Now it seemed to pass directly from the citadel through his skull, transmitted by the bone. *We stalled around too long,* he thought. *Now it has us. It won out because there are too many of us; we got to squabbling . . .*

Within his mind, a voice said, "Congratulations. By your fortitude, you have been successful."

A vast feeling pervaded him then, a sense of accomplishment.

"The odds against you were tremendous," the voice inside his mind continued. "Anyone else would have failed."

He knew then that everything was all right. They had been wrong.

"What you have done here," the voice declared, "you can continue to do all your life. You can always triumph over adversaries. By patience and persistence, you can win out. The universe isn't such an overwhelming place, after all . . . "

No, he realized with irony, it wasn't.

"They are just ordinary persons," the voice soothed. "So even though you're the only one, an individual against many, you have nothing to fear. Give it time — and don't worry."

"I won't," he said aloud.

The humming receded. The voice was gone.

After a long pause, Fowler said, "It's over."

"I don't get it," Pinario said.

"That was what it was supposed to do," Wiseman said. "It's a therapeutic toy. Helps give the child confidence. The disassembling of the soldiers" — he grinned — "ends the separation between him and the world. He becomes one with it. And, in doing so, conquers it."

"Then it's harmless," Fowler said.

"All this work for nothing," Pinario groused. To the bomb expert, he said, "I'm sorry we got you up here for nothing."

The citadel had now opened its gates wide. Twelve soldiers, once more intact, issued forth. The cycle was complete; the assault could begin again.

Suddenly Wiseman said, "I'm not going to release it."

"What?" Pinario said. "Why not?"

"I don't trust it," Wiseman said. "It's too complicated for what it actually does."

"Explain," Fowler demanded.

"There's nothing to explain," Wiseman said. "Here's this immensely intricate gadget, and all it does is take itself apart and then reassemble itself. There *must* be more, even if we can't — "

"It's therapeutic," Pinario put in.

Fowler said, "I'll leave it up to you, Leon. If you have doubts, then don't release it. We can't be too careful."

"Maybe I'm wrong," Wiseman said, "but I keep thinking to myself: *What did they actually build this for?* I feel we still don't know."

"And the American Cowboy Suit," Pinario added. "You don't want to release that either."

"Only the game," Wiseman said. "Syndrome, or whatever it's called." Bending down, he watched the soldiers as they hustled toward the citadel. Bursts of smoke, again … activity, feigned attacks, careful withdrawals …

"What are you thinking?" Pinario asked, scrutinizing him.

"Maybe it's a diversion," Wiseman said. "To keep our minds involved. So we won't notice something else." That was his intuition, but he couldn't pin it down. "A red herring," he said. "While something else takes place. That's why it's so complicated. We were *supposed* to suspect it. That's why they built it."

Baffled, he put his foot down in front of a soldier. The soldier took refuge behind his shoe, hiding from the monitors of the citadel.

"There must be something right before our eyes," Fowler said, "that we're not noticing."

"Yes." Wiseman wondered if they would ever find it. "Anyhow," he said, "we're keeping it here, where we can observe it."

Seating himself nearby, he prepared to watch the soldiers. He made himself comfortable for a long, long wait.

At six o'clock that evening, Joe Hauck, the sales manager for Appeley's Children's Store, parked his car before his house, got out, and strode up the stairs.

Under his arm he carried a large flat package, a "sample" that he had appropriated.

"Hey!" his two kids, Bobby and Lora, squealed as he let himself in. "You got something for us, Dad?" They crowded around him, blocking his path. In the kitchen, his wife looked up from the table and put down her magazine.

"A new game I picked for you," Hauck said. He unwrapped the package, feeling genial. There was no reason why he shouldn't help himself to one of the new games; he had been on the phone for weeks, getting the stuff through

Import Standards — and after all was said and done, only one of the three items had been cleared.

As the kids went off with the game, his wife said in a low voice, "More corruption in high places." She had always disapproved of his bringing home items from the store's stock.

"We've got thousands of them," Hauck said. "A warehouse full. Nobody'll notice one missing."

At the dinner table, during the meal, the kids scrupulously studied every word of the instructions that accompanied the game. They were aware of nothing else.

"Don't read at the table," Mrs. Hauck said reprovingly.

Leaning back in his chair, Joe Hauck continued his account of the day. "And after all that time, what did they release? One lousy item. We'll be lucky if we can push enough to make a profit. It was that Shock Troop gimmick that would really have paid off. And that's tied up indefinitely."

He lit a cigarette and relaxed, feeling the peacefulness of his home, the presence of his wife and children.

His daughter said, "Dad, do you want to play? It says the more who play, the better."

"Sure," Joe Hauck said.

While his wife cleared the table, he and his children spread out the board, counters, dice and paper money and shares of stock. Almost at once he was deep in the game, totally involved; his childhood memories of game-playing swam back, and he acquired shares of stock with cunning and originality, until, toward the conclusion of the game, he had cornered most of the syndromes.

He settled back with a sigh of contentment. "That's that," he declared to his children. "Afraid I had a head start. After all, I'm not new to this type of game." Getting hold of the valuable holdings on the board filled him with a powerful sense of satisfaction. "Sorry to have to win, kids."

His daughter said, "You didn't win."

"You lost," his son said.

"*What?*" Joe Hauck exclaimed.

"The person who winds up with the most stock *loses*," Lora said.

She showed him the instructions. "See? The idea is to get rid of your stocks. Dad, you're out of the game."

"The heck with that," Hauck said, disappointed. "That's no kind of game." His satisfaction vanished. "That's no fun."

"Now we two have to play out the game," Bobby said, "to see who finally wins."

As he got up from the board, Joe Hauck grumbled, "I don't get it. What would anybody see in a game where the winner winds up with nothing at all?"

Behind him, his two children continued to play. As stock and money changed hands, the children became more and more animated. When the game entered its final stages, the children were in a state of ecstatic concentration.

"They don't know Monopoly," Hauck said to himself, "so this screwball game doesn't seem strange to them."

Anyhow, the important thing was that the kids enjoyed playing Syndrome; evidently it would sell, and that was what mattered. Already the two youngsters were learning the naturalness of surrendering their holdings. They gave up their stocks and money avidly, with a kind of trembling abandon.

Glancing up, her eyes bright, Lora said, "It's the best educational toy you ever brought home, Dad!"

IF THERE WERE NO BENNY CEMOLI

SCAMPERING ACROSS the unplowed field the three boys shouted as they saw the ship: it had landed, all right, just where they expected, and they were the first to reach it.

"Hey, that's the biggest I ever saw!" Panting, the first boy halted. "That's not from Mars; that's from farther. It's from all the way out, I know it is." He became silent and afraid as he saw the size of it. And then looking up into the sky he realized that an armada had arrived, exactly as everyone had expected. "We better go tell," he said to his companions.

Back on the ridge, John LeConte stood by his steam-powered chauffeur-driven limousine, impatiently waiting for the boiler to warm. *Kids got there first*, he said to himself with anger. *Whereas I'm supposed to.* And the children were ragged; they were merely farm boys.

"Is the phone working today?" LeConte asked his secretary.

Glancing at his clipboard, Mr. Fall said, "Yes, sir. Shall I put through a message to Oklahoma City?" He was the skinniest employee ever assigned to LeConte's office. The man evidently took nothing for himself, was positively uninterested in food. And he was efficient.

LeConte murmured, "The immigration people ought to hear about this outrage."

He sighed. It had all gone wrong. The armada from Proxima Centauri had after ten years arrived and none of the early-warning devices had detected it in advance of its landing. Now Oklahoma City would have to deal with the outsiders here on home ground — a psychological disadvantage which LeConte felt keenly.

Look at the equipment they've got, he thought as he watched the commercial

173

ships of the flotilla begin to lower their cargos. *Why, hell, they make us look like provincials.* He wished that his official car did not need twenty minutes to warm up; he wished —

Actually, he wished that CURB did not exist.

Centaurus Urban Renewal Bureau, a do-gooding body unfortunately vested with enormous inter-system authority. It had been informed of the Misadventure back in 2170 and had started into space like a phototropic organism, sensitive to the mere physical light created by the hydrogen-bomb explosions. But LeConte knew better than that. Actually the governing organizations in the Centaurian system knew many details of the tragedy because they had been in radio contact with other planets of the Sol system. Little of the native forms on Earth had survived. He himself was from Mars; he had headed a relief mission seven years ago, had decided to stay because there were so many opportunities here on Earth, conditions being what they were . . .

This is all very difficult, he said to himself as he stood waiting for his steam-powered car to warm. *We got here first, but CURB does outrank us: we must face that awkward fact. In my opinion, we've done a good job of rebuilding. Of course, it isn't like it was before . . . but ten years is not long. Give us another twenty and we'll have the trains running again. And our recent road-building bonds sold quite successfully, in fact were oversubscribed.*

"Call for you, sir, from Oklahoma City," Mr. Fall said, holding out the receiver of the portable field-phone.

"Ultimate Representative in the Field John LeConte, here," LeConte said into it loudly. "Go ahead; I say go ahead."

"This is Party Headquarters," the dry official voice at the other end came faintly, mixed with static, in his ear. "We've received reports from dozens of alert citizens in Western Oklahoma and Texas of an immense — "

"It's here," LeConte said. "I can see it. I'm just about ready to go out and confer with its ranking members, and I'll file a full report at the usual time. So it wasn't necessary for you to check up on me." He felt irritable.

"Is the armada heavily armed?"

"Naw," LeConte said. "It appears to be comprised of bureaucrats and trade officials and commercial carriers. In other words, vultures."

The Party desk-man said, "Well, go and make certain they understand that their presence here is resented by the native population as well as the Relief of War-torn Areas Administrating Council. Tell them that the legislature will be calling to pass a special bill expressing indignation at this intrusion into domestic matters by an inter-system body."

"I know, I know," LeConte said. "It's all been decided; I know."

His chauffeur called to him, "Sir, your car is ready now."

The Party desk-man concluded, "Make certain they understand that you can't negotiate with them; you have no power to admit them to Earth. Only the Council can do that and of course it's adamantly against that."

LeConte hung up the phone and hurried to his car.

Despite the opposition of the local authorities, Peter Hood of CURB decided to locate his headquarters in the ruins of the old Terran capital, New York City. This would lend prestige to the CURBmen as they gradually widened the circle of the organization's influence. At last, of course, the circle would embrace the planet. But that would take decades.

As he walked through the ruins of what had once been a major train yard, Peter Hood thought to himself that when the task was done he himself would have long been retired. Not much remained of the pre-tragedy culture here. The local authorities — the political nonentities who had flocked in from Mars and Venus, as the neighboring planets were called — had done little. And yet he admired their efforts.

To the members of his staff walking directly behind him he said, "You know, they have done the hard part for us. We ought to be grateful. It is not easy to come into a totally destroyed area, as they've done."

His man Fletcher observed, "They got back a good return."

Hood said, "Motive is not important. They have achieved results." He was thinking of the official who had met them in his steam car; it had been solemn and formal, carrying complicated trappings. When these locals had first arrived on the scene years ago *they* had not been greeted, except perhaps by radiation-seared, blackened survivors who had stumbled out of cellars and gaped sightlessly. He shivered.

Coming up to him, a CURBman of minor rank saluted and said, "I think we've managed to locate an undamaged structure in which your staff could be housed for the time being. It's underground." He looked embarrassed. "Not what we had hoped for. We'd have to displace the locals to get anything attractive."

"I don't object," Hood said. "A basement will do."

"The structure," the minor CURBman said, "was once a great homeostatic newspaper, the *New York Times*. It printed itself directly below us. At least, according to the maps. We haven't located the newspaper yet; it was customary for the homeopapes to be buried a mile or so down. As yet we don't know how much of this one survived."

"But it would be valuable," Hood agreed.

"Yes," the CURBman said. "Its outlets are scattered all over the planet; it must have had a thousand different editions which it put out daily. How many outlets function — " He broke off. "It's hard to believe that the local politicos made no efforts to repair any of the ten or eleven world-wide homeopapes, but that seems to be the case."

"Odd," Hood said. Surely it would have eased their task. The post-tragedy job of reuniting people into a common culture depended on newspapers, ionization in the atmosphere making radio and TV reception difficult if not impossible. "This makes me instantly suspicious," he said, turning to his staff. "Are they perhaps not trying to rebuild after all? Is their work merely a pretense?"

It was his own wife Joan who spoke up. "They may simply have lacked the ability to place the homeopapes on an operational basis."

Give them the benefit of the doubt, Hood thought. *You're right.*

"So the last edition of the *Times*," Fletcher said, "was put on the lines the day the Misadventure occurred. And the entire network of newspaper communication and news-creation had been idle since. I can't respect these politicos; it shows they're ignorant of the basics of a culture. By reviving the homeopapes we can do more to re-establish the pre-tragedy culture than they've done in ten thousand pitiful projects." His tone was scornful.

Hood said, "You may misunderstand, but let it go. Let's hope that the cephalon of the pape is undamaged. We couldn't possibly replace it." Ahead he saw the yawning entrance which the CURBmen crews had cleared. This was to be his first move, here on the ruined planet, restoring this immense self-contained entity to its former authority. Once it had resumed its activity he would be freed for other tasks; the homeopape would take some of the burden from him.

A workman, still clearing debris away, muttered, "Jeez, I never saw so many layers of junk. You'd think they deliberately bottled it up down here." In his hands, the suction furnace which he operated glowed and pounded as it absorbed material, converting it to energy, leaving an increasingly enlarged opening.

"I'd like a report as soon as possible as to its condition," Hood said to the team of engineers who stood waiting to descend into the opening. "How long it will take to revive it, how much — " He broke off.

Two men in black uniforms had arrived. Police, from the Security ship. One, he saw, was Otto Dietrich, the ranking investigator accompanying the armada from Centaurus, and he felt tense automatically; it was a reflex for all of them — he saw the engineers and the workmen cease momentarily and then, more slowly, resume their work.

"Yes," he said to Dietrich. "Glad to see you. Let's go off to this side room and talk there." He knew beyond a doubt what the investigator wanted; he had been expecting him.

Dietrich said, "I won't take up too much of your time, Hood. I know you're quite busy. What is this, here?" He glanced about curiously, his scrubbed, round, alert face eager.

In a small side room, converted to a temporary office, Hood faced the two policemen. "I am opposed to prosecution," he said quietly. "It's been too long. Let them go."

Dietrich, tugging thoughtfully at his ear, said, "But war crimes are war crimes, even four decades later. Anyhow, what argument can there be? We're required by law to prosecute. *Somebody* started the war. They may well hold positions of responsibility now, but that hardly matters."

"How many police troops have you landed?" Hood asked.

"Two hundred."

"Then you're ready to go to work."

"We're ready to make inquiries. Sequester pertinent documents and initiate litigation in the local courts. We're prepared to enforce cooperation, if that's what you mean. Various experienced personnel have been distributed to key points." Dietrich eyed him. "All this is necessary; I don't see the problem. Did you intend to protect the guilty parties — make use of their so-called abilities on your staff?"

"No," Hood said evenly.

Dietrich said, "Nearly eighty million people died in the Misfortune. Can you forget that? Or is it that since they were merely local people, not known to us personally — "

"It's not that," Hood said. He knew it was hopeless; he could not communicate with the police mentality. "I've already stated my objections. I feel it serves no purpose at this late date to have trials and hangings. Don't request use of my staff in this; I'll refuse on the grounds that I can spare no one, not even a janitor. Do I make myself clear?"

"You idealists," Dietrich sighed. "This is strictly a noble task confronting us ... to rebuild, correct? What you don't or won't see is that these people will start it all over again, one day, unless we take steps now. We owe it to future generations. To be harsh now is the most humane method, in the long run. Tell me, Hood. What is this site? What are you resurrecting here with such vigor?"

"The *New York Times*," Hood said.

"It has, I assume, a morgue? We can consult its backlog of information? That would prove valuable in building up our cases."

Hood said, "I can't deny you access to material we uncover."

Smiling, Dietrich said, "A day by day account of the political events leading up to the war would prove quite interesting. Who, for instance, held supreme power in the United States at the time of the Misfortune? No one we've talked to so far seems to remember." His smile increased.

*   *   *

Early the next morning the report from the corps of engineers reached Hood in his temporary office. The power supply of the newspaper had been totally destroyed. But the cephalon, the governing brain-structure which guided and oriented the homeostatic system, appeared to be intact. If a ship were brought close by, perhaps its power supply could be integrated into the newspaper's lines. Thereupon much more would be known.

"In other words," Fletcher said to Hood, as they sat with Joan eating breakfast, "it may come on and it may not. Very pragmatic. You hook it up and if it works you've done your job. What if it doesn't? Do the engineers intend to give up at that point?"

Examining his cup, Hood said, "This tastes like authentic coffee." He pondered. "Tell them to bring a ship in and start the homeopape up. And if it begins to print, bring me the edition at once." He sipped his coffee.

An hour later a ship of the line had landed in the vicinity and its power source had been tapped for insertion into the homeopape. The conduits were placed, the circuits cautiously closed.

Seated in his office, Peter Hood heard far underground a low rumble, a halting, uncertain stirring. They had been successful. The newspaper was returning to life.

The edition, when it was laid on his desk by a bustling CURBman, surprised him by its accuracy. Even in its dormant state, the newspaper had somehow managed not to fall behind events. Its receptors had kept going.

CURB LANDS, TRIP DECADE LONG,
PLANS CENTRAL ADMINISTRATION

Ten years after the Misfortune of a nuclear holocaust, the inter-system rehabilitation agency, CURB, has made its historic appearance on Earth's surface, landing from a veritable armada of craft — a sight which witnesses described as "overpowering both in scope and in significance." CURBman Peter Hood, named top co-ordinator by Centaurian authorities, immediately set up headquarters in the ruins of New York City and conferred with aides, declaring that he had come "not to punish the guilty but to re-establish the planet-wide culture by every means available, and to restore —

It was uncanny, Hood thought as he read the lead article. The varied news-gathering services of the homeopape had reached into his own life, had digested and then inserted into the lead article even the discussion between himself and Otto Dietrich. The newspaper was — had been — doing its job. Nothing of news-interest escaped it, even a discreet conversation carried on with no outsiders as witnesses. He would have to be careful.

Sure enough, another item, ominous in tone, dealt with the arrival of the black jacks, the police.

SECURITY AGENCY VOWS "WAR CRIMINALS" TARGET
Captain Otto Dietrich, supreme police investigator arriving with the CURB armada from Proxima Centauri, said today that those responsible for the Misfortune of a decade ago "would have to pay for their crimes" before the bar of Centaurian justice. Two hundred black-uniformed police, it was learned by the *Times*, have already begun exploratory activities designed to —

The newspaper was warning Earth about Dietrich, and Hood could not help feeling grim relish. The *Times* had not been set up to serve merely the occupying hierarchy. It served everyone, including those Dietrich intended to try. Each step of the police activity would no doubt be reported in full detail. Dietrich, who liked to work in anonymity, would not enjoy this. But the authority to maintain the newspaper belonged to Hood.

And he did not intend to shut it off.

One item on the first page of the paper attracted his further notice; he read it, frowning and a little uneasy.

CEMOLI BACKERS RIOT IN UPSTATE NEW YORK
Supporters of Benny Cemoli, gathered in the familiar tent cities associated with the colorful political figure, clashed with local citizens armed with hammers, shovels, and boards, both sides claiming victory in the two-hour melee which left twenty injured and a dozen hospitalized in hastily-erected first aid stations. Cemoli, garbed as always in his toga-style red robes, visited the injured, evidently in good spirits, joking and telling his supporters that "it won't be long now" an evident reference to the organization's boast that it would march on New York City in the near future to establish what Cemoli deems "social justice and true equality for the first time in world history." It should be recalled that prior to his imprisonment at San Quentin —

Flipping a switch on his intercom system, Hood said, "Fletcher, check into activities up in the north of the county. Find out about some sort of a political mob gathering there."

Fletcher's voice came back. "I have a copy of the *Times*, too, sir. I see the item about this Cemoli agitator. There's a ship on the way up there right now; should have a report within ten minutes." Fletcher paused. "Do you think — it'll be necessary to bring in any of Dietrich's people?"

"Let's hope not," Hood said shortly.

Half an hour later the CURB ship, through Fletcher, made its report.

Puzzled, Hood asked that it be repeated. But there was no mistake. The CURB field team had investigated thoroughly. They had found no sign whatsoever of any tent city or any group gathering. And citizens in the area whom they had interrogated had never heard of anyone named "Cemoli." And there was no sign of any scuffle having taken place, no first aid stations, no injured persons. Only the peaceful, semi-rural countryside.

Baffled, Hood read the item in the *Times* once more. There it was, in black and white, on the front page, along with the news about the landing of the CURB armada. What did it mean?

He did not like it at all.

Had it been a mistake to revive the great, old, damaged homeostatic newspaper?

From a sound sleep that night Hood was awakened by a clanging from far beneath the ground, an urgent racket that grew louder and louder as he sat up in bed, blinking and confused. Machinery roared. He heard the heavy rumbling movement as automatic circuits fitted into place, responding to instructions emanating from within the closed system itself.

"Sir," Fletcher was saying from the darkness. A light came on as Fletcher located the temporary overhead fixture. "I thought I should come in and wake you. Sorry, Mr. Hood."

"I'm awake," Hood muttered, rising from the bed and putting on his robe and slippers. "What's it doing?"

Fletcher said, "It's printing an extra."

Sitting up, smoothing her tousled blonde hair back, Joan said, "Good Lord. What about?" Wide-eyed, she looked from her husband to Fletcher.

"We'll have to bring in the local authorities," Hood said. "Confer with them." He had an intuition as to the nature of the extra roaring through the presses at this moment. "Get that LeConte, the politico who met us on our arrival. Wake him up and fly him here immediately. We need him."

It took almost an hour to obtain the presence of the haughty, ceremonious local potentate and his staff member. The two of them in their elaborate uniforms at last put in an appearance at Hood's office, both of them indignant. They faced Hood silently, waiting to hear what he wanted.

In his bathrobe and slippers Hood sat at his desk, a copy of the *Times'* extra before him; he was reading it once more as LeConte and his man entered.

NEW YORK POLICE REPORT CEMOLI LEGIONS
ON MOVE TOWARD CITY,
BARRICADES ERECTED, NATIONAL GUARD ALERTED

He turned the paper, showing the headlines to the two Earthmen. "Who is this man?" he said.

After a moment LeConte said, "I — don't know."

Hood said, "Come on, Mr. LeConte."

"Let me read the article," LeConte said nervously. He scanned it in haste; his hands trembled as he held the newspaper. "Interesting," he said at last. "But I can't tell you a thing. It's news to me. You must understand that our communications have been sparse, since the Misfortune, and it's entirely possible that a political movement could spring up without our — "

"Please," Hood said. "Don't make yourself absurd."

Flushing, LeConte stammered, "I'm doing the best I can, summoned out of my bed in the middle of the night."

There was a stir, and through the office doorway came the rapidly-moving figure of Otto Dietrich, looking grim. "Hood," he said without preamble, "there's a *Times* kiosk near my headquarters. It just posted this." He held up a copy of the extra. "The damn thing is running this off and distributing it throughout the world, isn't it? However, we have crack teams up in that area and they report absolutely nothing, no road blocks, no militia-style troops on the move, no activity of any sort."

"I know," Hood said. He felt weary. And still, from beneath them, the deep rumble continued, the newspaper printing its extra, informing the world of the march by Benny Cemoli's supporters on New York City — a fantasy march, evidently, a product manufactured entirely within the cephalon of the newspaper itself.

"Shut it off," Dietrich said.

Hood shook his head. "No. I want to know more."

"That's no reason," Dietrich said. "Obviously, it's defective. Very seriously damaged, not working properly. You'll have to search elsewhere for your world-wide propaganda network." He tossed the newspaper down on Hood's desk.

To LeConte, Hood said, "Was Benny Cemoli active before the war?"

There was silence. Both LeConte and his assistant Mr. Fall were pale and tense; they faced him tight-lipped, glancing at each other.

"I am not much for police matters," Hood said to Dietrich, "but I think you could reasonably step in here."

Dietrich, understanding, said, "I agree. You two men are under arrest. Unless you feel inclined to talk a little more freely about this agitator in the red toga." He nodded to two of his police, who stood by the office doorway; they stepped obediently forward.

As the two policemen came up to him, LeConte said, "Come to think of it, there was such a person. But — he was very obscure."

"Before the war?" Hood asked.

"Yes." LeConte nodded slowly. "He was a joke. As I recall, and it's difficult ... a fat, ignorant clown from some backwoods area. He had a little radio station or something over which he broadcast. He peddled some sort of anti-radiation box which you installed in your house, and it made you safe from bomb-test fallout."

Now his staff member Mr. Fall said, "I remember. He even ran for the UN senate. But he was defeated, naturally."

"And that was the last of him?" Hood asked.

"Oh yes," LeConte said. "He died of Asian flu soon after. He's been dead for fifteen years."

In a helicopter, Hood flew slowly above the terrain depicted in the *Times* articles, seeing for himself that there was no sign of political activity. He did not feel really assured until he had seen with his own eyes that the newspaper had lost contact with actual events. The reality of the situation did not coincide with the *Times'* articles in any way; that was obvious. And yet — the homeostatic system continued on.

Joan, seated beside him, said, "I have the third article here, if you want to read it." She had been looking the latest edition over.

"No," Hood said.

"It says they're in the outskirts of the city," she said. "They broke through the police barricades and the governor has appealed for UN assistance."

Thoughtfully, Fletcher said, "Here's an idea. One of us, preferably you, Hood, should write a letter to the *Times.*"

Hood glanced at him.

"I think I can tell you exactly how it should be worded," Fletcher said. "Make it a simple inquiry. You've followed the accounts in the paper about Cemoli's movement. Tell the editor — " Fletcher paused. "That you feel sympathetic *and you'd like to join the movement.* Ask the paper how."

To himself, Hood thought, *In other words ask the newspaper to put me in touch with Cemoli.* He had to admire Fletcher's idea. It was brilliant, in a crazy sort of way. It was as if Fletcher had been able to match the derangement of the newspaper by a deliberate shift from common sense on his own part. He would participate in the newspaper's delusion. Assuming there was a Cemoli and a march on New York, he was asking a reasonable question.

Joan said, "I don't want to sound stupid, but how does one go about mailing a letter to a homeopape?"

"I've looked into that," Fletcher said. "At each kiosk set up by the paper there's a letter-slot, next to the coin-slot where you pay for your paper. It was the law when the homeopapes were set up originally, decades ago. All we need is your husband's signature." Reaching into his jacket, he brought out an envelope. "The letter's written."

Hood took the letter, examined it. *So we desire to be part of the mythical fat clown's throng,* he said to himself. "Won't there be a headline reading CURB CHIEF JOINS MARCH ON EARTH CAPITAL?" he asked Fletcher, feeling a trace of wry amusement. "Wouldn't a good, enterprising homeopape make front page use of a letter such as this?"

Obviously Fletcher had not thought of that; he looked chagrined. "I suppose we had better get someone else to sign it," he admitted. "Some minor person attached to your staff." He added, "I could sign it myself."

Handing him the letter back, Hood said, "Do so. It'll be interesting to see what response, if any, there is." *Letters to the editor,* he thought. *Letters to a vast, complex, electronic organism buried deep in the ground, responsible to no one, guided solely by its own ruling circuits. How would it react to this external ratification of its delusion? Would the newspaper be snapped back to reality?*

It was, he thought, *as if the newspaper, during these years of this enforced silence, had been dreaming, and now, reawakened, it had allowed portions of its former dreams to materialize in its pages along with its accurate, perceptive accounts of the actual situation. A blend of figments and sheer, stark reporting. Which ultimately would triumph? Soon, evidently, the unfolding story of Benny Cemoli would have the toga-wearing spellbinder in New York; it appeared that the march would succeed. And what then? How could this be squared with the arrival of CURB, with all its enormous inter-system authority and power? Surely the homeopape, before long, would have to face the incongruity.*

One of the two accounts would have to cease ... but Hood had an uneasy intuition that a homeopape which had dreamed for a decade would not readily give up its fantasies. *Perhaps,* he thought, *the news of us, of CURB and its task of rebuilding Earth, will fade from the pages of the* Times, *will be given a steadily decreasing coverage each day, farther back in the paper. And at last only the exploits of Benny Cemoli will remain.*

It was not a pleasant anticipation. It disturbed him deeply. *As if,* he thought, *we are only real so long as the* Times *writes about us; as if we were dependent for our existence on it.*

Twenty-four hours later, in its regular edition, the *Times* printed Fletcher's letter. In print it struck Hood as flimsy and contrived — surely the homeopape could not be taken in by it, and yet here it was. It had managed to pass each of the steps in the pape's processing.

Dear Editor:
    Your coverage of the heroic march on the decadent plutocratic stronghold of New York City has fired my enthusiasm. How does an ordinary citizen become a part of this history in the making? Please inform me at once, as I am eager to join Cemoli and endure the rigors and triumphs with the others.
                    Cordially,
                    Rudolf Fletcher

*   *   *

Beneath the letter, the homeopape had given an answer; Hood read it rapidly.

Cemoli's stalwarts maintain a recruiting office in downtown New York; address, 460 Bleekman St., New York 32. You might apply there, if the police haven't cracked down on these quasi-legal activities, in view of the current crisis.

Touching a button on his desk, Hood opened the direct line to police headquarters. When he had the chief investigator, he said, "Dietrich, I'd like a team of your men; we have a trip to make and there may be difficulties."

After a pause Dietrich said dryly, "So it's not all noble reclamation after all. Well, we've already dispatched a man to keep an eye on the Bleekman Street address. I admire your letter scheme. It may have done the trick." He chuckled.

Shortly, Hood and four black-uniformed Centaurian policemen flew by 'copter above the ruins of New York City, searching for the remains of what had once been Bleekman Street. By the use of a map they managed after half an hour to locate themselves.

"There," the police captain in charge of the team said, pointing. "That would be it, that building used as a grocery store." The 'copter began to lower.

It was a grocery store, all right. Hood saw no signs of political activity, no persons loitering, no flags or banners. And yet — something ominous seemed to lie behind the commonplace scene below, the bins of vegetables parked out on the sidewalk, the shabby women in long cloth coats who stood picking over the winter potatoes, the elderly proprietor with his white cloth apron sweeping with his broom. It was too natural, too easy. It was *too* ordinary.

"Shall we land?" the police captain asked him.

"Yes," Hood said. "And be ready."

The proprietor, seeing them land in the street before his grocery store, laid his broom carefully to one side and walked toward them. He was, Hood saw, a Greek. He had a heavy mustache and slightly wavy gray hair, and he gazed at them with innate caution, knowing at once that they did not intend him any good. Yet he had decided to greet them with civility; he was not afraid of them.

"Gentlemen," the Greek grocery store owner said, bowing slightly. "What can I do for you?" His eyes roved speculatively over the black Centaurian police uniforms, but he showed no expression, no reaction.

Hood said, "We've come to arrest a political agitator. You have nothing to be alarmed about." He started toward the grocery store; the team of police followed, their side arms drawn.

"Political agitation here?" the Greek said. "Come on. It is impossible."

He hurried after them, panting, alarmed now. "What have I done? Nothing at all; you can look around. Go ahead." He held open the door of the store, ushering them inside. "See right away for yourself."

"That's what we intend to do," Hood said. He moved with agility, wasting no time on conspicuous portions of the store; he strode directly on through.

The back room lay ahead, the warehouse with its cartons of cans, cardboard boxes stacked up on every side. A young boy was busy making a stock inventory; he glanced up, startled, as they entered. *Nothing here*, Hood thought. *The owner's son at work, that's all*. Lifting the lid of a carton Hood peered inside. Cans of peaches. And beside that a crate of lettuce. He tore off a leaf, feeling futile and — disappointed.

The police captain said to him in a low voice, "Nothing, sir."

"I see that," Hood said, irritably.

A door to the right led to a closet. Opening it, he saw brooms and a mop, a galvanized pail, boxes of detergents. And —

There were drops of paint on the floor.

The closet, some time recently, had been repainted. When he bent down and scratched with his nail he found the paint still tacky.

"Look at this," he said, beckoning the police captain over.

The Greek, nervously, said, "What's the matter, gentlemen? You find something dirty and report to the board of health, is that it? Customers have complained — tell me the truth, please. Yes, it is fresh paint. We keep everything spick and span. Isn't that in the public interest?"

Running his hands across the wall of the broom closet, the police captain said quietly, "Mr. Hood, there was a doorway here. Sealed up now, very recently." He looked expectantly toward Hood, awaiting instructions.

Hood said, "Let's go in."

Turning to his subordinates, the police captain gave a series of orders. From the ship, equipment was dragged, through the store, to the closet; a controlled whine arose as the police began the task of cutting into the wood and plaster.

Pale, the Greek said, "This is outrageous. I will sue."

"Right," Hood agreed. "Take us to court." Already a portion of the wall had given way. It fell inward with a crash, and bits of rubble spilled down onto the floor. A white cloud of dust rose, then settled.

It was not a large room which Hood saw in the glare of the police flashlights. Dusty, without windows, smelling stale and ancient . . . the room had not been inhabited for a long, long time, he realized, and he warily entered. It was empty. Just an abandoned storeroom of some kind, its wooden walls scaling and dingy. Perhaps before the Misfortune the grocery store had possessed a larger inventory. More stocks had been available then, but now this room was not needed. Hood moved about, flashing his beam of light up to the ceiling and then down to the floor. Dead flies, entombed here ... and, he saw, a few live ones which crept haltingly in the dust.

"Remember," the police captain said, "it was boarded up just now, within the last three days. Or at least the painting was just now done, to be absolutely accurate about it."

"These flies," Hood said. "They're not even dead yet." So it had not even been three days. Probably the boarding-up had been done yesterday.

What had this room been used for? He turned to the Greek, who had come after them, still tense and pale, his dark eyes flickering rapidly with concern. *This is a smart man*, Hood realized. *We will get little out of him.*

At the far end of the storeroom the police flashlights picked out a cabinet, empty shelves of bare, rough wood. Hood walked toward it.

"Okay," the Greek said thickly, swallowing. "I admit it. We have kept bootleg gin stored here. We became scared. You Centaurians — " He looked around at them with fear. "You're not like our local bosses; we know them, they understand us. You! You can't be reached. But we have to make a living." He spread his hands, appealing to them.

From behind the cabinet the edge of something protruded. Barely visible, it might never have been noticed. A paper which had fallen there, almost out of sight; it had slipped down farther and farther. Now Hood took hold of it and carefully drew it out. Back up the way it had come.

The Greek shuddered.

It was, Hood saw, a picture. A heavy, middle-aged man with loose jowls stained black by the grained beginnings of a beard, frowning, his lips set in defiance. A big man, wearing some kind of uniform. Once this picture had hung on the wall and people had come here and looked at it, paid respect to it. He knew who it was. This was Benny Cemoli, at the height of his political career, the leader glaring bitterly at the followers who had gathered here. So this was the man.

No wonder the *Times* showed such alarm.

To the Greek grocery store owner, Hood said, holding up the picture, "Tell me. Is this familiar to you?"

"No, no," the Greek said. He wiped perspiration from his face with a large red handkerchief. "Certainly not." But obviously, it was.

Hood said, "You're a follower of Cemoli, aren't you?"

There was silence.

"Take him along," Hood said to the police captain. "And let's start back." He walked from the room, carrying the picture with him.

As he spread the picture out on his desk, Hood thought, *It isn't merely a fantasy of the* Times. *We know the truth now. The man is real and twenty-four hours ago this portrait of him hung on a wall, in plain sight. It would still be there this moment, if CURB had not put in its appearance. We frightened them. The Earth people have a lot to hide from us, and they know it. They are taking steps, rapidly and effectively, and we will be lucky if we can —*

Interrupting his thoughts, Joan said, "Then the Bleekman Street address really was a meeting place for them. The pape was correct."

"Yes," Hood said.

"Where is he now?"

I wish I knew, Hood thought.

"Has Dietrich seen the picture yet?"

"Not yet," Hood said.

Joan said, "He was responsible for the war and Dietrich is going to find it out."

"No one man," Hood said, "could be solely responsible."

"But he figured largely," Joan said. "That's why they've gone to so much effort to eradicate all traces of his existence."

Hood nodded.

"Without the *Times*," she said, "would we ever have guessed that such a political figure as Benny Cemoli existed? We owe a lot to the pape. They overlooked it or weren't able to get to it. Probably they were working in such haste; they couldn't think of everything, even in ten years. It must be hard to obliterate *every* surviving detail of a planet-wide political movement, especially when its leader managed to seize absolute power in the final phase."

"Impossible to obliterate," Hood said. *A closed-off storeroom in the back of a Greek grocery store... that was enough to tell us what we needed to know. Now Dietrich's men can do the rest. If Cemoli is alive they will eventually find him, and if he's dead — they'll be hard to convince, knowing Dietrich. They'll never stop looking now.*

"One good thing about this," Joan said, "is that now a lot of innocent people will be off the hook. Dietrich won't go around prosecuting them. He'll be busy tracking down Cemoli."

True, Hood thought. And that was important. The Centaurian police would be thoroughly occupied for a long time to come, and that was just as well for everyone, including CURB and its ambitious program of reconstruction.

If there had never been a Benny Cemoli, he thought suddenly, *it would almost have been necessary to invent him.* An odd thought... he wondered how it happened to come to him. Again he examined the picture, trying to infer as much as possible about the man from this flat likeness. How had Cemoli sounded? Had he gained power through the spoken word, like so many demagogues before him? And his writing... Maybe some of it would turn up. Or even tape recordings of speeches he had made, the actual *sound* of the man. And perhaps video tapes as well. Eventually it would all come to light; it was only a question of time. *And then we will be able to experience for ourselves how it was to live under the shadow of such a man*, he realized.

The line from Dietrich's office buzzed. He picked up the phone.

"We have the Greek here," Dietrich said. "Under drug-guidance he's made a number of admissions; you may be interested."

"Yes," Hood said.

Dietrich said, "He tells us he's been a follower for seventeen years, a real old-timer in the Movement. They met twice a week in the back of his grocery store, in the early days when the Movement was small and relatively powerless. That picture you have — I haven't seen it, of course, but Stavros, our Greek gentleman, told me about it — that portrait is actually obsolete in the sense that several more recent ones have been in vogue among the faithful for some time now. Stavros hung onto it for sentimental reasons. It reminded him of the old days. Later on when the Movement grew in strength, Cemoli stopped showing up at the grocery store, and the Greek lost out in any personal contact with him. He continued to be a loyal dues-paying member, but it became abstract for him."

"What about the war?" Hood asked.

"Shortly before the war Cemoli seized power in a coup here in North America, through a march on New York City, during a severe economic depression. Millions were unemployed and he drew a good deal of support from them. He tried to solve the economic problems through an aggressive foreign policy — attacked several Latin American republics which were in the sphere of influence of the Chinese. That seems to be it, but Stavros is a bit hazy about the big picture ... we'll have to fill in more from other enthusiasts as we go along. From some of the younger ones. After all, this one is over seventy years old."

Hood said, "You're not going to prosecute him, I hope."

"Oh, no. He's simply a source of information. When he's told us all he has on his mind we'll let him go back to his onions and canned apple sauce. He's harmless."

"Did Cemoli survive the war?"

"Yes," Dietrich said. "But that was ten years ago. Stavros doesn't know if the man is still alive now. Personally I think he is, and we'll go on that assumption until it's proved false. We have to."

Hood thanked him and hung up.

As he turned from the phone he heard, beneath him, the low, dull rumbling. The homeopape had once more started into life.

"It's not a regular edition," Joan said, quickly consulting her wristwatch. "So it must be another extra. This is exciting, having it happen like this; I can't wait to read the front page."

What has Benny Cemoli done now? Hood wondered. *According to the* Times, *in its misphased chronicling of the man's epic ... what stage, actually taking place years ago, has now been reached. Something climactic, deserving of an extra. It will be interesting, no doubt of that. The* Times *knows what is fit to print.*

He, too, could hardly wait.

In downtown Oklahoma City, John LeConte put a coin into the slot of the kiosk which the *Times* had long ago established there. The copy of the *Times'* latest extra slid out, and he picked it up and read the headline briefly, spending only a moment on it to verify the essentials. Then he crossed the sidewalk and stepped once more into the rear seat of his chauffeur-driven steam car.

Mr. Fall said circumspectly, "Sir, here is the primary material, if you wish to make a word-by-word comparison." The secretary held out the folder, and LeConte accepted it.

The car started up. Without being told, the chauffeur drove in the direction of Party headquarters. LeConte leaned back, lit a cigar and made himself comfortable.

On his lap, the newspaper blazed up its enormous headlines.

CEMOLI ENTERS COALITION UN GOVERNMENT,
TEMPORARY CESSATION OF HOSTILITIES

To his secretary, LeConte said, "My phone, please."

"Yes sir." Mr. Fall handed him the portable field-phone. "But we're almost there. And it's always possible, if you don't mind my pointing it out, that they may have tapped us somewhere along the line."

"They're busy in New York," LeConte said. "Among the ruins." *In an area that hasn't mattered as long as I can remember,* he said to himself. However, possibly Mr. Fall's advice was good; he decided to skip the phone call. "What do you think of this last item?" he asked his secretary, holding up the newspaper.

"Very success-deserving," Mr. Fall said, nodding.

Opening his briefcase, LeConte brought out a tattered, coverless textbook. It had been manufactured only an hour ago, and it was the next artifact to be planted for the invaders from Proxima Centaurus to discover. This was his own contribution, and he was personally quite proud of it. The book outlined in massive detail Cemoli's program of social change; the revolution depicted in language comprehensible to school children.

"May I ask," Mr. Fall said, "if the Party hierarchy intends for them to discover a corpse?"

"Eventually," LeConte said. "But that will be several months from now." Taking a pencil from his coat pocket he wrote in the tattered textbook, crudely, as if a pupil had done it:

DOWN WITH CEMOLI.

Or was that going too far? No, he decided. There would be resistance. Certainly of the spontaneous, school boy variety. He added:

WHERE ARE THE ORANGES?

Peering over his shoulder, Mr. Fall said, "What does that mean?"

"Cemoli promises oranges to the youth," LeConte explained. "Another empty boast which the revolution never fulfills. That was Stavros's idea ... he being a grocer. A nice touch." *Giving it,* he thought, *just that much more semblance of verisimilitude. It's the little touches that have done it.*

"Yesterday," Mr. Fall said, "when I was at Party headquarters, I heard an audio tape that had been made. Cemoli addressing the UN. It was uncanny; if you didn't know — "

"Who did they get to do it?" LeConte asked, wondering why he hadn't been in on it.

"Some nightclub entertainer here in Oklahoma City. Rather obscure, of course. I believe he specializes in all sorts of characterizations. The fellow gave it a bombastic, threatening quality ... I must admit I enjoyed it."

And meanwhile, LeConte thought, *there are no war-crimes trials. We who were leaders during the war, on Earth and on Mars, we who held responsible posts — we are safe, at least for a while. And perhaps it will be forever. If our strategy continues to work. And if our tunnel to the cephalon of the homeopape, which took us five years to complete, isn't discovered. Or doesn't collapse.*

The steam car parked in the reserved space before Party headquarters; the chauffeur came around to open the door and LeConte got leisurely out, stepping forth into the light of day, with no feeling of anxiety. He tossed his cigar into the gutter and then sauntered across the sidewalk, into the familiar building.

NOVELTY ACT

LIGHTS BURNED LATE in the great communal apartment building Abraham Lincoln, because this was All Souls night: the residents, all six hundred of them, were required by their charter to attend, down in the subsurface community hall. They filed in briskly, men, women and children; at the door Bruce Corley, operating their rather expensive new identification reader, checked each of them in turn to be sure that no one from outside, from another communal apartment building, got in. The residents submitted good-naturedly, and it all went very fast.

"Hey Bruce, how much'd it set us back?" asked old Joe Purd, oldest resident in the building; he had moved in with his wife and two children the day the building, in May of 1980, had been built. His wife was dead now and the children had grown up, married and moved on, but Joe remained.

"Plenty," Bruce Corley said, "but it's error-proof; I mean, it isn't just subjective." Up to now, in his permanent job as sergeant of arms, he had admitted people merely by his ability to recognize them. But that way he had at last let in a pair of goons from Red Robin Hill Manor and they had disrupted the entire meeting with their questions and comments. It would not happen again.

Passing out copies of the agenda, Mrs. Wells smiled fixedly and chanted, "Item 3 A, Appropriation for Roof Repairs, has been moved to 4 A. Please make a note of that." The residents accepted their agendas and then divided into two streams flowing to opposite sides of the hall; the liberal faction of the building seated themselves on the right and the conservatives on the left, each conspicuously ignoring the existence of the other. A few uncommitted persons — newer residents or odd-balls — took seats in the rear, self-conscious and silent as the room buzzed with many small conferences. The tone,

191

the mood of the room, was tolerant, but the residents knew that tonight there was going to be a clash. Presumably, both sides were prepared. Here and there documents, petitions, newspaper clippings rustled as they were read and exchanged, handed back and forth.

On the platform, seated at the table with the four governing building trustees, chairman Donald Klugman felt sick at his stomach. A peaceful man, he shrank from these violent squabbles. Even seated in the audience he found it too much for him, and here tonight he would have to take active part; time and tide had rotated the chair around to him, as it did to each resident in turn, and of course it would be the night the school issue reached its climax.

The room had almost filled and now Patrick Doyle, the current building sky pilot, looking none too happy in his long white robe, raised his hands for silence. "The opening prayer," he called huskily, cleared his throat and brought forth a small card. "Everyone please shut their eyes and bow their heads." He glanced at Klugman and the trustees, and Klugman nodded for him to continue. "Heavenly Father," Doyle said, "we the residents of the communal apartment building Abraham Lincoln beseech You to bless our assembly tonight. Um, we ask that in Your mercy You enable us to raise the funds for the roof repairs which seem imperative. We ask that our sick be healed and our unemployed find jobs and that in processing applicants wishing to live amongst us we show wisdom in whom we admit and whom we turn away. We further ask that no outsiders get in and disrupt our law-abiding, orderly lives and we ask in particularly that lastly, if it be Thy will, that Nicole Thibodeaux be free of her sinus headaches which have caused her not to appear before us on TV lately, and that those headaches not have anything to do with that time two years ago, which we all recall, when that stagehand allowed that weight to fall and strike her on the head, sending her to the hospital for several days. Anyhow, amen."

The audience agreed, "Amen."

Rising from his chair, Klugman said, "Now, before the business of the meeting, we'll have a few minutes of our own talent displayed for our enjoyment. First, the three Fettersmoller girls from apartment number 205. They will do a soft-shoe dance to the tune of 'I'll Build a Stairway to the Stars.' " He reseated himself, and onto the stage came the three little blonde-haired children, familiar to the audience from many talent shows in the past.

As the Fettersmoller girls in their striped pants and glittery silver jackets shuffled smilingly through their dance, the door to the outside hall opened and a late-comer, Edgar Stone, appeared.

He was late, this evening, because he had been grading test papers of his next-door neighbor, Mr. Ian Duncan, and as he stood in the doorway his mind was still on the test and the poor showing which Duncan — whom he barely knew — had made. It seemed to him that without even having finished the test he could see that Duncan had failed.

On the stage the Fettersmoller girls sang in their scratchy voices, and Stone wondered why he had come. Perhaps for no more reason than to avoid the fine, it being mandatory for the residents to be here, tonight. These amateur talent shows, put on so often, meant nothing to him; he recalled the old days when the TV set had carried entertainment, good shows put on by professionals. Now of course all the professionals who were any good were under contract to the White House, and the TV had become educational, not entertaining. Mr. Stone thought of great old late-late movies with comics such as Jack Lemmon and Shirley MacLaine, and then he looked once more at the Fettersmoller girls and groaned.

Corley, hearing him, glanced at him severely.

At least he had missed the prayer. He presented his identification to Corley's new machine and it allowed him to pass down the aisle toward a vacant seat. Was Nicole watching this, tonight? Was a White House talent scout present somewhere in the audience? He saw no unfamiliar faces. The Fettersmoller girls were wasting their time. Seating himself, he closed his eyes and listened, unable to endure watching. They'll never make it, he thought. They'll have to face it, and so will their ambitious parents; they're untalented, like the rest of us ... Abraham Lincoln Apartments has added little to the cultural store of the nation, despite its sweaty, strenuous determination, and you are not going to be able to change that.

The hopelessness of the Fettersmoller girls' position made him remember once more the test papers which Ian Duncan, trembling and waxen-faced, had pressed into his hands early that morning. If Duncan failed he would be even worse-off than the Fettersmoller girls because he would not even be living at Abraham Lincoln; he would drop out of sight — their sight, anyhow — and would revert to a despised and ancient status: he would find himself once more living in a dorm, working on a manual gang as they had all done back in their teens.

Of course he would also be refunded the money which he had paid for his apartment, a large sum which represented the man's sole major investment in life. From one standpoint, Stone envied him. What would I do, he asked himself as he sat eyes closed, if I had my equity back right now, in a lump sum? Perhaps, he thought, I'd emigrate. Buy one of those cheap, illegal jalopies they peddle at those lots which —

Clapping hands roused him. The girls had finished, and he, too, joined in the applause. On the platform, Klugman waved for silence. "Okay, folks, I know you enjoyed that, but there's lots *more* in store, tonight. And then there's the business part of the meeting; we mustn't forget that." He grinned at them.

Yes, Stone thought. The business. And he felt tense, because he was one of the radicals at Abraham Lincoln who wanted to abolish the building's grammar school and send their children to a public grammar school where they would be exposed to children from other buildings entirely.

It was the kind of idea which met much opposition. And yet, in the last weeks, it had gained support. What a broadening experience it would be; their children would discover that people in other apartment buildings were no different from themselves. Barriers between people of all apartments would be torn down and a new understanding would come about.

At least, that was how it struck Stone, but the conservatives did not see it that way. Too soon, they said, for such mixing. There would be outbreaks of fights as the children clashed over which building was superior. In time it would happen ... but not now, not so soon.

Risking the severe fine, Ian Duncan missed the assembly and remained in his apartment that evening, studying official Government texts on the religio-political history of the United States — *relpols*, as they were called. He was weak in this, he knew; he could barely comprehend the economic factors, let alone all the religious and political ideologies that had come and gone during the twentieth century, directly contributing to the present situation. For instance, the rise of the Democratic-Republican Party. Once it had been two parties, engaging in wasteful quarrels, in struggles for power, just the way buildings fought now. The two parties had merged, about 1985. Now there was just the one party, which had ruled a stable and peaceful society, and everyone belonged to it. Everyone paid dues and attended meetings and voted, each four years, for a new President — for the man they thought Nicole would like best.

It was nice to know that they, the people, had the power to decide who would become Nicole's husband, each four years; in a sense it gave to the electorate supreme power, even above Nicole herself. For instance, this last man, Taufic Negal. Relations between him and the First Lady were quite cool, indicating that she did not like this most recent choice very much. But of course being a lady she would never let on.

When did the position of First Lady first begin to assume stature greater than that of President? the *relpol* text inquired. In other words, when did our society become matriarchal, Ian Duncan said to himself. Around about 1990; I know the answer to that. There were glimmerings before that; the change came gradually. Each year the President became more obscure, the First Lady became better known, more liked, by the public. It was the public which brought it about. Was it a need for mother, wife, mistress, or perhaps all three? Anyhow they got what they wanted; they got Nicole and she is certainly all three and more besides.

In the corner of his living room the television set said *taaaaang*, indicating that it was about to come on. With a sigh, Ian Duncan closed the official U.S. Government text book and turned his attention to the screen. A special, dealing with activities at the White House, he speculated. One more tour, perhaps, or a thorough scrutiny (in massively-detailed depth) of a new hobby or pursuit of Nicole's. Has she taken up collecting bone-china cups? If so, we will have to view each and every Royal Albert blue.

Sure enough, the round, wattled features of Maxwell Jamison, the White House news secretary, appeared on the screen. Raising his hand, Jamison made his familiar gesture of greeting. "Evening, people of this land of ours," he said solemnly. "Have you ever wondered what it would be like to descend to the bottom of the Pacific Ocean? Nicole has, and to answer that question she has assembled in the Tulip Room of the White House three of the world's foremost oceanographers. Tonight she will ask them for their stories, and you will hear them, too, as they were taped live, just a short while ago through the facilities of the Unified Triadic Networks' Public Affairs Bureau."

And now to the White House, Ian Duncan said to himself. At least vicariously. We who can't find our way there, who have no talents which might interest the First Lady even for one evening: we get to see in anyhow, through the carefully-regulated window of our television set.

Tonight he did not really want to watch, but it seemed expedient to do so; there might be a surprise quiz on the program, at the end. And a good grade on a surprise quiz might well offset the bad grade he had surely made on the recent political test, now being corrected by his neighbor Mr. Stone.

On the screen bloomed now lovely, tranquil features, the pale skin and dark, intelligent eyes, the wise and yet pert face of the woman who had come to monopolize their attention, on whom an entire nation, almost an entire planet, dwelt obsessively. At the sight of her, Ian Duncan felt engulfed by fear. He had failed her; his rotten test results were somehow known to her and although she would say nothing, the disappointment was there.

"Good evening," Nicole said in her soft, slightly-husky voice.

"It's this way," Ian Duncan found himself mumbling. "I don't have a head for abstractions; I mean, all this religio-political philosophy — it makes no sense to me. Couldn't I just concentrate on concrete reality? I ought to be baking bricks or turning out shoes." I ought to be on Mars, he thought, on the frontier. I'm flunking out here; at thirty-five I'm washed up, *and she knows it*. Let me go, Nicole, he thought in desperation. Don't give me any more tests, because I don't have a chance of passing them. Even this program about the ocean's bottom; by the time it's over I'll have forgotten all the data. I'm no use to the Democratic-Republican Party.

He thought about his brother, then. Al could help me. Al worked for Loony Luke, at one of his jalopy jungles, peddling the little tin and plastic ships that even defeated people could afford, ships that could, if luck was with them, successfully make a one-way trip to Mars. Al, he said to himself, you could get me a jalopy — wholesale.

On the TV screen, Nicole was saying, "And really, it is a world of much enchantment, with luminous entities far surpassing in variety and in sheer delightful wonder anything found on other planets. Scientists compute that there are more forms of life in the ocean — "

Her face faded, and a sequence showing odd, grotesque fish segued into its place. This is part of the deliberate propaganda line, Ian Duncan realized. An effort to take our minds off of Mars and the idea of getting away from the Party ... and from her. On the screen a bulbous-eyed fish gaped at him, and his attention, despite himself, was captured. Chrissakes, he thought, it is a weird world down there. Nicole, he thought, you've got me trapped. If only Al and I had succeeded; we might be performing right now for you, and we'd be happy. While you interviewed world-famous oceanographers Al and I would be discreetly playing in the background, perhaps one of the Bach "Two Part Inventions."

Going to the closet of his apartment, Ian Duncan bent down and carefully lifted a cloth-wrapped object into the light. We had so much youthful faith in this, he recalled. Tenderly, he unwrapped the jug; then, taking a deep breath, he blew a couple of hollow notes on it. The Duncan Brothers and Their Two-man Jug Band, he and Al had been, playing their own arrangements for two jugs of Bach and Mozart and Stravinsky. But the White House talent scout — the skunk. He had never even given them a fair audition. It had been done, he told them. Jesse Pigg, the fabulous jug-artist from Alabama, had gotten to the White House first, entertaining and delighting the dozen and one members of the Thibodeaux family gathered there with his version of "Derby Ram" and "John Henry" and the like.

"But," Ian Duncan had protested, "this is *classical* jug. We play late Beethoven sonatas."

"We'll call you," the talent scout had said briskly. "If Nicky shows an interest at any time in the future."

Nicky! He had blanched. Imagine being that intimate with the First Family. He and Al, mumbling pointlessly, had retired from the stage with their jugs, making way for the next act, a group of dogs dressed up in Elizabethan costumes portraying characters from Hamlet. The dogs had not made it, either, but that was little consolation.

"I am told," Nicole was saying, "that there is so little light in the ocean depths that, well, observe this strange fellow." A fish, sporting a glowing lantern before him, swam across the TV screen.

Startling him, there came a knock on the apartment door. With anxiety Duncan answered it; he found his neighbor Mr. Stone standing there, looking nervous.

"You weren't at All Souls?" Mr. Stone said. "Won't they check and find out?" He held in his hands Ian Duncan's corrected test.

Duncan said, "Tell me how I did." He prepared himself.

Entering the apartment, Stone shut the door after him. He glanced at the

TV set, saw Nicole seated with the oceanographers, listened for a moment to her, then abruptly said in a hoarse voice, "You did fine." He held out the test.

Duncan said, "I passed?" He could not believe it. He accepted the papers, examined them with incredulity. And then he understood what had happened. Stone had conspired to see that he passed; he had falsified the score, probably out of humanitarian motives. Duncan raised his head and they looked at each other, neither speaking. This is terrible, Duncan thought. What'll I do now? His reaction amazed him, but there it was.

I wanted to fail, he realized. Why? So I can get out of here, so I would have an excuse to give up all this, my apartment and my job, and go. Emigrate with nothing more than the shirt on my back, in a jalopy that falls to pieces the moment it comes to rest in the Martian wilderness.

"Thanks," he said glumly.

In a rapid voice, Stone said, "You can do the same for me sometime."

"Oh yeah, be happy to," Duncan said.

Scuttling back out of the apartment, Stone left him alone with the TV set, his jug and the falsely-corrected test papers, and his thoughts.

Al, you've got to help me, he said to himself. You've got to get me out of this; I can't even fail on my own.

In the little structure at the back of Jalopy Jungle No. 3, Al Duncan sat with his feet on the desk, smoking a cigarette and watching passers-by, the sidewalk and people and stores of downtown Reno, Nevada. Beyond the gleam of the new jalopies parked with flapping banners and streamers cascading from them he saw a shape waiting, hiding beneath the sign that spelled out LOONY LUKE.

And he was not the only person to see the shape; along the sidewalk came a man and woman with a small boy trotting ahead of them, and the boy, with an exclamation, hopped up and down, gesturing excitedly. "Hey, Dad, look! You know what it is? Look, it's the papoola."

"By golly," the man said with a grin, "so it is. Look, Marion, there's one of those Martian creatures, hiding there under that sign. What do you say we go over and chat with it?" He started in that direction, along with the boy. The woman, however, continued along the sidewalk.

"Come on, Mom!" the boy urged.

In his office, Al lightly touched the controls of the mechanism within his shirt. The papoola emerged from beneath the LOONY LUKE sign, and Al caused it to waddle on its six stubby legs toward the sidewalk, its round, silly hat slipping over one antenna, its eyes crossing and uncrossing as it made out the sight of the woman. The tropism being established, the papoola trudged after her, to the delight of the boy and his father.

"Look, Dad, it's following Mom! Hey Mom, turn around and see!"

The woman glanced back, saw the platter-like organism with its orange bug-shaped body, and she laughed. Everybody loves the papoola, Al thought to himself. See the funny Martian papoola. Speak, papoola; say hello to the nice lady who's laughing at you.

The thoughts of the papoola, directed at the woman, reached Al. It was greeting her, telling her how nice it was to meet her, soothing and coaxing her until she came back up the sidewalk toward it, joining her boy and husband so that now all three of them stood together, receiving the mental impulses emanating from the Martian creature which had come here to Earth with no hostile plans, no capacity to cause trouble. The papoola loved them, too, just as they loved it; it told them so right now — it conveyed to them the gentleness, the warm hospitality which it was accustomed to on its own planet.

What a wonderful place Mars must be, the man and woman were no doubt thinking, as the papoola poured out its recollections, its attitude. Gosh, it's not cold and schizoid, like Earth society; nobody spies on anybody else, grades their innumerable political tests, reports on them to building Security committees week in, week out. Think of it, the papoola was telling them as they stood rooted to the sidewalk, unable to pass on. You're your own boss, there, free to work your land, believe your own beliefs, become *yourself*. Look at you, afraid even to stand here listening. Afraid to —

In a nervous voice the man said to his wife, "We better go."

"Oh no," the boy said pleadingly. "I mean, gee, how often do you get to talk to a papoola? It must belong to that jalopy jungle, there." The boy pointed, and Al found himself under the man's keen, observing scrutiny.

The man said, "Of course. They landed here to sell jalopies. It's working on us right now, softening us up." The enchantment visibly faded from his face. "There's the man sitting in there operating it."

But, the papoola thought, what I tell you is still true. Even if it is a sales pitch. You could go there, to Mars, yourself. You and your family can see with your own eyes — if you have the courage to break free. Can you do it? Are you a real man? Buy a Loony Luke jalopy ... buy it while you still have the chance, because you know that someday, maybe not so long from now, the law is going to crack down. And there will be no more jalopy jungles. No more crack in the wall of the authoritarian society through which a few — a few lucky people — can escape.

Fiddling with the controls at his midsection, Al turned up the gain. The force of the papoola's psyche increased, drawing the man in, taking control of him. You must buy a jalopy, the papoola urged. Easy payment plan, service warranty, many models to choose from. The man took a step toward the lot. Hurry, the papoola told him. Any second now the authorities may close down the lot and your opportunity will be gone forever.

"This is how they work it," the man said with difficulty. "The animal snares people. Hypnosis. We have to leave." But he did not leave; it was too late: he was going to buy a jalopy, and Al, in the office with his control box, was reeling the man in.

Leisurely, Al rose to his feet. Time to go out and close the deal. He shut off the papoola, opened the office door and stepped outside onto the lot — and saw a once-familiar figure threading its way among the jalopies, toward him. It was his brother Ian and he had not seen him in years. Good grief, Al thought. What's he want? And at a time like this —

"Al," his brother called, gesturing. "Can I talk with you a second? You're not too busy, are you?" Perspiring and pale, he came closer, looking about in a frightened way. He had deteriorated since Al had last seen him.

"Listen," Al said, with anger. But already it was too late; the couple and their boy had broken away and were moving rapidly on down the sidewalk.

"I don't mean to bother you," Ian mumbled.

"You're not bothering me," Al said as he gloomily watched the three people depart. "What's the trouble, Ian? You don't look very well; are you sick? Come on in the office." He led his brother inside and shut the door.

Ian said, "I came across my jug. Remember when we were trying to make it to the White House? Al, we have to try once more. Honest to God, I can't go on like this; I can't stand to be a failure at what we agreed was the most important thing in our lives." Panting, he mopped at his forehead with his handkerchief, his hands trembling.

"I don't even have my jug any more," Al said presently.

"You must. Well, we could each record our parts separately on my jug and then synthesize them on one tape, and present that to the White House. This trapped feeling; I don't know if I can go on living with it. I have to get back to playing. If we started practicing right now on the 'Goldberg Variations' in two months we — "

Al broke in, "You still live at that place? That Abraham Lincoln?"

Ian nodded.

"And you still have that position down in Palo Alto, you're still a gear inspector?" He could not understand why his brother was so upset. "Hell, if worse comes to worst you can emigrate. Jug-playing is out of the question; I haven't played for years, since I last saw you in fact. Just a minute." He dialed the knobs of the mechanism which controlled the papoola; near the sidewalk the creature responded and began to return slowly to its spot beneath the sign.

Seeing it, Ian said, "I thought they were all dead."

"They are," Al said.

"But that one out there moves and — "

"It's a fake," Al said. "A puppet. I control it." He showed his brother the control box. "It brings in people off the sidewalk. Actually, Luke is supposed to have a real one on which these are modeled. Nobody knows for sure and the law can't touch Luke because technically he's now a citizen of Mars; they can't make him cough up the real one, if he does have it." Al seated himself and lit a cigarette. "Fail your *relpol* test," he said to Ian, "lose your apartment and get back your original deposit; bring me the money and I'll see that you get a damn fine jalopy that'll carry you to Mars. Okay?"

"I tried to fail my test," Ian said, "but they won't let me. They doctored the results. They don't want me to get away."

"Who's 'they'?"

"The man in the next apartment. Ed Stone, his name is. He did it deliberately; I saw the look on his face. Maybe he thought he was doing me a favor ... I don't know." He looked around him. "This is a nice little office you have here. You sleep in it, don't you? And when it moves, you move with it."

"Yeah," Al said, "we're always ready to take off." The police had almost gotten him a number of times, even though the lot could obtain orbital velocity in six minutes. The papoola had detected their approach, but not sufficiently far in advance for a comfortable escape; generally it was hurried and disorganized, with part of his inventory of jalopies being left behind.

"You're just one jump ahead of them," Ian mused. "And yet it doesn't bother you. I guess it's all in your attitude."

"If they get me," Al said, "Luke will bail me out." The shadowy, powerful figure of his boss was always there, backing him up, so what did he have to worry about? The jalopy tycoon knew a million tricks. The Thibodeaux clan limited their attacks on him to deep-think articles in popular magazines and on TV, harping on Luke's vulgarity and the shoddiness of his vehicles; they were a little afraid of him, no doubt.

"I envy you," Ian said. "Your poise. Your calmness."

"Doesn't your apartment building have a sky pilot? Go talk to him."

Ian said bitterly, "That's no good. Right now it's Patrick Doyle and he's as bad off as I am. And Don Klugman, our chairman, is even worse off; he's a bundle of nerves. In fact our whole building is shot through with anxiety. Maybe it has to do with Nicole's sinus headaches."

Glancing at his brother, Al saw that he was actually serious. The White House and all it stood for meant that much to him; it still dominated his life, as it had when they were boys. "For your sake," Al said quietly, "I'll get my jug out and practice. We'll make one more try."

Speechless, Ian gaped at him in gratitude.

Seated together in the business office of the Abraham Lincoln, Don Klugman and Patrick Doyle studied the application which Mr. Ian Duncan of no. 304 had filed with them. Ian desired to appear in the twice-weekly talent show, and at a time when a White House talent scout was present. The request, Klugman saw, was routine, except that Ian proposed to do his act in conjunction with another individual *who did not live at Abraham Lincoln.*

Doyle said, "It's his brother. He told me once; the two of them used to have this act, years ago. Baroque music on two jugs. A novelty."

"What apartment house does his brother live in?" Klugman asked. Approval of the application would depend on how relations stood between the Abraham Lincoln and the other building.

"None. He sells jalopies for that Loony Luke — you know. Those cheap little ships that get you just barely to Mars. He lives on one of the lots, I understand. The lots move around; it's a nomadic existence. I'm sure you've heard."

"Yes," Klugman agreed, "and it's totally out of the question. We can't have that act on our stage, not with a man like that involved in it. There's no reason why Ian Duncan can't play his jug; it's a basic political right and I wouldn't be surprised if it's a satisfactory act. But it's against our tradition to have an outsider participate; our stage is for our own people exclusively, always has been and always will. So there's no need even to discuss this." He eyed the sky pilot critically.

"True," Doyle said, "but it is a blood relative of one of our people, right? It's legal for one of us to invite a relative to watch the talent shows ... so why not let him participate? This means a lot to Ian; I think you know he's been failing, lately. He's not a very intelligent person. Actually, he should be doing a manual job, I suppose. But if he has artistic ability, for instance this jug concept — "

Examining his documents, Klugman saw that a White House scout would be attending a show at the Abraham Lincoln in two weeks. The best acts at the building would of course be scheduled that night ... the Duncan Brothers and Their Baroque Jug Band would have to compete successfully in order to obtain that privilege, and there were a number of acts which — Klugman thought — were probably superior. After all, *jugs* ... and not even electronic jugs, at that.

"All right," he said aloud to Doyle. "I agree."

"You're showing your humane side," the sky pilot said, with a grin of sentimentality which disgusted Klugman. "And I think we'll all enjoy the Bach and Vivaldi as played by the Duncan Brothers on their inimitable jugs."

Klugman, wincing, nodded.

On the big night, as they started into the auditorium on floor one of Abraham Lincoln Apartments, Ian Duncan saw, trailing along behind his brother, the flat, scuttling shape of the Martian creature, the papoola. He stopped short. "You're bringing that along?"

Al said, "You don't understand. Don't we have to win?"

After a pause, Ian said, "Not that way." He understood, all right; the papoola would take on the audience as it had taken on sidewalk traffic. It would exert its extra-sensory influence on them, coaxing out a favorable decision. So much for the ethics of a jalopy salesman, Ian realized. To his brother, this seemed perfectly normal; if they couldn't win by their jug-playing they would win through the papoola.

"Aw," Al said, gesturing, "don't be your own worst enemy. All we're engaged in here is a little subliminal sales technique, such as they've been using for a century — it's an ancient, reputable method of swinging public opinion your way. I mean, let's face it; we haven't played the jug professionally in years." He touched the controls at his waist and the papoola hurried forward to catch up with them. Again Al touched the controls —

And in Ian's mind a persuasive thought came, *Why not?* Everyone else does it.

With difficulty he said, "Get that thing off me, Al."

Al shrugged. And the thought, which had invaded Ian's mind from without, gradually withdrew. And yet, a residue remained. He was no longer sure of his position.

"It's nothing compared to what Nicole's machinery can accomplish," Al pointed out, seeing the expression on his face. "One papoola here and there, and that planet-wide instrument that Nicole has made out of TV — there you have the real danger, Ian. The papoola is crude; you know you're being worked on. Not so when you listen to Nicole. The pressure is so subtle and so complete — "

"I don't know about that," Ian said, "I just know that unless we're successful, unless we get to play at the White House, life as far as I'm concerned isn't worth living. And nobody put that idea in my head. It's just the way I feel; it's my own idea, dammit." He held the door open, and Al passed on into the auditorium, carrying his jug by the handle. Ian followed, and a moment later the two of them were on the stage, facing the partially-filled hall.

"Have you ever seen her?" Al asked.

"I see her all the time."

"I mean in reality. In person. So to speak, in the flesh."

"Of course not," Ian said. That was the whole point of their being successful, of getting to the White House. They would see her really, not just the TV image; it would no longer be a fantasy — it would be true.

"I saw her once," Al said. "I had just put the lot down, Jalopy Jungle No. 3, on a main business avenue in Shreveport, La. It was early in the morning, about eight o'clock. I saw official cars coming; naturally I thought it was the police — I started to take off. But it wasn't. It was a motorcade, with Nicole in it, going to dedicate a new apartment building, the largest yet."

"Yes," Ian said. "The Paul Bunyan." The football team from Abraham Lincoln played annually against its team, and always lost. The Paul Bunyan had over ten thousand residents, and all of them came from administrative-class backgrounds; it was an exclusive apartment building of active Party members, with uniquely high monthly payments.

"You should have seen her," Al said thoughtfully as he sat facing the audience, his jug on his lap. He tapped the papoola with his foot; it had taken up a position beneath his chair, out of sight. "Yes," he murmured, "you really should. It's not the same as on TV, Ian. Not at all."

Ian nodded. He had begun to feel apprehensive, now; in a few minutes they would be introduced. Their test had come.

Seeing him gripping his jug tautly, Al said, "Shall I use the papoola or not? It's up to you." He raised a quizzical brow.

Ian said, "Use it."

"Okay," Al said, reaching his hand inside his coat. Leisurely, he stroked the controls. And, from beneath his chair, the papoola rolled forth, its antennae twitching drolly, its eyes crossing and uncrossing.

At once the audience became alert; people leaned forward to see, some of them chuckling with delight.

"Look," a man said excitedly. It was old Joe Purd, as eager as a child. "It's the papoola!"

A woman rose to her feet to see more clearly, and Ian thought to himself, *Everyone loves the papoola.* We'll win, whether we can play the jug or not. And then what? Will meeting Nicole make us even more unhappy than we are? Is that what we'll get out of this: hopeless, massive discontent? An ache, a longing which can never be satisfied in this world?

It was too late to back out, now. The doors of the auditorium had shut and Don Klugman was rising from his chair, rapping for order. "Okay, folks," he said into his lapel microphone. "We're going to have a little display of some talent, right now, for everyone's enjoyment. As you see on your programs, first in order is a fine group, the Duncan Brothers and their Classical Jugs with a medley of Bach and Handel tunes that ought to set your feet tapping." He beamed archly at Ian and Al, as if saying, How does that suit you as an intro?

Al paid no attention; he manipulated his controls and gazed thoughtfully at the audience, then at last picked up his jug, glanced at Ian and then tapped his foot. "The Little Fugue in G Minor" opened their medley, and Al began to blow on the jug, sending forth the lively theme.

Bum, bum, bum. Bum-bum bum-bum bum bum de bum. DE bum, DE bum, de de-de bum ... His cheeks puffed out red and swollen as he blew.

The papoola wandered across the stage, then lowered itself, by a series of gangly, foolish motions, into the first row of the audience. It had begun to go to work.

The news posted on the communal bulletin board outside the cafeteria of the Abraham Lincoln that the Duncan Brothers had been chosen by the talent scout to perform at the White House astounded Edgar Stone. He read the announcement again and again, wondering how the little nervous, cringing man had managed to do it.

There's been cheating, Stone said to himself. Just as I passed him on his political tests ... he's got somebody else to falsify a few results for him along the talent line: He himself had heard the jugs; he had been present at that program, and the Duncan Brothers, Classical Jugs, were simply not that good. They were *good*, admittedly ... but intuitively he knew that more was involved.

Deep inside him he felt anger, a resentment that he had falsified Duncan's test-score. I put him on the road to success, Stone realized; I saved him. And now he's on his way to the White House.

No wonder Duncan did so poorly on his political test, Stone said to himself. He was busy practicing on his jug; he has no time for the commonplace realities which the rest of us have to cope with. It must be great to be an artist, Stone thought with bitterness. You're exempt from all the rules, you can do as you like.

He sure made a fool out of me, Stone realized.

Striding down the second floor hall, Stone arrived at the office of the building sky pilot; he rang the bell and the door opened, showing him the sight of the sky pilot deep in work at his desk, his face wrinkled with fatigue. "Um, father," Stone said, "I'd like to confess. Can you spare a few minutes? It's very urgently on my mind, my sins I mean."

Rubbing his forehead, Patrick Doyle nodded. "Jeez," he murmured. "It either rains or it pours; I've had ten residents in today so far, using the confessionator. Go ahead." He pointed to the alcove which opened onto his office. "Sit down and plug yourself in. I'll be listening while I fill out these 4–10 forms from Boise."

Filled with wrathful indignation, his hands trembling, Edgar Stone attached the electrodes of the confessionator to the correct spots of his scalp, and then, picking up the microphone, began to confess. The tape-drums of the machine turned as he spoke. "Moved by a false pity," he said, "I infracted a rule of the building. But mainly I am concerned not with the act itself but with the motives behind it; the act merely is the outgrowth of a false attitude toward my fellow residents. This person, my neighbor Mr. Duncan, did poorly in his recent *relpol* test and I foresaw him being evicted from Abraham Lincoln. I identified with him because subconsciously I regard myself as a failure, both as a resident of this building and as a man, so I falsified his score to indicate that he had passed. Obviously, a new *relpol* test will have to be given to Mr. Duncan and the one which I scored will have to be voided." He eyed the sky pilot, but there was no reaction.

That will take care of Ian Duncan and his Classical Jug, Stone said to himself.

By now the confessionator had analyzed his confession; it popped a card out, and Doyle rose to his feet wearily to receive it. After a careful study he glanced up. "Mr. Stone," he said, "the view expressed here is that your confession is no confession. What do you really have on your mind? Go back and begin all over; you haven't probed down deeply enough and brought up the genuine material. And I suggest you start out by confessing that you misconfessed consciously and deliberately."

"No such thing," Stone said, but his voice — even to him — sounded feeble. "Perhaps I could discuss this with you informally. I did falsify Ian Duncan's test score. Now, maybe my motives for doing it — "

Doyle interrupted, "Aren't you jealous of Duncan now? What with his success with the jug, White House-ward?"

There was silence.

"This could be," Stone admitted at last. "But it doesn't change the fact that by all rights Ian Duncan shouldn't be living here; he should be evicted, my motives notwithstanding. Look it up in the Communal Apartment-building Code. I know there's a section covering a situation like this."

"But you can't get out of here," the sky pilot said, "without confessing; you have to satisfy the machine. You're attempting to force eviction of a neighbor to fulfill your own emotional needs. Confess that, and then perhaps we can discuss the code ruling as it pertains to Duncan."

Stone groaned and once more attached the electrodes to his scalp. "All right," he grated. "I hate Ian Duncan because he's artistically gifted and I'm not. I'm willing to be examined by a twelve-resident jury of my neighbors to see what the penalty for my sin is — but I insist that Duncan be given another *relpol* test! I won't give up on this; he has no right to be living here among us. It's morally and legally *wrong*."

"At least you're being honest, now," Doyle said.

"Actually," Stone said, "I enjoy jug band playing; I liked their music, the other night. But I have to act in what I believe to be the communal interest."

The confessionator, it seemed to him, snorted in derision as it popped a second card. But perhaps it was only his imagination.

"You're just getting yourself deeper," Doyle said, reading the card. "Look at this." He passed the card to Stone. "Your mind is a riot of confused, ambivalent motives. When was the last time you confessed?"

Flushing, Stone mumbled, "I think last August. Pepe Jones was the sky pilot, then."

"A lot of work will have to be done with you," Doyle said, lighting a cigarette and leaning back in his chair.

The opening number on their White House performance, they had decided after much discussion and argument, would be the Bach "Chaconne in D." Al had always liked it, despite the difficulties involved, the double-stopping and all. Even thinking about the "Chaconne" made Ian nervous. He wished, now that it had been decided, that he had held out for the simpler "Fifth Unaccompanied Cello Suite." But too late now. Al had sent the information on to the White House A & R — artists and repertory — secretary, Harold Slezak.

Al said, "Don't worry; you've got the number two jug in this. Do you mind being second jug to me?"

"No," Ian said. It was a relief, actually; Al had the far more difficult part.

Outside the perimeter of Jalopy Jungle No. 3 the papoola moved, criss-crossing the sidewalk in its gliding, quiet pursuit of a sales prospect. It was only ten in the morning and no one worth collaring had come along, as yet. Today the lot had set down in the hilly section of Oakland, California, among the winding tree-lined streets of the better residential section. Across from the lot, Ian could see the Joe Louis, a peculiarly-shaped but striking apartment building of a thousand units, mostly occupied by well-to-do Negroes. The building, in the morning sun, looked especially neat and cared for. A guard, with badge and gun, patrolled the entrance, stopping anyone who did not live there from entering.

"Slezak has to okay the program," Al reminded him. "Maybe Nicole won't want to hear the 'Chaconne'; she's got very specialized tastes and they're changing all the time."

In his mind Ian saw Nicole, propped up in her enormous bed, in her pink, frilly robe, her breakfast on a tray beside her as she scanned the program schedules presented to her for her approval. Already she's heard about us, he thought. *She knows of our existence.* In that case, we really do exist. Like a child that has to have its mother watching what it does; we're brought into being, validated consensually, by Nicole's gaze.

And when she takes her eye off us, he thought, then what? What happens to us afterward? Do we disintegrate, sink back into oblivion?

Back, he thought, into random, unformed atoms. Where we came from ... the world of nonbeing. The world we've been in all our lives, up until now.

"And," Al said, "she may ask us for an encore. She may even request a particular favorite. I've researched it, and it seems she sometimes asks to hear Schumann's 'The Happy Farmer.' Got that in mind? We'd better work up 'The Happy Farmer,' just in case." He blew a few toots on his jug, thoughtfully.

"I can't do it," Ian said abruptly. "I can't go on. It means too much to me. Something will go wrong; we won't please her and they'll boot us out. And we'll never be able to forget it."

"Look," Al began. "We have the papoola. And that gives us — " He broke off. A tall, stoop-shouldered elderly man in an expensive natural-fiber blue pin-stripe suit was coming up the sidewalk. "My God, it's Luke himself," Al said. He looked frightened. "I've only seen him twice before in my life. Something must be wrong."

"Better reel in the papoola," Ian said. The papoola had begun to move toward Loony Luke.

With a bewildered expression on his face Al said, "I can't." He fiddled desperately with the controls at his waist. "It won't respond."

The papoola reached Luke, and Luke bent down, picked it up and continued on toward the lot, the papoola under his arm.

"He's taken precedence over me," Al said. He looked at his brother numbly.

The door of the little structure opened and Loony Luke entered. "We received a report that you've been using this on your own time, for purposes of your own," he said to Al, his voice low and gravelly. "You were told not to do that; the papoolas belong to the lots, not to the operators."

Al said, "Aw, come on, Luke."

"You ought to be fired," Luke said, "but you're a good salesman so I'll keep you on. Meanwhile, you'll have to make your quota without help." Tightening his grip on the papoola, he started back out. "My time is valuable; I have to go." He saw Al's jug. "That's not a musical instrument; it's a thing to put whiskey in."

Al said, "Listen, Luke, this is publicity. Performing for Nicole means that the network of jalopy jungles will gain prestige; got it?"

"I don't want prestige," Luke said, pausing at the door. "There's no catering to Nicole Thibodeaux by me; let her run her society the way she wants and I'll run the jungles the way I want. She leaves me alone and I leave her alone and that's fine with me. Don't mess it up. Tell Slezak you can't appear and forget about it; no grown man in his right senses would be hooting into an empty bottle anyhow."

"That's where you're wrong," Al said. "Art can be found in the most mundane daily walks of life, like in these jugs for instance."

Luke, picking his teeth with a silver toothpick, said, "Now you don't have a papoola to soften the First Family up for you. Better think about that ... do you really expect to make it without the papoola?"

After a pause Al said to Ian, "He's right. The papoola did it for us. But — hell, let's go on anyhow."

"You've got guts," Luke said. "But no sense. Still, I have to admire you. I can see why you've been a top notch salesman for the organization; you don't give up. Take the papoola the night you perform at the White House and then return it to me the next morning." He tossed the round, bug-like creature to Al; grabbing it, Al hugged it against his chest like a big pillow. "Maybe it would be good publicity for the jungles," Luke said. "But I know this. Nicole doesn't like us. Too many people have slipped out of her hands by means of us; we're a leak in mama's structure and mama knows it." He grinned, showing gold teeth.

Al said, "Thanks, Luke."

"But I'll operate the papoola," Luke said. "By remote. I'm a little more skilled than you; after all, I *built* them."

"Sure," Al said. "I'll have my hands full playing anyhow."

"Yes," Luke said, "you'll need both hands for that bottle."

Something in Luke's tone made Ian Duncan uneasy. What's he up to? he wondered. But in any case he and his brother had no choice; they had to have the papoola working for them. And no doubt Luke could do a good job of operating it; he had already proved his superiority over Al, just now, and as Luke said, Al would be busy blowing away on his jug. But still —

"Loony Luke," Ian said, "have you ever met Nicole?" It was a sudden thought on his part, an unexpected intuition.

"Sure," Luke said steadily. "Years ago. I had some hand puppets; my Dad and I traveled around putting on puppet shows. We finally played the White House."

"What happened there?" Ian asked.

Luke, after a pause, said, "She didn't care for us. Said something about our puppets being indecent."

And you hate her, Ian realized. You never forgave her. "Were they?" he asked Luke.

"No," Luke answered. "True, one act was a strip show; we had follies girl puppets. But nobody ever objected before. My Dad took it hard but it didn't bother me." His face was impassive.

Al said, "Was Nicole the First Lady that far back?"

"Oh yes," Luke said. "She's been in office for seventy-three years; didn't you know that?"

"It isn't possible," both Al and Ian said, almost together.

"Sure it is," Luke said. "She's a really old woman, now. A grandmother. But she still looks good, I guess. You'll know when you see her."

Stunned, Ian said, "On TV —"

"Oh yeah," Luke agreed. "On TV she looks around twenty. But look in the history books yourself; figure it out. The facts are all there."

The facts, Ian realized, mean nothing when you can see with your own eyes that she's as young-looking as ever. And we see that every day.

Luke, you're lying, he thought. We know it; we all know it. My brother saw her; Al would have said, if she was really like that. You hate her; that's your motive. Shaken, he turned his back to Luke, not wanting to have anything to do with the man, now. Seventy-three years in office — that would make Nicole almost ninety, now. He shuddered at the idea; he blocked it out of his thoughts. Or at least he tried to.

"Good luck, boys," Luke said, chewing on his toothpick.

In his sleep Ian Duncan had a terrible dream. A hideous old woman with greenish, wrinkled claws scrabbled at him, whining for him to do something — he did not know what it was because her voice, her words, blurred into indistinction, swallowed by her broken-toothed mouth, lost in the twisting thread of saliva which found its way to her chin. He struggled to free himself . . .

"Chrissake," Al's voice came to him. "Wake up; we have to get the lot moving; we're supposed to be at the White House in three hours."

Nicole, Ian realized as he sat up groggily. It was her I was dreaming about; ancient and withered, but still her. "Okay," he muttered as he rose unsteadily from the cot. "Listen, Al," he said, "suppose she is old, like Loony Luke says? What then? What'll we do?"

"We'll perform," Al said. "Play our jugs."

"But I couldn't live through it," Ian said. "My ability to adjust is just too brittle. This is turning into a nightmare; Luke controls the papoola and Nicole is old — what's the point of our going on? Can't we go back to just seeing her on the TV and maybe once in our lifetime at a great distance like you did in Shreveport? That's good enough for me, now. I want that, the image; okay?"

"No," Al said doggedly. "We have to see this through. Remember, you can always emigrate to Mars."

The lot had already risen, was already moving toward the East Coast and Washington, D.C.

When they landed, Slezak, a rotund, genial little individual, greeted them warmly; he shook hands with them as they walked toward the service entrance of the White House. "Your program is ambitious," he bubbled, "but if you can fulfill it, fine with me, with us here, the First Family I mean, and in particular the First Lady herself who is actively enthusiastic about all forms of original artistry. According to your biographical data you two made a thorough study of primitive disc recordings from the early nineteen hundreds, as early as 1920, of jug bands surviving from the U.S. Civil War, so you're authentic juggists except of course you're classical, not folk."

"Yes sir," Al said.

"Could you, however, slip in one folk number?" Slezak asked as they passed the guards at the service entrance and entered the White House, the long, carpeted corridor with its artificial candles set at intervals. "For instance, we suggest 'Rockabye My Sarah Jane.' Do you have that in your repertoire? If not — "

"We have it," Al said shortly. "We'll add it toward the end."

"Fine," Slezak said, prodding them amiably ahead of him. "Now may I ask what this creature you carry is?" He eyed the papoola with something less than enthusiasm. "Is it alive?"

"It's our totem animal," Al said.

"You mean a superstitious charm? A mascot?"

"Exactly," Al said. "With it we assuage anxiety." He patted the papoola's head. "And it's part of our act; it dances while we play. You know, like a monkey."

"Well I'll be darned," Slezak said, his enthusiasm returning. "I see, now.

Nicole will be delighted; she loves soft, furry things." He held a door open ahead of them.

And there she sat.

How could Luke have been so wrong? Ian thought. She was even lovelier than on TV, and much more distinct; that was the main difference, the fabulous authenticity of her appearance, its reality to the senses. The senses knew the difference. Here she sat, in faded blue-cotton trousers, moccasins on her feet, a carelessly-buttoned white shirt through which he could see — or imagined he could see — her tanned, smooth skin … how informal she was, Ian thought. Lacking in pretense or show. Her hair cut short, exposing her beautifully-formed neck and ears. And, he thought, so darn young. She did not look even twenty. And the vitality. The TV could not catch that, the delicate glow of color and line all about her.

"Nicky," Slezak said, "these are the classical juggists."

She glanced up, sideways; she had been reading a newspaper. Now she smiled. "Good morning," she said. "Did you have breakfast? We could serve you some Canadian bacon and butterhorns and coffee if you want." Her voice, oddly, did not seem to come from her; it materialized from the upper part of the room, almost at the ceiling. Looking that way, Ian saw a series of speakers and he realized that a glass barrier separated Nicole from them, a security measure to protect her. He felt disappointed and yet he understood why it was necessary. If anything happened to her —

"We ate, Mrs. Thibodeaux," Al said. "Thanks." He, too, was glancing up at the speakers.

We ate Mrs. Thibodeaux, Ian thought crazily. Isn't it actually the other way around? Doesn't she, sitting here in her blue-cotton pants and shirt, doesn't she devour *us*?

Now the President, Taufic Negal, a slender, dapper, dark man, entered behind Nicole, and she lifted her face up to him and said, "Look, Taffy, they have one of those papoolas with them — won't that be fun?"

"Yes," the President said, smiling, standing beside his wife.

"Could I see it?" Nicole asked Al. "Let it come here." She made a signal, and the glass wall began to lift.

Al dropped the papoola and it scuttled toward Nicole, beneath the raised security barrier; it hopped up, and all at once Nicole held it in her strong hands, gazing down at it intently.

"Heck," she said, "it's not alive; it's just a toy."

"None survived," Al said. "As far as we know. But this is an authentic model, based on remains found on Mars." He stepped toward her —

The glass barrier settled in place. Al was cut off from the papoola and he stood gaping foolishly, seemingly very upset. Then, as if by instinct, he touched the controls at his waist. Nothing happened for a time and then, at last, the papoola stirred. It slid from Nicole's hands and hopped back to the floor. Nicole exclaimed in amazement, her eyes bright.

"Do you want it, dear?" her husband asked. "We can undoubtedly get you one, even several."

"What does it do?" Nicole asked Al.

Slezak bubbled, "It dances, ma'am, when they play; it has rhythm in its bones — correct, Mr. Duncan? Maybe you could play something now, a shorter piece, to show Mrs. Thibodeaux." He rubbed his hands together.

Al and Ian looked at each other.

"S-sure," Al said. "Uh, we could play that little Schubert thing, that arrangement of 'The Trout.' Okay, Ian, get set." He unbuttoned the protective case from his jug, lifted it out and held it awkwardly. Ian did the same. "This is Al Duncan, here, at the first jug," Al said. "And besides me is my brother Ian at the second jug, bringing you a concert of classical favorites, beginning with a little Schubert." And then, at a signal from Al, they both began to play.

Bump bump-bump BUMP-BUMP buuump bump, ba-bump-bump bup-bup-bup-bup-bupppp.

Nicole giggled.

We've failed, Ian thought. God, the worst has come about: we're ludicrous. He ceased playing; Al continued on, his cheeks red and swelling with the effort of playing. He seemed unaware that Nicole was holding her hand up to cover her laughter, her amusement at them and their efforts. Al played on, by himself, to the end of the piece, and then he, too, lowered his jug.

"The papoola," Nicole said, as evenly as possible. "It didn't dance. Not one little step — why not?" And again she laughed, unable to stop herself.

Al said woodenly, "I — don't have control of it; it's on remote, right now." To the papoola he said, "You better dance."

"Oh really, this is wonderful," Nicole said. "Look," she said to her husband, "he has to *beg* it to dance. Dance, whatever your name is, papoola-thing from Mars, or rather imitation papoola-thing from Mars." She prodded the papoola with the toe of her moccasin, trying to nudge it into life. "Come on, little synthetic ancient cute creature, all made out of wires. Please."

The papoola leaped at her. It bit her.

Nicole screamed. A sharp *pop* sounded from behind her, and the papoola vanished into particles that swirled. A White House security guard stepped into sight, his rifle in his hands, peering intently at her and at the floating particles; his face was calm but his hands and the rifle quivered. Al began to curse to himself, chanting the words over and over again, the same three or four, unceasingly.

"Luke," he said then, to his brother. "He did it. Revenge. It's the end of us." He looked gray, worn-out. Reflexively he began wrapping his jug up once more, going through the motions step by step.

"You're under arrest," a second White House guard said, appearing behind them and training his gun on the two of them.

"Sure," Al said listlessly, his head nodding, wobbling vacuously. "We had nothing to do with it so arrest us."

Getting to her feet with the assistance of her husband, Nicole walked toward Al and Ian. "Did it bite me because I laughed?" she said in a quiet voice.

Slezak stood mopping his forehead. He said nothing; he merely stared at them sightlessly.

"I'm sorry," Nicole said. "I made it angry, didn't I? It's a shame; we would have enjoyed your act."

"Luke did it," Al said.

" 'Luke.' " Nicole studied him. "Loony Luke, you mean. He owns those dreadful jalopy jungles that come and go only a step from illegality. Yes, I know who you mean; I remember him." To her husband she said, "I guess we'd better have him arrested, too."

"Anything you say," her husband said, writing on a pad of paper.

Nicole said, "This whole jug business ... it was just a cover-up for an action hostile to us, wasn't it? A crime against the state. We'll have to rethink the entire philosophy of inviting performers here ... perhaps it's been a mistake. It gives too much access to anyone who has hostile intentions toward us. I'm sorry." She looked sad and pale, now; she folded her arms and stood rocking back and forth, lost in thought.

"Believe me, Nicole," Al began.

Introspectively, she said, "I'm not Nicole; don't call me that. Nicole Thibodeaux died years ago. I'm Kate Rupert, the fourth one to take her place. I'm just an actress who looks enough like the original Nicole to be able to keep this job, and I wish sometimes, when something like this happens, that I didn't have it. I have no real authority. There's a council somewhere that governs ... I've never even seen them." To her husband she said, "They know about this, don't they?"

"Yes," he said, "they've already been informed."

"You see," she said to Al, "he, even the President, has more actual power than I." She smiled wanly.

Al said, "How many attempts have there been on your life?"

"Six or seven," she said. "All for psychological reasons. Unresolved Oedipal complexes or something like that. I don't really care." She turned to her husband, then. "I really think these two men here — " She pointed at Al and Ian. "They don't seem to know what's going on; maybe they are innocent." To her husband and Slezak and the security guards she said, "Do they have to be destroyed? I don't see why you couldn't just eradicate a part of their memory-cells and let them go. Why wouldn't that do?"

Her husband shrugged. "If you want it that way."

"Yes," she said. "I'd prefer that. It would make my job easier. Take them to the medical center at Bethesda and then let's go on; let's give an audience to the next performers."

A security guard nudged Ian in the back with his gun. "Down the corridor, please."

"Okay," Ian murmured, gripping his jug. But what happened? he wondered. I don't quite understand. This woman isn't Nicole and even worse there is no Nicole anywhere; there's just the TV image, the illusion, and behind it, behind her, another group entirely rules. A council of some kind. But who are they and how did they get power? Will we ever know? We came so far; we almost seem to know what's really going on. The actuality behind the illusion ... can't they tell us the rest? What difference would it make now? How —

"Goodbye," Al was saying to him.

"What?" he said, horrified. "Why do you say that? They're going to let us go, aren't they?"

Al said, "We won't remember each other. Take my word for it; we won't be allowed to keep any ties like that. So — " He held out his hand. "So goodbye, Ian. We made it to the White House. You won't remember that either, but it's true; we did do it." He grinned crookedly.

"Move along," the security guard said to them.

Holding their jugs, the two of them moved down the corridor, toward the door and the waiting black medical van beyond.

It was night, and Ian Duncan found himself at a deserted street corner, cold and shivering, blinking in the glaring white light of an urban monorail loading platform. What am I doing here? he asked himself, bewildered. He looked at his wristwatch; it was eight o'clock. I'm supposed to be at the All Souls Meeting, aren't I? he thought dazedly.

I can't miss another one, he realized. Two in a row — it's a terrible fine; it's economic ruin. He began to walk.

The familiar building, Abraham Lincoln with all its network of towers and windows, lay extended ahead; it was not far and he hurried, breathing deeply, trying to keep up a good steady pace. It must be over, he thought. The lights in the great central subsurface auditorium were not lit. Damn it, he breathed in despair.

"All Souls is over?" he said to the doorman as he entered the lobby, his identification held out.

"You're a little confused, Mr. Duncan," the doorman said, putting away his gun. "All Souls was last night; this is Friday."

Something's gone wrong, Ian realized. But he said nothing; he merely nodded and hurried on toward the elevator.

As he emerged from the elevator on his own floor, a door opened and a furtive figure beckoned to him. "Hey, Duncan."

It was Corley. Warily, because an encounter like this could be disastrous, Ian approached him. "What is it?"

"A rumor," Corley said in a rapid, fear-filled voice. "About your last *relpol* test — some irregularity. They're going to rouse you at five or six A.M. tomorrow morning and spring a surprise quiz on you." He glanced up and down the hall. "Study the late 1980s and the religio-collectivist movements in particular. Got it?"

"Sure," Ian said, with gratitude. "And thanks a lot. Maybe I can do the same — " He broke off, because Corley had hurried back into his own apartment and shut the door; Ian was alone.

Certainly very nice of him, he thought as he walked on. Probably saved my hide, kept me from being forcibly ejected right out of here forever.

When he reached his apartment he made himself comfortable, with all his reference books on the political history of the United States spread out around him. I'll study all night, he decided. Because I have to pass that quiz; I have no choice.

To keep himself awake, he turned on the TV. Presently the warm, familiar being, the presence of the First Lady, flowed into motion and began to fill the room.

" ... and at our musical tonight," she was saying, "we will have a saxophone quartet which will play themes from Wagner's operas, in particular my favorite, 'Die Meistersinger.' I believe we will truly all find this a deeply rewarding and certainly an enriching experience to cherish. And, after that, my husband the President and I have arranged to bring you once again an old favorite of yours, the world renown cellist, Henri LeClercq, in a program of Jerome Kern and Cole Porter." She smiled, and at his pile of reference books, Ian Duncan smiled back.

I wonder how it would be to play at the White House, he said to himself. To perform before the First Lady. Too bad I never learned to play any kind of musical instrument. I can't act, write poems, dance or sing — nothing. So what hope is there for me? Now, if I had come from a musical family, if I had had a father or brothers to teach me how. ...

Glumly, he scratched a few notes on the rise of the French Christian Fascist Party of 1975. And then, drawn as always to the TV set, he put his pen down and turned to face the set. Nicole was now exhibiting a piece of Delft tile which she had picked up, she explained, in a little shop in Vermont. What lovely clear colors it had ... he watched, fascinated, as her strong, slim fingers caressed the shiny surface of the baked enamel tile.

"See the tile," Nicole was murmuring in her husky voice. "Don't you wish you had a tile like that? Isn't it lovely?"

"Yes," Ian Duncan said.

"How many of you would like someday to see such a tile?" Nicole asked. "Raise your hands."

Ian raised his hand hopefully.

"Oh, a whole lot of you," Nicole said, smiling her intimate, radiant smile. "Well, perhaps later we will have another tour of the White House. Would you like that?"

Hopping up and down in his chair, Ian said, "Yes, I'd like that."

On the TV screen she was smiling directly at him, it seemed. And so he smiled back. And then, reluctantly, feeling a great weight descend over him, he at last turned back to his reference books. Back to the harsh realities of his daily, endless life.

Against the window of his apartment something bumped and a voice called at him thinly, "Ian Duncan, I don't have much time."

Whirling, he saw outside in the night darkness a shape drifting, an egg-like construction that hovered. Within it a man waved at him energetically, still calling. The egg gave off a dull *putt-putt* noise, its jets idling as the man kicked open the hatch of the vehicle and then lifted himself out.

Are they after me already on this quiz? Ian Duncan asked himself. He stood up, feeling helpless. So soon ... I'm not ready, yet.

Angrily, the man in the vehicle spun the jets until their steady white exhaust firing met the surface of the building; the room shuddered and bits of plaster broke away. The window itself collapsed as the heat of the jets crossed it. Through the gap exposed the man yelled once more, trying to attract Ian Duncan's faculties.

"Hey, Duncan! Hurry up! I have your brother already; he's on his way in another ship!" The man, elderly, wearing an expensive natural-fiber blue pin-stripe suit, lowered himself with dexterity from the hovering egg-shaped vehicle and dropped feet-first into the room. "We have to get going if we're to make it. You don't remember me? Neither did Al. Boy, I take off my hat to them."

Ian Duncan stared at him, wondering who he was and who Al was and what was happening.

"Mama's psychologists did a good, good job of working you over," the elderly man panted. "That Bethesda — it must be quite a place. I hope they never get me there." He came toward Ian, caught hold of him by the shoulder. "The police are shutting down all my jalopy jungles; I have to beat it to Mars and I'm taking you along with me. Try to pull yourself together; I'm Loony Luke — you don't remember me now but you will after we're all on Mars and you see your brother again. *Come on.*" Luke propelled him toward the gap in the wall of the room, where once had been a window, and toward the vehicle — it was called a jalopy, Ian realized — drifting beyond.

"Okay," Ian said, wondering what he should take with him. What would he need on Mars? Toothbrush, pajamas, a heavy coat? He looked frantically around his apartment, one last look at it. Far off police sirens sounded.

Luke scrambled back into the jalopy, and Ian followed, taking hold of the elderly man's extended hand. The floor of the jalopy crawled with bright orange bug-like creatures whose antennae waved at him. Papoolas, he remembered, or something like that.

You'll be all right now, the papoolas were thinking. Don't worry; Loony Luke got you away in time, just barely in time. Now just relax.

"Yes," Ian said. He lay back against the side of the jalopy and relaxed; for the first time in many years he felt at peace.

The ship shot upward into the night emptiness and the new planet which lay beyond.

WATERSPIDER

I

THAT MORNING, as he carefully shaved his head until it glistened, Aaron Tozzo pondered a vision too unfortunate to be endured. He saw in his mind fifteen convicts from Nachbaren Slager, each man only one inch high, in a ship the size of a child's balloon. The ship, traveling at almost the speed of light, continued on forever, with the men aboard neither knowing nor caring what became of them.

The worst part of the vision was just that in all probability it was true.

He dried his head, rubbed oil into his skin, then touched the button within his throat. When contact with the Bureau switchboard had been established, Tozzo said, "I admit we can do nothing to get those fifteen men back, but at least we can refuse to send any more."

His comment, recorded by the switchboard, was passed on to his co-workers. They all agreed; he listened to their voices chiming in as he put on his smock, slippers and overcoat. Obviously, the flight had been an error; even the public knew that now. But —

"But we're going on," Edwin Fermeti, Tozzo's superior, said above the clamor. "We've already got the volunteers."

"Also from Nachbaren Slager?" Tozzo asked. Naturally the prisoners there would volunteer; their lifespan at the camp was no more than five or six years. And if this flight to Proxima were successful, the men aboard would obtain their freedom. They would not have to return to any of the five inhabited planets within the Sol System.

"Why does it matter where they originate?" Fermeti said smoothly.

Tozzo said, "Our effort should be directed toward improving the U.S.

Department of Penology, instead of trying to reach other stars." He had a sudden urge to resign his position with the Emigration Bureau and go into politics as a reform candidate.

Later, as he sat at the breakfast table, his wife patted him sympathetically on the arm. "Aaron, you haven't been able to solve it yet, have you?"

"No," he admitted shortly. "And now I don't even care." He did not tell her about the other ship loads of convicts which had fruitlessly been expended; it was forbidden to discuss that with anyone not employed by a department of the Government.

"Could they be re-entering on their own?"

"No. Because mass was lost here, in the Sol System. To re-enter they have to obtain equal mass back, to replace it. That's the whole point." Exasperated, he sipped his tea and ignored her. Women, he thought. Attractive but not bright. "They need mass back," he repeated. "Which would be fine if they were making a round trip, I suppose. But this is an attempt to colonize; it's not a guided tour that returns to its point of origin."

"How long does it take them to reach Proxima?" Leonore asked. "All reduced like that, to an inch high."

"About four years."

Her eyes grew large. "That's marvelous."

Grumbling at her, Tozzo pushed his chair back from the table and rose. I wish they'd take her, he said to himself, since she imagines it's so marvelous. But Leonore would be too smart to volunteer.

Leonore said softly, "Then I was right. The Bureau *has* sent people. You as much as admitted it just now."

Flushing, Tozzo said, "Don't tell anybody; none of your female friends especially. Or it's my job." He glared at her.

On that hostile note, he set off for the Bureau.

As Tozzo unlocked his office door, Edwin Fermeti hailed him. "You think Donald Nils is somewhere on a planet circling Proxima at this very moment?" Nils was a notorious murderer who had volunteered for one of the Bureau's flights. "I wonder — maybe he's carrying around a lump of sugar five times his size."

"Not really very funny," Tozzo said.

Fermeti shrugged. "Just hoping to relieve the pessimism. I think we're all getting discouraged." He followed Tozzo into his office. "Maybe we should volunteer ourselves for the next flight." It sounded almost as if he meant it, and Tozzo glanced quickly at him. "Joke," Fermeti said.

"One more flight," Tozzo said, "and if it fails, I resign."

"I'll tell you something," Fermeti said. "We have a new tack." Now Tozzo's co-worker Craig Gilly had come sauntering up. To the two men, Fermeti said, "We're going to try using pre-cogs in obtaining our formula for re-entry." His eyes flickered as he saw their reaction.

Astonished, Gilly said, "But all the pre-cogs are dead. Destroyed by Presidential order twenty years ago."

Tozzo, impressed, said, "He's going to dip back into the past to obtain a pre-cog. Isn't that right, Fermeti?"

"We will, yes," his superior said, nodding. "Back to the golden age of pre-cognition. The twentieth century."

For a moment Tozzo was puzzled. And then he remembered.

During the first half of the twentieth century so many pre-cogs — people with the ability to read the future — had come into existence that an organized guild had been formed with branches in Los Angeles, New York, San Francisco and Pennsylvania. This group of pre-cogs, all knowing one another, had put out a number of periodicals which had flourished for several decades. Boldly and openly, the members of the pre-cog guild had proclaimed in their writings their knowledge of the future. And yet — as a whole, their society had paid little attention to them.

Tozzo said slowly, "Let me get this straight. You mean you're going to make use of the Department of Archaeology's time-dredges to scoop up a famous pre-cog of the past?"

Nodding, Fermeti said, "And bring him here to help us, yes."

"But how can he help us? He would have no knowledge of our future, only of his own."

Fermeti said, "The Library of Congress has already given us access to its virtually complete collection of pre-cog journals of the twentieth century." He smiled crookedly at Tozzo and Gilly, obviously enjoying the situation. "It's my hope — and my expectation — that among this great body of writings we will find an article *specifically dealing with our re-entry problem*. The chances, statistically speaking, are quite good ... they wrote about innumerable topics of future civilization, as you know."

After a pause, Gilly said, "Very clever. I think your idea may solve our problem. Speed-of-light travel to other star systems may yet become a possibility."

Sourly, Tozzo said, "Hopefully, before we run out of convicts." But he, too, liked his superior's idea. And, in addition, he looked forward to seeing face to face one of the famous twentieth century pre-cogs. Theirs had been one brief, glorious period — sadly, long since ended.

Or not so brief, if one dated it as starting with Jonathan Swift, rather than with H. G. Wells. Swift had written of the two moons of Mars and their unusual orbital characteristics years before telescopes had proved their existence. And so today there was a tendency in the textbooks to include him.

II

It took the computers at the Library of Congress only a short while to scan the brittle, yellowed volumes, article by article, and to select the sole contribution dealing with deprivation of mass and restoration as the modus operandi of interstellar space travel. Einstein's formula that as an object increased its velocity its mass increased proportionally had been so fully accepted, so completely unquestioned, that no one in the twentieth century had paid any attention to the particular article, which had been put in print in August of 1955 in a pre-cog journal called *If*.

In Fermeti's office, Tozzo sat beside his superior as the two of them pored over the photographic reproduction of the journal. The article was titled *Night Flight*, and it ran only a few thousand words. Both men read it avidly, neither speaking until they had finished.

"Well?" Fermeti said, when they had come to the end.

Tozzo said, "No doubt of it. That's our Project, all right. A lot is garbled; for instance he calls the Emigration Bureau 'Outward, Incorporated,' and believes it to be a private commercial firm." He referred to the text. "It's really uncanny, though. You're obviously this character, Edmond Fletcher; the names are similar but still a little off, as is everything else. And I'm Alison Torelli." He shook his head admiringly. "Those pre-cogs ... having a mental image of the future that was always askew and yet in the main — "

"In the main correct," Fermeti finished. "Yes, I agree. This *Night Flight* article definitely deals with us and the Bureau's Project ... herein called *Waterspider*, because it has to be done in one great leap. Good lord, that would have been a perfect name, had we thought of it. Maybe we can still call it that."

Tozzo said slowly, "But the pre-cog who wrote *Night Flight* ... in no place does he actually give the formula for mass-restoration or even for mass-deprivation. He just simply says that 'we have it.' " Taking the reproduction of the journal, he read aloud from the article:

Difficulty in restoring mass to the ship and its passengers at the termination of the flight had proved a stumbling block for Torelli and his team of researchers and yet they had at last proved successful. After the fateful implosion of the *Sea Scout*, the initial ship to —

"And that's all," Tozzo said. "So what good does it do us? Yes, this pre-cog experienced our present situation a hundred years ago — *but he left out the technical details*."

There was silence.

At last Fermeti said thoughtfully, "That doesn't mean he didn't *know* the technical data. We know today that the others in his guild were very often trained scientists." He examined the biographical report. "Yes, while not actually using his pre-cog ability he worked as a chicken-fat analyst for the University of California."

"Do you still intend to use the time-dredge to bring him up to the present?"

Fermeti nodded. "I only wish the dredge worked both ways. If it could be used with the future, not the past, we could avoid having to jeopardize the safety of this pre-cog — " He glanced down at the article. "This Poul Anderson."

Chilled, Tozzo said, "What hazard is there?"

"We may not be able to return him to his own time. Or — " Fermeti paused. "We might lose part of him along the way, wind up with only half of him. The dredge has bisected many objects before."

"And this man isn't a convict at Nachbaren Slager," Tozzo said. "So you don't have that rationale to fall back on."

Fermeti said suddenly, "We'll do it properly. We'll reduce the jeopardy by sending a team of men back to that time, back to 1954. They can apprehend this Poul Anderson and see that *all of him* gets into the time-dredge, not merely the top half or the left side."

So it had been decided. The Department of Archaeology's time-dredge would go back to the world of 1954 and pick up the pre-cog Poul Anderson; there was nothing further to discuss.

Research conducted by the U.S. Department of Archaeology showed that in September of 1954 Poul Anderson had been living in Berkeley, California, on Grove Street. In that month he had attended a top-level meeting of pre-cogs from all over the United States at the Sir Francis Drake Hotel in San Francisco. It was probable that there, in that meeting, basic policy for the next year had been worked out, with Anderson, and other experts, participating.

"It's really very simple," Fermeti explained to Tozzo and Gilly. "A pair of men will go back. They will be provided with forged identification showing them to be part of the nation-wide pre-cog organization ... squares of cellophane-enclosed paper which are pinned to the coat lapel. Naturally, they will be wearing twentieth century garments. They will locate Poul Anderson, single him out and draw him off to one side."

"And tell him what?" Tozzo said skeptically.

"That they represent an unlicensed amateur pre-cog organization in Battlecreek, Michigan, and that they have constructed an amusing vehicle built to resemble a time-travel dredge of the future. They will ask Mr. Anderson, who was actually quite famous in his time, to pose by their humbug dredge, and then they will ask for a shot of him within. Our research shows that, according to his contemporaries, Anderson was mild and easy-going, and also that at these yearly top-strategy assemblies he often became convivial enough to enter into the mood of optimism generated by his fellow pre-cogs."

Tozzo said, "You mean he sniffed what they called 'airplane dope'? He was a 'glue-sniffer'?"

With a faint smile, Fermeti said, "Hardly. That was a mania among adolescents and did not become widespread in fact until a decade later. No, I am speaking about imbibing alcohol."

PHILIP K. DICK

"I see," Tozzo said, nodding.

Fermeti continued, "In the area of difficulties, we must cope with the fact that at this top-secret session, Anderson brought along his wife Karen, dressed as a Maid of Venus in gleaming breast-cups, short skirt and helmet, and that he also brought their new-born daughter Astrid. Anderson himself did not wear any disguise for purposes of concealing his identity. He had no anxieties, being a quite stable person, as were most twentieth century pre-cogs.

"However, during the discussion periods between formal sessions, the pre-cogs, minus their wives, circulating about, playing poker and arguing, some of them it is said stoning one another — "

"Stoning?"

"Or, as it was put, becoming stoned. In any case, they gathered in small groups in the antechambers of the hotel, and it is at such an occasion that we expect to nab him. In the general hubbub his disappearance would not be noted. We would expect to return him to that exact time, or at least no more than a few hours later or earlier ... preferably not earlier because *two* Poul Andersons at the meeting might prove awkward."

Tozzo, impressed, said, "Sounds foolproof."

"I'm glad you like it," Fermeti said tartly, "because you will be one of the team sent."

Pleased, Tozzo said, "Then I had better get started learning the details of life in the mid twentieth century." He picked up another issue of *If*. This one, May of 1971, had interested him as soon as he had seen it. Of course, this issue would not be known yet to the people of 1954 ... but eventually they would see it. And once having seen it they would never forget it ...

Ray Bradbury's first textbook to be serialized, he realized as he examined the journal. *The Fisher of Men*, it was called, and in it the great Los Angeles pre-cog had anticipated the ghastly Gutmanist political revolution which was to sweep the inner planets. Bradbury had warned against Gutman, but the warning had gone — of course — unheeded. Now Gutman was dead and the fanatical supporters had dwindled to the status of random terrorists. But had the world listened to Bradbury —

"Why the frown?" Fermeti asked him. "Don't you want to go?"

"Yes," Tozzo said thoughtfully. "But it's a terrible responsibility. These are no ordinary men."

"That is certainly the truth," Fermeti said, nodding.

III

Twenty-four hours later, Aaron Tozzo stood surveying himself in his mid twentieth century clothing and wondering if Anderson would be deceived, if he actually could be duped into entering the dredge.

The costume certainly was perfection itself. Tozzo had even been equipped with the customary waist-length beard and handlebar mustache so popular circa 1950 in the United States. And he wore a wig.

Wigs, as everyone knew, had at that time swept the United States as the fashion note par excellence; men and women had both worn huge powdered perukes of bright colors, reds and greens and blues and of course dignified grays. It was one of the most amusing occurrences of the twentieth century.

Tozzo's wig, a bright red, pleased him. Authentic, it had come from the Los Angeles Museum of Cultural History, and the curator had vouched for it being a man's, not a woman's. So the fewest possible chances of detection were being taken. Little risk existed that they would be detected as members of another, future culture entirely.

And yet, Tozzo was still uneasy.

However, the plan had been arranged; now it was time to go. With Gilly, the other member selected, Tozzo entered the time-dredge and seated himself at the controls. The Department of Archaeology had provided a full instruction manual, which lay open before him. As soon as Gilly had locked the hatch, Tozzo took the bull by the horns (a twentieth century expression) and started up the dredge.

Dials registered. They were spinning backward into time, back to 1954 and the San Francisco Pre-Cog Congress.

Beside him, Gilly practiced mid twentieth century phrases from a reference volume. "Diz muz be da blace ... " Gilly cleared his throat. "Kilroy was here," he murmured. "Wha' hoppen? Like man, let's cut out; this ball's a drag." He shook his head. "I can't grasp the exact sense of these phrases," he apologized to Tozzo. "Twenty-three skidoo."

Now a red light glowed; the dredge was about to conclude its journey. A moment later its turbines halted.

They had come to rest on the sidewalk outside the Sir Francis Drake Hotel in downtown San Francisco.

On all sides, people in quaint archaic costumes dragged along on foot. And, Tozzo saw, there were no monorails; all the visible traffic was surface-bound. What a congestion, he thought, as he watched the automobiles and buses moving inch by inch along the packed streets. An official in blue waved traffic ahead as best he could, but the entire enterprise, Tozzo could see, was an abysmal failure.

"Time for phase two," Gilly said. But he, too, was gaping at the stalled surface vehicles. "Good grief," he said, "look at the incredibly short skirts of the women; why, the knees are virtually exposed. Why don't the women die of whisk virus?"

"I don't know," Tozzo said, "but I do know we've got to get into the Sir Francis Drake Hotel."

Carefully, they opened the port of the time-dredge and stepped out. And then Tozzo realized something. There had been an error. Already.

The men of this decade were clean-shaven.

"Gilly," he said rapidly, "we've got to shed our beards and mustaches." In an instant he had pulled Gilly's off, leaving his bare face exposed. But the wig; that was correct. All the men visible wore head-dress of some type; Tozzo saw few if any bald men. The women, too, had luxurious wigs ... or were they wigs? Could they perhaps be *natural* hair?

In any case, both he and Gilly now would pass. Into the Sir Francis Drake, he said to himself, leading Gilly along.

They darted lithely across the sidewalk — it was amazing how slowly the people of this time-period walked — and into the inexpressibly old-fashioned lobby of the hotel. Like a museum, Tozzo thought as he glanced about him. I wish we could linger ... but they could not.

"How's our identification?" Gilly said nervously. "Is it passing inspection?" The business with the facehair had upset him.

On each of their lapels they carried the expertly made false identification. It worked. Presently they found themselves ascending by a lift, or rather elevator, to the correct floor.

The elevator let them off in a crowded foyer. Men, all clean-shaven, with wigs or natural hair, stood in small clusters everywhere, laughing and talking. And a number of attractive women, some of them in garments called leotards, which were skin-tight, loitered about smilingly. Even though the styles of the times required their breasts to be covered, they were a sight to see.

Sotto voce, Gilly said, "I am stunned. In this room are some of the — "

"I know," Tozzo murmured. Their Project could wait, at least a little while. Here was an unbelievably golden opportunity to see these pre-cogs, actually to talk to them and listen to them ...

Here came a tall, handsome man in a dark suit that sparkled with tiny specks of some unnatural material, some variety of synthetic. The man wore glasses and his hair, everything about him, had a tanned, dark look. The name on his identification ... Tozzo peered.

The tall, good-looking man was A. E. van Vogt.

"Say," another individual, perhaps a pre-cog enthusiast, was saying to van Vogt, stopping him. "I read both versions of your *World of Null A* and I still didn't quite get that about it being *him*; you know, at the end. Could you explain that part to me? And also when they started into the tree and then just — "

van Vogt halted. A soft smile appeared on his face and he said. "Well, I'll tell you a secret. I start out with a plot and then the plot sort of folds up. So then I have to have another plot to finish the rest of the story."

Going over to listen, Tozzo felt something magnetic about van Vogt. He was so tall, so spiritual. Yes, Tozzo said to himself; that was the word, a healing spirituality. There was a quality of innate goodness which emanated from him.

All at once van Vogt said, "There goes a man with my pants." And without a further word to the enthusiast, stalked off and disappeared into the crowd.

Tozzo's head swam. To actually have seen and heard A. E. van Vogt —

"Look," Gilly was saying, plucking at his sleeve. "That enormous, genial-looking man seated over there; that's Howard Browne, who edited the pre-cog journal *Amazing* at this time-period."

"I have to catch a plane," Howard Browne was saying to anyone who would listen to him. He glanced about him in a worried anxiety, despite his almost physical geniality.

"I wonder," Gilly said, "if Doctor Asimov is here."

We can ask, Tozzo decided. He made his way over to one of the young women wearing a blonde wig and green leotards. "WHERE IS DOCTOR ASIMOV?" he asked clearly in the argot of the times.

"Who's to know?" the girl said.

"Is he here, miss?"

"Naw," the girl said.

Gilly again plucked at Tozzo's sleeve. "We must find Poul Anderson, remember? Enjoyable as it is to talk to this girl — "

"I'm inquiring about Asimov," Tozzo said brusquely. After all, Isaac Asimov had been the founder of the entire twenty-first century positronic robot industry. How could he not be here?

A burly outdoorish man strode by them, and Tozzo saw that this was Jack Vance. Vance, he decided, looked more like a big game hunter than anything else ... we must beware of him, Tozzo decided. If we got into any altercation Vance could take care of us easily.

He noticed now that Gilly was talking to the blonde-wigged girl in the green leotards. "MURRAY LEINSTER?" Gilly was asking. "The man whose paper on parallel time is still at the very forefront of theoretical studies; isn't he — "

"I dunno," the girl said, in a bored tone of voice.

A group had gathered about a figure opposite them; the central person whom everybody was listening to was saying, " ... all right, if like Howard Browne you prefer air travel, fine. But I say it's risky. I don't fly. In fact even riding in a car is dangerous. I generally lie down in the back." The man wore a short-cropped wig and a bow tie; he had a round, pleasant face but his eyes were intense.

It was Ray Bradbury, and Tozzo started toward him at once.

"Stop!" Gilly whispered angrily. "Remember what we came for."

And, past Bradbury, seated at the bar, Tozzo saw an older, care-weathered man in a brown suit wearing small glasses and sipping a drink. He recognized the man from drawings in early Gernsback publications; it was the fabulously unique pre-cog from the New Mexico region, Jack Williamson.

"I thought *Legion of Time* was the finest novel-length science-fiction work I ever read," an individual, evidently another pre-cog enthusiast, was saying to Jack Williamson, and Williamson was nodding in pleasure.

"That was originally going to be a short story," Williamson said. "But it grew. Yes, I like that one, too."

Meanwhile Gilly had wandered on, into an adjoining room. He found, at a table, two women and a man in deep conversation. One of the women, dark-haired and handsome, with bare shoulders, was — according to her identification plate — Evelyn Paige. The taller woman he discovered was the renowned Margaret St. Clair, and Gilly at once said:

"Mrs. St. Clair, your article entitled *The Scarlet Hexapod* in the September 1959 *If* was one of the finest — " And then he broke off.

Because Margaret St. Clair had not written that yet. Knew in fact nothing about it. Flushing with nervousness, Gilly backed away.

"Sorry," he murmured. "Excuse me; I became confused."

Raising an eyebrow, Margaret St. Clair said, "In the September 1959 issue, you say? What are you, a man from the future?"

"Droll," Evelyn Paige said, "but let's continue." She gave Gilly a hard stare from her black eyes. "Now Bob, as I understand what you're saying — " She addressed the man opposite her, and Gilly saw now to his delight that the dire-looking cadaverous individual was none other than Robert Bloch.

Gilly said, "Mr. Bloch, your article in *Galaxy: Sabbatical,* was — "

"You've got the wrong person, my friend," Robert Bloch said. "I never wrote any piece entitled *Sabbatical.*"

Good Lord, Gilly realized. I did it again; *Sabbatical* is another work which has not been written yet. I had better get away from here. He moved back toward Tozzo ... and found him standing rigidly.

Tozzo said, "I've found Anderson."

At once, Gilly turned, also rigid.

Both of them had carefully studied the pictures provide by the Library of Congress. There stood the famous pre-cog, tall and slender and straight, even a trifle thin, with curly hair — or wig — and glasses, a warm glint of friendliness in his eyes. He held a whiskey glass in one hand, and he was discoursing with several other pre-cogs. Obviously he was enjoying himself.

"Um, uh, let's see," Anderson was saying, as Tozzo and Gilly came quietly up to join the group. "Pardon?" Anderson cupped his ear to catch what one of the other pre-cogs was saying. "Oh, uh, yup, that's right." Anderson nodded. "Yup, Tony, uh, I agree with you one hundred per cent."

The other pre-cog, Tozzo realized, was the superb Tony Boucher, whose pre-cognition of the religious revival of the next century had been almost supernatural. The word-by-word description of the Miracle in the Cave involving the robot … Tozzo gazed at Boucher with awe, and then he turned back to Anderson.

"Poul," another pre-cog said. "I'll tell you how the Italians intended to get the British to leave if they did invade in 1943. The British would stay at hotels, the best, naturally. The Italians would overcharge them."

"Oh, yes, yes," Anderson said, nodding and smiling, his eyes twinkling. "And then the British, being gentlemen, would say nothing — "

"But they'd leave the next day," the other pre-cog finished, and all in the group laughed, except for Gilly and Tozzo.

"Mr. Anderson," Tozzo said tensely, "we're from an amateur pre-cog organization at Battlecreek, Michigan and we would like to photograph you beside our model of a time-dredge."

"Pardon?" Anderson said, cupping his ear.

Tozzo repeated what he had said, trying to be audible above the background racket. At last Anderson seemed to understand.

"Oh, um, well, where is it?" Anderson asked obligingly.

"Downstairs on the sidewalk," Gilly said. "It was too heavy to bring up."

"Well, uh, if it won't take too awfully long," Anderson said, "which I doubt it will." He excused himself from the group and followed after them as they started toward the elevator.

"It's steam-engine building time," a heavy-set man called to them as they passed. "Time to build steam engines, Poul."

"We're going downstairs," Tozzo said nervously.

"Walk downstairs on your heads," the pre-cog said. He waved goodbye goodnaturedly, as the elevator came and the three of them entered it.

"Kris is jolly today," Anderson said.

"And how," Gilly said, using one of his phrases.

"Is Bob Heinlein here?" Anderson asked Tozzo as they descended. "I understand he and Mildred Clingerman went off somewhere to talk about cats and nobody has seen them come back."

"That's the way the ball bounces," Gilly said, trying out another twentieth century phrase.

Anderson cupped his ear, smiled hesitantly, but said nothing.

At last, they emerged on the sidewalk. At the sight of their time-dredge, Anderson blinked in astonishment.

"I'll be gosh darned," he said, approaching it. "That's certainly imposing. Sure, I'd, uh, be happy to pose beside it." He drew his lean, angular body erect, smiling that warm, almost tender smile that Tozzo had noticed before. "Uh, how's this?" Anderson inquired, a little timidly.

With an authentic twentieth century camera taken from the Smithsonian, Gilly snapped a picture. "Now inside," he requested, and glanced at Tozzo.

"Why, uh, certainly," Poul Anderson said, and stepped up the stairs and into the dredge. "Gosh, Karen would, uh, like this," he said as he disappeared inside. "I wish to heck she'd come along."

Tozzo followed swiftly. Gilly slammed the hatch shut, and, at the control board, Tozzo, with the instruction manual in hand, punched buttons.

The turbines hummed, but Anderson did not seem to hear them; he was engrossed in staring at the controls, his eyes wide.

"Gosh," he said.

The time-dredge passed back to the present, with Anderson still lost in his scrutiny of the controls.

IV

Fermeti met them. "Mr. Anderson," he said, "this is an incredible honor." He held out his hand, but now Anderson was peering through the open hatch past him, at the city beyond; he did not notice the offered hand.

"Say," Anderson said, his face twitching. "Um, what's, uh, this?"

He was staring at the monorail system primarily, Tozzo decided. And this was odd, because at least in Seattle there had been monorails back in Anderson's time ... or had there been? Had that come later? In any case, Anderson now wore a massively perplexed expression.

"Individual cars," Tozzo said, standing close beside him. "Your monorails had only group cars. Later on, after your time, it was made possible for each citizen's house to have a monorail outlet; the individual brought his car out of its garage and onto the rail-terminal, from which point he joined the collective structure. Do you see?"

But Anderson remained perplexed; his expression in fact had deepened.

"Um," he said, "what do you mean 'my time'? Am I dead?" He looked morose now. "I thought it would be more along the lines of Valhalla, with Vikings and such. Not futuristic."

"You're not dead, Mr. Anderson," Fermeti said. "What you're facing is the culture-syndrome of the mid twenty-first century. I must tell you, sir, that you've been napped. But you will be returned; I give you both my personal and official word."

Anderson's jaw dropped, but he said nothing; he continued to stare.

Donald Nils, notorious murderer, sat at the single table in the reference room of the Emigration Bureau's interstellar speed-of-light ship and computed that he was, in Earth figures, an inch high. Bitterly, he cursed. "It's cruel and unusual punishment," he grated aloud. "It's against the Constitution." And then he remembered that he had volunteered, in order to get out of Nachbaren Slager. That goddam hole, he said to himself. Anyhow, I'm out of there.

And, he said to himself, even if I'm only an inch high I've still made myself captain of this lousy ship, and if it ever gets to Proxima I'll be captain of the entire lousy Proxima System. I didn't study with Gutman himself for nothing. And if that don't beat Nachbaren Slager, I don't know what does ...

His second-in-command, Pete Bailly, stuck his head into the reference room. "Hey, Nils, I have been looking over the micro-repro of this particular old pre-cog journal *Astounding* like you told me, this Venus Equilateral article about matter transmission, and I mean even though I was the top vid repairman in New York City that don't mean I can build one of *these* things." He glared at Nils. "That's asking a lot."

Nils said tightly, "We've got to get back to Earth."

"You're out of luck," Bailly told him. "Better settle for Prox."

Furiously, Nils swept the micro-reproductions from the table, onto the floor of the ship. "That damn Bureau of Emigration! They tricked us!"

Bailly shrugged. "Anyhow we got plenty to eat and a good reference library and 3-D movies every night."

"By the time we get to Prox," Nils snarled, "we'll have seen every movie — " He calculated. "Two thousand times."

"Well, then don't watch. Or we can run them backwards. How's your research coming?"

"I got going the micro of an article in *Space Science Fiction*," Nils said thoughtfully, "called *The Variable Man*. It tells about faster-than-light transmission. You disappear and then reappear. Some guy named Cole is going to perfect it, according to the old-time pre-cog who wrote it." He brooded about that. "If we could build a faster-than-light ship we could return to Earth. We could take over."

"That's crazy talk," Bailly said.

Nils regarded him. "I'm in command."

"Then," Bailly said, "we got a nut in command. There's no returning to Terra; we better build our lives on Proxima's planets and forget forever about our home. Thank God we got women aboard. My God, even if we did get back ... what could one-inch high people accomplish? We'd be jeered at."

"Nobody jeers at me," Nils said quietly.

But he knew Bailly was right. They'd be lucky if they could research the micros of the old pre-cog journals in the ship's reference room and develop for themselves a way of landing safely on Proxima's planets ... even *that* was asking a lot.

We'll succeed, Nils said to himself. As long as everyone obeys me, does exactly as I tell them, with no dumb questions.

Bending, he activated the spool of the December 1962 *If*. There was an article in it that particularly interested him ... and he had four years ahead of him in which to read, understand, and finally apply it.

*   *   *

Fermeti said, "Surely your pre-cog ability helped prepare you for this, Mr. Anderson." His voice faltered with nervous strain, despite his efforts to control it.

"How about taking me back now?" Anderson said. He sounded almost calm.

Fermeti, after shooting a swift glance at Tozzo and Gilly, said to Anderson, "We have a technical problem, you see. That's why we brought you here to our own time-continuum. You see — "

"I think you had better, um, take me back," Anderson broke in. "Karen'll get worried." He craned his neck, peering in all directions. "I knew it would be somewhat on this order," he murmured. His face twitched. "Not too different from what I expected ... what's that tall thing over there? Looks like what the old blimps used to catch onto."

"That," Tozzo said, "is a prayer tower."

"Our problem," Fermeti said patiently, "is dealt with in your article *Night Flight* in the August 1955 *If*. We've been able to deprive an interstellar vehicle of its mass, but so far restoration of mass has — "

"Uh, oh, yes," Anderson said, in a preoccupied way. "I'm working on that yarn right now. Should have that off to Scott in another couple of weeks." He explained, "My agent."

Fermeti considered a moment and then said, "Can you give us the formula for mass-restoration, Mr. Anderson?"

"Um," Poul Anderson said slowly, "Yes, I guess that would be the correct term. Mass-restoration ... I could go along with that." He nodded. "I haven't worked out any formula; I didn't want to make the yarn too technical. I guess I could make one up, if that's what they wanted." He was silent, then, apparently having withdrawn into a world of his own; the three men waited, but Anderson said nothing more.

"Your pre-cog ability," Fermeti said.

"Pardon?" Anderson said, cupping his ear. "Pre-cog?" He smiled shyly. "Oh, uh, I wouldn't go so far as to say that. I know John believes in all that, but I can't say as I consider a few experiments at Duke University as proof."

Fermeti stared at Anderson a long time. "Take the first article in the January 1953 *Galaxy*," he said quietly. "*The Defenders* ... about the people living beneath the surface and the robots up above, pretending to fight the war but actually not, actually faking the reports so interestingly that the people — "

"I read that," Poul Anderson agreed. "Very good, I thought, except for the ending. I didn't care too much for the ending."

Fermeti said, "You understand, don't you, that those exact conditions came to pass in 1996, during World War Three? That by means of the article we were able to penetrate the deception carried on by our surface robots? That virtually every word of that article was exactly prophetic — "

"Phil Dick wrote that," Anderson said. "*The Defenders*."

"Do you know him?" Tozzo inquired.

"Met him yesterday at the Convention," Anderson said. "For the first time. Very nervous fellow, was almost afraid to come in."

Fermeti said, "Am I to understand that *none of you are aware that you are pre-cogs?*" His voice shook, completely out of control now.

"Well," Anderson said slowly, "some sf writers believe in it. I think Alf Van Vogt does." He smiled at Fermeti.

"But don't you understand?" Fermeti demanded. "You described *us* in an article — you accurately described our Bureau and its interstellar Project!"

After a pause, Anderson murmured, "Gosh, I'll be darned. No, I didn't know that. Um, thanks a lot for telling me."

Turning to Tozzo, Fermeti said, "Obviously we'll have to recast our entire concept of the mid twentieth century." He looked weary.

Tozzo said, "For our purposes their ignorance doesn't matter. Because the pre-cognitive ability was there anyhow, whether they recognized it or not." That, to him, was perfectly clear.

Anderson, meanwhile, had wandered off a little and stood now inspecting the display window of a nearby gift store. "Interesting bric-a-brac in there. I ought to pick up something for Karen while I'm here. Would it be all right — " He turned questioningly to Fermeti. "Could I step in there for a moment and look around?"

"Yes, yes," Fermeti said irritably.

Poul Anderson disappeared inside the gift shop, leaving the three of them to argue the meaning of their discovery.

"What we've got to do," Fermeti said, "is sit him down in the situation familiar to him: *before a typewriter*. We must persuade him to compose an article on deprivation of mass and its subsequent restoration. Whether he himself takes the article to be factual or not has no bearing; it still will be. The Smithsonian must have a workable twentieth century typewriter and 8½ by 11 white sheets of paper. Do you agree?"

Tozzo, meditating, said, "I'll tell you what I think. It was a cardinal error to permit him to go into that gift shop."

"Why is that?" Fermeti said.

"I see his point," Gilly said excitedly. "We'll never see Anderson again; he's skipped out on us through the pretext of gift-shopping for his wife."

Ashen-faced, Fermeti turned and raced into the gift ship. Tozzo and Gilly followed.

The store was empty. Anderson had eluded them; he was gone.

As he loped silently out the back door of the gift shop, Poul Anderson thought to himself, I don't believe they'll get me. At least not right away.

I've got too much to do while I'm here, he realized. What an opportunity! When I'm an old man I can tell Astrid's children about this.

Thinking of his daughter Astrid reminded him of one very simple fact, however. Eventually he had to go back to 1954. Because of Karen and the baby. No matter what he found here — for him it was temporary.

But meanwhile ... first I'll go to the library, *any* library, he decided. And get a good look at history books that'll tell me what took place in the intervening years between 1954 and now.

I'd like to know, he said to himself, about the Cold War, how the U.S. and Russia came out. And — space explorations. I'll bet they put a man on Luna by 1975. Certainly, they're exploring space now; heck, they even have a time-dredge so they must have *that*.

Ahead Poul Anderson saw a doorway. It was open and without hesitation he plunged into it. Another shop of some kind, but this one larger than the gift shop.

"Yes sir," a voice said, and a bald-headed man — they all seemed to be bald-headed here — approached him. The man glanced at Anderson's hair, his clothes ... however the clerk was polite; he made no comment. "May I help you?" he asked.

"Um," Anderson said, stalling. What did this place sell, anyhow? He glanced around. Gleaming electronic objects of some sort. But what did they do?

The clerk said, "Haven't you been nuzzled lately, sir?"

"What's that?" Anderson said. *Nuzzled?*

"The new spring nuzzlers have arrived, you know," the clerk said, moving toward the gleaming spherical machine nearest him. "Yes," he said to Poul, "you do strike me as very, very faintly introve — no offense meant, sir, I mean, it's legal to be introved." The clerk chuckled. "For instance, your rather odd clothing ... made it yourself, I take it? I must say, sir, to make your own clothing is highly introve. Did you weave it?" The clerk grimaced as if tasting something bad.

"No," Poul said, "as a matter of fact it's my best suit."

"Heh, heh," the clerk said. "I share the joke, sir; quite witty. But what about your head? You haven't shaved your head in *weeks*."

"Nope," Anderson admitted. "Well, maybe I do need a nuzzler." Evidently everyone in this century had one; like a TV set in his own time, it was a necessity, in order for one to be part of the culture.

"How many in your family?" the clerk said. Bringing out a measuring tape, he measured the length of Poul's sleeve.

"Three," Poul answered, baffled.

"How old is the youngest?"

"Just born," Poul said.

The clerk's face lost all its color. "Get out of here," he said quietly. "Before I call for the polpol."

"Um, what's that? Pardon?" Poul said, cupping his ear and trying to hear, not certain he had understood.

"You're a criminal," the clerk mumbled. "You ought to be in Nachbaren Slager."

"Well, thanks anyhow," Poul said, and backed out of the store, onto the sidewalk; his last glimpse was of the clerk still staring at him.

"Are you a foreigner?" a voice asked, a woman's voice. At the curb she had halted her vehicle. It looked to Poul like a bed; in fact, he realized, it was a bed. The woman regarded him with astute calm, her eyes dark and intense. Although her glistening shaved head somewhat upset him, he could see that she was attractive.

"I'm from another culture," Poul said, finding himself unable to keep his eyes from her figure. Did all the women dress like this here in this society? Bare shoulders, he could understand. But not —

And the bed. The combination of the two was too much for him. What kind of business was she in, anyhow? And in public. What a society this was ... morals had changed since his own time.

"I'm looking for the library," Poul said, not coming too close to the vehicle which was a bed with motor and wheels, a tiller for steering.

The woman said, "The library is one bight from here."

"Um," Poul said, "what's a 'bight'?"

"Obviously, you're wanging me," the woman said. All visible parts of her flushed a dark red. "It's not funny. Any more than your disgustingly hairy head is. Really, both your wanging and your head are not amusing, at least not to me." And yet she did not go on; she remained where she was, regarding him somberly. "Perhaps you need help," she decided. "Perhaps I should pity you. You know of course that the polpol could pick you up any time they want."

Poul said, "Could I, um, buy you a cup of coffee somewhere and we could talk? I'm really anxious to find the library."

"I'll go with you," the woman agreed. "Although I have no idea what 'coffee' is. If you touch me I'll nilp at once."

"Don't do that," Poul said, "it's unnecessary; all I want to do is look up some historical material." And then it occurred to him that he could make good use of any technical data he could get his hands on.

What one volume might he smuggle back to 1954 which would be of great value? He racked his brains. An almanac. A dictionary ... a school text on science which surveyed all the fields for laymen; yes, that would do it. A seventh grade text or a high school text. He could rip the covers off, throw them away, put the pages inside his coat.

Poul said, "Where's a school? The closest school." He felt the urgency of it, now. He had no doubt that they were after him, close behind.

"What is a 'school'?" the woman asked.

"Where your children go," Poul said.

The woman said quietly, "You poor sick man."

V

For a time Tozzo and Fermeti and Gilly stood in silence. And then Tozzo said in a carefully controlled voice, "You know what's going to happen to him, of course. Polpol will pick him up and mono-express him to Nachbaren Slager. Because of his appearance. He may even be there already."

Fermeti sprinted at once for the nearest vidphone. "I'm going to contact the authorities at Nachbaren Slager. I'll talk to Potter; we can trust him, I think."

Presently Major Potter's heavy, dark features formed on the vidscreen. "Oh, hello, Fermeti. You want more convicts, do you?" He chuckled. "You use them up even faster than we do."

Behind Potter, Fermeti caught a glimpse of the open recreation area of the giant internment camp. Criminals, both political and nonpol, could be seen roaming about, stretching their legs, some of them playing dull, pointless games which, he knew, went on and on, sometimes for months, each time they were out of their work-cells.

"What we want," Fermeti said, "is to prevent an individual being brought to you at all." He described Poul Anderson. "If he's monoed there, call me at once. And don't harm him. You understand? We want him back safe."

"Sure," Potter said easily. "Just a minute; I'll have a scan put on our new admissions." He touched a button to his right and a 315-R computer came on; Fermeti heard its low hum. Potter touched buttons and then said, "This'll pick him out if he's monoed here. Our admissions-circuit is prepared to reject him."

"No sign yet?" Fermeti asked tensely.

"Nope," Potter said, and purposefully yawned.

Fermeti broke the connection.

"Now what?" Tozzo said. "We could possibly trace him by means of a Ganymedean sniffer-sponge." They were a repellent life form, though; if one managed to find its quarry it fastened at once to its blood system leech-wise. "Or do it mechanically," he added. "With a detec beam. We have a print of Anderson's EEG pattern, don't we? But that would really bring in the polpol." The detec beam by law belonged only to the polpol; after all, it was the artifact which had, at last, tracked down Gutman himself.

Fermeti said bluntly, "I'm for broadcasting a planet-wide Type II alert.

That'll activate the citizenry, the average informer. They'll know there's an automatic reward for any Type II found."

"But he could be manhandled that way," Gilly pointed out. "By a mob. Let's think this through."

After a pause Tozzo said, "How about trying it from a purely cerebral standpoint? If you had been transported from the mid twentieth century to our continuum, what would you want to do? *Where would you go?*"

Quietly, Fermeti said, "To the nearest spaceport, of course. To buy a ticket to Mars or the outplanets — routine in our age but utterly out of the question at mid twentieth century."

They looked at one another.

"But Anderson doesn't know where the spaceport is," Gilly said. "It'll take him valuable time to orient himself. We can go there directly by express subsurface mono."

A moment later the three Bureau of Emigration men were on their way.

"A fascinating situation," Gilly said, as they rode along, jiggling up and down, facing one another in the monorail first-class compartment. "We totally misjudged the mid twentieth century mind; it should be a lesson to us. Once we've regained possession of Anderson we should make further inquiries. For instance, the Poltergeist Effect. What was their interpretation of it? And table-tapping — did they recognize it for what it was? Or did they merely consign it to the realm of the so-called 'occult' and let it go at that?"

"Anderson may hold the clue to these questions and many others," Fermeti said. "But our central problem remains the same. We must induce him to complete the mass-restoration formula in precise mathematical terms, rather than vague, poetic allusions."

Thoughtfully, Tozzo said, "He's a brilliant man, that Anderson. Look at the ease by which he eluded us."

"Yes," Fermeti agreed. "We mustn't underestimate him. We did that, and it's rebounded." His face was grim.

Hurrying up the almost-deserted sidestreet, Poul Anderson wondered why the woman had regarded him as sick. And the mention of children had set off the clerk in the store, too. Was birth illegal now? Or was it regarded as sex had been once, as something too private to speak of in public?

In any case, he realized, if I plan to stay here I've got to shave my head. And, if possible, acquire different clothing.

There must be barbershops. And, he thought, the coins in my pockets; they're probably worth a lot to collectors.

He glanced about, hopefully. But all he saw were tall, luminous plastic and metal buildings which made up the city, structures in which incomprehensible transactions took place. They were as alien to him as —

Alien, he thought, and the word lodged chokingly in his mind. Because —

something had oozed from a doorway ahead of him. And now his way was blocked — deliberately, it seemed — by a slime mold, dark yellow in color, as large as a human being, palpitating visibly on the sidewalk. After a pause the slime mold undulated toward at him at a regular, slow rate. A human evolutionary development? Poul Anderson wondered, recoiling from it. Good Lord ... and then he realized what he was seeing.

This era had space travel. He was seeing a creature from another planet.

"Um," Poul said, to the enormous mass of slime mold, "can I bother you a second to ask a question?"

The slime mold ceased to undulate forward. And in Poul's brain a thought formed which was not his own. "I catch your query. In answer: I arrived yesterday from Callisto. But I also catch a number of unusual and highly interesting thoughts in addition ... you are a time traveler from the past." The tone of the creature's emanations was one of considerate, polite amusement — and interest.

"Yes," Poul said. "From 1954."

"And you wish to find a barbershop, a library and a school. All at once, in the precious time remaining before they capture you." The slime mold seemed solicitous. "What can I do to help you? I could absorb you, but it would be a permanent symbiosis, and you would not like that. You are thinking of your wife and child. Allow me to inform you as to the problem regarding your unfortunate mention of children. Terrans of this period are experiencing a mandatory moratorium on childbirth, because of the almost infinite sporting of the previous decades. There was a war, you see. Between Gutman's fanatical followers and the more liberal legions of General McKinley. The latter won."

Poul said, "Where should I go? I'm confused." His head throbbed and he felt tired. Too much had happened. Just a short while ago he had been standing with Tony Boucher in the Sir Francis Drake Hotel, drinking and chatting ... and now this. Facing this great slime mold from Callisto. It was difficult — to say the least — to make such an adjustment.

The slime mold was transmitting to him. "I am accepted here while you, their ancestor, are regarded as odd. Ironic. To me, you look quite like them, except for your curly brown hair and of course your silly clothing." The creature from Callisto pondered. "My friend, the polpol are the political police, and they search for deviants, followers of the defeated Gutman, who are terrorists now, and hated. Many of these followers are drawn from the potentially criminal classes. That is, the non-conformists, the so-called introves. Individuals who set their own subjective value-system up in place of the objective system in vogue. It is a matter of life and death to the Terrans, since Gutman almost won."

"I'm going to hide," Poul decided.

"But where? You can't really. Not unless you wish to go underground and join the Gutmanites, the criminal class of bomb-throwers ... and you won't want to do that. Let us stroll together, and if anyone challenges you, I will say you're my servant. You have manual extensors and I have not. And I have, by a quirk, decided to dress you oddly and to have you retain your head-hair. The responsibility then becomes mine. It is actually not unusual for higher out-world organisms to employ Terran help."

"Thanks," Poul said tautly, as the slime mold resumed its slow forward motion along the sidewalk. "But there are things I want to do — "

"I am on my way to the zoo," the slime mold continued.

An unkind thought came to Poul.

"Please," the slime mold said. "Your anachronistic twentieth century humor is not appreciated. I am not an inhabitant of the zoo; it is for life forms of low mental order such as Martian glebs and trawns. Since the initiation of interplanetary travel, zoos have become the center of — "

Poul said, "Could you lead me to the space terminal?" He tried to make his request sound casual.

"You take a dreadful risk," the slime mold said, "in going to any public place. The polpol watch constantly."

"I still want to go." If he could board an interplanetary ship, if he could leave Earth, see other worlds —

But they would erase his memory; all at once he realized that, in a rush of horror. *I've got to make notes*, he told himself. At once!

"Do, um, you have a pencil?" he asked the slime mold. "Oh, wait; I have one. Pardon me." Obviously the slime mold didn't.

On a piece of paper from his coat pocket — it was convention material of some sort — he wrote hurriedly, in brief, disjointed phrases, what had happened to him, what he had seen in the twenty-first century. Then he quickly stuck the paper back in his pocket.

"A wise move," the slime mold said. "And now to the spaceport, if you will accompany me at my slow pace. And, as we go, I will give you details of Terra's history from your period on." The slime mold moved down the sidewalk. Poul accompanied it eagerly; after all, what choice did he have? "The Soviet Union. That was tragic. Their war with Red China in 1983 which finally involved Israel and France ... regrettable, but it did solve the problem of what to do with France — a most difficult nation to deal with in the latter half of the twentieth century."

On his piece of paper Poul jotted that down, too.

"After France had been defeated — " The slime mold went on, as Poul scratched against time.

Fermeti said, "We must glin, if we're to catch Anderson before he boards a ship." And by "glin" he did not mean glinning a little; he meant a full search with the cooperation of the polpol. He hated to bring them in, and yet their help now seemed vital. Too much time had passed and Anderson had not yet been found.

The spaceport lay ahead, a great disk miles in diameter, with no vertical obstructions. In the center was the Burned Spot, seared by years of tail-exhausts from landing and departing ships. Fermeti liked the spaceport, because here the denseness of the close-packed buildings of the city abruptly ceased. Here was *openness*, such as he recalled from childhood ... if one dared to think openly of childhood.

The terminal building was set hundreds of feet beneath the rexeroid layer built to protect the waiting people in case of an accident above. Fermeti reached the entrance of the descent ramp, then halted impatiently to wait for Tozzo and Gilly to catch up with him.

"I'll nilp," Tozzo said, but without enthusiasm. And he broke the band on his wrist with a single decisive motion.

The polpol ship hovered overhead at once.

"We're from the Emigration Bureau," Fermeti explained to the polpol lieutenant. He outlined their Project, described — reluctantly — their bringing Poul Anderson from his time-period to their own.

"Hair on head," the polpol lieutenant nodded. "Quaint duds. Okay, Mr. Fermeti; we'll glin until we find him." He nodded, and his small ship shot off.

"They're efficient," Tozzo admitted.

"But not likeable," Fermeti said, finishing Tozzo's thought.

"They make me uncomfortable," Tozzo agreed. "But I suppose they're supposed to."

The three of them stepped onto the descent ramp — and dropped at breathtaking speed to level one below. Fermeti shut his eyes, wincing at the loss of weight. It was almost as bad as takeoff itself. Why did everything have to be so rapid, these days? It certainly was not like the previous decade, when things had gone leisurely.

They stepped from the ramp, shook themselves, and were approached instantly by the building's polpol chief.

"We have a report on your man," the gray-uniformed officer told them.

"He hasn't taken off?" Fermeti said. "Thank God." He looked around.

"Over there," the officer said, pointing.

At a magazine rack, Poul Anderson was looking intently at the display.

It took only a moment for the three Emigration Bureau officials to surround him.

"Oh, uh, hello," Anderson said. "While I was waiting for my ship I thought I'd take a look and see what's still in print."

Fermeti said, "Anderson, we require your unique abilities. I'm sorry, but we're taking you back to the Bureau."

All at once Anderson was gone. Soundlessly, he had ducked away; they saw his tall, angular form become smaller as he raced for the gate to the field proper.

Reluctantly, Fermeti reached within his coat and brought out a sleep-gun. "There's no other choice," he murmured, and squeezed.

The racing figure tumbled, rolled. Fermeti put the sleep-gun away and in a toneless voice said, "He'll recover. A skinned knee, nothing worse." He glanced at Gilly and Tozzo. "Recover at the Bureau, I mean."

Together, the three of them advanced toward the prone figure on the floor of the spaceport waiting room.

"You may return to your own time-continuum," Fermeti said quietly, "when you've given us the mass-restoration formula." He nodded, and a Bureau workman approached, carrying the ancient Royal typewriter.

Seated in the chair across from Fermeti in the Bureau's inner business office, Poul Anderson said, "I don't use a portable."

"You must cooperate," Fermeti informed him. "We have the scientific know-how to restore you to Karen; remember Karen and remember your newly-born daughter at the Congress in San Francisco's Sir Francis Drake Hotel. Without full cooperation from you, Anderson, there will be no cooperation from the Bureau. Surely, with your pre-cog ability you can see that."

After a pause Anderson said, "Um, I can't work unless I have a pot of fresh coffee brewing around me at all times, somewhere."

Curtly, Fermeti signaled. "We'll obtain coffee beans for you," he declared. "But the brewing is up to you. We'll also supply a pot from the Smithsonian collection and there our responsibility ends."

Taking hold of the carriage of the typewriter, Anderson began to inspect it. "Red and black ribbon," he said. "I always use black. But I guess I can make do." He seemed a trifle sullen. Inserting a sheet of paper, he began to type. At the top of the page appeared the words:
NIGHT FLIGHT
— Poul Anderson
"You say *If* bought it?" he asked Fermeti.
"Yes," Fermeti replied tensely.
Anderson typed:

Difficulties at Outward, Incorporated had begun to nettle Edmond Fletcher. For one thing, an entire ship had disappeared, and although the individuals aboard were not personally known to him he felt a twinge of responsibility. Now, as he lathered himself with hormone-impregnated soap

"He starts at the beginning," Fermeti said bitingly. "Well, if there's no alternative we'll simply have to bear with him." Musingly, he murmured, "I wonder how long it takes ... I wonder how fast he writes. As a pre-cog he can see what's coming next; it should help him to do it in a hurry." Or was that just wishful thinking?

"Have the coffee beans arrived yet?" Anderson asked, glancing up.

"Any time now," Fermeti said.

"I hope some of the beans are Colombian," Anderson said.

Long before the beans arrived the article was done.

Rising stiffly, uncoiling his lengthy limbs, Poul Anderson said, "I think you have what you want, there. The mass restoration formula is on typescript page 20."

Eagerly, Fermeti turned the pages. Yes, there it was; peering over his shoulder, Tozzo saw the paragraph:

If the ship followed a trajectory which would carry it into the star Proxima, it would, he realized, regain its mass through a process of leeching solar energy from the great star-furnace itself. Yes, it was Proxima itself which held the key to Torelli's problem, and now, after all this time, it had been solved. The simple formula revolved in his brain.

And, Tozzo saw, there lay the formula. As the article said, the mass would be regained from solar energy converted into matter, the ultimate source of power in the universe. The answer had stared them in the face all this time!

Their long struggle was over.

"And now," Poul Anderson said, "I'm free to go back to my own time?"

Fermeti said simply, "Yes."

"Wait," Tozzo said to his superior. "There's evidently something you don't understand." It was a section which he had read in the instruction manual attached to the time-dredge. He drew Fermeti to one side, where Anderson could not hear. "He can't be sent back to his own time with the knowledge he has now."

"What knowledge?" Fermeti inquired.

"That — well, I'm not certain. Something to do with our society, here. What I'm trying to tell you is this: the first rule of time travel, according to the manual, is don't change the past. In this situation just bringing Anderson here has changed the past merely by exposing him to our society."

Pondering, Fermeti said, "You may be correct. While he was in that gift shop he may have picked up some object which, taken back to his own time, might revolutionize their technology."

"Or at the magazine rack at the spaceport," Tozzo said. "Or on his trip between those two points. And — *even the knowledge that he and his colleagues are pre-cogs.*"

"You're right," Fermeti said. "The memory of this trip must be wiped from his brain." He turned and walked slowly back to Poul Anderson. "Look here," he addressed him. "I'm sorry to tell you this, but everything that's happened to you must be wiped from your brain."

After a pause, Anderson said, "That's a shame. Sorry to hear that." He looked downcast. "But I'm not surprised," he murmured. He seemed philosophical about the whole affair. "It's generally handled this way."

Tozzo asked, "Where can this alteration of the memory cells of his brain be accomplished?"

"At the Department of Penology," Fermeti said. "Through the same channels we obtained the convicts." Pointing his sleep-gun at Poul Anderson he said, "Come along with us. I regret this ... but it has to be done."

VI

At the Department of Penology, painless electroshock removed from Poul Anderson's brain the precise cells in which his most recent memories were stored. Then, in a semi-conscious state, he was carried back into the time-dredge. A moment later he was on his trip back to the year 1954, to his own society and time. To the Sir Francis Drake Hotel in downtown San Francisco, California and his waiting wife and child.

When the time-dredge returned empty, Tozzo, Gilly and Fermeti breathed a sigh of relief and broke open a bottle of hundred-year-old Scotch which Fermeti had been saving. The mission had been successfully accomplished; now they could turn their attention back to the Project.

"Where's the manuscript that he wrote?" Fermeti said, putting down his glass to look all around his office.

There was no manuscript to be found. And, Tozzo noticed, the antique Royal typewriter which they had brought from the Smithsonian — it was gone, too. But why?

Suddenly chill fear traveled up him. He understood.

"Good Lord," he said thickly. He put down his glass. "Somebody get a copy of the journal with his article in it. At once."

Fermeti said, "What is it, Aaron? Explain."

"When we removed his memory of what had happened we made it impossible for him to write the article for the journal," Tozzo said. "He must have based *Night Flight* on his experience with us, here." Snatching up the August 1955 copy of *If* he turned to the table-of-contents page.

No article by Poul Anderson was listed. Instead, on page 78, he saw Philip K. Dick's *The Mold of Yancy* listed instead.

They had changed the past after all. And now the formula for their Project was gone — gone entirely.

"We shouldn't have tampered," Tozzo said in a hoarse voice. "We should never have brought him out of the past." He drank a little more of the century-old Scotch, his hands shaking.

"Brought who?" Gilly said, with a puzzled look.

"Don't you remember?" Tozzo stared at him, incredulous.

"What's this discussion about?" Fermeti said impatiently. "And what are you two doing in my office? You both should be busy at work." He saw the bottle of Scotch and blanched. "How'd that get open?"

His hands trembling, Tozzo turned the pages of the journal over and over again. Already, the memory was growing diffuse in his mind; he struggled in vain to hold onto it. They had brought someone from the past, a pre-cog, wasn't it? But who? A name, still in his mind but dimming with each passing moment ... Anderson or Anderton, something like that. And in connection with the Bureau's interstellar mass-deprivation Project.

Or was it?

Puzzled, Tozzo shook his head and said in bewilderment, "I have some peculiar words in my mind. *Night Flight*. Do either of you happen to know what it refers to?"

"*Night Flight*," Fermeti echoed. "No, it means nothing to me. I wonder, though — it certainly would be an effective name for our Project."

"Yes," Gilly agreed. "That must be what it refers to."

"But our Project is called *Waterspider*, isn't it?" Tozzo said. At least he thought it was. He blinked, trying to focus his faculties.

"The truth of the matter, " Fermeti said, "is that we've never titled it." Brusquely, he added, "But I agree with you; that's an even better name for it. *Waterspider*. Yes, I like that."

The door of the office opened and there stood a uniformed, bonded messenger. "From the Smithsonian," he informed them. "You requested this." He produced a parcel, which he laid on Fermeti's desk.

"I don't remember ordering anything from the Smithsonian," Fermeti said. Opening it cautiously he found a can of roasted, ground coffee beans, still vacuum packed, over a century old.

The three men looked at one another blankly.

"Strange," Torelli murmured. "There must be some mistake."

"Well," Fletcher said, "in any case, back to Project *Waterspider*."

Nodding, Torelli and Gilman turned in the direction of their own office on the first floor of Outward, Incorporated, the commercial firm at which they has worked and the project on which they had labored, with so many heartaches and setbacks, for so long.

At the Science Fiction Convention at the Sir Francis Drake Hotel, Poul Anderson looked around him in bewilderment. Where had he been? Why had he gone out of the building? And it was an hour later; Tony Boucher and Jim

Gunn had left for dinner by now, and he saw no sign of his wife Karen and the baby, either.

The last he remembered was two fans from Battlecreek who wanted him to look at a display outside on the sidewalk. Perhaps he had gone to see that. In any case, he had no memory of the interval.

Anderson groped about in his coat pocket for his pipe, hoping to calm his oddly jittery nerves — and found, not his pipe, but instead a folded piece of paper.

"Got anything for our auction, Poul?" a member of the Convention committee asked, halting beside him. "The auction is just about to start — we have to hurry."

Still looking at the paper from his pocket, Poul murmured, "Um, you mean something here with me?"

"Like a typescript of some published story, the original manuscript or earlier versions or notes. You know." He paused, waiting.

"I seem to have some notes in my pocket," Poul said, still glancing over them. They were in his handwriting but he didn't remember having made them. A time-travel story, from the look of them. Must have been from those Bourbons and water, he decided, and not enough to eat. "Here," he said uncertainly, "it isn't much but I guess you can auction these." He took one final glance at them. "Notes for a story about a political figure called Gutman and a kidnapping in time. Intelligent slime mold, too, I notice." On impulse, he handed them over.

"Thanks," the man said, and hurried on toward the other room, where the auction was being held.

"I bid ten dollars," Howard Browne called, smiling broadly. "Then I have to catch a bus to the airport." The door closed after him.

Karen, with Astrid, appeared beside Poul. "Want to go into the auction?" she asked her husband. "Buy an original Finlay?"

"Um, sure," Poul Anderson said, and with his wife and child walked slowly after Howard Browne.

WHAT THE DEAD MEN SAY

I

THE BODY of Louis Sarapis, in a transparent plastic shatterproof case, had lain on display for one week, exciting a continual response from the public. Distended lines filed past with the customary sniffling, pinched faces, distraught elderly ladies in black cloth coats.

In a corner of the large auditorium in which the casket reposed, Johnny Barefoot impatiently waited for his chance at Sarapis's body. But he did not intend merely to view it; his job, detailed in Sarapis's will, lay in another direction entirely. As Sarapis's public relations manager, his job was — simply — to bring Louis Sarapis back to life.

"Keerum," Barefoot murmured to himself, examining his wristwatch and discovering that two more hours had to pass before the auditorium doors could be finally closed. He felt hungry. And the chill, issuing from the quick-pack envelope surrounding the casket, had increased his discomfort minute by minute.

His wife Sarah Belle approached him, then, with a thermos of hot coffee. "Here, Johnny." She reached up and brushed the black, shiny Chiricahua hair back from his forehead. "You don't look so good."

"No," he agreed. "This is too much for me. I didn't care for him much when he was alive — I certainly don't like him any better this way." He jerked his head at the casket and the double line of mourners.

Sarah Belle said softly, "Nil nisi bonum."

He glowered at her, not sure of what she had said. Some foreign language, no doubt. Sarah Belle had a college degree.

"To quote Thumper Rabbit," Sarah Belle said, smiling gently, " 'if you

245

can't say nothing good, don't say nothing at all.' " She added, "From *Bambi*, an old film classic. If you attended the lectures at the Museum of Modern Art with me every Monday night — "

"Listen," Johnny Barefoot said desperately, "I don't want to bring the old crook back to life, Sarah Belle; how'd I get myself into this? I thought sure when the embolism dropped him like a cement block it meant I could kiss the whole business goodbye forever." But it hadn't quite worked out that way.

"Unplug him," Sarah Belle said.

"W-what?"

She laughed. "Are you afraid to? Unplug the quick-pack power source and he'll warm up. And no resurrection, right?" Her blue-gray eyes danced with amusement. "Scared of him, I guess. Poor Johnny." She patted him on the arm. "I should divorce you, but I won't; you need a mama to take care of you."

"It's wrong," he said. "Louis is completely helpless, lying there in the casket. It would be — unmanly to unplug him."

Sarah Belle said quietly, "But someday, sooner or later, you'll have to confront him, Johnny. And when he's in half-life you'll have the advantage. So it will be a good time; you might come out of it intact." Turning, she trotted off, hands thrust deep in her coat pockets because of the chill.

Gloomily, Johnny lit a cigarette and leaned against the wall behind him. His wife was right, of course. A half-lifer was no match, in direct physical tête-à-tête, for a living person. And yet — he still shrank from it, because ever since childhood he had been in awe of Louis, who had dominated 3-4 shipping, the Earth to Mars commercial routes, as if he were a model rocket-ship enthusiast pushing miniatures over a paper-mâché board in his basement. And now, at his death, at seventy years of age, the old man through Wilhelmina Securities controlled a hundred related — and non-related — industries on both planets. His net worth could not be calculated, even for tax purposes; it was not wise, in fact, to try, even for Government tax experts.

It's my kids, Johnny thought; *I'm thinking about them, in school back in Oklahoma.* To tangle with old Louis would be okay if he wasn't a family man ... nothing meant more to him than the two little girls and of course Sarah Belle, too. *I got to think of them, not myself*, he told himself now as he waited for the opportunity to remove the body from the casket in accordance with the old man's detailed instructions. *Let's see. He's probably got about a year in total half-life time, and he'll want it divided up strategically, like at the end of each fiscal year. He'll probably proportion it out over two decades, a month here and there, then towards the end as he runs out, maybe just a week. And then — days.*

And finally old Louis would be down to a couple of hours; the signal would be weak, the dim spark of electrical activity hovering in the frozen brain cells ... it would flicker, the words from the amplifying equipment would fade, grow indistinct. And then — silence, at last the grave. But that might be twenty-five years from now; it would be the year 2100 before the old man's cephalic processes ceased entirely.

Johnny Barefoot, smoking his cigarette rapidly, thought back to the day he had slouched anxiously about the personnel office of Archimedean Enterprises, mumbling to the girl at the desk that he wanted a job; he had some brilliant ideas that were for sale, ideas that would help untangle the knot of strikes, the spaceport violence growing out of jurisdictional overlapping by rival unions — ideas that would, in essence, free Sarapis of having to rely on union labor at all. It was a dirty scheme, and he had known it then, but he had been right; it was worth money. The girl had sent him on to Mr. Pershing, the Personnel Manager, and Pershing had sent him to Louis Sarapis.

"You mean," Sarapis had said, "I launch from the *ocean?* From the Atlantic, out past the three mile limit?"

"A union is a national organization," Johnny had said. "Neither outfit has a jurisdiction on the high seas. But a business organization is international."

"I'd need men out there; I'd need the same number, even more. Where'll I get them?"

"Go to Burma or India or the Malay States," Johnny had said. "Get young unskilled laborers and bring them over. Train them yourself on an indentured servant basis. In other words, charge the cost of their passage against their earnings." It was peonage, he knew. And it appealed to Louis Sarapis. A little empire on the high seas, worked by men who had no legal rights. Ideal.

Sarapis had done just that and hired Johnny for his public relations department; that was the best place for a man who had brilliant ideas of a non-technical nature. In other words, an uneducated man: a *noncol.* A useless misfit, an outsider. A loner lacking college degrees.

"Hey Johnny," Sarapis had said once. "How come since you're so bright you never went to school? Everyone knows that's fatal, nowadays. Self-destructive impulse, maybe?" He had grinned, showing his stainless-steel teeth.

Moodily, he had replied, "You've got it, Louis. I want to die. I hate myself." At that point he had recalled his peonage idea. But that had come after he had dropped out of school, so it couldn't have been that. "Maybe I should see an analyst," he had said.

"Fakes," Louis had told him. "All of them — I know because I've had six on my staff, working for me exclusively at one time or another. What's wrong with you is you're an envious type; if you can't have it big you don't want it, you don't want the climb, the long struggle."

But I've got it big, Johnny Barefoot realized, had realized even then. *This is big, working for you. Everyone wants to work for Louis Sarapis; he gives all sorts of people jobs.*

The double lines of mourners that filed past the casket ... he wondered if all these people could be employees of Sarapis or relatives of employees.

Either that or people who had benefited from the public dole that Sarapis had pushed through Congress and into law during the depression three years ago. Sarapis, in his old age the great daddy for the poor, the hungry, the out of work. Soup kitchens, with lines there, too. Just as now.

Perhaps the same people had been in those lines who were here today.

Startling Johnny, an auditorium guard nudged him. "Say, aren't you Mr. Barefoot, the P.R. man for old Louis?"

"Yes," Johnny said. He put out his cigarette and then began to unscrew the lid of the thermos of coffee which Sarah Belle had brought him. "Have some," he said. "Or maybe you're used to the cold in these civic halls." The City of Chicago had lent this spot for Louis to lie in state; it was gratitude for what he had done here in this area. The factories he had opened, the men he had put on the payroll.

"I'm not used," the guard said, accepting a cup of coffee. "You know, Mr. Barefoot, I've always admired you because you're a noncol, and look how you rose to a top job and lots of salary, not to mention fame. It's an inspiration to us other noncols."

Grunting, Johnny sipped his own coffee.

"Of course," the guard said, "I guess it's really Sarapis we ought to thank; he gave you the job. My brother-in-law worked for him; that was back five years ago when nobody in the world was hiring except Sarapis. You hear what an old skinflint he was — wouldn't permit the unions to come in, and all. But he gave so many old folks pensions ... my father was living on a Sarapis pension-plan until the day he died. And all those bills he got through Congress; they wouldn't have passed any of the welfare for the needy bills without pressure from Sarapis."

Johnny grunted.

"No wonder there're so many people here today," the guard said. "I can see why. Who's going to help the little fellow, the noncols like you and me, now that he's gone?"

Johnny had no answer, for himself or for the guard.

As owner of the Beloved Brethren Mortuary, Herbert Schoenheit von Vogelsang found himself required by law to consult with the late Mr. Sarapis's legal counsel, the well-known Mr. Claude St. Cyr. In this connection it was essential for him to know precisely how the half-life periods were to be proportioned out; it was his job to execute the technical arrangements.

The matter should have been routine, and yet a snag developed almost at once. He was unable to get in touch with Mr. St. Cyr, trustee for the estate.

Drat, Schoenheit von Vogelsang thought to himself as he hung up the unresponsive phone. *Something must be wrong; this is unheard of in connection with a man so important.*

He had phoned from the bin — the storage vaults in which the half-lifers were kept in perpetual quick-pack. At this moment, a worried-looking clerical sort of individual waited at the desk with a claim check stub in his hand. Obviously he had shown up to collect a relative. Resurrection Day — the holiday on which the half-lifers were publicly honored — was just around the corner; the rush would soon be beginning.

"Yes sir," Herb said to him, with an affable smile. "I'll take your stub personally."

"It's an elderly lady," the customer said. "About eighty, very small and wizened. I didn't want just to talk to her; I wanted to take her out for a while." He explained, "My grandmother."

"Only a moment," Herb said, and went back into the bin to search out number 3054039-B.

When he located the correct party he scrutinized the lading report attached; it gave but fifteen days of half-life remaining. Automatically, he pressed a portable amplifier into the hull of the glass casket, tuned it, listened at the proper frequency for indication of cephalic activity.

Faintly from the speaker came, " ... and then Tillie sprained her ankle and we never thought it'd heal; she was so foolish about it, wanting to start walking immediately ... "

Satisfied, he unplugged the amplifier and located a union man to perform the actual task of carting 3054039-B to the loading platform, where the customer could place her in his 'copter or car.

"You checked her out?" the customer asked as he paid the money due.

"Personally," Herb answered. "Functioning perfectly." He smiled at the customer. "Happy Resurrection Day, Mr. Ford."

"Thank you," the customer said, starting off for the loading platform.

When I pass, Herb said to himself, *I think I'll will my heirs to revive me one day a century. That way I can observe the fate of all mankind.* But that meant a rather high maintenance cost to the heirs, and no doubt sooner or later they would kick over the traces, have the body taken out of quick-pack and — God forbid — buried.

"Burial is barbaric," Herb murmured aloud. "Remnant of the primitive origins of our culture."

"Yes sir," his secretary Miss Beasman agreed, at her typewriter.

In the bin, several customers communed with their half-lifer relations, in rapt quiet, distributed at intervals along the aisles which separated the caskets. It was a tranquil sight, these faithfuls, coming as they did so regularly, to pay homage. They brought messages, news of what took place in the outside world; they cheered the gloomy half-lifers in these intervals of cerebral activity. And — they paid Herb Schoenheit von Vogelsang; it was a profitable business, operating a mortuary.

"My dad seems a little frail," a young man said, catching Herb's attention.

"I wonder if you could take a moment to check him over. I'd really appreciate it."

"Certainly," Herb said, accompanying the customer down the aisle to his deceased relative. The lading report showed only a few days remaining; that explained the vitiated quality of cerebration. But still — he turned up the gain, and the voice from the half-lifer became a trifle stronger. *He's almost at an end*, Herb thought. It was obvious that the son did not want to see the lading, did not actually care to know that contact with his dad was diminishing, finally. So Herb said nothing; he merely walked off, leaving the son to commune. Why tell him? Why break the bad news?

A truck had now appeared at the loading platform, and two men hopped down from it, wearing familiar pale blue uniforms. Atlas Interplan Van and Storage, Herb realized. Delivering another half-lifer, or here to pick up one which had expired. He strolled toward them. "Yes, gentlemen," he said.

The driver of the truck leaned out and said, "We're here to deliver Mr. Louis Sarapis. Got room all ready?"

"Absolutely," Herb said at once. "But I can't get hold of Mr. St. Cyr to make arrangements for the schedule. When's he to be brought back?"

Another man, dark-haired, with shiny-button black eyes, emerged from the truck. "I'm John Barefoot. According to the terms of the will I'm in charge of Mr. Sarapis. He's to be brought back to life immediately; that's the instructions I'm charged with."

"I see," Herb said, nodding. "Well, that's fine. Bring him in and we'll plug him right in."

"It's cold, here," Barefoot said. "Worse than the auditorium."

"Well of course," Herb answered.

The crew from the van began wheeling the casket. Herb caught a glimpse of the dead man, the massive, gray face resembling something cast from a break-mold. *Impressive old pirate*, he thought. *Good thing for us all he's dead finally, in spite of his charity work. Because who wants charity? Especially his.* Of course, Herb did not say that to Barefoot; he contented himself with guiding the crew to the prearranged spot.

"I'll have him talking in fifteen minutes," he promised Barefoot, who looked tense. "Don't worry; we've had almost no failures at this stage; the initial residual charge is generally quite vital."

"I suppose it's later," Barefoot said, "as it dims ... then you have the technical problems."

"Why does he want to be brought back so soon?" Herb asked.

Barefoot scowled and did not answer.

"Sorry," Herb said, and continued tinkering with the wires which had to be seated perfectly to the cathode terminals of the casket. "At low temperatures," he murmured, "the flow of current is virtually unimpeded. There's no measurable resistance at minus 150. So — " He fitted the anode cap in place.

"The signal should bounce out clear and strong." In conclusion, he clicked the amplifier on.

A hum. Nothing more.

"Well?" Barefoot said.

"I'll recheck," Herb said, wondering what had gone afoul.

"Listen," Barefoot said quietly, "if you slip up here and let the spark flicker out — " It was not necessary for him to finish; Herb knew.

"Is it the Democratic-Republican National Convention that he wants to participate in?" Herb asked. The Convention would be held later in the month, in Cleveland. In the past, Sarapis had been quite active in the behind-the-scenes activities at both the Democratic-Republican and the Liberal Party nominating conventions. It was said, in fact, that he had personally chosen the last Democratic-Republican Presidential candidate, Alfonse Gam. Tidy, handsome Gam had lost, but not by very much.

"Are you still getting nothing?" Barefoot asked.

"Um, it seems — " Herb said.

"Nothing. Obviously." Now Barefoot looked grim. "If you can't rouse him in another ten minutes *I'll* get hold of Claude St. Cyr and we'll take Louis out of your mortuary and lodge charges of negligence against you."

"I'm doing what I can," Herb said, perspiring as he fiddled with the leads to the casket. "We didn't perform the quick-pack installation, remember; there may have been a slip-up at that point."

Now static supervened over the steady hum.

"Is that him coming in?" Barefoot demanded.

"No," Herb admitted, thoroughly upset by now. It was, in fact, a bad sign.

"Keep trying," Barefoot said. But it was unnecessary to tell Herbert Schoenheit von Vogelsang that; he was struggling desperately, with all he had, with all his years of professional competence in this field. And still he achieved nothing; Louis Sarapis remained silent.

I'm not going to be successful, Herb realized in fear. *I don't understand why, either. WHAT'S WRONG? A big client like this, and it has to get fouled up.* He toiled on, not looking at Barefoot, not daring to.

At the radio telescope at Kennedy Slough, on the dark side of Luna, Chief Technician Owen Angress discovered that he had picked up a signal emanating from a region one light-week beyond the solar system in the direction of Proxima. Ordinarily such a region of space would have held little of interest for the U.N. Commission on Deep-Space Communications, but this, Owen Angress realized, was unique.

What reached him, thoroughly amplified by the great antennae of the radio telescope, was, faintly but clearly, a human voice.

" ... probably let it slide by," the voice was declaring. "If I know them, and I believe I do. That Johnny; he'd revert without my keeping my eye on him, but at least he's not a crook like St. Cyr. I did right to fire St. Cyr. Assuming I can make it stick ... " The voice faded momentarily.

What's out there? Angress wondered, dazedly. "At one fifty-second of a light-year," he murmured, making a quick mark on the deep-space map which he had been recharting. "Nothing. That's just empty dust-clouds." He could not understand what the signal implied; was it being bounced back to Luna from some nearby transmitter? Was this, in other words, merely an echo?

Or was he reading his computation incorrectly?

Surely this couldn't be correct. Some individual ruminating at a transmitter out beyond the solar system ... a man not in a hurry, thinking aloud in a kind of half-slumbering attitude, as if free-associating ... it made no sense.

I'd better report this to Wycoff at the Soviet Academy of Sciences, he said to himself. Wycoff was his current supervisor; next month it would be Jamison of MIT. *Maybe it's a long-haul ship that —*

The voice filtered in clearly once again. " ... that Gam is a fool; did wrong to select him. Know better now but too late. Hello?" The thoughts became sharp, the words more distinct. "Am I coming back? — for god's sake, it's about time. Hey! Johnny! Is that you?"

Angress picked up the telephone and dialed the code for the line to the Soviet Union.

"Speak up, Johnny!" the voice from the speaker demanded plaintively. "Come on, son; I've got so damn much on my mind. So much to do. Convention's started yet, has it? Got no sense of time stuck in here, can't see or hear; wait'll you get here and you'll find out ... " Again the voice faded.

This is exactly what Wycoff likes to call a "phenomenon," Angress realized. *And I can understand why.*

II

On the evening television news, Claude St. Cyr heard the announcer babbling about a discovery made by the radio telescope on Luna, but he paid little attention: he was busy mixing martinis for his guests.

"Yes," he said to Gertrude Harvey, "ironic as it is, I drew up the will myself, including the clause that automatically dismissed me, canceled my services out of existence the moment he died. And I'll tell you why Louis did that; he had paranoid suspicions of me, so he figured that with such a clause he'd insure himself against being — " He paused as he measured out the iota of dry wine which accompanied the gin. "Being prematurely dispatched." He grinned, and Gertrude, arranged decoratively on the couch beside her husband, smiled back.

"A lot of good it did him," Phil Harvey said.

"Hell," St. Cyr protested. "I had nothing to do with his death; it was an embolus, a great fat clot stuck like a cork in a bottleneck." He laughed at the image. "Nature's own remedy."

Gertrude said, "Listen. The TV; it's saying something strange." She rose, walked over to it and bent down, her ear close to the speaker.

"It's probably that oaf Kent Margrave," St. Cyr said. "Making another political speech." Margrave had been their President now for four years; a Liberal, he had managed to defeat Alfonse Gam, who had been Louis Sarapis' hand-picked choice for the office. Actually Margrave, for all his faults, was quite a politician; he had managed to convince large blocs of voters that having a puppet of Sarapis' for their President was not such a good idea.

"No," Gertrude said, carefully arranging her skirt over her bare knees. "This is — the space agency, I think. Science."

"Science!" St. Cyr laughed. "Well, then let's listen; I admire science. Turn it up." *I suppose they've found another planet in the Orionus System*, he said to himself. *Something more for us to make the goal of our collective existence.*

"A voice," the TV announcer was saying, "emanating from outer space, tonight has scientists both in the United States and the Soviet Union completely baffled."

"Oh no," St. Cyr choked. "A voice from outer space — please, no more." Doubled up with laughter, he moved off, away from the TV set; he could not bear to listen any more. "That's what we need," he said to Phil. "A voice that turns out to be — you know Who it is."

"Who?" Phil asked.

"God, of course. The radio telescope at Kennedy Slough has picked up the voice of God and now we're going to receive another set of divine commandments or at least a few scrolls." Removing his glasses he wiped his eyes with his Irish linen handkerchief.

Dourly, Phil Harvey said, "Personally I agree with my wife; I find it fascinating."

"Listen, my friend," St. Cyr said, "you know it'll turn out to be a transistor radio that some Jap student lost on a trip between Earth and Callisto. And the radio just drifted on out of the solar system entirely and now the telescope has picked it up and it's a huge mystery to all the scientists." He became more sober. "Shut it off, Gert; we've got serious things to consider."

Obediently but reluctantly she did so. "Is it true, Claude," she asked, rising to her feet, "that the mortuary wasn't able to revive old Louis? That he's not in half-life as he's supposed to be by now?"

"Nobody tells me anything from the organization, now," St. Cyr answered. "But I did hear a rumor to that effect." He knew, in fact, that it was so; he had many friends within Wilhelmina, but he did not like to talk about these surviving links. "Yes, I suppose that's so," he said.

Gertrude shivered. "Imagine not coming back. How dreadful."

"But that was the old natural condition," her husband pointed out as he drank his martini. "Nobody had half-life before the turn of the century."

"But we're used to it," she said stubbornly.

To Phil Harvey, St. Cyr said, "Let's continue our discussion."

Shrugging, Harvey said, "All right. If you really feel there's something to discuss." He eyed St. Cyr critically. "I could put you on my legal staff, yes. If that's what you're sure you want. But I can't give you the kind of business that Louis could. It wouldn't be fair to the legal men I have in there now."

"Oh, I recognize that," St. Cyr said. After all, Harvey's drayage firm was small in comparison with the Sarapis outfits; Harvey was in fact a minor figure in the 3-4 shipping business.

But that was precisely what St. Cyr wanted. Because he believed that within a year with the experience and contacts he had gained working for Louis Sarapis he could depose Harvey and take over Elektra Enterprises.

Harvey's first wife had been named Elektra. St. Cyr had known her, and after she and Harvey had split up St. Cyr had continued to see her, now in a more personal — and more spirited — way. It had always seemed to him that Elektra Harvey had obtained a rather bad deal; Harvey had employed legal talent of sufficient caliber to outwit Elektra's attorney ... who had been, as a matter of fact, St. Cyr's junior law partner, Harold Faine. Ever since her defeat in the courts, St. Cyr had blamed himself; why hadn't he taken the case personally? But he had been so tied up with Sarapis business ... it had simply not been possible.

Now, with Sarapis gone and his job with Atlas, Wilhelmina and Archimedean over, he could take some time to rectify the imbalance; he could come to the aid of the woman (he admitted it) whom he loved.

But that was a long step from this situation; first he had to get into Harvey's legal staff — at any cost. Evidently, he was succeeding.

"Shall we shake on it, then?" he asked Harvey, holding out his hand.

"Okay," Harvey said, not very much stirred by the event. He held out his hand, however, and they shook. "By the way," he said, then, "I have some knowledge — fragmentary but evidently accurate — as to why Sarapis cut you off in his will. And it isn't what you said at all."

"Oh?" St. Cyr said, trying to sound casual.

"My understanding is that he suspected someone, possibly you, of desiring to prevent him from returning to half-life. That you were going to select a particular mortuary which certain contacts of yours operate ... and they'd somehow fail to revive the old man." He eyed St. Cyr. "And oddly, that seems to be exactly what has happened."

There was silence.

Gertrude said, at last, "Why would Claude not want Louis Sarapis to be resurrected?"

"I have no idea," Harvey said. He stroked his chin thoughtfully. "I don't even fully understand half-life itself. Isn't it true that the half-lifer often finds himself in possession of a sort of insight, of a new frame of reference, a perspective, that he lacked while alive?"

"I've heard psychologists say that," Gertrude agreed. "It's what the old theologists called *conversion.*"

"Maybe Claude was afraid of some insight that Louis might show up with," Harvey said. "But that's just conjecture."

"Conjecture," Claude St. Cyr agreed, "in its entirety, including that as to any such plan as you describe; in actual fact I know absolutely no one in the mortuary business." His voice was steady, too; he made it come out that way. But this all was very sticky, he said to himself. Quite awkward.

The maid appeared, then, to tell them that dinner was ready. Both Phil and Gertrude rose, and Claude joined them as they entered the dining room together.

"Tell me," Phil Harvey said to Claude. "Who is Sarapis' heir?"

St. Cyr said, "A granddaughter who lives on Callisto; her name is Kathy Egmont and she's an odd one ... she's about twenty years old and already she's been in jail five times, mostly for narcotics addiction. Lately, I understand, she's managed to cure herself of the drug habit and now she's a religious convert of some kind. I've never met her but I've handled volumes of correspondence passing between her and old Louis."

"And she gets the entire estate, when it's out of probate? With all the political power inherent in it?"

"Haw," St. Cyr said. "Political power can't be willed, can't be passed on. All Kathy gets is the economic syndrome. It functions, as you know, through the parent holding company licensed under the laws of the state of Delaware, Wilhelmina Securities, and that's hers, if she cares to make use of it — if she can understand what it is she's inheriting."

Phil Harvey said, "You don't sound very optimistic."

"All the correspondence from her indicates — to me at least — that she's a sick, criminal type, very eccentric and unstable. The very last sort I'd like to see inherit Louis's holdings."

On that note, they seated themselves at the dinner table.

In the night, Johnny Barefoot heard the phone, drew himself to a sitting position and fumbled until his hands touched the receiver. Beside him in the bed Sarah Belle stirred as he said gratingly, "Hello. Who the hell is it?"

A fragile female voice said, "I'm sorry, Mr. Barefoot ... I didn't mean to wake you up. But I was told by my attorney to call you as soon as I arrived on Earth." She added, "This is Kathy Egmont, although actually my real name is Mrs. Kathy Sharp. Do you know who I am?"

"Yes," Johnny said, rubbing his eyes and yawning. He shivered from the cold of the room; beside him, Sarah Belle drew the covers back up over her shoulders and turned the other way. "Want me to come and pick you up? Do you have a place to stay?"

"I have no friends here on Terra," Kathy said. "But the spaceport people told me that the Beverely is a good hotel, so I'm going there. I started from Callisto as soon as I heard that my grandfather had died."

"You made good time," he said. He hadn't expected her for another twenty-four hours.

"Is there any chance — " The girl sounded timid. "Could I possibly stay with you, Mr. Barefoot? It scares me, the idea of a big hotel where no one knows me."

"I'm sorry," he said at once. "I'm married." And then he realized that such a retort was not only inappropriate ... it was actually abusive. "What I mean is," he explained, "I have no spare room. You stay at the Beverely tonight and tomorrow we'll find you a more acceptable apartment."

"All right," Kathy said. She sounded resigned but still anxious. "Tell me, Mr. Barefoot, what luck have you had with my grandfather's resurrection? Is he in half-life, now?"

"No," Johnny said. "It's failed, so far. They're working on it."

When he had left the mortuary, five technicians had been busy at work, trying to discover what was wrong.

Kathy said, "I thought it might work out that way."

"Why?"

"Well, my grandfather — he was so different from everyone else. I realize you know that, perhaps even better than I ... after all, you were with him daily. But — I just couldn't imagine him inert, the way the half-lifers are. Passive and helpless, you know. Can you imagine him like that, after all he's done?"

Johnny said, "Let's talk tomorrow; I'll come by the hotel about nine. Okay?"

"Yes, that's fine. I'm glad to have met you, Mr. Barefoot. I hope you'll stay on with Archimedean, working for me. Goodbye." The phone clicked; she had rung off.

My new boss, Johnny said to himself. *Wow.*

"Who was that?" Sarah Belle murmured. "At this hour?"

"The owner of Archimedean," Johnny said. "My employer."

"Louis Sarapis?" His wife sat up at once. "Oh ... you mean his granddaughter; she's here already. What's she sound like?"

"I can't tell," he said meditatively. "Frightened, mostly. It's a finite, small world she comes from, compared with Terra, here." He did not tell his wife the things he knew about Kathy, her drug addiction, her terms in jail.

"Can she take over now?" Sarah Belle asked. "Doesn't she have to wait until Louis's half-life is over?"

"Legally, he's dead. His will has come into force." *And*, he thought acidly, *he's not in half-life anyhow; he's silent and dead in his plastic casket, in his quick-pack, which evidently wasn't quite quick enough.*

"How do you think you'll get along with her?"

"I don't know," he said candidly. "I'm not even sure I'm going to try." He did not like the idea of working for a woman, especially one younger than himself. And one who was — at least according to hearsay — virtually psychopathic. But on the phone she had certainly not sounded psychopathic. He mulled that over in his mind, wide-awake now.

"She's probably very pretty," Sarah Belle said. "You'll probably fall in love with her and desert me."

"Oh no," he said. "Nothing as startling as that. I'll probably try to work for her, drag out a few miserable months, and then give up and look elsewhere." *And meanwhile*, he thought, *WHAT ABOUT LOUIS? Are we, or are we not, going to be able to revive him?* That was the really big unknown.

If the old man could be revived, he could direct his granddaughter; even though legally and physically dead, he could continue to manage his complex economic and political sphere, to some extent. But right now this was simply not working out, and the old man had planned on being revived at once, certainly before the Democratic-Republican Convention. Louis certainly knew — or rather had known — what sort of person he was willing his holdings to. Without help she surely could not function. *And*, Johnny thought, *there's little I can do for her. Claude St. Cyr could have, but by the terms of the will he's out of the picture entirely. So what is left? We must keep trying to revive old Louis, even if we have to visit every mortuary in the United States, Cuba and Russia.*

"You're thinking confused thoughts," Sarah Belle said. "I can tell by your expression." She turned on the small lamp by the bed, and was now reaching for her robe. "Don't try to solve serious matters in the middle of the night."

This must be how half-life feels, he thought groggily. He shook his head, trying to clear it, to wake up fully.

The next morning he parked his car in the underground garage of the Beverely and ascended by elevator to the lobby and the front desk where he was greeted by the smiling day clerk. It was not much of a hotel, Johnny decided. Clean, however; a respectable family hotel which probably rented many of its units by the month, some no doubt to elderly retired people. Evidently Kathy was accustomed to living modestly.

In answer to his query, the clerk pointed to the adjoining coffee shop. "You'll find her in there, eating breakfast. She said you might be calling, Mr. Barefoot."

In the coffee shop he found a good number of people having breakfast; he stopped short, wondering which was Kathy. The dark-haired girl with the stilted, frozen features, over in the far corner out of the way? He walked toward her. Her hair, he decided, was dyed. Without makeup she looked unnaturally pale; her skin had a stark quality, as if she had known a good deal of suffering, and not the sort that taught or informed one, made one into a "better" person. It had been pure pain, with no redemptive aspects, he decided as he studied her.

"Kathy?" he asked.

The girl turned her head. Her eyes, empty; her expression totally flattened. In a little voice she said, "Yes. Are you John Barefoot?" As he came up to the booth and seated himself opposite her she watched as if she imagined he would spring at her, hurl himself on her and — God forbid — sexually assault her. *It's as if she's nothing more than a lone, small animal*, he thought. *Backed into a corner to face the entire world.*

The color, or rather lack of it, could stem from the drug addiction, he decided. But that did not explain the flatness of her tone, and her utter lack of facial expression. And yet — she was pretty. She had delicate, regular features ... animated, they would have been interesting. And perhaps they had been, once. Years ago.

"I have only five dollars left," Kathy said. "After I paid for my one-way ticket and my hotel and my breakfast. Could you — " She hesitated. "I'm not sure exactly what to do. Could you tell me ... do I own anything yet? Anything that was my grandfather's? That I could borrow against?"

Johnny said, "I'll write you a personal check for one hundred dollars and you can pay me back sometime." He got out his checkbook.

"Really?" She looked stunned, and now, faintly, she smiled. "How trusting of you. Or are you trying to impress me? You were my grandfather's public relations man, weren't you? How were you dealt with in the will? I can't remember; it's all happened so fast, it's been so blurred."

"Well," he said, "I wasn't fired, as was Claude St. Cyr."

"Then you're staying on." That seemed to relieve her mind. "I wonder ... would it be correct to say you're now working for *me*?"

"You could say that," Johnny said. "Assuming you feel you need a P.R. man. Maybe you don't. Louis wasn't sure, half the time."

"Tell me what efforts have been made to resurrect him."

He explained to her, briefly, what he had done.

"And this is not generally known?" she asked.

"Definitely not. I know it, a mortuary owner with the unnatural name of Herb Schoenheit von Vogelsang knows it, and possibly news has trickled to a few high people in the drayage business, such as Phil Harvey. Even Claude St. Cyr may know it, by now. Of course, as time goes on and Louis has nothing to say, no political pronouncements for the press — "

"We'll have to make them up," Kathy said. "And pretend they're from him. That will be your job, Mr. Funnyfoot." She smiled once more. "Press-releases by my grandfather, until he's finally revived or we give up. Do you think we'll have to give up?" After a pause she said softly, "I'd like to see him. If I may. If you think it's all right."

"I'll take you there, to the Blessed Brethren Mortuary. I have to go there within the hour anyhow."

Nodding, Kathy resumed eating her breakfast.

As Johnny Barefoot stood beside the girl, who gazed intently at the transparent casket, he thought bizarrely, *Maybe she'll rap on the glass and say, "Grandfather, you wake up." And,* he thought, *maybe that will accomplish it. Certainly nothing else has.*

Wringing his hands, Herb Schoenheit von Vogelsang burbled miserably, "I just don't understand it, Mr. Barefoot. We worked all night, in relays, and we just aren't getting a single spark. And yet we ran an electrocephalograph and the 'gram shows faint but unmistakable cerebral activity. So the after-life is there, but we can't seem to contact it. We've got probes at every part of the skull, now, as you can see." He pointed to the maze of hair-wires connecting the dead man's head to the amplifying equipment surrounding the casket. "I don't know what else we can do, sir."

"Is there measurable brain metabolism?" Johnny asked.

"Yes sir. We called in outside experts and they detected it; it's a normal amount, too, just what you'd expect, immediately after death."

Kathy said calmly, "I know it's hopeless. He's too big a man for this. This is for aged relatives. For grandmothers, to be trotted out once a year on Resurrection Day." She turned away from the casket. "Let's go," she said to Johnny.

Together, he and the girl walked along the sidewalk from the mortuary, neither speaking. It was a mild spring day, and the trees here and there at the curb had small pink flowers. Cherry trees, Johnny decided.

"Death," Kathy murmured, at last. "And rebirth. A technological miracle. Maybe when Louis saw what it was like on the other side he changed his mind about coming back ... maybe he just doesn't *want* to return."

"Well," Johnny said, "the electrical spark is there; he's inside there, thinking something." He let Kathy take his arm as they crossed the street. "Someone told me," he said quietly, "that you're interested in religion."

"Yes, I am," Kathy said quietly. "You see, when I was a narcotics addict I took an overdose — never mind of what — and as a result my heart action ceased. I was officially, medically, dead for several minutes; they brought me back by open-chest heart massage and electroshock ... you know. During that time I had an experience, probably much like what those who go into half-life have experienced."

"Was it better than here?"

"No," she said. "But it was different. It was — dreamlike. I don't mean vague or unreal. I mean the logic, the weightlessness; you see, that's the main difference. You're free of gravity. It's hard to realize how important that is, but just think how many of the characteristics of the dream derive from that one fact."

Johnny said, "And it changed you."

"I managed to overcome the oral addictive aspects of my personality, if that's what you mean. I learned to control my appetites. My greed." At a newspaper stand Kathy halted to read the headlines. "Look," she said.

VOICE FROM OUTER SPACE BAFFLES SCIENTISTS

"Interesting," Johnny said.

Kathy, picking up the newspaper, read the article which accompanied the headline. "How strange," she said. "They've picked up a sentient, living entity ... here, you can read it, too." She passed the newspaper to him. "I did that, when I died ... I drifted out, free of the solar system, first planetary gravity then the sun's. I wonder who it is." Taking the newspaper back she reread the article.

"Ten cents, sir or madam," the robot vender said, suddenly.

Johnny tossed it the dime.

"Do you think it's my grandfather?" Kathy asked.

"Hardly," Johnny said.

"I think it is," Kathy said, staring past him, deep in thought. "I know it is; look, it began one week after his death, and it's one light-week out. The time fits, and here's the transcript of what it's saying." She pointed to the column. "All about you, Johnny, and about me and about Claude St. Cyr, that lawyer he fired, and the Convention; it's all there, but garbled. That's the way your thoughts run, when you're dead; all compressed, instead of in sequence." She smiled up at Johnny. "So we've got a terrible problem. We can hear him, by use of the radio telescope at Kennedy Slough. But he can't hear us."

"You don't actually — "

"Oh, I do," she said matter-of-factly. "I knew he wouldn't settle for half-life; this is a whole, entire life he's leading now, out in space, there, beyond the last planet of our system. And there isn't going to be any way we can interfere with him; whatever it is he's doing — " She began to walk on, once more; Johnny followed. "Whatever it is, it's going to be at least as much as he did when he was alive here on Terra. You can be sure of that. Are you afraid?"

"Hell," Johnny protested, "I'm not even convinced, let alone afraid." And yet — perhaps she was right. She seemed so certain about it. He could not help being a little impressed, a little convinced.

"You should be afraid," Kathy said. "He may be very strong, out there. He may be able to do a lot. Affect a lot ... affect us, what we do and say and believe.

Even without the radio telescope — he may be reaching us, even now. Subliminally."

"I don't believe it," Johnny said. But he did, in spite of himself. She was right; it was just what Louis Sarapis would do.

Kathy said, "We'll know more when the Convention begins, because that's what he cares about. He failed to get Gam elected last time, and that was one of the few times in his life that he was beaten."

"Gam!" Johnny echoed, amazed. "That has-been? Is he even still in existence? Why, he completely disappeared, four years ago — "

"My grandfather won't give up with him," Kathy said meditatively. "And he is alive; he's a turkey farmer or some such thing, on Io. Perhaps it's ducks. Anyhow, he's there. Waiting."

"Waiting for what?"

Kathy said, "For my grandfather to contact him again. As he did before, four years ago, at the Convention then."

"No one would vote for Gam again!" Repelled, he gazed at her.

Smiling, Kathy said nothing. But she squeezed his arm, hugging him. As if, he thought, she were afraid again, as she had been in the night, when he had talked to her. Perhaps even more so.

III

The handsome, dapper, middle-aged man wearing vest and narrow, old-fashioned necktie, rose to his feet as Claude St. Cyr entered the outer office of St. Cyr and Faine, on his way to court. "Mr. St. Cyr — "

Glancing at him, St. Cyr murmured, "I'm in a rush; you'll have to make an appointment with my secretary." And then he recognized the man. He was talking to Alfonse Gam.

"I have a telegram," Gam said. "From Louis Sarapis." He reached into his coat pocket.

"Sorry," St. Cyr said stiffly. "I'm associated with Mr. Phil Harvey now; my business relationship with Mr. Sarapis was terminated several weeks ago." But he paused, curious. He had met Gam before; at the time of the national campaign, four years ago, he had seen a good deal of the man — in fact, he had represented Gam in several libel suits, one with Gam as the plaintiff, the other as defendant. He did not like the man.

Gam said, "This wire arrived the day before yesterday."

"But Sarapis has been — " Claude St. Cyr broke off. "Let me see it." He held out his hand, and Gam passed him the wire.

It was a statement from Louis Sarapis to Gam, assuring Gam of Louis's utter and absolute support in the forthcoming struggle at the Convention. And Gam was correct; the wire was dated only three days before. It did not make sense.

"I can't explain it, Mr. St. Cyr," Gam said dryly. "But it sounds like Louis. He wants me to run again. As you can see. It never occurred to me; as far as I'm concerned I'm out of politics and in the guinea-fowl business. I thought you might know something about this, who sent it and why." He added, "Assuming that old Louis didn't."

St. Cyr said, "How could Louis have sent it?"

"I mean, written it before his death and had someone send it just the other day. Yourself, perhaps." Gam shrugged. "Evidently it wasn't you. Perhaps Mr. Barefoot, then." He reached out for his wire.

"Do you actually intend to run again?" St. Cyr asked.

"If Louis wants me to."

"And lose again? Drag the party to defeat again, just because of one stubborn, vindictive old man — " St. Cyr broke off. "Go back to raising guinea fowl. Forget politics. You're a loser, Gam. Everyone in the party knows it. Everyone in America, in fact."

"How can I contact Mr. Barefoot?"

St. Cyr said, "I have no idea." He started on.

"I'll need legal help," Gam said.

"For what? Who's suing you now? You don't need legal help, Mr. Gam; you need medical help, a psychiatrist to explain why you want to run again. Listen — " He leaned toward Gam. "If Louis alive couldn't get you into office, Louis dead certainly can't." He went on, then, leaving Gam standing there.

"Wait," Gam said.

Reluctantly, Claude St. Cyr turned around.

"This time I'm going to win," Gam said. He sounded as if he meant it; his voice, instead of its usual reedy flutter, was firm.

Uneasy, St. Cyr said, "Well, good luck. To both you and Louis."

"Then he *is* alive." Gam's eyes flickered.

"I didn't say that; I was being ironic."

Gam said thoughtfully, "But he is alive; I'm sure of it. I'd like to find him. I went to some of the mortuaries, but none of them had him, or if they did they wouldn't admit it. I'll keep looking; I want to confer with him." He added, "That's why I came here from Io."

At that point, St. Cyr managed to break away and depart. *What a nonentity,* he said to himself. *A cypher, nothing but a puppet of Louis's.* He shuddered. *God protect us from such a fate: that man as our President.*

Imagine us all *becoming like Gam!*

It was not a pleasant thought; it did not inspire him for the day ahead. And he had a good deal of work on his shoulders.

This was the day that he, as attorney for Phil Harvey, would make Mrs. Kathy Sharp — the former Kathy Egmont — an offer for Wilhelmina Securities. An exchange of stock would be involved; voting stock, redistributed in such a fashion that Harvey gained control of Wilhelmina. The worth of the corporation being almost impossible to calculate, Harvey was offering not money but real estate in exchange; he had enormous tracts of land on Ganymede, deeded to him by the Soviet Government a decade ago in exchange for technical assistance he had rendered it and its colonies.

The chance of Kathy accepting was nil.

And yet, the offer had to be made. The next step — he shrank from even thinking about it — involved a fracas to the death in the area of direct economic competition, between Harvey's drayage firm and hers. And hers, he knew, was now in a state of decay; there had been union trouble since the old man's death. The thing that Louis hated the most had started to take place: union organizers had begun to move in on Archimedean.

He himself sympathized with the unions; it was about time they came onto the scene. Only the old man's dirty tactics and his boundless energy, not to speak of his ruthless, eternal imagination, had kept them out. Kathy had none of these. And Johnny Barefoot —

What can you ask of a noncol? St. Cyr asked himself caustically. *Brilliant strategy-purse out of the sow's ear of mediocrity?*

And Barefoot had his hands full building up Kathy's image before the public; he had barely begun to succeed in that when the union squabbles broke out. An ex-narcotics addict and religious nut, a woman who had a criminal record ... Johnny had his work cut out for him.

Where he had been productive lay in the area of the woman's physical appearance. She looked sweet, even gentle and pure; almost saintly. And Johnny had seized on this. Instead of quoting her in the press he had photographed her, a thousand wholesome poses: with dogs, children, at county fairs, at hospitals, involved in charity drives — the whole business.

But unfortunately Kathy had spoiled the image he had created, spoiled it in a rather unusual way.

Kathy maintained — simply — that she was in communication with her grandfather. That it was he who lay a light-week out in space, picked up by Kennedy Slough. She heard him, as the rest of the world did ... and by some miracle he heard her, too.

St. Cyr, riding the self-service elevator up to the 'copter port on the roof, laughed aloud. Her religious crankery couldn't be kept from the gossip columnists ... Kathy had said too much in public places, in restaurants and small, famous bars. And even with Johnny beside her. Even he couldn't keep her quiet.

Also, there had been that incident at that party in which she had taken off her clothes, declaring the hour of purification to be momentarily arriving; she had daubed herself in certain spots with crimson nail polish, as well, a sort of ritual ceremony ... of course she had been drinking.

And this is the woman, St. Cyr thought, *who operates Archimedean.*

The woman we must oust, for our good and *the public's*. It was, to him, practically a mandate in the name of the people. Virtually a public service to be performed, and the only one who did not see it that way was Johnny.

St. Cyr thought, *Johnny LIKES her. There's the motive.*

I wonder, he mused, *what Sarah Belle thinks of that.*

Feeling cheerful, St. Cyr entered his 'copter, closed the hatch and inserted his key in the ignition. And then he thought once again of Alfonse Gam. And his good humor vanished at once; again he felt glum.

There are two people, he realized, *who are acting on the assumption that old Louis Sarapis is alive; Kathy Egmont Sharp and Alfonse Gam.*

Two most unsavory people, too. And, in spite of himself, he was being forced to associate with both of them. It seemed to be his fate.

He thought, *I'm no better off than I was with old Louis. In some respects, I'm even worse off.*

The 'copter rose into the sky, on its way to Phil Harvey's building in downtown Denver.

Being late, he snapped on the little transmitter, picked up the microphone and put in a call to Harvey. "Phil," he said, "Can you hear me? This is St. Cyr and I'm on my way west." He listened, then.

— Listened, and heard from the speaker a far-off weird babble, a murmur as if many words were being blended into a confusion. He recognized it; he had come onto it several times now, on the TV news programs.

" ... spite of personal attacks, much superior to Chambers, who couldn't win an election for house of ill repute janitor. You keep up faith in yourself, Alfonse. People know a good man, value him; you wait. Faith moves mountains. I ought to know, look what I've accomplished in my life ... "

It was, St. Cyr realized, the entity a light-week out, now emitting an even more powerful signal; like sunspots, it beclouded normal transmission channels. He cursed, scowled, then snapped off the receiver.

Fouling up communications, he said to himself. *Must be against the law; I ought to consult the FCC.*

Shaken, he piloted his 'copter on, across open farm land.

My God, he thought, *it did sound like old Louis!*

Could Kathy Egmont Sharp possibly be right?

At the Michigan plant of Archimedean, Johnny Barefoot appeared for his appointment with Kathy and found her in a state of gloom.

"Don't you see what's happening?" she demanded, facing him across the office which had once been Louis's. "I'm not managing things right at all; everybody knows that. Don't you know that?" Wild-eyed, she stared at him.

"I don't know that," Johnny said. But inside he did know it; she was correct. "Take it easy and sit down," he said. "Harvey and St. Cyr will be here any minute now, and you want to be in command of yourself when you meet with them." It was a meeting which he had hoped to avoid. But, he had realized, sooner or later it would take place, and so he had let Kathy agree to it.

Kathy said, "I — have something terrible to tell you."

"What is it? It can't be so terrible." He set himself, waiting in dread to hear.

"I'm back on drugs, Johnny. All this responsibility and pressure; it's too much for me. I'm sorry." She gazed down at the floor sadly.

"What is the drug?"

"I'd rather not say. It's one of the amphetamines. I've read the literature; I know it can cause a psychosis, in the amounts I'm taking. But I don't care." Panting, she turned away, her back to him. He saw, now, how thin she had gotten. And her face was gaunt, hollow-eyed; he now understood why. The overdosage of amphetamines wasted the body away, turned matter into energy. Her metabolism was altered so that she became, as the addiction returned, a pseudo-hyperthyroid, with all the somatic processes speeded up.

Johnny said, "I'm sorry to hear it." He had been afraid of this. And yet when it had come he had not understood; he had had to wait until she told him. "I think," he said, "you should be under a doctor's care." He wondered where she got the drug. But probably for her, with her years of experience, it was not difficult.

"It makes a person very unstable emotionally," Kathy said. "Given to sudden rages and also crying jags. I want you to know that, so you won't blame me. So you'll understand that it's the drug." She tried to smile; he saw her making the effort.

Going over to her he put his hand on her shoulder. "Listen," he said, "when Harvey and St. Cyr get here, I think you better accept their offer."

"Oh," she said, nodding. "Well."

"And then," he said, "I want you to go voluntarily into a hospital."

"The cookie factory," Kathy said bitterly.

"You'd be better off," he said, "without the responsibility you have, here at Archimedean. What you need is deep, protracted rest. You're in a state of mental and physical fatigue, but as long as you're taking that amphetamine — "

"Then it doesn't catch up with me," Kathy finished. "Johnny, I can't sell out to Harvey and St. Cyr."

"Why not?"

"Louis wouldn't want me to. He — " She was silent a moment. "He says no."

Johnny said, "Your health, maybe your life — "

"My sanity, you mean, Johnny."

"You have too much personally at stake," he said. "The hell with Louis.

The hell with Archimedean; you want to find yourself in a mortuary, too, in half-life? It's not worth it; it's just property, and you're a living creature."

She smiled. And then, on the desk, a light came on and a buzzer sounded. The receptionist outside said, "Mrs. Sharp, Mr. Harvey and Mr. St. Cyr are here, now. Shall I send them in?"

"Yes," she answered.

The door opened, and Claude St. Cyr and Phil Harvey came swiftly in. "Hey, Johnny," St. Cyr said. He seemed to be in a confident mood; beside him, Harvey looked confident, too.

Kathy said, "I'll let Johnny do most of the talking."

He glanced at her. *Did that mean she had agreed to sell?* He said, "What kind of deal is this? What do you have to offer in exchange for a controlling interest in Wilhelmina Securities of Delaware? I can't imagine what it could be."

"Ganymede," St. Cyr said. "An entire moon." He added, "Virtually."

"Oh yes," Johnny said. "The USSR land deed. Has it been tested in the international courts?"

"Yes," St. Cyr said, "and found totally valid. Its worth is beyond estimate. And each year it will increase, perhaps double, in value. My client will put that up. It's a good offer, Johnny; you and I know each other, and you know when I say it that it's true."

Probably it was, Johnny decided. It was in many respects a generous offer; Harvey was not trying to bilk Kathy.

"Speaking for Mrs. Sharp," Johnny began. But Kathy cut him off.

"No," she said in a quick, brisk voice. "I can't sell. He says not to."

Johnny said, "You've already given me authority to negotiate, Kathy."

"Well," she said in a hard voice, "I'm taking it back."

"If I'm to work with you and for you at all," Johnny said, "you must go on my advice. We've already talked it over and agreed — "

The phone in the office rang.

"Listen to him yourself," Kathy said. She picked up the phone and held it out to Johnny. "He'll tell you."

Johnny accepted the phone and put it to his ear. "Who is this?" he demanded. And then he heard the drumming. The far-off uncanny drumming noise, as if something were scratching at a long metal wire.

" ... imperative to retain control. Your advice absurd. She can pull herself together; she's got the stuff. Panic reaction; you're scared because she's ill. A good doctor can fix her up. Get a doctor for her; get medical help. Get an attorney and be sure she stays out of the hands of the law. Make sure her supply of drugs is cut. Insist on ... " Johnny yanked the receiver away from his ear, refusing to hear more. Trembling, he hung the phone back up.

"You heard him," Kathy said. "Didn't you? *That was Louis.*"

"Yes," Johnny said.

"He's grown," Kathy said. "Now we can hear him direct; it's not just the radio telescope at Kennedy Slough. I heard him last night, clearly, for the first time, as I lay down to go to sleep."

To St. Cyr and Harvey, Johnny said, "We'll have to think your proposition over, evidently. We'll have to get an appraisal of the worth of the unimproved real estate you're offering and no doubt you want an audit of Wilhelmina. That will take time." He heard his voice shake; he had not gotten over the shock of picking up the telephone and hearing the living voice of Louis Sarapis.

After making an appointment with St. Cyr and Harvey to meet with them once more later in the day, Johnny took Kathy out to a late breakfast; she had admitted, reluctantly, that she had eaten nothing since the night before.

"I'm just not hungry," she explained, as she sat picking listlessly at her plate of bacon and eggs, toast with jam.

"Even if that was Louis Sarapis," Johnny said, "you don't — "

"It was. Don't say 'even'; you know it's him. He's gaining power all the time, out there. Perhaps from the sun."

"So it's Louis," he said doggedly. "Nonetheless, you have to act in your own interest, not in his."

"His interests and mine are the same," Kathy said. "They involve maintaining Archimedean."

"Can he give you the help you need? Can he supply what's missing? He doesn't take your drug-addiction seriously; that's obvious. All he did was preach at me." He felt anger. "That's damn little help, for you or for me, in this situation."

"Johnny," she said, "I feel him near me all the time; I don't need the TV or the phone — I *sense* him. It's my mystical bent, I think. My religious intuition; it's helping me maintain contact with him." She sipped a little orange juice.

Bluntly, Johnny said, "It's your amphetamine psychosis, you mean."

"I won't go into the hospital, Johnny. I won't sign myself in; I'm sick but not that sick. I can get over this bout on my own, because I'm not alone. I have my grandfather. And — " She smiled at him. "I have you. In spite of Sarah Belle."

"You won't have me, Kathy," he said quietly, "unless you sell to Harvey. Unless you accept the Ganymede real estate."

"You'd quit?"

"Yes," he said.

After a pause, Kathy said, "My grandfather says go ahead and quit." Her eyes were dark, enlarged, and utterly cold.

"I don't believe he'd say that."

"Then talk to him."

"How?"

Kathy pointed to the TV set in the corner of the restaurant. "Turn it on and listen."

Rising to his feet, Johnny said, "I don't have to; I've already given my decision. I'll be at my hotel, if you should change your mind." He walked away from the table, leaving her sitting there. Would she call after him? He listened as he walked. She did not call.

A moment later he was out of the restaurant, standing on the sidewalk. She had called his bluff, and so it ceased to be a bluff; it became the real thing. He actually had quit.

Stunned, he walked aimlessly on. And yet — he had been right. He knew that. It was just that ... damn her, he thought. Why didn't she give in? Because of Louis, he realized. Without the old man she would have gone ahead and done it, traded her controlling, voting stock for the Ganymede property. Damn Louis Sarapis, not her, he thought furiously.

What now? he asked himself. Go back to New York? Look for a new job? For instance approach Alfonse Gam? There was money in that, if he could land it. Or should he stay here in Michigan, hoping that Kathy would change her mind?

She can't keep on, he decided. *No matter what Sarapis tells her. Or rather, what she believes he's telling her. Whichever it is.*

Hailing a cab, he gave the driver the address of his hotel room. A few moments later he was entering the lobby of the Antler Hotel, back where he had started early in the morning. Back to the forbidding empty room, this time merely to sit and wait. To hope that Kathy would change her mind and call him. This time he had no appointment to go to; the appointment was over.

When he reached his hotel room he heard his phone ringing.

For a moment Johnny stood at the door, key in hand, listening to the phone on the other side of the door, the shrill noise reaching him as he stood in the hall. *Is it Kathy?* he wondered. *Or is it* him?

He put the key in the lock, turned it and entered the room; sweeping the receiver off its hook he said, "Hello."

Drumming and far-off, the voice, in the middle of its monotonous monologue, its recitation to itself, was murmuring, " ... no good at all, Barefoot, to leave her. Betrayal of your job; thought you understood your responsibilities. Same to her as it was to me, and you never would have walked off in a fit of pique and left me. I deliberately left the disposition of my body to you so you'd stay on. You can't ... " At that point Johnny hung up, chilled.

The phone rang again, at once.

This time he did not take it off the hook. *The hell with you*, he said to himself. He walked to the window and stood looking down at the street below, thinking to himself of the conversation he had held with old Louis years ago, the one that had made such an impression in his mind. The conversation in which it had come out that he had failed to go to college because he wanted to die. Looking down at the street below, he thought, *Maybe I ought to jump. At least there'd be no more phones ... no more of* it.

The worse part, he thought, *is its* senility. *Its thoughts are not clear, not distinct; they're dream-like; irrational. The old man is not genuinely alive. He is not even in half-life. This is a dwindling away of consciousness toward a nocturnal state. And we are forced to listen to it as it unwinds, as it develops step by step, to final, total death.*

But even in this degenerative state, it had desires. It *wanted*, and strongly. It wanted him to do something; it wanted Kathy to do something; the remnants of Louis Sarapis were vital and active, and clever enough to find ways of pursuing him, of getting what was wanted. It was a travesty of Louis's wishes during his lifetime, and yet it could not be ignored; it could not be escaped.

The phone continued to ring.

Maybe it isn't Louis, he thought then. *Maybe it's Kathy.* Going to it he lifted the receiver. And put it back down at once. The drumming once more, the fragments of Louis Sarapis's personality ... he shuddered. *And is it just here, is it selective?*

He had a terrible feeling that it was *not* selective.

Going to the TV set at the far end of the room he snapped the switch. The screen grew into lighted animation, and yet, he saw, it was strangely blurred. The dim outlines of — it seemed to be a face.

And everyone, he realized, *is seeing this.* He turned to another channel. Again the dully-formed features, the old man half-materialized here on the television screen. And from the set's speaker the murmur of indistinct words. " ... told you time and again your primary responsibility is to ... " Johnny shut the set off; the ill-formed face and words sank out of existence, and all that remained, once more, was the ringing phone.

He picked up the phone and said, "Louis, can you hear me?"

" ... when election time comes they'll see. A man with the spirit to campaign a second time, take the financial responsibility, after all it's only for the wealthy men, now, the cost of running ... " The voice droned on. No, the old man could not hear him. It was not a conversation; it was a monologue. It was not authentic communication.

And yet the old man knew what was occurring on Earth; he seemed to understand, to somehow see, that Johnny had quit his job.

Hanging up the phone he seated himself and lit a cigarette.

I can't go back to Kathy, he realized, *unless I'm willing to change my mind and advise her not to sell. And that's impossible; I can't do that. So that's out. What is there left for me?*

How long can Sarapis hound me? Is there any place I can go?

Going to the window once more he stood looking down at the street below.

At a newsstand, Claude St. Cyr tossed down coins, picked up the newspaper.

"Thank you, sir or madam," the robot vender said.

The lead article ... St. Cyr blinked and wondered if he had lost his mind. He could not grasp what he was reading — or rather unable to read. It made no sense; the homeostatic news-printing system, the fully automated micro-relay newspaper, had evidently broken down. All he found was a procession of words, randomly strung together. It was worse than *Finnegans Wake*.

Or was it random? One paragraph caught his eye.

At the hotel window now ready to leap. If you expect to conduct any more business with her you better get over there. She's dependent on him, needs a man since her husband, that Paul Sharp, abandoned her. The Antler Hotel, room 604. I think you have time. Johnny is too hot-headed; shouldn't have tried to bluff her. With my blood you can't be bluffed and she's got my blood, I

St. Cyr said rapidly to Harvey, who stood beside him, "Johnny Barefoot's in a room at the Antler Hotel about to jump, and this is old Sarapis telling us, warning us. We better get over there."

Glancing at him, Harvey said, "Barefoot's on our side; we can't afford to have him take his life. But why would Sarapis — "

"Let's just get over there," St. Cyr said, starting toward his parked 'copter. Harvey followed on the run.

IV

All at once the telephone stopped ringing. Johnny turned from the window — and saw Kathy Sharp standing by it, the receiver in her hand. "He called me," she said. "And he told me, Johnny, where you were and what you were going to do."

"Nuts," he said, "I'm not going to do anything." He moved back from the window.

"He thought you were," Kathy said.

"Yes, and that proves he can be wrong." His cigarette, he saw, had burned down to the filter; he dropped it into the ashtray on the dresser and stubbed it out.

"My grandfather was always fond of you," Kathy said. "He wouldn't like anything to happen to you."

Shrugging, Johnny said, "As far as I'm concerned I have nothing to do with Louis Sarapis any more."

Kathy had put the receiver to her ear; she paid no attention to Johnny — she was listening to her grandfather, he saw, and so he ceased talking. It was futile.

"He says," Kathy said, "that Claude St. Cyr and Phil Harvey are on their way up here. He told them to come, too."

"Nice of him," he said shortly.

Kathy said, "I'm fond of you, too, Johnny. I can see what my grandfather found about you to like and admire. You genuinely take my welfare seriously, don't you? Maybe I could go into the hospital voluntarily, for a short period anyhow, a week or a few days."

"Would that be enough?" he asked.

"It might." She held the phone out to him. "He wants to talk to you. I think you'd better listen; he'll find a way to reach you, in any case. And you know that."

Reluctantly, Johnny accepted the phone.

" ... trouble is you're out of a job and that depresses you. If you're not working you feel you don't amount to anything; that's the kind of person you are. I like that. The same way myself. Listen, I've got a job for you. At the Convention. Doing publicity to make sure Alfonse Gam is nominated; you'd do a swell job. Call Gam. Call Alfonse Gam. Johnny, call Gam. Call — "

Johnny hung up the phone.

"I've got a job," he told Kathy. "Representing Gam. At least Louis says so."

"Would you do that?" Kathy asked. "Be his P.R. man at the nominating convention?"

He shrugged. Why not? Gam had the money; he could and would pay well. And certainly he was no worse than the President, Kent Margrave. And — *I must get a job,* Johnny realized. *I have to live. I've got a wife and two children; this is no joke.*

"Do you think Gam has a chance this time?" Kathy asked.

"No, not really. But miracles in politics do happen; look at Richard Nixon's incredible comeback in 1968."

"What is the best route for Gam to follow?"

He eyed her. "I'll talk that over with him. Not with you."

"You're still angry," Kathy said quietly. "Because I won't sell. Listen, Johnny. Suppose I turned Archimedean over to you."

After a moment he said, "What does Louis say to that?"

"I haven't asked him."

"You know he'd say no. I'm too inexperienced. I know the operation, of course; I've been with it from the start. But — "

"Don't sell yourself short," Kathy said softly.

"Please," Johnny said. "Don't lecture me. Let's try to stay friends; cool, distant friends." *And if there's one thing I can't stand,* he said to himself, *it's being lectured by a woman. And for my own good.*

The door of the room burst open. Claude St. Cyr and Phil Harvey leaped inside, then saw Kathy, saw him with her, and sagged. "So he got you to come here, too," St. Cyr said to her, panting for breath.

"Yes," she said. "He was very concerned about Johnny." She patted him on the arm. "See how many friends you have? Both warm and cool?"

"Yes," he said. But for some reason felt deeply, miserably sad.

That afternoon Claude St. Cyr found time to drop by the house of Elektra Harvey, his present employer's ex-wife.

"Listen, doll," St. Cyr said, "I'm trying to do good for you in this present deal. If I'm successful — " He put his arms around her and gave her a bear hug. "You'll recover a little of what you lost. Not all, but enough to make you a trifle happier about life in general." He kissed her and, as usual, she responded; she squirmed effectively, drew him down to her, pressed close in a manner almost uncannily satisfying. It was very pleasant, and in addition it lasted a long time. And that was *not* usual.

Stirring, moving away from him finally, Elektra said, "By the way, can you tell me what ails the phone and the TV? I can't call — there always seems to be someone on the line. And the picture on the TV screen; it's all fuzzy and distorted, and it's always the same, just a sort of *face*."

"Don't worry about it," Claude said. "We're working on that right now; we've got a crew of men out scouting." His men were going from mortuary to mortuary; eventually they'd find Louis's body. And then this nonsense would come to an end ... to everyone's relief.

Going to the sideboard to fix drinks, Elektra Harvey said, "Does Phil know about us?" She measured out bitters into the whiskey glasses, three drops to each.

"No," St. Cyr said, "and it's none of his business anyhow."

"But Phil has a strong prejudice about ex-wives. He wouldn't like it. He'd get ideas about you being disloyal; since he dislikes me, you're supposed to, too. That's what Phil calls 'integrity'."

"I'm glad to know that," St. Cyr said, "but there's damn little I can do about it. Anyhow, he isn't going to find out."

"I can't help being worried, though," Elektra said, bringing him his drink. "I was tuning the TV, you see, and — I know this sounds crazy, but it actually seemed to me — " She broke off. "Well, I actually thought I heard the TV announcer mention us. But he was sort of mumbling, or the reception was bad. But anyhow I did hear that, your name and mine." She looked soberly up at him, while absent-mindedly rearranging the strap of her dress.

Chilled, he said, "Dear, it's ridiculous." Going over to the TV set he clicked it on.

Good Lord, he thought. *Is Louis Sarapis everywhere? Does he see everything we do from that locus of his out there in deep space?*

It was not exactly a comforting thought, especially since he was trying to involve Louis's granddaughter in a business deal which the old man disapproved of.

He's getting back at me, St. Cyr realized as he reflexively tuned the television set with numbed fingers.

Alfonse Gam said, "As a matter of fact, Mr. Barefoot, I intended to call you. I have a wire from Mr. Sarapis advising me to employ you. I do think, however, we'll have to come up with something entirely new. Margrave has a considerable advantage over us."

"True," Johnny admitted. "But let's be realistic; we're going to get help this time. Help from Louis Sarapis."

"Louis helped last time," Gam pointed out, "and it wasn't sufficient."

"But his help now will be on a different order." *After all,* Johnny thought, *the old man controls all the communication media, the newspapers, radio and TV, even the telephones, God forbid.* With such power Louis could do almost anything he chose.

He hardly needs me, he thought caustically. But he did not say that to Alfonse Gam; apparently Gam did not understand about Louis and what Louis could do. And after all, a job was a job.

"Have you turned on a TV set lately?" Gam asked. "Or tried to use the phone, or even bought a newspaper? There's nothing but a sort of decaying gibberish coming out. If that's Louis, he's not going to be much help at the Convention. He's — disjointed. Just rambles."

"I know," Johnny said guardedly.

"I'm afraid whatever scheme Louis had for his half-life period has gone wrong," Gam said. He looked morose; he did not look like a man who expected to win an election. "Your admiration for Louis is certainly greater than mine, at this stage," Gam said. "Frankly, Mr. Barefoot, I had a long talk with Mr. St. Cyr, and his concepts were totally discouraging. I'm determined to press on, but frankly — " He gestured. "Claude St. Cyr told me to my face I'm a loser."

"You're going to believe St. Cyr? He's on the other side, now, with Phil Harvey." Johnny was astonished to find the man so naive, so pliable.

"I told him I was going to win," Gam murmured. "But honest to God, this drivel from every TV set and phone — it's awful. It discourages me; I want to get as far away from it as possible."

Presently Johnny said, "I understand."

"Louis didn't use to be like that," Gam said plaintively. "He just drones on, now. Even if he can swing the nomination to me ... do I want it? I'm tired, Mr. Barefoot. Very tired." He was silent, then.

"If you're asking me to give you pep," Johnny said, "you've got the wrong man." The voice from the phone and the TV affected him much the same way. Much too much for him to say anything encouraging to Gam.

"You're in P.R.," Gam said. "Can't you generate enthusiasm where there is none? Convince me, Barefoot, and then I'll convince the world." From his pocket he brought a folded-up telegram. "This is what came from Louis, the other day. Evidently he can interfere with the telegraph lines as well as the other media." He passed it over and Johnny read it.

"Louis was more coherent then," Johnny said. "When he wrote this."

"That's what I mean! He's deteriorating rapidly. When the Convention begins — and it's only one more day, now — what'll he be like? I sense something dreadful, here. And I don't care to get mixed up in it." He added, "And yet I want to run. So Barefoot — you deal with Louis for me; you can be the go-between." He added, "The psychopomp."

"What's that mean?"

"The go-between God and man," Gam said.

Johnny said, "If you use words like that you won't get the nomination; I can promise you that."

Smiling wryly, Gam said, "How about a drink?" He started from his living room, toward the kitchen. "Scotch? Bourbon?"

"Bourbon," Johnny said.

"What do you think of the girl, Louis's granddaughter?"

"I like her," he said. And that was true; he certainly did.

"Even though she's a psychotic, a drug addict, been in jail and on top of that a religious nut?"

"Yes," Johnny said tightly.

"I think you're crazy," Gam said, returning with the drinks. "But I agree with you. She's a good person. I've known her for some time, as a matter of fact. Frankly, I don't know why she took the bent that she has. I'm not a psychologist ... probably though it has something to do with Louis. She has a peculiar sort of devotion to him, a kind of loyalty that's both infantile and fanatic. And, to me, touchingly sweet."

Sipping his drink, Johnny said, "This is terrible bourbon."

"Old Sir Muskrat," Gam said, grimacing. "I agree."

"You better serve a better drink," Johnny said, "or you really are through in politics."

"That's why I need you," Gam said. "You see?"

"I see," Johnny said, carrying his drink into the kitchen to pour it back in the bottle — and to take a look at the Scotch instead.

"How are you going about getting me elected?" Alfonse Gam asked.

Johnny said, "I — think our best approach, our only approach, is to make use of the sentimentality people feel about Louis's death. I saw the lines of mourners; it was impressive, Alfonse. Day after day they came. When he was alive, many persons feared him, feared his power. But now they can breathe easier; he's gone, and the frightening aspects of — "

Gam interrupted. "But Johnny, he's not gone; that's the whole point. You know that gibbering *thing* on the phones and on TV — that's him!"

"But they don't know it," Johnny said. "The public is baffled — just as the first person to pick it up was baffled. That technician at Kennedy Slough."

Emphatically, he said, "Why should they connect an electrical emanation one light-week away from Earth with Louis Sarapis?"

After a moment Gam said, "I think you're making an error, Johnny. But Louis said to hire you, and I'm going to. And you have a free hand; I'll depend on your expertise."

"Thanks," Johnny said. "You can depend on me." But inside, he was not so sure. *Maybe the public is smarter than I realize*, he thought. *Maybe I'm making a mistake*. But what other approach was there? None that he could dream up; either they made use of Gam's tie with Louis or they had absolutely nothing by which to recommend him.

A slender thread on which to base the campaign for nomination — and only a day before the Convention convened. He did not like it.

The telephone in Gam's living room rang.

"That's probably him," Gam said. "You want to talk to him? To be truthful, I'm afraid to take it off the hook."

"Let it ring," Johnny said. He agreed with Gam; it was just too damn unpleasant.

"But we can't evade him," Gam pointed out. "If he wants to get in touch with us; if it isn't the phone it's the newspaper. And yesterday I tried to use my electric typewriter ... instead of the letter I intended to compose I got the same mishmash — I got a text from *him*."

Neither of them moved to take the phone, however. They let it ring on.

"Do you want an advance?" Gam asked. "Some cash?"

"I'd appreciate it," Johnny said. "Since today I quit my job with Archimedean."

Reaching into his coat for his wallet, Gam said, "I'll give you a check." He eyed Johnny. "You like her but you can't work with her; is that it?"

"That's it," Johnny said. He did not elaborate, and Gam did not press him any further. Gam was, if nothing else, gentlemanly. And Johnny appreciated it.

As the check changed hands the phone stopped ringing.

Was there a link between the two? Johnny wondered. Or was it just chance? No way to tell. Louis seemed to know everything ... anyhow, this was what Louis had wanted; he had told both of them that.

"I guess we did the right thing," Gam said tartly. "Listen, Johnny. I hope you can get back on good terms with Kathy Egmont Sharp. For her sake; she needs help. Lots of it."

Johnny grunted.

"Now that you're not working for her, make one more try," Gam said. "Okay?"

"I'll think about it," Johnny said.

"She's a very sick girl, and she's got a lot of responsibility now. You know that, too. Whatever caused the rift between you — try to come to some kind of understanding *before it's too late*. That's the only proper way."

Johnny said nothing. But he knew, inside him, that Gam was right.

And yet — how did he do it? He didn't know how. *How to you approach a psychotic person?* he wondered. *How do you repair such a deep rift?* It was hard enough in regular situations ... and this had so many overtones.

If nothing else, this had Louis mixed in it. And Kathy's feelings about Louis. Those would have to change. The blind adoration — that would have to cease.

"What does your wife think of her?" Gam asked.

Startled, he said, "Sarah Belle? She's never met Kathy." He added, "Why do you ask?"

Gam eyed him and said nothing.

"Damn odd question," Johnny said.

"Damn odd girl, that Kathy," Gam said. "Odder than you think, my friend. There's a lot you don't know." He did not elaborate.

To Claude St. Cyr, Phil Harvey said, "There's something I want to know. Something we must have the answer to, or we'll never get control of the voting stock of Wilhelmina. *Where's the body?*"

"We're looking," St. Cyr said patiently. "We're trying all of the mortuaries, one by one. But money's involved; undoubtedly someone's paying them to keep quiet, and if we want them to talk — "

"That girl," Harvey said, "is going on instructions from beyond the grave. Despite the fact that Louis is devolving ... she still pays attention to him. It's — unnatural." He shook his head, repelled.

"I agree," St. Cyr said. "In fact, you expressed it perfectly. This morning when I was shaving — I picked him up on the TV." He shuddered visibly. "I mean, it's coming at us from every side, now."

"Today," Harvey said, "is the first day of the Convention." He looked out of the window, at the cars and people. "Louis's attention will be tied up there, trying to swing the vote onto Alfonse Gam. That's where Johnny is, working for Gam — that was Louis's idea. Now perhaps we can operate with more success. Do you see? Maybe he's forgotten about Kathy; my God, he can't watch everything at once."

St. Cyr said quietly, "But Kathy is not at Archimedean now."

"Where is she, then? In Delaware? At Wilhelmina Securities? It ought to be easy to find her."

"She's sick," St. Cyr said. "In a hospital, Phil. She was admitted during the late evening, last night. For her drug addiction, I presume."

There was silence.

"You know a lot," Harvey said finally. "Where'd you learn this, anyhow?"

"From listening to the phone and the TV. But I don't know where the hospital is. It could even be off Earth, on Luna or on Mars, even back where she came from. I got the impression she's extremely ill. Johnny's abandoning her set her back greatly." He gazed at his employer somberly. "That's all I know, Phil."

"Do you think Johnny Barefoot knows where she is?"

"I doubt it."

Pondering, Harvey said, "I'll bet she tries to call him. I'll bet he either knows or will know, soon. If we only could manage to put a snoop-circuit on his phone ... get his calls routed through here."

"But the phones," St. Cyr said wearily. "All it is now — just the gibberish. The interference from Louis." He wondered what became of Archimedean Enterprises if Kathy was declared unable to manage her affairs, if she was forcibly committed. Very complicated, depending on whether Earth law or —

Harvey was saying, "We can't find her and we can't find the body. And meanwhile the Convention's on, and they'll nominate that wretched Gam, that creature of Louis's. And next we know, he'll be President." He eyed St. Cyr with antagonism. "So far you haven't done me much good, Claude."

"We'll try all the hospitals. But there's tens of thousands of them. And if it isn't in this area it could be anywhere." He felt helpless. *Around and around we go*, he thought, *and we get nowhere.*

Well, we can keep monitoring the TV, he decided. *That's some help.*

"I'm going to the Convention," Harvey announced. "I'll see you later. If you should come up with something — which I doubt — you can get in touch with me there." He strode to the door, and a moment later St. Cyr found himself alone.

Doggone it, St. Cyr said to himself. *What'll I do now? Maybe I ought to go to the Convention, too.* But there was one more mortuary he wanted to check; his men had been there, but he also wanted to give it a try personally. It was just the sort that Louis would have liked, run by an unctuous individual named, revoltingly, Herbert Schoenheit von Vogelsang, which meant, in German, Herbert Beauty of the Bird's Song — a fitting name for a man who ran the Beloved Brethren Mortuary in downtown Los Angeles, with branches in Chicago and New York and Cleveland.

When he reached the mortuary, Claude St. Cyr demanded to see Schoenheit von Vogelsang personally. The place was doing a rush business; Resurrection Day was just around the corner and the petite bourgeoisie, who flocked in great numbers to just such ceremonies, were lined up waiting to retrieve their half-lifer relatives.

"Yes sir," Schoenheit von Vogelsang said, when at last he appeared at the counter in the mortuary's business office. "You asked to speak to me."

St. Cyr laid his business card down on the counter; the card still described

him as legal consultant for Archimedean Enterprises. "I am Claude St. Cyr,"
he declared. "You may have heard of me."

Glancing at the card, Schoenheit von Vogelsang blanched and mumbled,
"I give you my word, Mr. St. Cyr, we're trying, we're really trying. We've spent
out of our own funds over a thousand dollars in trying to make contact with
him; we've had high-gain equipment flown in from Japan where it was developed and made. And still no results." Tremulously, he backed away from the
counter. "You can come and see for yourself. Frankly, I believe someone's
doing it on purpose; a complete failure like this can't occur naturally, if you
see what I mean."

St. Cyr said, "Let me see him."

"Certainly." The mortuary owner, pale and agitated, led the way through
the building into the chill bin, until, at last, St. Cyr saw ahead the casket
which had lain in state, the casket of Louis Sarapis. "Are you planning any
sort of litigation?" the mortuary owner asked fearfully. "I assure you, we — "

"I'm here," St. Cyr stated, "merely to take the body. Have your men load it
onto a truck for me."

"Yes, Mr. St. Cyr," Herb Schoenheit von Vogelsang said in meek obe-
dience; he waved two mortuary employees over and began giving them
instructions. "Do you have a truck with you, Mr. St. Cyr?" he asked.

"You may provide it," St. Cyr said, in a forbidding voice.

Shortly, the body in its casket was loaded onto a mortuary truck, and the
driver turned to St. Cyr for instructions.

St. Cyr gave him Phil Harvey's address.

"And the litigation," Herb Schoenheit von Vogelsang was murmuring, as
St. Cyr boarded the truck to sit beside the driver. "You don't infer malpractice
on our part, do you, Mr. St. Cyr? Because if you do — "

"The affair is closed as far as we're concerned," St. Cyr said to him
laconically, and signaled the driver to drive off.

As soon as they left the mortuary, St. Cyr began to laugh.

"What strikes you so funny?" the mortuary driver asked.

"Nothing," St. Cyr said, still chuckling.

When the body in its casket, still deep in its original quick-pack, had been
left off at Harvey's home and the driver had departed, St. Cyr picked up the
telephone and dialed. But he found himself unable to get through to the
Convention Hall. All he heard, for his trouble, was the weird distant drumming, the monotonous litany of Louis Sarapis — he hung up, disgusted but at
the same time grimly determined.

We've had enough of that, St. Cyr said to himself. *I won't wait for Harvey's
approval; I don't need it.*

Searching the living room he found, in a desk drawer, a heat gun. Pointing
it at the casket of Louis Sarapis he pressed the trigger.

The envelope of quick-pack steamed up, the casket itself fizzed as the plastic melted. Within, the body blackened, shriveled, charred away at last into a baked, coal-like clinker, small and nondescript.

Satisfied, St. Cyr returned the heat gun to the desk drawer.

Once more he picked up the phone and dialed.

In his ear the monotonous voice intoned, " ... no one but Gam can do it; Gam's the man what am — good slogan for you, Johnny. Gam's the man what am; remember that. I'll do the talking. Give me the mike and I'll tell them; Gam's the man what am. Gam's — "

Claude St. Cyr slammed down the phone, turned to the blackened deposit that had been Louis Sarapis; he gaped mutely at what he could not comprehend. The voice, when St. Cyr turned on the television set, emanated from that, too, just as it had been doing; nothing had changed.

The voice of Louis Sarapis was not originating in the body. Because the body was gone. There simply was no connection between them.

Seating himself in a chair, Claude St. Cyr got out his cigarettes and shakily lit up, trying to understand what this meant. It seemed almost as if he had it, almost had the explanation.

But not quite.

V

By monorail — he had left his 'copter at the Beloved Brethren Mortuary — Claude St. Cyr numbly made his way to Convention Hall. The place, of course, was packed; the noise was terrible. But he managed to obtain the services of a robot page; over the public address system, Phil Harvey's presence was requested in one of the side rooms used as meeting places by delegations wishing to caucus in secret.

Harvey appeared, disheveled from shoving through the dense pack of spectators and delegates. "What is it, Claude?" he asked, and then he saw his attorney's face. "You better tell me," he said quietly.

St. Cyr blurted, "The voice we hear. It isn't Louis! It's someone else trying to sound like Louis!"

"How do you know?"

He told him.

Nodding, Harvey said, "And it definitely was Louis's body you destroyed; there was no deceit there at the mortuary — you're positive of that."

"I'm not positive," St. Cyr said. "But I think it was; I believe it now and I believed it at the time." It was too late to find out now, in any case, not enough remained of the body for such an analysis to be successfully made.

"But who could it be, then?" Harvey said. "My God, it's coming to us from beyond the solar system — could it be nonterrestrials of some kind? Some sort of echo or mockery, a non-living reaction unfamiliar to us? An inert process without intent?"

St. Cyr laughed. "You're babbling, Phil. Cut it out."

Nodding, Harvey said, "Whatever you say, Claude. If you think it's someone here — "

"I don't know," St. Cyr said candidly. "But I'd guess it's someone right on this planet, someone who knew Louis well enough to have introjected his characteristics sufficiently thoroughly to imitate them." He was silent, then. That was as far as he could carry his logical processes ... beyond that he saw nothing. It was a blank, and a frightening one at that.

There is, he thought, *an element of the deranged in it. What we took to be decay — it's more a form of madness than degeneration. Or is madness itself degeneration?* He did not know; he wasn't trained in the field of psychiatry, except regarding its legal aspects. And the legal aspects had no application, here.

"Has anyone nominated Gam yet?" he asked Harvey.

"Not yet. It's expected to come sometime today, though. There's a delegate from Montana who'll do it, the rumor is."

"Johnny Barefoot is here?"

"Yes." Harvey nodded. "Busy as can be, lining up delegates. In and out of the different delegations, very much in evidence. No sign of Gam, of course. He won't come in until the end of the nominating speech and then of course all hell will break loose. Cheering and parading and waving banners ... the Gam supporters are all prepared."

"Any indication of — " St. Cyr hesitated. "What we've assumed to be Louis? His presence?" *Or its presence*, he thought. *Whatever it is.*

"None as yet," Harvey said.

"I think we'll hear from it," St. Cyr said. "Before the day is over."

Harvey nodded; he thought so, too.

"Are you afraid of it?" St. Cyr asked.

"Sure," Harvey said. "A thousand times more so than ever, now that we don't even know who or what it is."

"You're right to take that attitude," St. Cyr said. He felt the same way.

"Perhaps we should tell Johnny," Harvey said.

St. Cyr said, "Let him find out on his own."

"All right, Claude," Harvey said. "Anything you say. After all, it was you who finally found Louis's body; I have complete faith in you."

In a way, St. Cyr thought, *I wish I hadn't found it. I wish I didn't know what I know now; we were better off believing it was old Louis talking to us from every phone, newspaper and TV set.*

That was bad — but this is far worse. Although, he thought, *it seems to me that the answer is there, somewhere, just waiting.*

I must try, he told himself. *Try to get it. TRY!*

* * *

Off by himself in a side room, Johnny Barefoot tensely watched the events of the Convention on closed-circuit TV. The distortion, the invading presence from one light-week away, had cleared for a time, and he could see and hear the delegate from Montana delivering the nominating speech for Alfonse Gam.

He felt tired. The whole process of the Convention, its speeches and parades, its tautness, grated on his nerves, ran contrary to his disposition. *So damn much show*, he thought. Display for what? If Gam wanted to gain the nomination he could get it, and all the rest of this was purposeless.

His own thoughts were on Kathy Egmont Sharp.

He had not seen her since her departure for U.C. Hospital in San Francisco. At this point he had no idea of her condition, whether she had responded to therapy or not.

The deep intuition could not be evaded that she had not.

How sick really was Kathy? Probably very sick, with or without drugs; he felt that strongly. Perhaps she would never be discharged from U.C. Hospital; he could imagine that.

On the other hand — if she wanted out, he decided, *she would find a way to get out*. That he intuited, too, even more strongly.

So it was up to her. She had committed herself, gone into the hospital voluntarily. And she would come out — if she ever did — the same way. No one could compel Kathy ... she was simply not that sort of person. And that, he realized, could well be a symptom of the illness-process.

The door to the room opened. He glanced up from the TV screen.

And saw Claude St. Cyr standing in the entrance. St. Cyr held a heat gun in his hand, pointed at Johnny. He said, "Where's Kathy?"

"I don't know," Johnny said. He got slowly, warily, to his feet.

"You do. I'll kill you if you don't tell me."

"Why?" he said, wondering what had brought St. Cyr to this point, this extreme behavior.

St. Cyr said, "Is it on Earth?" Still holding the gun pointed at Johnny he came toward him.

"Yes," Johnny said, with reluctance.

"Give me the name of the city."

"What are you going to do?" Johnny said. "This isn't like you, Claude; you used to always work within the law."

St. Cyr said, "I think the voice is Kathy. I know it's not Louis, now; we have that to go on but beyond that it's just a guess. *Kathy is the only one I know deranged enough, deteriorated enough*. Give me the name of the hospital."

"The only way you could know it isn't Louis," Johnny said, "would be to destroy the body."

"That's right," St. Cyr said, nodding.

Then you have, Johnny realized. *You found the correct mortuary; you got to Herb Schoenheit von Vogelsang.* So that was that.

The door to the room burst open again; a group of cheering delegates, Gam supporters, marched in, blowing horns and hurling streamers, carrying huge hand-painted placards. St. Cyr turned toward them, waving his gun at them — and Johnny Barefoot sprinted past the delegates, to the door and out into the corridor.

He ran down the corridor and a moment later emerged at the great central hall in which Gam's demonstration was in full swing. From the loudspeakers mounted at the ceiling a voice boomed over and over.

"Vote for Gam, the man what am. Gam, Gam, vote for Gam, vote for Gam, the one fine man; vote for Gam who really am. Gam, Gam, Gam, he really am — "

Kathy, he thought. *It can't be you; it just can't.* He ran on, out of the hall, squeezing past the dancing, delirious delegates, past the glazed-eyed men and women in their funny hats, their banners wiggling . . . he reached the street, the parked 'copters and cars, throngs of people clustered about, trying to push inside.

If it is you, he thought, *then you're too sick ever to come back. Even if you want to, will yourself to. Had you been waiting for Louis to die, is that it? Do you hate us? Or are you afraid of us? What explains what it is you're doing . . . what's the reason for it?*

He hailed a 'copter marked TAXI. "To San Francisco," he instructed the driver.

Maybe you're not conscious that you're doing it, he thought. *Maybe it's an autonomous process, rising out of your unconscious mind. Your mind split into two portions, one on the surface which we see, the other one —*

The one we hear.

Should we feel sorry for you? he wondered. *Or should we hate you, fear you? HOW MUCH HARM CAN YOU DO? I guess that's the real issue. I love you,* he thought. *In some fashion, at least. I care about you, and that's a form of love, not such as I feel toward my wife or my children, but it is a concern. Damn it,* he thought, *this is dreadful. Maybe St. Cyr is wrong; maybe it isn't you.*

The 'copter swept upward into the sky, cleared the buildings and turned west, its blade spinning at peak velocity.

On the ground, standing in front of the convention hall, St. Cyr and Phil Harvey watched the 'copter go.

"Well, so it worked," St. Cyr said. "I got him started moving. I'd guess he's on his way either to Los Angeles or to San Francisco."

A second 'copter slid up before them, hailed by Phil Harvey; the two men entered it and Harvey said, "You see the taxi that just took off? Stay behind it, just within sight. But don't let it catch a glimpse of you if you can help it."

"Heck," the driver said, "If I can see it, it can see me." But he clicked on his meter and began to ascend. Grumpily, he said to Harvey and St. Cyr, "I don't like this kind of stuff; it can be dangerous."

"Turn on your radio," St. Cyr told him. "If you want to hear something that's dangerous."

"Aw hell," the driver said, disgusted. "The radio don't work; some kind of interference, like sun spots or maybe some amateur operator — I lost a lot of fares because the dispatcher can't get hold of me. I think the police ought to do something about it, don't you?"

St. Cyr said nothing. Beside him, Harvey peered at the 'copter ahead.

When he reached U.C. Hospital at San Francisco, and had landed at the field on the main building's roof, Johnny saw the second ship circling, not passing on, and he knew that he was right; he had been followed all the way. But he did not care. It didn't matter.

Descending by means of the stairs, he came out on the third floor and approached a nurse. "Mrs. Sharp," he said. "Where is she?"

"You'll have to ask at the desk," the nurse said. "And visiting hours aren't until — "

He rushed on until he found the desk.

"Mrs. Sharp's room is 309," the bespectacled, elderly nurse at the desk said. "But you must have Doctor Gross's permission to visit her. And I believe Doctor Gross is having lunch right now and probably won't be back until two o'clock, if you'd care to wait." She pointed to a waiting room.

"Thanks," he said. "I'll wait." He passed through the waiting room and out the door at the far end, down the corridor, watching the numbers on the doors until he saw room number 309. Opening the door he entered the room, shut the door after him and looked around for her.

There was the bed, but it was empty.

"Kathy," he said.

At the window, in her robe, she turned, her face sly, bound up by hatred; her lips moved and, staring at him, she said with loathing, "I want Gam because he am." Spitting at him, she crept toward him, her hands raised, her fingers writhing. "Gam's a man, a *real* man," she whispered, and he saw, in her eyes, the dissolved remnants of her personality expire even as he stood there. "Gam, gam, gam," she whispered, and slapped him.

He retreated. "It's you," he said. "Claude St. Cyr was right. Okay. I'll go." He fumbled for the door behind him, trying to get it open. Panic passed through him, like a wind, then; he wanted nothing but to get away. "Kathy," he said, "let go." Her nails had dug into him, into his shoulder, and she hung onto him, peering sideways into his face, smiling at him.

"You're dead," she said. "Go away. I smell you, the dead inside you."

"I'll go," he said, and managed to find the handle of the door. She let go of him, then; he saw her right hand flash up, the nails directed at his face, possibly his eyes — he ducked, and her blow missed him. "I want to get away," he said, covering his face wtih his arms.

Kathy whispered, "I am Gam, I am. I'm the only one who am. Am alive. Gam, alive." She laughed. "Yes, I will," she said, mimicking his voice perfectly. "Claude St. Cyr was right; okay, I'll go. I'll go. I'll go." She was now between him and the door. "The window," she said. "Do it now, what you wanted to do when I stopped you." She hurried toward him, and he retreated, backward, step by step, until he felt the wall behind him.

"It's all in your mind," he said, "this hate. Everyone is fond of you; I am, Gam is, St. Cyr and Harvey are. What's the point of this?"

"The point," Kathy said, "is that I show you what you're really like. Don't you know yet? You're even worse than me. I'm just being honest."

"Why did you pretend to be Louis?" he said.

"I am Louis," Kathy said. "When he died he didn't go into half-life because I ate him; he became me. I was waiting for that. Alfonse and I had it all worked out, the transmitter out there with the recorded tape ready — we frightened you, didn't we? You're all scared, too scared to stand in his way. He'll be nominated; he's been nominated already, I feel it, I know it."

"Not yet," Johnny said.

"But it won't be long," Kathy said. "And I'll be his wife." She smiled at him. "And you'll be dead, you and the others." Coming at him she chanted, "I am Gam, I am Louis and when you're dead I'll be you, Johnny Barefoot, and all the rest; I'll eat you all." She opened her mouth wide and he saw the sharp, jagged, pale-as-death teeth.

"And rule over the dead," Johnny said, and hit her with all his strength, on the side of her face, near the jaw. She spun backward, fell, and then at once was up and rushing at him. Before she could catch him he sprinted away, to one side, caught then a glimpse of her distorted, shredded features, ruined by the force of his blow — and then the door to the room opened, and St. Cyr and Phil Harvey, with two nurses, stood there. Kathy stopped. He stopped, too.

"Come on, Barefoot," St. Cyr said, jerking his head.

Johnny crossed the room and joined them.

Tying the sash of her robe, Kathy said matter-of-factly, "So it was planned; he was to kill me, Johnny was to. And the rest of you would all stand and watch and enjoy it."

"They have an immense transmitter out there," Johnny said. "They placed it a long time ago, possibly years back. All this time they've been waiting for Louis to die; maybe they even killed him, finally. The idea's to get Gam nominated and elected, while keeping everyone terrorized with that transmission. She's sick, much sicker than we realized, even sicker than *you* realized. Most of all it was under the surface where it didn't show."

St. Cyr shrugged. "Well, she'll have to be certified." He was calm but unusually slow-spoken. "The will named me as trustee; I can represent the estate against her, file the commitment papers and then come forth at the sanity hearing."

"I'll demand a jury trial," Kathy said. "I can convince a jury of my sanity; it's actually quite easy and I've been through it before."

"Possibly," St. Cyr said. "But anyhow the transmitter will be gone; by that time the authorities will be out there."

"It'll take months to reach it," Kathy said. "Even by the fastest ship. And by then the election will be over; Alfonse will be President."

St. Cyr glanced at Johnny Barefoot. "Maybe so," he murmured.

"That's why we put it out so far," Kathy said. "It was Alfonse's money and my ability; I inherited Louis's ability — you see. I can do anything. Nothing is impossible for me if I want it; all I have to do is want it *enough.*"

"You wanted me to jump," Johnny said. "And I didn't."

"You would have," Kathy said, "in another minute. If they hadn't come in." She seemed quite poised, now. "You will, eventually; I'll keep after you. And there's no place you can hide; you know I'll follow you and find you. All three of you." Her gaze swept from one of them to the next, taking them all in.

Harvey said, "I've got a little power and wealth, too. I think we can defeat Gam, even if he's nominated."

"You have power," Kathy said, "but not imagination. What you have isn't enough. Not against me." She spoke quietly, with complete confidence.

"Let's go," Johnny said, and started down the hall, away from room 309 and Kathy Egmont Sharp.

Up and down San Francisco's hilly streets Johnny walked, hands in his pockets, ignoring the buildings and people, seeing nothing, merely walking on and on. Afternoon faded, became evening; the lights of the city came on and he ignored that, too. He walked block after block until his feet ached, burned, until he became aware that he was very hungry — that it was now ten o'clock at night and he had not eaten anything since morning. He stopped, then, and looked around him.

Where were Claude St. Cyr and Phil Harvey? He could not remember having parted from them; he did not even remember leaving the hospital. But Kathy; he remembered that. He could not forget it even if he wanted to. And he did not want to. It was too important ever to be forgotten, by any of them who had witnessed it, understood it.

At a newsstand he saw the massive, thick-black headlines.

GAM WINS NOMINATION, PROMISES BATTLING CAMPAIGN
FOR NOVEMBER ELECTION

So she did get that, Johnny thought. *They did, the two of them; they got what they're after exactly. And now — all they have to do is defeat Kent Margrave. And that thing out there, a light-week away; it's still yammering. And will be for months.*

They'll win, he realized.

At a drugstore he found a phone booth; entering it he put money into the slot and dialed Sarah Belle, his own home phone number.

The phone clicked in his ear. And then the familiar monotonous voice chanted, "Gam in November, Gam in November; win with Gam, President Alfonse Gam, our man — I am for Gam. *I am for Gam. For GAM!"* He rang off, then, and left the phone booth. It was hopeless.

At the counter of the drugstore he ordered a sandwich and coffee; he sat eating mechanically, filling the requirements of his body without pleasure or desire, eating by reflex until the food was gone and it was time to pay the bill. *What can I do?* he asked himself. *What can anyone do? All the means of communication are gone; the media have been taken over.* They *have the radio, TV, newspapers, phone, wire services … everything that depends on microwave transmission or open-gap electric circuitry. They've captured it all, left nothing for us, the opposition, by which to fight back.*

Defeat, he thought. *That's the dreary reality that lies ahead for us. And then, when they enter office, it'll be our — death.*

"That'll be a dollar ten," the counter girl said.

He paid for his meal and left the drugstore.

When a 'copter marked TAXI came spiraling by, he hailed it.

"Take me home," he said.

"Okay," the driver said amiably. "Where is home, buddy?"

He gave him the address in Chicago and then settled back for the long ride. He was giving up; he was quitting, going back to Sarah Belle, to his wife and children. The fight — for him — apparently was over.

When she saw him standing in the doorway, Sarah Belle said, "Good God, Johnny — you look terrible." She kissed him, led him inside, into the warm, familiar living room. "I thought you'd be out celebrating."

"*Celebrating?*" he said hoarsely.

"Your man won the nomination." She went to put the coffee pot on for him.

"Oh yeah," he said, nodding. "That's right. I was his P.R. man; I forgot."

"Better lie down," Sarah Belle said. "Johnny, I've never seen you look so beaten; I can't understand it. What happened to you?"

He sat down on the couch and lit a cigarette.

"What can I do for you?" she asked, with anxiety.

"Nothing," he said.

"Is that Louis Sarapis on all the TV and phones? It sounds like him. I was talking with the Nelsons and they said it's Louis's exact voice."

"No," he said. "It's not Louis. Louis is dead."

"But his period of half-life — "

"No," he said. "He's dead. Forget about it."

"You know who the Nelsons are, don't you? They're the new people who moved into the apartment that — "

"I don't want to talk," he said. "Or be talked at."

Sarah Belle was silent, for a minute. And then she said, "One thing they said — you won't like to hear it, I guess. The Nelsons are plain, quite commonplace people ... they said even if Alfonse Gam got the nomination they wouldn't vote for him. They just don't like him."

He grunted.

"Does that made you feel bad?" Sarah Belle asked. "I think they're reacting to the pressure, Louis's pressure on the TV and phones; they just don't care for it. I think you've been excessive in your campaign, Johnny." She glanced at him hesitantly. "That's the truth; I have to say it."

Rising to his feet, he said, "I'm going to visit Phil Harvey. I'll be back later on."

She watched him go out the door, her eyes darkened with concern.

When he was admitted to Phil Harvey's house he found Phil and Gertrude Harvey and Claude St. Cyr sitting together in the living room, each with a glass in hand, but no one speaking. Harvey glanced up briefly, saw him, and then looked away.

"Are we going to give up?" he asked Harvey.

Harvey said, "I'm in touch with Kent Margrave. We're going to try to knock out the transmitter. But it's a million to one shot, at that distance. And with even the fastest missile it'll take a month."

"But that's at least something," Johnny said. It would at least be before the election; it would give them several weeks in which to campaign. "Does Margrave understand the situation?"

"Yes," Claude St. Cyr said. "We told him virtually everything."

"But that's not enough," Phil Harvey said. "There's one more thing we must do. You want to be in on it? Draw for the shortest match?" He pointed to the coffee table; on it Johnny saw three matches, one of them broken in half. Now Phil Harvey added a fourth match, a whole one.

St. Cyr said, "Her first. Her right away, as soon as possible. And then later on if necessary, Alfonse Gam."

Weary, cold fright filled Johnny Barefoot.

"Take a match," Harvey said, picking up the four matches, arranging and rearranging them in his hand and then holding out the four even tops to the people in the room. "Go ahead, Johnny. You got here last so I'll have you go first."

"Not me," he said.

"Then we'll draw without you," Gertrude Harvey said, and picked a match. Phil held the remaining ones out to St. Cyr and he drew one also. Two remained in Phil Harvey's hand.

"I was in love with her," Johnny said. "I still am."

Nodding, Phil Harvey said, "Yes, I know."

His heart leaden, Johnny said, "Okay. I'll draw." Reaching, he selected one of the two matches.

It was the broken one.

"I got it," he said. "It's me."

"Can you do it?" Claude St. Cyr asked him.

He was silent for a time. And then he shrugged and said, "Sure. I can do it. Why not?" *Why not indeed?* he asked himself. *A woman that I was falling in love with; certainly I can murder her. Because it has to be done. There is no other way out for us.*

"It may not be as difficult as we think," St. Cyr said. "We've consulted some of Phil's technicians and we picked up some interesting advice. Most of their transmissions are coming from nearby, not a light-week away by any means. I'll tell you how we know. Their transmissions have kept up with changing events. For example, your suicide-attempt at the Antler Hotel. *There was no time-lapse there or anywhere else.*"

"And they're not supernatural, Johnny," Gertrude Harvey said.

"So the first thing to do," St. Cyr continued, "is to find their base here on Earth or at least here in the solar system. It could be Gam's guinea fowl ranch on Io. Try there, if you find she's left the hospital."

"Okay," Johnny said, nodding slightly.

"How about a drink?" Phil Harvey said to him.

Johnny nodded.

The four of them, seated in a circle, drank, slowly and in silence.

"Do you have a gun?" St. Cyr asked.

"Yes." Rising to his feet he set his glass down.

"Good luck," Gertrude said, after him.

Johnny opened the front door and stepped outside alone, out into the dark, cold evening.

ORPHEUS WITH CLAY FEET

AT THE OFFICES of Concord Military Service Consultants, Jesse Slade looked through the window at the street below and saw everything denied him in the way of freedom, flowers and grass, the opportunity for a long and unencumbered walk into new places. He sighed.

"Sorry, sir," the client opposite his desk mumbled apologetically. "I guess I'm boring you."

"Not at all," Slade said, reawakening to his onerous duties. "Let's see … " He examined the papers which the client, a Mr. Walter Grossbein, had presented to him. "Now you feel, Mr. Grossbein, that your most favorable chance to elude military service lies in the area of a chronic ear-trouble deemed by civilian doctors in the past *acute labyrinthitis*. Hmmm." Slade studied the pertinent documents.

His duties — and he did not enjoy them — lay in locating for clients of the firm a way out of military service. The war against the Things had not been conducted properly, of late; many casualties from the Proxima region had been reported — and with the reports had come a rush of business for Concord Military Service Consultants.

"Mr. Grossbein," Slade said thoughtfully, "I noticed when you entered my office that you tended to list to one side."

"Did I?" Mr. Grossbein asked, surprised.

"Yes, and I thought to myself, That man has a severe impairment of his sense of balance. That's related to the ear, you know, Mr. Grossbein. Hearing, from an evolutionary standpoint, is an outgrowth of the sense of balance. Some water creatures of a low order incorporate a grain of sand and make use of it as a drop-weight within their fluid body, and by that method tell if they're going up or down."

Mr. Grossbein said, "I believe I understand."

"Say it, then," Jesse Slade said.

"I — frequently list to one side or another as I walk."

"And at night?"

Mr. Grossbein frowned, and then said happily, "I, uh, find it almost impossible to orient myself at night, in the dark, when I can't see."

"Fine," Jesse Slade said, and begin writing on the client's military service form B-30. "I think this will get you an exemption," he said.

Happily, the client said, "I can't thank you enough."

Oh yes you can, Jesse Slade thought to himself. You can thank us to the tune of fifty dollars. After all, without us you might be a pale, lifeless corpse in some gully on a distant planet, not far from now.

And, thinking about distant planets, Jesse Slade felt once more the yearning. The need to escape from his small office and the process of dealing with gold-bricking clients whom he had to face, day after day.

There must be another life than this, Slade said to himself. Can this really be all there is to existence?

Far down the street outside his office window a neon sign glowed night and day. Muse Enterprises, the sign read, and Jesse Slade knew what it meant. I'm going in there, he said to himself. Today. When I'm on my ten-thirty coffee break; I won't even wait for lunch time.

As he put on his coat, Mr. Hnatt, his supervisor, entered the office and said, "Say, Slade, what's up? Why the fierce trapped look?"

"Um, I'm getting out, Mr. Hnatt," Slade told him. "Escaping. I've told fifteen thousand men how to escape military service; now it's my turn."

Mr. Hnatt clapped him on the back. "Good idea, Slade; you're overworked. Take a vacation. Take a time-travel adventure to some distant civilization — it'll do you good."

"Thanks, Mr. Hnatt," Slade said, "I'll do just that." And left his office as fast as his feet would carry him, out of the building and down the street to the glowing neon sign of Muse Enterprises.

The girl behind the counter, blonde-haired, with dark green eyes and a figure that impressed him more for its engineering aspects, its suspension so to speak, smiled at him and said, "Our Mr. Manville will see you in a moment, Mr. Slade. Please be seated. You'll find authentic nineteenth century *Harper's Weeklies* over on the table, there." She added, "And some twentieth century *Mad Comics*, those great classics of lampoonery equal to Hogarth."

Tensely, Mr. Slade seated himself and tried to read; he found an article in *Harper's Weekly* telling that the Panama Canal was impossible and had already been abandoned by its French designers — that held his attention for a moment (the reasoning was so logical, so convincing) but after a few moments his old ennui and restlessness, like a chronic fog, returned. Rising to his feet he once more approached the desk.

"Mr. Manville isn't here yet?" he asked hopefully.

From behind him a male voice said, "You, there at the counter."

Slade turned. And found himself facing a tall, dark-haired man with an intense expression, eyes blazing.

"You," the man said, "are in the *wrong century*."

Slade gulped.

Striding toward him, the dark-haired man said, "I am Manville, sir." He held out his hand and they shook. "You must go away," Manville said. "Do you understand, sir? As soon as possible."

"But I want to use your services," Slade mumbled.

Manville's eyes flashed. "I mean away into the past. What's your name?" He gestured emphatically. "Wait, it's coming to me. Jesse Slade, of Concord, up the street, there."

"Right," Slade said, impressed.

"All right, now down to business," Mr. Manville said. "Into my office." To the exceptionally-constructed girl at the counter he said, "No one is to disturb us, Miss Frib."

"Yes, Mr. Manville," Miss Frib said. "I'll see to that, don't you fear, sir."

"I know that, Miss Frib." Mr. Manville ushered Slade into a well-furnished inner office. Old maps and prints decorated the walls; the furniture — Slade gaped. Early American, with wood pegs instead of nails. New England maple and worth a fortune.

"Is it all right ... " he began.

"Yes, you may actually sit on that Directorate chair," Mr. Manville told him. "But be careful; it scoots out from under you if you lean forward. We keep meaning to put rubber casters on it or some such thing." He looked irritated now, at having to discuss such trifles. "Mr. Slade," he said brusquely, "I'll speak plainly; obviously you're a man of high intellect and we can skip the customary circumlocutions."

"Yes," Slade said, "please do."

"Our time-travel arrangements are of a specific nature; hence the name 'Muse.' Do you grasp the meaning, here?"

"Um," Slade said, at a loss but trying. "Let's see. A muse is an organism that functions to — "

"That inspires," Mr. Manville broke in impatiently. "Slade, you are — let's face it — not a creative man. That's why you feel bored and unfulfilled. Do you paint? Compose? Make welded iron sculpture out of spaceship bodies and discarded lawn chairs? You don't. You do nothing; you're utterly passive. Correct?"

Slade nodded. "You've hit it, Mr. Manville."

"I've hit nothing," Mr. Manville said irritably. "You don't follow me,

Slade. Nothing will make you creative because you don't have it within you. You're too ordinary. I'm not going to get you started finger-painting or basket-weaving; I'm no Jungian analyst who believes art is the answer." Leaning back he pointed his finger at Slade. "Look, Slade. We can help you, but you must be willing to help yourself first. Since you're not creative, the best you can hope for — and we can assist you here — is to inspire others who are creative. Do you see?"

After a moment Slade said, "I see, Mr. Manville. I do."

"Right," Manville said, nodding. "Now, you can inspire a famous musician, like Mozart or Beethoven, or a scientist such as Albert Einstein, or a sculptor such as Sir Jacob Epstein — any one of a number of people, writers, musicians, poets. You could, for example, meet Sir Edward Gibbon during his travels to the Mediterranean and fall into a casual conversation with him and say something to this order... Hmmm, look at the ruins of this ancient civilization all around us. I wonder, how does a mighty empire such as Rome come to fall into decay? Fall into ruin... fall apart... "

"Good Lord," Slade said fervently, "I see, Manville; I get it. I repeat the word 'fall' over and over again to Gibbon, and due to me he gets the idea of his great history of Rome, the *Decline and Fall of the Roman Empire*. And — " He felt himself tremble. "I helped."

" 'Helped'?" Manville said. "Slade, that's hardly the word. Without you there would have been no such work. You, Slade, could be Sir Edward's muse." He leaned back, got out an Upmann cigar, circa 1915, and lit up.

"I think," Slade said, "I'd like to mull this over. I want to be sure I inspire the proper person; I mean, they all deserve to be inspired, but — "

"But you want to find *the* person in terms of your own psychic needs," Manville agreed, puffing fragrant blue smoke. "Take our brochure." He passed a large shiny multi-color 3-D pop-up booklet to Slade. "Take this home, read it, and come back to us when you're ready."

Slade said, "God bless you, Mr. Manville."

"And calm down," Manville said. "The world isn't going to end... we know that here at Muse because we've looked." He smiled, and Slade managed to smile back.

Two days later Jesse Slade returned to Muse Enterprises. "Mr. Manville," he said, "I know whom I want to inspire." He took a deep breath. "I've thought and thought and what would mean to the most to me would be if I could go back to Vienna and inspire Ludwig van Beethoven with the idea for the Choral Symphony, you know, that theme in the fourth movement that the baritone sings that goes bum-bum de-da de-da bum-bum, daughters of Elysium; you know." He flushed. "I'm no musician, but all my life I've admired the Beethoven Ninth and especially —

"It's been done," Manville said.

"Eh?" He did not understand.

"It's been taken, Mr. Slade." Manville looked impatient as he sat at his great oak rolltop desk, circa 1910. Bringing out a thick metal-staved black binder he turned the pages. "Two years ago a Mrs. Ruby Welch of Montpelier, Idaho went back to Vienna and inspired Beethoven with the theme for the choral movement of his Ninth." Manville slammed the binder shut and regarded Slade. "Well? What's your second choice?"

Stammering, Slade said, "I'd — have to think. Give me time."

Examining his watch, Manville said shortly, "I'll give you two hours. Until three this afternoon. Good day, Slade." He rose to his feet, and Slade automatically rose, too.

An hour later, in his cramped office at Concord Military Service Consultants, Jesse Slade realized in a flashing single instant who and what he wanted to inspire. At once he put on his coat, excused himself to sympathetic Mr. Hnatt, and hurried down the street to Muse Enterprises.

"Well, Mr. Slade," Manville said, seeing him enter. "Back so soon. Come into the office." He strode ahead, leading the way. "All right, let's have it." He shut the door after the two of them.

Jesse Slade licked his dry lips and then, coughing, said, "Mr. Manville, I want to go back and inspire — well, let me explain. You know the great science fiction of the golden age, between 1930 and 1970?"

"Yes, yes," Manville said impatiently, scowling as he listened.

"When I was in college," Slade said, "getting my M.A. in English lit, I had to read a good deal of twentieth century science fiction, of course. Of the greats there were three writers who stood out. The first was Robert Heinlein with his future history. The second, Isaac Asimov with his Foundation epic series. And — " He took a deep, shuddering breath. "The man I did my paper on. Jack Dowland. Of the three of them, Dowland was considered the greatest. His future history of the world began to appear in 1957, in both magazine form — as short stories — and in book form, as complete novels. By 1963, Dowland was regarded as — "

Mr. Manville said, "Hmmm." Getting out the black binder, he began to thumb through it. "Twentieth century science fiction ... a rather specialized interest — fortunately for you. Let's see."

"I hope," Slade said quietly, "it hasn't been taken."

"Here is one client," Mr. Manville said. "Leo Parks of Vacaville, California. He went back and inspired A. E. van Vogt to avoid love stories and westerns and try science fiction." Turning more pages, Mr. Manville said, "And last year a client of Muse Enterprises, Miss Julie Oxenblut of Kansas City, Kansas asked to be permitted to inspire Robert Heinlein in his future history ... was it Heinlein you said, Mr. Slade?"

"No," Slade said, "it was Jack Dowland, the greatest of the three. Heinlein was great, but I did much research on this, Mr. Manville, and Dowland was greater."

"No, it hasn't been done," Manville decided, closing up the black binder. From his desk drawer he brought out a form. "You fill this out, Mr. Slade," he said, "and then we'll begin to roll on this matter. Do you know the year and the place at which Jack Dowland began work on his future history of the world?"

"I do," Slade said. "He was living in a little town on the then Route 40 in Nevada, a town called Purpleblossom, consisted of three gas stations, a cafe, a bar, and a general store. Dowland had moved there to get atmosphere; he wanted to write stories of the Old West in the form of TV scripts. He hoped to make a good deal of money."

"I see you know your subject," Manville said, impressed.

Slade continued, "While living in Purpleblossom he did write a number of TV western scripts but somehow he found them unsatisfactory. In any case, he remained there, trying other fields such as children's books and articles on teen-age pre-marital sex for the slick magazines of the times ... and then, all at once, in the year 1956, he suddenly turned to science fiction and immediately produced the greatest novelette seen to date in that field. That was the consensus gentium of the time, Mr. Manville, and I have read the story and I agree. It was called THE FATHER ON THE WALL and it still appears in anthologies now and then; it's the kind of story that will never die. And the magazine in which it appeared, *Fantasy & Science Fiction*, will always be remembered for having published Dowland's first epic in its August 1957 issue."

Nodding, Mr. Manville said, "And this is the magnus opus which you wish to inspire. This, and all that followed."

"You have it right, sir," Mr. Slade said.

"Fill out your form," Manville said, "and we'll do the rest." He smiled at Slade and Slade, confident, smiled back.

The operator of the time-ship, a short, heavy-set, crew-cut young man with strong features, said briskly to Slade, "Okay, bud; you ready or not? Make up your mind."

Slade, for one last time, inspected his twentieth century suit which Muse Enterprises had provided him — one of the services for the rather high fee which he had found himself paying. Narrow necktie, cuffless trousers, and Ivy League striped shirt ... yes, Slade decided, from what he knew of the period it was authentic, right down to the sharp-pointed Italian shoes and the colorful stretch socks. He would pass without any difficulty as a citizen of the U.S. of 1956, even in Purpleblossom, Nevada.

"Now listen," the operator said, as he fastened the safety belt around Slade's middle, "you got to remember a couple of things. First of all, the only way you can get back to 2040 is with me; you can't *walk* back. And second, you got to be careful not to change the past — I mean, stick to your one simple task of inspiring this individual, this Jack Dowland, *and let it go at that.*"

"Of course," Slade said, puzzled at the admonition.

"Too many clients," the operator said, "you'd be surprised how many, go wild when they get back into the past; they get delusions of power and want to make all sorts of changes — eliminate wars, hunger and poverty — you know. Change history."

"I won't do that," Slade said. "I have no interest in abstract cosmic ventures on that order." To him, inspiring Jack Dowland was cosmic enough. And yet he could empathize enough to understand the temptation. In his own work he had seen all kinds of people.

The operator slammed shut the hatch of the time-ship, made certain that Slade was strapped in properly, and then took his own seat at the controls. He snapped a switch and a moment later Slade was on his way to his vacation from monotonous office work — back to 1956 and the nearest he would come to a creative act in his life.

The hot midday Nevada sun beat down, blinding him; Slade squinted, peered about nervously for the town of Purpleblossom. All he saw was dull rock and sand, the open desert with a single narrow road passing among the joshua plants.

"To the right," the operator of the time-ship said, pointing. "You can walk there in ten minutes. You understand your contract, I hope. Better get it out and read it."

From the breast pocket of his 1950-style coat, Slade brought the long yellow contract form with Muse Enterprises. "It says you'll give me thirty-six hours. That you'll pick me up in this spot and that it's my responsibility to be here; if I'm not, and can't be brought back to my own time, the company is not liable."

"Right," the operator said, and re-entered the time-ship. "Good luck, Mr. Slade. Or, as I should call you, Jack Dowland's muse." He grinned, half in derision, half in friendly sympathy, and then the hatch shut after him.

Jesse Slade was alone on the Nevada desert, a quarter mile outside the tiny town of Purpleblossom.

He began to walk, perspiring, wiping his neck with his handkerchief.

There was no problem to locating Jack Dowland's house, since only seven houses existed in the town. Slade stepped up onto the rickety wooden porch, glancing at the yard with its trash can, clothes line, discarded plumbing fixtures ... parked in the driveway he saw a dilapidated car of some archaic sort — archaic even for the year 1956.

He rang the bell, adjusted his tie nervously, and once more in his mind rehearsed what he intended to say. At this point in his life, Jack Dowland had written no science fiction; that was important to remember — it was in fact the entire point. This was the critical nexus in his life — history, this fateful ringing of his doorbell. Of course Dowland did not know that. What was he doing within the house? Writing? Reading the funnies of a Reno newspaper? Sleeping?

Footsteps. Tautly, Slade prepared himself.

The door opened. A young woman wearing light-weight cotton trousers, her hair tied back with a ribbon, surveyed him calmly. What small, pretty feet she had, Slade noticed. She wore slippers; her skin was smooth and shiny, and he found himself gazing intently, unaccustomed to seeing so much of a woman exposed. Both ankles were completely bare.

"Yes?" the woman asked pleasantly but a trifle wearily. He saw now that she had been *vacuuming*; there in the living room was a tank type G.E. vacuum cleaner ... its existence here proving that historians were wrong; the tank type cleaner had *not* vanished in 1950 as was thought.

Slade, thoroughly prepared, said smoothly, "Mrs. Dowland?" The woman nodded. Now a small child appeared to peep at him past its mother. "I'm a fan of your husband's monumental — " Oops, he thought, that wasn't right. "Ahem," he corrected himself, using a twentieth century expression often found in books of that period. "Tsk-tsk," he said. "What I mean to say is this, madam. I know well the works of your husband Jack. I am here by means of a lengthy drive across the desert badlands to observe him in his habitat." He smiled hopefully.

"You know Jack's work?" She seemed surprised, but thoroughly pleased.

"On the telly," Slade said. "Fine scripts of his." He nodded.

"You're English, are you?" Mrs. Dowland said. "Well, did you want to come in?" She held the door wide. "Jack is working right now up in the attic ... the children's noise bothers him. But I know he'd like to stop and talk to you, especially since you drove so far. You're Mr. — "

"Slade," Slade said. "Nice abode you possess, here."

"Thank you." She led the way into a dark, cool kitchen in the center of which he saw a round plastic table with wax milk carton, melmac plate, sugar bowl, two coffee cups and other amusing objects thereon. "JACK!" she called at the foot of a flight of stairs. "THERE'S A FAN OF YOURS HERE; HE WANTS TO SEE YOU!"

Far off above them a door opened. The sound of a person's steps, and then, as Slade stood rigidly, Jack Dowland appeared, young and good-look-ing, with slightly-thinning brown hair, wearing a sweater and slacks, his lean, intelligent face beclouded with a frown. "I'm at work," he said curtly. "Even though I do it at home it's a job like any other." He gazed at Slade. "What do you want? What do you mean you're a 'fan' of my work? *What* work? Christ, it's been two months since I sold anything; I'm about ready to go out of my mind."

Slade said, "Jack Dowland, that is because you have yet to find your proper genre." He heard his voice tremble; this was the moment.

"Would you like a beer, Mr. Slade?" Mrs. Dowland asked.

"Thank you, miss," Slade said. "Jack Dowland," he said, "I am here to inspire you."

"Where are you from?" Dowland said suspiciously. "And how come you're wearing your tie that funny way?"

"Funny in what respect?" Slade asked, feeling nervous.

"With the knot at the bottom instead of up around your adam's apple." Dowland walked around him, now, studying him critically. "And why's your head shaved? You're too young to be bald."

"The custom of this period," Slade said feebly. "Demands a shaved head. At least in New York."

"Shaved head my ass," Dowland said. "Say, what are you, some kind of a crank? What do you want?"

"I want to praise you," Slade said. He felt angry now; a new emotion, indignation, filled him — he was not being treated properly and he knew it.

"Jack Dowland," he said, stuttering a little, "I know more about your work than you do; I know your proper genre is science fiction and not television westerns. Better listen to me; I'm your muse." He was silent, then, breathing noisily and with difficulty.

Dowland stared at him, and then threw back his head and laughed.

Also smiling, Mrs. Dowland said, "Well, I knew Jack had a muse but I assumed it was female. Aren't all muses female?"

"No," Slade said angrily. "Leon Parks of Vacaville, California, who inspired A. E. van Vogt, was male." He seated himself at the plastic table, his legs being too wobbly, now, to support him. "Listen to me, Jack Dowland — "

"For God's sake," Dowland said, "either call me Jack or Dowland but not both; it's not natural the way you're talking. Are you on tea or something?" He sniffed intently.

"Tea," Slade echoed, not understanding. "No, just a beer, please."

Dowland said, "Well get to the point. I'm anxious to be back at work. Even if it's done at home it *is* work."

It was now time for Slade to deliver his encomium. He had prepared it carefully; clearing his throat he began. "Jack, if I may call you that, I wonder why the hell you haven't tried science fiction. I figure that — "

"I'll tell you why," Jack Dowland broke in. He paced back and forth, his hands in his trousers pockets. "Because there's going to be a hydrogen war. The future's black. Who wants to write about it? Keeerist." He shook his head. "And anyhow who reads that stuff? Adolescents with skin trouble. Misfits. And it's junk. Name me one good science fiction story, just one. I picked up a magazine on a bus once when I was in Utah. Trash! I wouldn't write that trash even if it paid well, and I looked into it and it doesn't pay well — around one half cent a word. And who can live on that?" Disgustedly, he started toward the stairs. "I'm going back to work."

"Wait," Slade said, feeling desperate. All was going wrong. "Hear me out, Jack Dowland."

"There you go with that funny talk again," Dowland said. But he paused, waiting. "Well?" he demanded.

Slade said, "Mr. Dowland, I am from the future." He was not supposed to say that — Mr. Manville had warned him severely — but it seemed at the moment to be the only way out for him, the only thing that would stop Jack Dowland from walking off.

"What?" Dowland said loudly. "The *what?*"

"I am a time-traveler," Slade said feebly, and was silent.

Dowland walked back toward him.

When he arrived at the time-ship, Slade found the short-set operator seated on the ground before it, reading a newspaper. The operator glanced up, grinned and said, "Back safe and sound, Mr. Slade. Come on, let's go." He opened the hatch and guided Slade within.

"Take me back," Slade said. "Just take me back."

"What's the matter? Didn't you enjoy your inspiring?"

"I just want to go back to my own time," Slade said.

"Okay," the operator said, raising an eyebrow. He strapped Slade into his seat and then took his own beside him.

When they reached Muse Enterprises, Mr. Manville was waiting for them. "Slade," he said, "come inside." His face was dark. "I have a few words to say to you."

When they were alone in Manville's office, Slade began, "He was in a bad mood, Mr. Manville. Don't blame me." He hung his head, feeling empty and futile.

"You — " Manville stared down at him in disbelief. "You *failed* to inspire him! That's never happened before!"

"Maybe I can go back again," Slade said.

"My God," Manville said, "you not only didn't inspire him — you turned him *against* science fiction."

"How did you find this out?" Slade said. He had hoped to keep it quiet, make it his own secret to carry with him to the grave.

Manville said bitingly, "All I had to do was keep my eye on the reference books dealing with literature of the twentieth century. Half an hour after you left, the entire texts on Jack Dowland, including the half-page devoted to his biography in the Britannica — vanished."

Slade said nothing; he stared at the floor.

"So I researched it," Manville said. "I had the computers at the University of California look up all extant citations on Jack Dowland."

"Were there any?" Slade mumbled.

"Yes," Manville said. "There were a couple. Minute, in rarified technical articles dealing comprehensively and exhaustively with that period. Because of you, Jack Dowland is now completely unknown to the public — *and was so even during his own day.*" He waved a finger at Slade, panting with wrath. "Because of you, Jack Dowland never wrote his epic future history of mankind. Because of your so-called 'inspiration' he continued to write scripts for TV westerns — and died at forty-six an utterly anonymous hack."

"No science fiction at *all?*" Slade asked, incredulous. Had he done that badly? He couldn't believe it; true, Dowland had bitterly repulsed every suggestion Slade had made — true, he had gone back up to his attic in a peculiar frame of mind after Slade had made his point. But —

"All right," Manville said, "there exists *one* science fiction work by Jack Dowland. Tiny, mediocre and totally unknown." Reaching into his desk drawer he grabbed out a yellowed, ancient magazine which he tossed to Slade. "One short story called ORPHEUS WITH CLAY FEET, under the pen name Philip K. Dick. Nobody read it then, nobody reads it now — it was an account of a visit to Dowland by — " He glared furiously at Slade. "By a well-intentioned idiot from the future with deranged visions of *inspiring* him to write a mythological history of the world to come. Well, Slade? What do you say?"

Slade said heavily, "He used my visit as the basis for the story. Obviously."

"And it made him the only money he ever earned as a science fiction writer — dissapointingly little, barely enough to justify his effort and time. You're in the story, I'm in the story — Lord, Slade, you must have told him everything."

"I did," Slade said. "To convince him."

"Well, he wasn't convinced; he thought you were a nut of some kind. He wrote the story obviously in a bitter frame of mind. Let me ask you this: was he busy working when you arrived?"

"Yes," Slade said, "but Mrs. Dowland said — "

"There is — was — no Mrs. Dowland! Dowland never married! That must have been a neighbor's wife whom Dowland was having an affair with. No wonder he was furious; you broke in on his assignation with that girl, whoever she was. She's in the story, too; he put everything in and then gave up his house in Purpleblossom, Nevada and moved to Dodge City, Kansas."

There was silence.

"Um," Slade said at last, "well, could I try again? With someone else? I was thinking on the way back about Paul Ehrlich and his magic bullet, his discovery of the cure for — "

"Listen," Manville said. "I've been thinking, too. You're going back but not to inspire Doctor Ehrlich or Beethoven or Dowland or anybody like that, anybody useful to society."

With dread, Slade glanced up.

"You're going back," Manville said between his teeth, "to *uninspire* people like Adolf Hitler and Karl Marx and Sanrome Clinger — "

"You mean you think I'm so ineffectual ... " Slade mumbled.

"Exactly. We'll start with Hitler in his period of imprisonment after his first abortive attempt to seize power in Bavaria. The period in which he dictated *Mein Kampf* to Rudolf Hess. I've discussed this with my superiors and it's all worked out; you'll be there as a fellow prisoner, you understand? And you'll recommend to Adolf Hitler, just as you recommended to Jack Dowland, that he write. In this case, a detailed autobiography laying out in detail his political program for the world. And if everything goes right — "

"I understand," Slade murmured, staring at the floor again. "It's a — I'd say an inspired idea, but I'm afraid I've given onus to that word by now."

"Don't credit me with the idea," Manville said. "I got it out of Dowland's wretched story, ORPHEUS WITH CLAY FEET; that's how he resolved it at the end." He turned the pages of the ancient magazine until he came to the part he wanted. "Read that, Slade. You'll find that it carries you up to your encounter with me, and then you go off to do research on the Nazi Party so that you can best uninspire Adolf Hitler not to write his autobiography and hence possibly prevent World War Two. And if you fail to uninspire Hitler, we'll try you on Stalin, and if you fail to uninspire Stalin, then — "

"All right," Slade muttered, "I understand; you don't have to spell it out to me."

"And you'll do it," Manville said, "because in ORPHEUS WITH CLAY FEET you agree. So it's all decided already."

Slade nodded. "Anything. To make amends."

To him Manville said, "You idiot. How could you have done so badly?"

"It was an off-day for me," Slade said. "I'm sure I could do better the next time." Maybe with Hitler, he thought. Maybe I can do a terrific job of uninspiring him, better than anyone else ever did in uninspiring anyone in history.

"We'll call you the null-muse," Manville said.

"Clever idea," Slade said.

Wearily, Manville said, "Don't compliment me; compliment Jack Dowland. It was in his story, too. At the very last."

"And that's how it ends?" Slade asked.

"No," Manville said, "it ends with me presenting you with a bill — the costs of sending you back to uninspire Adolf Hitler. Five hundred dollars, in advance." He held out his hand. "Just in case you never get back here."

Resignedly, in misery, Jesse Slade reached as slowly as possible into his twentieth century coat pocket for his wallet.

THE DAYS OF PERKY PAT

AT TEN IN THE MORNING a terrific horn, familiar to him, hooted Sam Regan out of his sleep, and he cursed the careboy upstairs; he knew the racket was deliberate. The careboy, circling, wanted to be certain that flukers — and not merely wild animals — got the care parcels that were to be dropped.

We'll get them, we'll get them, Sam Regan said to himself as he zipped his dust-proof overalls, put his feet into boots and then grumpily sauntered as slowly as possible toward the ramp. Several other flukers joined him, all showing similar irritation.

"He's early today," Tod Morrison complained. "And I'll bet it's all staples, sugar and flour and lard — nothing interesting like say candy."

"We ought to be grateful," Norman Schein said.

"Grateful!" Tod halted to stare at him. "GRATEFUL?"

"Yes," Schein said. "What do you think we'd be eating without them: If they hadn't seen the clouds ten years ago."

"Well," Tod said sullenly, "I just don't like them to come *early*; I actually don't exactly mind their coming, as such."

As he put his shoulders against the lid at the top of the ramp, Schein said genially, "That's mighty tolerant of you, Tod boy. I'm sure the careboys would be pleased to hear your sentiments."

Of the three of them, Sam Regan was the last to reach the surface; he did not like the upstairs at all, and he did not care who knew it. And anyhow, no one could compel him to leave the safety of the Pinole Fluke-pit; it was entirely his business, and he noted now that a number of his fellow flukers had elected to remain below in their quarters, confident that those who did answer the horn would bring them back something.

"It's bright," Tod murmured, blinking in the sun.

The care ship sparkled close overhead, set against the gray sky as if hanging from an uneasy thread. Good pilot, this drop, Tod decided. He, or rather *it*, just lazily handles it, in no hurry. Tod waved at the care ship, and once more the huge horn burst out its din, making him clap his hands to his ears. Hey, a joke's a joke, he said to himself. And then the horn ceased; the careboy had relented.

"Wave to him to drop," Norm Schein said to Tod. "You've got the wigwag."

"Sure," Tod said, and began laboriously flapping the red flag, which the Martian creatures had long ago provided, back and forth, back and forth.

A projectile slid from the underpart of the ship, tossed out stabilizers, spiraled toward the ground.

"Sheoot," Sam Regan said with disgust. "It is staples; they don't have the parachute." He turned away, not interested.

How miserable the upstairs looked today, he thought as he surveyed the scene surrounding him. There, to the right, the uncompleted house which someone — not far from their pit — had begun to build out of lumber salvaged from Vallejo, ten miles to the north. Animals or radiation dust had gotten the builder, and so his work remained where it was; it would never be put to use. And, Sam Regan saw, an unusually heavy precipitate had formed since last he had been up here, Thursday morning or perhaps Friday; he had lost exact track. The darn dust, he thought. Just rocks, pieces of rubble, and the dust. World's becoming a dusty object with no one to whisk it off regularly. How about you? he asked silently of the Martian careboy flying in slow circles overhead. Isn't your technology limitless? Can't you appear some morning with a dust rag a million miles in surface area and restore our planet to pristine newness?

Or rather, he thought, to pristine *oldness*, the way it was in the "ol-days," as the children call it. We'd like that. While you're looking for something to give to us in the way of further aid, try that.

The careboy circled once more, searching for signs of writing in the dust: a message from the flukers below. I'll write that, Sam thought. BRING DUST RAG, RESTORE OUR CIVILIZATION. Okay, careboy?

All at once the care ship shot off, no doubt on its way back home to its base on Luna or perhaps all the way to Mars.

From the open fluke-pit hole, up which the three of them had come, a further head poked, a woman. Jean Regan, Sam's wife, appeared, shielded by a bonnet against the gray, blinding sun, frowning and saying, "Anything important? Anything *new*?"

" 'Fraid not," Sam said. The care parcel projectile had landed and he walked toward it, scuffing his boots in the dust. The hull of the projectile had cracked open from the impact and he could see the canisters already. It looked to be five thousand pounds of salt — might as well leave it up here so the animals wouldn't starve, he decided. He felt despondent.

How peculiarly anxious the careboys were. Concerned all the time that the mainstays of existence be ferried from their own planet to Earth. They must think we eat all day long, Sam thought. My God ... the pit was filled to capacity with stored foods. But of course it had been one of the smallest public shelters in Northern California.

"Hey," Schein said, stooping down by the projectile and peering into the crack opened along its side. "I believe I see something we can use." He found a rusted metal pole — once it had helped reinforce the concrete side of an ol-days public building — and poked at the projectile, stirring its release mechanism into action. The mechanism, triggered off, popped the rear half of the projectile open ... and there lay the contents.

"Looks like radios in that box," Tod said. "Transistor radios." Thoughtfully stroking his short black beard he said, "Maybe we can use them for something new in our layouts."

"Mine's already got a radio," Schein pointed out.

"Well, build an electronic self-directing lawn mower with the parts," Tod said. "You don't have that, do you?" He knew the Scheins' Perky Pat layout fairly well; the two couples, he and his wife with Schein and his, had played together a good deal, being almost evenly matched.

Sam Regan said, "Dibs on the radios, because I can use them." His layout lacked the automatic garage-door opener that both Schein and Tod had; he was considerably behind them.

"Let's get to work," Schein agreed. "We'll leave the staples here and just cart back the radios. If anybody wants the staples, let them come here and get them. Before the do-cats do."

Nodding, the other two men fell to the job of carting the useful contents of the projectile to the entrance of their fluke-pit ramp. For use in their precious, elaborate Perky Pat layouts.

Seated cross-legged with his whetstone, Timothy Schein, ten years old and aware of his many responsibilities, sharpened his knife, slowly and expertly. Meanwhile, disturbing him, his mother and father noisily quarreled with Mr. and Mrs. Morrison, on the far side of the partition. They were playing Perky Pat again. As usual.

How many times today they have to play that dumb game? Timothy asked himself. Forever, I guess. He could see nothing in it, but his parents played on anyhow. And they weren't the only ones; he knew from what other kids said, even from other fluke-pits, that their parents, too, played Perky Pat most of the day, and sometimes even on into the night.

His mother said loudly, "Perky Pat's going to the grocery store and it's got one of those electric eyes that opens the door. Look." A pause. "See, it opened for her, and now she's inside."

"She pushes a cart," Timothy's dad added, in support.

"No, she doesn't," Mrs. Morrison contradicted. "That's wrong. She gives her list to the grocer and he fills it."

"That's only in little neighborhood stores," his mother explained. "And this is a supermarket, you can tell because of the electric eye door."

"I'm sure all grocery stores had electric eye doors," Mrs. Morrison said stubbornly, and her husband chimed in with his agreement. Now the voices rose in anger; another squabble had broken out. As usual.

Aw, cung to them, Timothy said to himself, using the strongest word which he and his friends knew. What's a supermarket anyhow? He tested the blade of his knife — he had made it himself, originally, out of a heavy metal pan — and then hopped to his feet. A moment later he had sprinted silently down the hall and was rapping his special rap on the door of the Chamberlains' quarters.

Fred, also ten years old, answered. "Hi. Ready to go? I see you got that ol' knife of yours sharpened; what do you think we'll catch?"

"Not a do-cat," Timothy said. "A lot better than that; I'm tired of eating do-cat. Too peppery."

"Your parents playing Perky Pat?"

"Yeah."

Fred said, "My mom and dad have been gone for a long time, off playing with the Benteleys." He glanced sideways at Timothy, and in an instant they had shared their mute disappointment regarding their parents. Gosh, and maybe the darn game was all over the world, by now; that would not have surprised either of them.

"How come your parents play it?" Timothy asked.

"Same reason yours do," Fred said.

Hesitating, Timothy said, "Well, why? I don't know why they do; I'm asking you, can't you say?"

"It's because — " Fred broke off. "Ask them. Come on; let's get upstairs and start hunting." His eyes shone. "Let's see what we can catch and kill today."

Shortly, they had ascended the ramp, popped open the lid, and were crouching amidst the dust and rocks, searching the horizon. Timothy's heart pounded; this moment always overwhelmed him, the first instant of reaching the upstairs. The thrilling initial sight of the expanse. Because it was never the same. The dust, heavier today, had a darker gray color to it than before; it seemed denser, more mysterious.

Here and there, covered by many layers of dust, lay parcels dropped from past relief ships — dropped and left to deteriorate. Never to be claimed. And, Timothy saw, an additional new projectile which had arrived that morning.

Most of its cargo could be seen within; the grownups had not had any use for the majority of the contents, today.

"Look," Fred said softly.

Two do-cats — mutant dogs or cats; no one knew for sure — could be seen, lightly sniffing at the projectile. Attracted by the unclaimed contents.

"We don't want them," Timothy said.

"That one's sure nice and fat," Fred said longingly. But it was Timothy that had the knife; all he himself had was a string with a metal bolt on the end, a bull-roarer that could kill a bird or a small animal at a distance — but useless against a do-cat, which generally weighed fifteen to twenty pounds and sometimes more.

High up in the sky a dot moved at immense speed, and Timothy knew that it was a care ship heading for another fluke-pit, bringing supplies to it. Sure are busy, he thought to himself. Those careboys always coming and going; they never stop, because if they did, the grownups would die. Wouldn't that be too bad? he thought ironically. Sure be sad.

Fred said, "Wave to it and maybe it'll drop something." He grinned at Timothy, and then they both broke out laughing.

"Sure," Timothy said. "Let's see; what do I want?" Again the two of them laughed at the idea of them wanting something. The two boys had the entire upstairs, as far as the eye could see ... they had even more than the careboys had, and that was plenty, more than plenty.

"Do you think they know?" Fred said, "that our parents play Perky Pat with furniture made out of what they drop? I bet they don't know about Perky Pat; they never have seen a Perky Pat doll, and if they did they'd be really mad."

"You're right," Timothy said. "They'd be so sore they'd probably stop dropping stuff." He glanced at Fred, catching his eye.

"Aw no," Fred said. "We shouldn't tell them; your dad would beat you again if you did that, and probably me, too."

Even so, it was an interesting idea. He could imagine first the surprise and then the anger of the careboys; it would be fun to see that, see the reaction of the eight-legged Martian creatures who had so much charity inside their warty bodies, the cephalopodic univalve mollusk-like organisms who had voluntarily taken it upon themselves to supply succor to the waning remnants of the human race ... this was how they got paid back for their charity, this utterly wasteful, stupid purpose to which their goods were being put. This stupid Perky Pat game that all the adults played.

And anyhow it would be very hard to tell them; there was almost no communication between humans and careboys. They were too different. Acts, deeds, could be done, conveying something ... but not mere words, not mere *signs*. And anyhow —

A great brown rabbit bounded by to the right, past the half-completed house. Timothy whipped out his knife. "Oh boy!" he said aloud in excitement. "Let's go!" He set off across the rubbly ground, Fred a little behind him. Gradually they gained on the rabbit; swift running came easy to the two boys: they had done much practicing.

"Throw the knife!" Fred panted, and Timothy, skidding to a halt, raised his right arm, paused to take aim, and then hurled the sharpened, weighted knife. His most valuable, self-made possession.

It cleaved the rabbit straight through its vitals. The rabbit tumbled, slid, raising a cloud of dust.

"I bet we can get a dollar for that!" Fred exclaimed, leaping up and down. "The hide alone — I bet we can get fifty cents just for the darn hide!"

Together, they hurried toward the dead rabbit, wanting to get there before a red-tailed hawk or a day-owl swooped on it from the gray sky above.

Bending, Norman Schein picked up his Perky Pat doll and said sullenly, "I'm quitting; I don't want to play any more."

Distressed, his wife protested, "But we've got Perky Pat all the way downtown in her new Ford hardtop convertible and parked and a dime in the meter and she's shopped and now she's in the analyst's office reading *Fortune* — we're way ahead of the Morrisons! Why do you want to quit, Norm?"

"We just don't agree," Norman grumbled. "You say analysts charged twenty dollars an hour and I distinctly remember them charging only ten; nobody could charge twenty. So you're penalizing our side, and for what? The Morrisons agree it was only ten. Don't you?" he said to Mr. and Mrs. Morrison, who squatted on the far side of the layout which combined both couples' Perky Pat sets.

Helen Morrison said to her husband, "You went to the analyst more than I did; are you sure he charged only ten?"

"Well, I went mostly to group therapy," Tod said. "At the Berkeley State Mental Hygiene Clinic, and they charged according to your ability to pay. And Perky Pat is at a *private* psychoanalyst."

"We'll have to ask someone else," Helen said to Norman Schein. "I guess all we can do now this minute is suspend the game." He found himself being glared at by her, too, now, because by his insistence on the one point he had put an end to their game for the whole afternoon.

"Shall we leave it all set up?" Fran Schein asked. "We might as well; maybe we can finish tonight after dinner."

Norman Schein gazed down at their combined layout, the swanky shops, the well-lit streets with the parked new-model cars, all of them shiny, the split-level house itself, where Perky Pat lived and where she entertained Leonard, her boy friend. It was the *house* that he perpetually yearned for; the house was the real focus of the layout — of all the Perky Pat layouts, however much they might otherwise differ.

Perky Pat's wardrobe, for instance, there in the closet of the house, the big bedroom closet. Her capri pants, her white cotton short-shorts, her two-piece polka dot swimsuit, her fuzzy sweaters ... and there, in her bedroom, her hi-fi set, her collection of long playing records ...

It had been this way, once, really been like this in the ol-days. Norm Schein could remember his own l-p record collection, and he had once had clothes almost as swanky as Perky Pat's boy friend Leonard, cashmere jackets and tweed suits and Italian sportshirts and shoes made in England. He hadn't owned a Jaguar XKE sports car, like Leonard did, but he had owned a fine-looking old 1963 Mercedes-Benz, which he had used to drive to work.

We lived then, Norm Schein said to himself, *like Perky Pat and Leonard do now.* This is how it actually was.

To his wife he said, pointing to the clock radio which Perky Pat kept beside her bed, "Remember our G.E. clock radio? How it used to wake us up in the morning with classical music from that FM station, KSFR? The 'Wolf-gangers,' the program was called. From six A.M. to nine every morning."

"Yes," Fran said, nodding soberly. "And you used to get up before me; I knew I should have gotten up and fixed bacon and hot coffee for you, but it was so much fun just indulging myself, not stirring for half an hour longer, until the kids woke up."

"Woke up, hell; they were awake before we were," Norm said. "Don't you remember? They were in the back watching 'The Three Stooges' on TV until eight. Then I got up and fixed hot cereal for them, and then I went on to my job at Ampex down at Redwood City."

"Oh yes," Fran said. "The TV." Their Perky Pat did not have a TV set; they had lost it to the Regans in a game a week ago, and Norm had not yet been able to fashion another one realistic-looking enough to substitute. So, in a game, they pretended now that "the TV repairman had come for it." That was how they explained their Perky Pat not having something she really would have had.

Norm thought, Playing this game ... it's like being back there, back in the world before the war. That's why we play it, I suppose. He felt shame, but only fleetingly; the shame, almost at once, was replaced by the desire to play a little longer.

"Let's not quit," he said suddenly. "I'll agree the psychoanalyst would have charged Perky Pat twenty dollars. Okay?"

"Okay," both the Morrisons said together, and they settled back down once more to resume the game.

Tod Morrison had picked up their Perky Pat; he held it, stroking its blonde hair — theirs was blonde, whereas the Scheins' was a brunette — and fiddling with the snaps of its skirt.

"Whatever are you doing?" his wife inquired.

"Nice skirt she has," Tod said. "You did a good job sewing it."

Norm said, "Ever know a girl, back in the ol-days, that looked like Perky Pat?"

"No," Tod Morrison said somberly. "Wish I had, though. I *saw* girls like Perky Pat, especially when I was living in Los Angeles during the Korean War. But I just could never manage to know them personally. And of course there were really terrific girl singers, like Peggy Lee and Julie London ... they looked a lot like Perky Pat."

"Play," Fran said vigorously. And Norm, whose turn it was, picked up the spinner and spun.

"Eleven," he said. "That gets my Leonard out of the sports car repair garage and on his way to the race track." He moved the Leonard doll ahead.

Thoughtfully, Tod Morrison said, "You know, I was out the other day hauling in perishables which the careboys had dropped ... Bill Ferner was there, and he told me something interesting. He met a fluker from a fluke-pit down where Oakland used to be. And at that fluke-pit you know what they play? Not Perky Pat. They never have heard of Perky Pat."

"Well, what do they play, then?" Helen asked.

"They have another doll entirely." Frowning, Tod continued, "Bill says the Oakland fluker called it a Connie Companion doll. Ever hear of that?"

"A 'Connie Companion' doll," Fran said thoughtfully. "How strange. I wonder what she's like. Does she have a boy friend?"

"Oh sure," Tod said. "His name is Paul. Connie and Paul. You know, we ought to hike down there to that Oakland Fluke-pit one of these days and see what Connie and Paul look like and how they live. Maybe we could learn a few things to add to our own layouts."

Norm said, "Maybe we could play them."

Puzzled, Fran said, "Could a Perky Pat play a Connie Companion? Is that possible? I wonder what would happen?"

There was no answer from any of the others. Because none of them knew.

As they skinned the rabbit, Fred said to Timothy, "Where did the name 'fluker' come from? It's sure an ugly word; why do they use it?"

"A fluker is a person who lived through the hydrogen war," Timothy explained. "You know, by a fluke. A fluke of fate? See? Because almost everyone was killed; there used to be thousands of people."

"But what's a 'fluke,' then? When you say a 'fluke of fate —' "

"A fluke is when fate has decided to spare you," Timothy said, and that was all he had to say on the subject. That was all he knew.

Fred said thoughtfully, "But you and I, we're not flukers because we weren't alive when the war broke out. We were born after."

"Right," Timothy said.

"So anybody who calls me a fluker," Fred said, "is going to get hit in the eye with my bull-roarer."

"And 'careboy,' " Timothy said, "that's a made-up word, too. It's from when stuff was dumped from jet planes and ships to people in a disaster area. They were called 'care parcels' because they came from people who cared."

"I know that," Fred said. "I didn't ask that."

"Well, I told you anyhow," Timothy said.

The two boys continued skinning the rabbit.

Jean Regan said to her husband, "Have you heard about the Connie Companion doll?" She glanced down the long rough-board table to make sure none of the other families was listening. "Sam," she said, "I heard it from Helen Morrison; she heard it from Tod and he heard it from Bill Ferner, I think. So it's probably true."

"What's true?" Sam said.

"That in the Oakland Fluke-pit they don't have Perky Pat; they have Connie Companion ... and it occurred to me that maybe some of this — you know, this sort of emptiness, this boredom we feel now and then — maybe if we saw the Connie Companion doll and how she lives, maybe we could add enough to our own layout to — " She paused, reflecting. "To make it more complete."

"I don't care for the name," Sam Regan said. "Connie Companion; it sounds cheap." He spooned up some of the plain, utilitarian grain-mash which the careboys had been dropping, of late. And, as he ate a mouthful, he thought, I'll bet Connie Companion doesn't eat slop like this; I'll bet she eats cheeseburgers with all the trimmings, at a high-type drive-in.

"Could we make a trek down there?" Jean asked.

"To Oakland Fluke-pit?" Sam stared at her. "It's *fifteen miles*, all the way on the other side of the Berkeley Fluke-pit!"

"But this is important," Jean said stubbornly. "And Bill says that a fluker from Oakland came all the way up here, in search of electronic parts or something ... so if he can do it, we can. We've got the dust suits they dropped us. I know we could do it."

Little Timothy Schein, sitting with his family, had overheard her; now he spoke up. "Mrs. Regan, Fred Chamberlain and I, we could trek down that far, if you pay us. What do you say?" He nudged Fred, who sat beside him. "Couldn't we? For maybe five dollars."

Fred, his face serious, turned to Mrs. Regan and said, "We could get you a Connie Companion doll. For five dollars for *each* of us."

"Good grief," Jean Regan said, outraged. And dropped the subject.

But later, after dinner, she brought it up again when she and Sam were alone in their quarters.

"Sam, I've got to see it," she burst out. Sam, in a galvanized tub, was taking his weekly bath, so he had to listen to her. "Now that we know it exists we have to play against someone in the Oakland Fluke-pit; at least we can do that. Can't we? Please." She paced back and forth in the small room, her hands clasped tensely. "Connie Companion may have a Standard Station and an airport terminal with jet landing strip and color TV and a French restaurant where they serve escargot, like the one you and I went to when we were first married ... I just have to see her layout."

"I don't know," Sam said hesitantly. "There's something about Connie Companion doll that — makes me uneasy."

"What could it possibly be?"

"I don't know."

Jean said bitterly, "It's because you know her layout is so much better than ours and she's so much more than Perky Pat."

"Maybe that's it," Sam murmured.

"If you don't go, if you don't try to make contact with them down at the Oakland Fluke-pit, someone else will — someone with more ambition will get ahead of you. Like Norman Schein. He's not afraid the way you are."

Sam said nothing; he continued with his bath. But his hands shook.

A careboy had recently dropped complicated pieces of machinery which were, evidently, a form of mechanical computer. For several weeks the computers — if that was what they were — had sat about the pit in their cartons, unused, but now Norman Schein was finding something to do with one. At the moment he was busy adapting some of its gears, the smallest ones, to form a garbage disposal unit for his Perky Pat's kitchen.

Using the tiny special tools — designed and built by inhabitants of the fluke-pit — which were necessary in fashioning environmental items for Perky Pat, he was busy at his hobby bench. Thoroughly engrossed in what he was doing, he all at once realized that Fran was standing directly behind him, watching.

"I get nervous when I'm watched," Norm said, holding a tiny gear with a pair of tweezers.

"Listen," Fran said, "I've thought of something. Does this suggest anything to you?" She placed before him one of the transistor radios which had been dropped the day before.

"It suggests that garage-door opener already thought of," Norm said irritably. He continued with his work, expertly fitting the miniature pieces together in the sink drain of Pat's kitchen; such delicate work demanded maximum concentration.

Fran said, "It suggests that there must be radio *transmitters* on Earth somewhere, or the careboys wouldn't have dropped these."

"So?" Norm said, uninterested.

"Maybe our Mayor has one," Fran said. "Maybe there's one right here in our own pit, and we could use it to call the Oakland Fluke-pit. Representatives from there could meet us halfway ... say at the Berkeley Fluke-pit. And we could play there. So we wouldn't have that long fifteen mile trip."

Norman hesitated in his work; he set the tweezers down and said slowly, "I think possibly you're right." But if their Mayor Hooker Glebe had a radio transmitter, would he let them use it? And if he did —

"We can try," Fran urged. "It wouldn't hurt to try."

"Okay," Norm said, rising from his hobby bench.

The short, sly-faced man in Army uniform, the Mayor of the Pinole Fluke-pit, listened in silence as Norm Schein spoke. Then he smiled a wise, cunning smile. "Sure, I have a radio transmitter. Had it all the time. Fifty watt output. But why would you want to get in touch with the Oakland Fluke-pit?"

Guardedly, Norm said, "That's my business."

Hooker Glebe said thoughtfully, "I'll let you use it for fifteen dollars."

It was a nasty shock, and Norm recoiled. Good Lord; all the money he and his wife had — they needed every bill of it for use in playing Perky Pat. Money was the tender in the game; there was no other criterion by which one could tell if he had won or lost. "That's too much," he said aloud.

"Well, say ten," the Mayor said, shrugging.

In the end they settled for six dollars and a fifty cent piece.

"I'll make the radio contact for you," Hooker Glebe said. "Because you don't know how. It will take time." He began turning a crank at the side of the generator of the transmitter. "I'll notify you when I've made contact with them. But give me the money now." He held out his hand for it, and, with great reluctance, Norm paid him.

It was not until late that evening that Hooker managed to establish contact with Oakland. Pleased with himself, beaming in self-satisfaction, he appeared at the Scheins' quarters, during their dinner hour. "All set," he announced. "Say, you know there are actually *nine* fluke-pits in Oakland? I didn't know that. Which you want? I've got one with the radio code of Red Vanilla." He chuckled. "They're tough and suspicious down there; it was hard to get any of them to answer."

Leaving his evening meal, Norman hurried to the Mayor's quarters, Hooker puffing along after him.

The transmitter, sure enough, was on, and static wheezed from the speaker of its monitoring unit. Awkwardly, Norm seated himself at the microphone. "Do I just talk?" he asked Hooker Glebe.

"Just say, This is Pinole Fluke-pit calling. Repeat that a couple of times and then when they acknowledge, you say what you want to say." The Mayor fiddled with controls of the transmitter, fussing in an important fashion.

"This is Pinole Fluke-pit," Norm said loudly into the microphone.

Almost at once a clear voice from the monitor said, "This is Red Vanilla

Three answering." The voice was cold and harsh; it struck him forcefully as distinctly alien. Hooker was right.

"Do you have Connie Companion down there where you are?"

"Yes we do," the Oakland fluker answered.

"Well, I challenge you," Norman said, feeling the veins in his throat pulse with the tension of what he was saying. "We're Perky Pat in this area; we'll play Perky Pat against your Connie Companion. Where can we meet?"

"Perky Pat," the Oakland fluker echoed. "Yeah, I know about her. What would the stakes be, in your mind?"

"Up here we play for paper money mostly," Norman said, feeling that his response was somehow lame.

"We've got lots of paper money," the Oakland fluker said cuttingly. "That wouldn't interest any of us. What else?"

"I don't know." He felt hampered, talking to someone he could not see; he was not used to that. People should, he thought, be face to face, then you can see the other person's expression. This was not natural. "Let's meet halfway," he said, "and discuss it. Maybe we could meet at the Berkeley Fluke-pit; how about that?"

The Oakland fluker said, "That's too far. You mean lug our Connie Companion layout all that way? It's too heavy and something might happen to it."

"No, just to discuss rules and stakes," Norman said.

Dubiously, the Oakland fluker said, "Well, I guess we could do that. But you better understand — we take Connie Companion doll pretty damn seriously; you better be prepared to talk terms."

"We will," Norm assured him.

All this time Mayor Hooker Glebe had been cranking the handle of the generator; perspiring, his face bloated with exertion, he motioned angrily for Norm to conclude his palaver.

"At the Berkeley Fluke-pit," Norm finished. "In three days. And send your best player, the one who has the biggest and most authentic layout. Our Perky Pat layouts are works of art, you understand."

The Oakland fluker said, "We'll believe that when we see them. After all, we've got carpenters and electricians and plasterers here, building our layouts; I'll bet you're all unskilled."

"Not as much as you think," Norm said hotly, and laid down the microphone. To Hooker Glebe — who had immediately stopped cranking — he said, "We'll beat them. Wait'll they see the garbage disposal unit I'm making for my Perky Pat; did you know there were people back in the ol-days, I mean real alive human beings, who didn't have garbage disposal units?"

"I remember," Hooker said peevishly. "Say, you got a lot of cranking for your money; I think you gypped me, talking so long." He eyed Norm with such hostility that Norm began to feel uneasy. After all, the Mayor of the pit had the authority to evict any fluker he wished; that was their law.

"I'll give you the fire alarm box I just finished the other day," Norm said. "In my layout it goes at the corner of the block where Perky Pat's boy friend Leonard lives."

"Good enough," Hooker agreed, and his hostility faded. It was replaced, at once, by desire. "Let's see it, Norm. I bet it'll go good in my layout; a fire alarm box is just what I need to complete my first block where I have the mailbox. Thank you."

"You're welcome," Norm sighed, philosophically.

When he returned from the two-day trek to the Berkeley Fluke-pit his face was so grim that his wife knew at once that the parley with the Oakland people had not gone well.

That morning a careboy had dropped cartons of a synthetic tea-like drink; she fixed a cup of it for Norman, waiting to hear what had taken place eight miles to the south.

"We haggled," Norm said, seated wearily on the bed which he and his wife and child all shared. "They don't want money; they don't want goods — naturally not goods, because the darn careboys are dropping regularly down there, too."

"What will they accept, then?"

Norm said, "Perky Pat herself." He was silent, then.

"Oh good Lord," she said, appalled.

"But if we win," Norm pointed out, "we win Connie Companion."

"And the layouts? What about them?"

"We keep our own. It's just Perky Pat herself, not Leonard, not anything else."

"But," she protested, "what'll we *do* if we lose Perky Pat?"

"I can make another one," Norm said. "Given time. There's still a big supply of thermoplastics and artificial hair, here in the pit. And I have plenty of different paints; it would take at least a month, but I could do it. I don't look forward to the job, I admit. But — " His eyes glinted. "Don't look on the dark side; *imagine what it would be like to win Connie Companion doll*. I think we may well win; their delegate seemed smart and, as Hooker said, tough ... but the one I talked to didn't strike me as being very flukey. You know, on good terms with luck."

And, after all, the element of luck, of chance, entered into each stage of the game through the agency of the spinner.

"It seems wrong," Fran said, "to put up Perky Pat herself. But if you say so — " She managed to smile a little. "I'll go along with it. And if you won Connie Companion — who knows? You might be elected Mayor when

Hooker dies. Imagine, to have won somebody else's *doll* — not just the game, the money, but the *doll itself.*"

"I can win," Norm said soberly. "Because I'm very flukey." He could feel it in him, the same flukeyness that had got him through the hydrogen war alive, that had kept him alive ever since. You either have it or you don't, he realized. And I do.

His wife said, "Shouldn't we ask Hooker to call a meeting of everyone in the pit, and send the best player out of our entire group. So as to be the surest of winning."

"Listen," Norm Schein said emphatically. "I'm the best player. I'm going. And so are you; we make a good team, and we don't want to break it up. Anyhow, we'll need at least two people to carry Perky Pat's layout." All in all, he judged, their layout weighed sixty pounds.

His plan seemed to him to be satisfactory. But when he mentioned it to the others living in the Pinole Fluke-pit he found himself facing sharp disagreement. The whole next day was filled with argument.

"You can't lug your layout all that way yourselves," Sam Regan said. "Either take more people with you or carry your layout in a vehicle of some sort. Such as a cart." He scowled at Norm.

"Where'd I get a cart?" Norm demanded.

"Maybe something could be adapted," Sam said. "I'll give you every bit of help I can. Personally, I'd go along but as I told my wife this whole idea worries me." He thumped Norm on the back. "I admire your courage, you and Fran, setting off this way. I wish I had what it takes." He looked unhappy.

In the end, Norm settled on a wheelbarrow. He and Fran would take turns pushing it. That way neither of them would have to carry any load above and beyond their food and water, and of course knives by which to protect them from the do-cats.

As they were carefully placing the elements of their layout in the wheelbarrow, Norm Schein's boy Timothy came sidling up to them. "Take me along, Dad," he pleaded. "For fifty cents I'll go as guide and scout, and also I'll help you catch food along the way."

"We'll manage fine," Norm said. "You stay here in the fluke-pit; you'll be safer here." It annoyed him, the idea of his son tagging along on an important venture such as this. It was almost — sacreligious.

"Kiss us goodbye," Fran said to Timothy, smiling at him briefly; then her attention returned to the layout within the wheelbarrow. "I hope it doesn't tip over," she said fearfully to Norm.

"Not a chance," Norm said. "If we're careful." He felt confident.

A few moments later they began wheeling the wheelbarrow up the ramp to the lid at the top, to upstairs. Their journey to the Berkeley Fluke-pit had begun.

*   *   *

A mile outside the Berkeley Fluke-pit he and Fran began to stumble over empty drop-canisters and some only partly empty: remains of past care parcels such as littered the surface near their own pit. Norm Schein breathed a sigh of relief; the journey had not been so bad after all, except that his hands had become blistered from gripping the metal handles of the wheelbarrow, and Fran had turned her ankle so that now she walked with a painful limp. But it had taken them less time than he had anticipated, and his mood was one of buoyancy.

Ahead, a figure appeared, crouching low in the ash. A boy. Norm waved at him and called, "Hey, sonny — we're from the Pinole pit; we're supposed to meet a party from Oakland here ... do you remember me?"

The boy, without answering, turned and scampered off.

"Nothing to be afraid of," Norm said to his wife. "He's going to tell their Mayor. A nice old fellow named Ben Fennimore."

Soon several adults appeared, approaching warily.

With relief, Norm set the legs of the wheelbarrow down into the ash, letting go and wiping his face with his handkerchief. "Has the Oakland team arrived yet?" he called.

"Not yet," a tall, elderly man with a white armband and ornate cap answered. "It's you Schein, isn't it?" he said, peering. This was Ben Fennimore. "Back already with your layout." Now the Berkeley flukers had begun crowding around the wheelbarrow, inspecting the Scheins' layout. Their faces showed admiration.

"They have Perky Pat here," Norm explained to his wife. "But — " He lowered his voice. "Their layouts are only basic. Just a house, wardrobe and car ... they've built almost nothing. No imagination."

One Berkeley fluker, a woman, said wonderingly to Fran, "And you made each of the pieces of furniture yourselves?" Marveling, she turned to the man beside her. "See what they've accomplished, Ed?"

"Yes," the man answered, nodding. "Say," he said to Fran and Norm, "can we see it all set up? You're going to set it up in our pit, aren't you?"

"We are indeed," Norm said.

The Berkeley flukers helped push the wheelbarrow the last mile. And before long they were descending the ramp, to the pit below the surface.

"It's a big pit," Norm said knowingly to Fran. "Must be two thousand people here. This is where the University of California was."

"I see," Fran said, a little timid at entering a strange pit; it was the first time in years — since the war, in fact — that she had seen any strangers. And so many at once. It was almost too much for her; Norm felt her shrink back, pressing against him in fright.

When they had reached the first level and were starting to unload the wheelbarrow, Ben Fennimore came up to them and said softly, "I think the Oakland people have been spotted; we just got a report of activity upstairs. So be prepared." He added, "We're rooting for you, of course, because you're Perky Pat, the same as us."

"Have you ever seen Connie Companion doll?" Fran asked him.

"No ma'am," Fennimore answered courteously. "But naturally we've heard about it, being neighbors to Oakland and all. I'll tell you one thing ... we hear that Connie Companion doll is a bit older than Perky Pat. You know — more, um, *mature.*" He explained, "I just wanted to prepare you."

Norm and Fran glanced at each other. "Thanks," Norm said slowly. "Yes, we should be as much prepared as possible. How about Paul?"

"Oh, he's not much," Fennimore said. "Connie runs things; I don't even think Paul has a real apartment of his own. But you better wait until the Oakland flukers get here; I don't want to mislead you — my knowledge is all hearsay, you understand."

Another Berkeley fluker, standing nearby, spoke up. "I saw Connie once, and she's much more grown up than Perky Pat."

"How old do you figure Perky Pat is?" Norm asked him.

"Oh, I'd say seventeen or eighteen," Norm was told.

"And Connie?" He waited tensely.

"Oh, she might be twenty-five, even."

From the ramp behind them they heard noises. More Berkeley flukers appeared, and, after them, two men carrying between them a platform on which, spread out, Norm saw a great, spectacular layout.

This was the Oakland team, and they weren't a couple, a man and wife; they were both men, and they were hard-faced with stern, remote eyes. They jerked their heads briefly at him and Fran, acknowledging their presence. And then, with enormous care, they set down the platform on which their layout rested.

Behind them came a third Oakland fluker carrying a metal box, much like a lunch pail. Norm, watching, knew instinctively that in the box lay Connie Companion doll. The Oakland fluker produced a key and began unlocking the box.

"We're ready to begin playing any time," the taller of the Oakland men said. "As we agreed in our discussion, we'll use a numbered spinner instead of dice. Less chance of cheating that way."

"Agreed," Norm said. Hesitantly he held out his hand. "I'm Norman Schein and this is my wife and play-partner Fran."

The Oakland man, evidently the leader, said, "I'm Walter R. Wynn. This is my partner here, Charley Dowd, and the man with the box, that's Peter Foster. He isn't going to play; he just guards our layout." Wynn glanced about, at the Berkeley flukers, as if saying, I know you're all partial to Perky Pat, in here. But we don't care; we're not scared.

Fran said, "We're ready to play, Mr. Wynn." Her voice was low but controlled.

"What about money?" Fennimore asked.

"I think both teams have plenty of money," Wynn said. He laid out several thousand dollars in greenbacks, and now Norm did the same. "The money of course is not a factor in this, except as a means of conducting the game."

Norm nodded; he understood perfectly. Only the dolls themselves mattered. And now, for the first time, he saw Connie Companion doll.

She was being placed in her bedroom by Mr. Foster who evidently was in charge of her. And the sight of her took his breath away. Yes, she was older. A grown woman, not a girl at all ... the difference between her and Perky Pat was acute. And so life-like. Carved, not poured; she obviously had been whittled out of wood and then painted — she was not a thermoplastic. And her hair. It appeared to be genuine hair.

He was deeply impressed.

"What do you think of her?" Walter Wynn asked, with a faint grin.

"Very — impressive," Norm conceded.

Now the Oaklanders were studying Perky Pat. "Poured thermoplastic," one of them said. "Artificial hair. Nice clothes, though; all stitched by hand, you can see that. Interesting; what we heard was correct. Perky Pat isn't a grownup, she's just a teenager."

Now the male companion to Connie appeared; he was set down in the bedroom beside Connie.

"Wait a minute," Norm said. "You're putting Paul or whatever his name is, in her bedroom with her? Doesn't he have his own apartment?"

Wynn said, "They're married."

"*Married!*" Norman and Fran stared at him, dumbfounded.

"Why sure," Wynn said. "So naturally they live together. Your dolls, they're not, are they?"

"N-no," Fran said. "Leonard is Perky Pat's boy friend ... " Her voice trailed off. "Norm," she said, clutching his arm, "I don't believe him; I think he's just saying they're married to get the advantage. Because if they both start out from the same room — "

Norm said aloud, "You fellows, look here. It's not fair, calling them married."

Wynn said, "We're not 'calling' them married; they are married. Their names are Connie and Paul Lathrope, of 24 Arden Place, Piedmont. They've been married for a year, most players will tell you." He sounded calm.

Maybe, Norm thought, it's true. He was truly shaken.

"Look at them together," Fran said, kneeling down to examine the Oaklanders' layout. "In the same bedroom, in the same house. Why, Norm; do you see? There's just the one bed. A big double bed." Wild-eyed, she appealed to him. "How can Perky Pat and Leonard play against them?" Her voice shook. "It's not morally *right*."

"This is another type of layout entirely," Norm said to Walter Wynn. "This, that you have. Utterly different from what we're used to, as you can see." He pointed to his own layout. "I insist that in this game Connie and Paul *not* live together and *not* be considered married."

"But they are," Foster spoke up. "It's a fact. Look — their clothes are in the same closet." He showed them the closet. "And in the same bureau drawers." He showed them that, too. "And look in the bathroom. Two toothbrushes. His and hers, in the same rack. So you can see we're not making it up."

There was silence.

Then Fran said in a choked voice, "And if they're married — you mean they've been — intimate?"

Wynn raised an eyebrow, then nodded. "Sure, since they're married. Is there anything wrong with that?"

"Perky Pat and Leonard have never — " Fran began, and then ceased.

"Naturally not," Wynn agreed. "Because they're only going together. We understand that."

Fran said, "We just can't play. We can't." She caught hold of her husband's arm. "Let's go back to Pinole pit — please, Norman."

"Wait," Wynn said, at once. "If you don't play, you're conceding; you have to give up Perky Pat."

The three Oaklanders all nodded. And, Norm saw, many of the Berkeley flukers were nodding, too, including Ben Fennimore.

"They're right," Norm said heavily to his wife. "We'd have to give her up. We better play, dear."

"Yes," Fran said, in a dead, flat voice. "We'll play." She bent down and listlessly spun the needle of the spinner. It stopped at six.

Smiling, Walter Wynn knelt down and spun. He obtained a four.

The game had begun.

Crouching behind the strewn, decayed contents of a care parcel that had been dropped long ago, Timothy Schein saw coming across the surface of ash his mother and father, pushing the wheelbarrow ahead of them. They looked tired and worn.

"Hi," Timothy yelled, leaping out at them in joy at seeing them again; he had missed them very much.

"Hi, son," his father murmured, nodding. He let go of the handles of the wheelbarrow, then halted and wiped his face with his handkerchief.

Now Fred Chamberlain raced up, panting. "Hi, Mr. Schein; hi, Mrs. Schein. Hey, did you win? Did you beat the Oakland flukers? I bet you did, didn't you?" He looked from one of them to the other and then back.

In a low voice Fran said, "Yes, Freddy. We won."

Norm said, "Look in the wheelbarrow."

The two boys looked. And, there among Perky Pat's furnishings, lay another doll. Larger, fuller-figured, much older than Pat ... they stared at her and she stared up sightlessly at the gray sky overhead. So this is Connie Companion doll, Timothy said to himself. Gee.

"We were lucky," Norm said. Now several people had emerged from the pit and were gathering around them, listening. Jean and Sam Regan, Tod Morrison and his wife Helen, and now their Mayor, Hooker Glebe himself, waddling up excited and nervous, his face flushed, gasping for breath from the labor — unusual for him — of ascending the ramp.

Fran said,"We got a cancellation of debts card, just when we were most behind. We owed fifty thousand, and it made us even with the Oakland flukers. And then, after that, we got an advance ten squares card, and that put us right on the jackpot square, at least in our layout. We had a very bitter squabble, because the Oaklanders showed us that on their layout it was a tax lien slapped on real estate holdings square, but we had spun an odd number so that put us back on our own board." She sighed. "I'm glad to be back. It was hard, Hooker; it was a tough game."

Hooker Glebe wheezed, "Let's all get a look at the Connie Companion doll, folks." To Fran and Norm he said, "Can I lift her up and show them?"

"Sure," Norm said, nodding.

Hooker picked up Connie Companion doll. "She sure is realistic," he said, scrutinizing her. "Clothes aren't as nice as ours generally are; they look machine-made."

"They are," Norm agreed. "But she's carved, not poured."

"Yes, so I see." Hooker turned the doll about, inspecting her from all angles. "A nice job. She's — um, more filled-out than Perky Pat. What's this outfit she has on? Tweed suit of some sort."

"A business suit," Fran said. "We won that with her; they had agreed on that in advance."

"You see, she has a job," Norm explained. "She's a psychology consultant for a business firm doing marketing research. In consumer preferences. A high-paying position ... she earns twenty thousand a year, I believe Wynn said."

"Golly," Hooker said. "And Pat's just going to college; she's still in school." He looked troubled. "Well, I guess they were bound to be ahead of us in some ways. What matters is that you won." His jovial smile returned. "Perky Pat came out ahead." He held the Connie Companion doll up high, where everyone could see her. "Look what Norm and Fran came back with, folks!"

Norm said, "Be careful with her, Hooker." His voice was firm.

"Eh?" Hooker said, pausing. "Why, Norm?"

"Because," Norm said, "she's going to have a baby."

There was a sudden chill silence. The ash around them stirred faintly; that was the only sound.

"How do you know?" Hooker asked.

"They told us. The Oaklanders told us. And we won that, too — after a bitter argument that Fennimore had to settle." Reaching into the wheelbarrow he brought out a little leather pouch, from it he carefully took a carved pink new-born baby. "We won this too because Fennimore agreed that from a technical standpoint it's literally part of Connie Companion doll at this point."

Hooker stared a long, long time.

"She's married," Fran explained. "To Paul. They're not just going together. She's three months pregnant, Mr. Wynn said. He didn't tell us until after we won; he didn't want to, then, but they felt they had to. I think they were right; it wouldn't have done not to say."

Norm said, "And in addition there's actually an embryo outfit — "

"Yes," Fran said. "You have to open Connie up, of course, to see — "

"No," Jean Regan said. "Please, no."

Hooker said, "No, Mrs. Schein, don't." He backed away.

Fran said, "It shocked us of course at first, but — "

"You see," Norm put in, "it's logical; you have to follow the logic. Why, eventually Perky Pat — "

"No," Hooker said violently. He bent down, picked up a rock from the ash at his feet. "No," he said, and raised his arm. "You stop, you two. Don't say any more."

Now the Regans, too, had picked up rocks. No one spoke.

Fran said, at last, "Norm, we've got to get out of here."

"You're right," Tod Morrison told them. His wife nodded in grim agreement.

"You two go back down to Oakland," Hooker told Norman and Fran Schein. "You don't live here any more. You're different than you were. You — changed."

"Yes," Sam Regan said slowly, half to himself. "I was right; there was something to fear." To Norm Schein he said, "How difficult a trip is it to Oakland?"

"We just went to Berkeley," Norm said. "To the Berkeley Fluke-pit." He seemed baffled and stunned by what was happening. "My God," he said, "we can't turn around and push this wheelbarrow back all the way to Berkeley again — we're worn out, we need rest!"

Sam Regan said, "What if somebody else pushed?" He walked up to the Scheins, then, and stood with them. "I'll push the darn thing. You lead the way, Schein." He looked toward his own wife, but Jean did not stir. And she did not put down her handful of rocks.

Timothy Schein plucked at his father's arm. "Can I come this time, Dad? Please let me come."

"Okay," Norm said, half to himself. Now he drew himself together. "So we're not wanted here." He turned to Fran. "Let's go. Sam's going to push the wheelbarrow; I think we can make it back there before nightfall. If not, we can sleep out in the open; Timothy'll help protect us against the do-cats."

Fran said, "I guess we have no choice." Her face was pale.

"And take this," Hooker said. He held out the tiny carved baby. Fran Schein accepted it and put it tenderly back in its leather pouch. Norm laid Connie Companion back down in the wheelbarrow, where she had been. They were ready to start back.

"It'll happen up here eventually," Norm said, to the group of people, to the Pinole flukers. "Oakland is just more advanced; that's all."

"Go on," Hooker Glebe said. "Get started."

Nodding, Norm started to pick up the handles of the wheelbarrow, but Sam Regan moved him aside and took them himself. "Let's go," he said.

The three adults, with Timothy Schein going ahead of them with his knife ready — in case a do-cat attacked — started into motion, in the direction of Oakland and the south. No one spoke. There was nothing to say.

"It's a shame this had to happen," Norm said at last, when they had gone almost a mile and there was no further sign of the Pinole flukers behind them.

"Maybe not," Sam Regan said. "Maybe it's for the good." He did not seem downcast. And after all, he had lost his wife; he had given up more than anyone else, and yet — he had survived.

"Glad you feel that way," Norm said somberly.

They continued on, each with his own thoughts.

After a while, Timothy said to his father, "All these big fluke-pits to the south ... there's lots more things to do there, isn't there? I mean, you don't just sit around playing that game." He certainly hoped not.

His father said, "That's true, I guess."

Overhead, a care ship whistled at great velocity and then was gone again almost at once; Timothy watched it go but he was not really interested in it, because there was so much more to look forward to, on the ground and below the ground, ahead of them to the south.

His father murmured, "Those Oaklanders; their game, their particular doll, it taught them something. Connie had to grow and it forced them all to grow along with her. Our flukers never learned about that, not from Perky Pat. I wonder if they ever will. She'd have to grow up the way Connie did. Connie must have been like Perky Pat, once. A long time ago."

Not interested in what his father was saying — who really cared about dolls and games with dolls? — Timothy scampered ahead, peering to see what lay before them, the opportunities and possibilities, for him and for his mother and dad, for Mr. Regan also.

"I can't wait," he yelled back at his father, and Norm Schein managed a faint, fatigued smile in answer.

STAND-BY

AN HOUR BEFORE his morning program on channel six, ranking news clown Jim Briskin sat in his private office with his production staff, conferring on the report of an unknown possibly hostile flotilla detected at eight hundred astronomical units from the sun. It was big news, of course. But how should it be presented to his several-billion viewers scattered over three planets and seven moons?

Peggy Jones, his secretary, lit a cigarette and said, "Don't alarm them, Jim-Jam. Do it folksy-style." She leaned back, riffled the dispatches received by their commercial station from Unicephalon 40-D's teletypers.

It had been the homeostatic problem-solving structure Unicephalon 40-D at the White House in Washington, D.C. which had detected this possible external enemy; in its capacity as President of the United States it had at once dispatched ships of the line to stand picket duty. The flotilla appeared to be entering from another solar system entirely, but that fact of course would have to be determined by the picket ships.

"Folksy-style," Jim Briskin said glumly. "I grin and say, Hey look comrades — it's happened at last, the thing we all feared, ha ha." He eyed her. "That'll get baskets full of laughs all over Earth and Mars but just possibly not on the far-out moons." Because if there were some kind of attack it would be the farther colonists who would be hit first.

"No, they won't be amused," his continuity advisor Ed Fineberg agreed. He, too, looked worried; he had a family on Ganymede.

"Is there any lighter piece of news?" Peggy asked. "By which you could open your program? The sponsor would like that." She passed the armload of news dispatches to Briskin. "See what you can do. Mutant cow obtains voting franchise in court case in Alabama ... you know."

323

"I know," Briskin agreed as he began to inspect the dispatches. One such as his quaint account — it had touched the hearts of millions — of the mutant blue jay which learned, by great trial and effort, to sew. It had sewn itself and its progeny a nest, one April morning, in Bismark, North Dakota, in front of the TV cameras of Briskin's network.

One piece of news stood out; he knew intuitively, as soon as he saw it, that here he had what he wanted to lighten the dire tone of the day's news. Seeing it, he relaxed. The worlds went on with business as usual, despite this great news-break from eight hundred AUs. out.

"Look," he said, grinning. "Old Gus Schatz is dead. Finally."

"Who's Gus Schatz?" Peggy asked, puzzled. "That name ... it does sound familiar."

"The union man," Jim Briskin said. "You remember. The stand-by President, sent over to Washington by the union twenty-two years ago. He's dead, and the union — " He tossed her the dispatch: it was lucid and brief. "Now it's sending a new stand-by President over to take Schatz's place. I think I'll interview him. Assuming he can talk."

"That's right," Peggy said. "I keep forgetting. There still is a human stand-by in case Unicephalon fails. Has it ever failed?"

"No." Ed Fineberg said. "And it never will. So we have one more case of union featherbedding. The plague of our society."

"But still," Jim Briskin said, "people would be amused. The home life of the top stand-by in the country ... why the union picked him, what his hobbies are. What this man, whoever he is, plans to do during his term to keep from going mad with boredom. Old Gus learned to bind books; he collected rare old motor magazines and bound them in vellum with gold-stamped lettering."

Both Ed and Peggy nodded in agreement. "Do that," Peggy urged him. "You can make it interesting, Jim-Jam; you can make anything interesting. I'll place a call to the White House, or is the new man there yet?"

"Probably still at union headquarters in Chicago," Ed said. "Try a line there. Government Civil Servants' Union, East Division."

Picking up the phone, Peggy quickly dialed.

At seven o'clock in the morning Maximilian Fischer sleepily heard noises; he lifted his head from the pillow, heard the confusion growing in the kitchen, the landlady's shrill voice, then men's voices which were unfamiliar to him. Groggily, he managed to sit up, shifting his bulk with care. He did not hurry; the doc had said not to overexert, because of the strain on his already-enlarged heart. So he took his time dressing.

Must be after a contribution to one of the funds, Max said to himself. *It sounds like some of the fellas. Pretty early, though.* He did not feel alarmed. *I'm in good standing*, he thought firmly. *Nuthin' to fear.*

With care, he buttoned a fine pink and green-striped silk shirt, one of his favorites. *Gives me class*, he thought as with labored effort he managed to bend far enough over to slip on his authentic simulated deerskin pumps. *Be ready to meet them on an equality level*, he thought as he smoothed his thinning hair before the mirror. *If they shake me down too much I'll squawk directly to Pat Noble at the Noo York hiring hall; I mean, I don't have to stand for any stuff. I been in the union too long.*

From the other room a voice bawled, "Fischer — get your clothes on and come out. We got a job for you and it begins today."

A job, Max thought with mixed feelings; he did not know whether to be glad or sorry. For over a year now he had been drawing from the union fund, as were most of his friends. Well what do you know. *Cripes,* he thought; *suppose it's a hard job, like maybe I got to bend over all the time or move around.* He felt anger. *What a dirty deal. I mean, who do they think they are?* Opening the door, he faced them. "Listen," he began, but one of the union officials cut him off.

"Pack your things, Fischer. Gus Schatz kicked the bucket and you got to go down to Washington, D.C. and take over the number one stand-by; we want you there before they abolish the position or something and we have to go out on strike or go to court. Mainly, we want to get someone right in clean and easy with no trouble; you understand? Make the transition so smooth that no one hardly takes notice."

At once, Max said, "What's it pay?"

Witheringly, the union official said, "You got no decision to make in this; *you're picked.* You want your freeloader fund-money cut off? You want to have to get out at your age and look for work?"

"Aw come on," Max protested. "I can pick up the phone and dial Pat Noble — "

The union officials were grabbing up objects here and there in the apartment. "We'll help you pack. Pat wants you in the White House by ten o'clock this morning."

"Pat!" Max echoed. He had been sold out.

The union officials, dragging suitcases from the closet, grinned.

Shortly, they were on their way across the flatlands of the Midwest by monorail. Moodily, Maximilian Fischer watched the countryside flash past; he said nothing to the officials flanking him, preferring to mull the matter over and over in his mind. What could he recall about the number one stand-by job? It began at eight A.M. — he recalled reading that. And there always were a lot of tourists flocking through the White House to catch a glimpse of Unicephalon 40-D, especially the school kids ... and he disliked kids because they always jeered at him due to his weight. Cripes, he'd have a million of them filing by, because he had to be on the premises. By law, he had to be within a hundred yards of Unicephalon 40-D at all times, day and night, or was it fifty yards? Anyhow it practically was right on top, so if the homeo-static problem-solving system failed — *Maybe I better bone up on this*, he decided. *Take a TV educational course on government administration, just in case.*

To the union official on his right, Max asked, "Listen, goodmember, do I have any powers in this job you guys got me? I mean, can I — "

"It's a union job like every other union job," the official answered wearily. "You sit. You stand by. Have you been out of work that long, you don't remember?" He laughed, nudging his companion. "Listen, Fischer here wants to know what authority the job entails." Now both men laughed. "I tell you what, Fischer," the official drawled. "When you're all set up there in the White House, when you got your chair and bed and made all your arrange-ments for meals and laundry and TV viewing time, why don't you amble over to Unicephalon 40-D and just sort of whine around there, you know, scratch and whine, until it notices you."

"Lay off," Max muttered.

"And then," the official continued, "you sort of say, Hey Unicephalon, listen. I'm your buddy. How about a little 'I scratch your back, you scratch mine.' You pass an ordinance for me — "

"But what can he do in exchange?" the other union official asked.

"Amuse it. He can tell it the story of his life, how he rose out of poverty and obscurity and educated himself by watching TV seven days a week until finally, guess what, he rose all the way to the top; he got the job — " The official snickered. "Of stand-by President."

Maximilian, flushing, said nothing; he stared woodenly out of the mono-rail window.

When they reached Washington, D.C. and the White House, Maximilian Fischer was shown a little room. It had belonged to Gus, and although the faded old motor magazines had been cleared out, a few prints remained tacked on the walls: a 1963 Volvo S-122, a 1957 Peugeot 403 and other antique classics of a bygone age. And, on a bookcase, Max saw a hand-carved plastic model of a 1950 Studebaker Starlight coupe, with each detail perfect.

"He was making that when he croaked," one of the union officials said as he set down Max's suitcase. "He could tell you any fact there is about those old preturbine cars — any useless bit of car knowledge."

Max nodded.

"You got any idea what you're going to do?" the official asked him.

"Aw hell," Max said. "How could I decide so soon? Give me time." Moodily, he picked up the Studebaker Starlight coupe and examined its underside. The desire to smash the model car came to him; he put the car down, then, turning away.

"Make a rubber band ball," the official said.

"What?" Max said.

"The stand-by before Gus. Louis somebody-or-other... he collected rubber bands, made a huge ball, big as a house, by the time he died. I forget his name, but the rubber band ball is at the Smithsonian now."

There was a stir in the hallway. A White House receptionist, a middle-aged woman severely dressed, put her head in the room and said, "Mr. President, there's a TV news clown here to interview you. Please try to finish with him as quickly as possible because we have quite a few tours passing through the building today and some may want to look at you."

"Okay," Max said. He turned to face the TV news clown. It was Jim-Jam Briskin, he saw, the ranking clown just now. "You want to see me?" he asked Briskin haltingly. "I mean, you're sure it's *me* you want to interview?" He could not imagine what Briskin could find of interest about him. Holding out his hand he added, "This is my room, but these model cars and pics aren't mine; they were Gus's. I can't tell you nuthin' about them."

On Briskin's head the familiar flaming-red clown wig glowed, giving him in real life the same bizarre cast that the TV cameras picked up so well. He was older, however, than the TV image indicated, but he had the friendly, natural smile that everyone looked for: it was his badge of informality, a really nice guy, even-tempered but with a caustic wit when occasion demanded. Briskin was the sort of man who ... *well*, Max thought, *the sort of fella you'd like to see marry into your family.*

They shook hands. Briskin said, "You're on camera, Mr. Max Fischer. Or rather, Mr. President, I should say. This is Jim-Jam talking. For our literally billions of viewers located in every niche and corner of this far-flung solar system of ours, let me ask you this. How does it feel, sir, to know that if Unicephalon 40-D should fail, even momentarily, you would be catapulted into the most important post that has ever fallen onto the shoulders of a human being, that of actual, not merely stand-by, President of the United States? Does it worry you at night?" He smiled. Behind him the camera technicians swung their mobile lenses back and forth; lights burned Max's eyes and he felt the heat beginning to make him sweat under his arms and on his neck and upper lip. "What emotions grip you at this instant?" Briskin asked. "As you stand on the threshold of this new task for perhaps the balance of your life? What thoughts run through your mind, now that you're actually here in the White House?"

After a pause, Max said, "It's — a big responsibility." And then he realized, he saw, that Briskin was laughing at him, laughing silently as he stood there. Because it was all a gag Briskin was pulling. Out in the planets and moons his audience knew it, too; they knew Jim-Jam's humor.

"You're a large man, Mr. Fischer," Briskin said. "If I may say so, a stout man. Do you get much exercise? I ask this because with your new job you pretty well will be confined to this room, and I wondered what change in your life this would bring about."

"Well," Max said, "I feel of course that a Government employee should always be at his post. Yes, what you say is true; I have to be right here day and night, but that doesn't bother me. I'm prepared for it."

"Tell me," Jim Briskin said, "do you — " And then he ceased. Turning to the video technicians behind him he said in an odd voice, "We're off the air."

A man wearing headphones squeezed forward past the cameras. "On the monitor, listen." He hurriedly handed the headphones to Briskin. "We've been pre-empted by Unicephalon; it's broadcasting a news bulletin."

Briskin held the phones to his ear. His face writhed and he said, "Those ships at eight hundred AUs. They are hostile, it says." He glanced up sharply at his technicians, the red clown's wig sliding askew. "They've begun to attack."

Within the following twenty-four hours the aliens had managed not only to penetrate the Sol System but also to knock out Unicephalon 40-D.

News of this reached Maximilian Fischer in an indirect manner as he sat in the White House cafeteria having his supper.

"Mr. Maximilian Fischer?"

"Yeah," Max said, glancing up at the group of Secret Servicemen who had surrounded his table.

"You're President of the United States."

"Naw," Max said. "I'm the stand-by President; that's different."

The Secret Serviceman said, "Unicephalon 40-D is out of commission for perhaps as long as a month. So according to the amended Constitution, you're President and also Commander-in-Chief of the armed forces. We're here to guard you." The Secret Serviceman grinned ludicrously. Max grinned back. "Do you understand?" the Secret Serviceman asked. "I mean, does it penetrate?"

"Sure," Max said. Now he understood the buzz of conversation he had overheard while waiting in the cafeteria line with his tray. It explained why White House personnel had looked at him strangely. He set down his coffee cup, wiped his mouth with his napkin, slowly and deliberately, pretended to be absorbed in solemn thought. But actually his mind was empty.

"We've been told," the Secret Serviceman said, "that you're needed at once at the National Security Council bunker. They want your participation in finalization of strategy deliberations."

They walked from the cafeteria to the elevator.

"Strategy policy," Max said, as they descended. "I got a few opinions about that. I guess it's time to deal harshly with these alien ships, don't you agree?"

The Secret Servicemen nodded.

"Yes, we got to show we're not afraid," Max said. "Sure, we'll get finalization; we'll blast the buggers."

The Secret Servicemen laughed good-naturedly.

Pleased, Max nudged the leader of the group. "I think we're pretty goddam strong; I mean, the U.S.A. has got teeth."

"You tell 'em, Max," one of the Secret Servicemen said, and they all laughed aloud. Max included.

As they stepped from the elevator they were stopped by a tall, well-dressed man who said urgently, "Mr. President, I'm Jonathan Kirk, White House press secretary; I think before you go in there to confer with the NSC people you should address the nation in this hour of gravest peril. The public wants to see what their new leader is like." He held out a paper. "Here's a statement drawn up by the Political Advisory Board; it codifies your — "

"Nuts," Max said, handing it back without looking at it. "I'm the President, not you. Kirk? Burke? Shirk? Never heard of you. Show me the microphone and I'll make my own speech. Or get me Pat Noble; maybe he's got some ideas." And then he remembered that Pat had sold him out in the first place; Pat had gotten him into this. "Not him either," Max said. "Just give me the microphone."

"This is a time of crisis," Kirk grated.

"Sure," Max said, "so leave me alone; you keep out of my way and I'll keep out of yours. Ain't that right?" He slapped Kirk good-naturedly on the back. "And we'll both be better off."

A group of people with portable TV cameras and lighting appeared, and among them Max saw Jim-Jam Briskin, in the middle, with his staff.

"Hey, Jim-Jam," he yelled. "Look, I'm President now!"

Stolidly, Jim Briskin came toward him.

"I'm not going to be winding no ball of string," Max said. "Or making model boats, nuthin' like that." He shook hands warmly with Briskin. "I thank you," Max said. "For your congratulations."

"Congratulations," Briskin said, then, in a low voice.

"Thanks," Max said, squeezing the man's hand until the knuckles creaked. "Of course, sooner or later they'll get that noise-box patched up and I'll just be stand-by again. But — " He grinned gleefully around at all of them; the corridor was full of people now, from TV to White House staff members to Army officers and Secret Servicemen.

Briskin said, "You have a big task, Mr. Fischer."

"Yeah," Max agreed.

Something in Briskin's eyes said: *And I wonder if you can handle it. I wonder if you're the man to hold such power.*

"Surely I can do it," Max declared, into Briskin's microphone, for all the vast audience to hear.

"Possibly you can," Jim Briskin said, and on his face was dubiousness.

"Hey, you don't like me any more," Max said. "How come?"

Briskin said nothing, but his eyes flickered.

"Listen," Max said, "I'm President now; I can close down your silly network — I can send FBI men in any time I want. For your information I'm firing the Attorney General right now, whatever his name is, and putting in a man I know, a man I can trust."

Briskin said, "I see." And now he looked less dubious; conviction, of a sort which Max could not fathom, began to appear instead. "Yes," Jim Briskin said, "you have the authority to order that, don't you? *If* you're really President..."

"Watch out," Max said. "You're nothing compared to me, Briskin, even if you do have that great big audience." Then, turning his back on the cameras, he strode through the open door, into the NSC bunker.

Hours later, in the early morning, down in the National Security Council subsurface bunker, Maximilian Fischer listened sleepily to the TV set in the background as it yammered out the latest news. By now, intelligence sources had plotted the arrival of thirty more alien ships in the Sol System. It was believed that seventy in all had entered. Each was being continually tracked.

But that was not enough, Max knew. Sooner or later he would have to give the order to attack the alien ships. He hesitated. After all, who were they? Nobody at CIA knew. How strong were they? Not known either. And — would the attack be successful?

And then there were domestic problems. Unicephalon had continually tinkered with the economy, priming it when necessary, cutting taxes, lowering interest rates ... that had ceased with the problem-solver's destruction. *Jeez,* Max thought dismally. *What do I know about unemployment? I mean, how can I tell what factories to reopen and where?*

He turned to General Tompkins, Chairman of the Joint Chiefs of Staff, who sat beside him examining a report on the scrambling of the tactical defensive ships protecting Earth. "They got all them ships distributed right?" he asked Tompkins.

"Yes, Mr. President," General Tompkins answered.

Max winced. But the general did not seem to have spoken ironically; his tone had been respectful. "Okay," Max murmured. "Glad to hear that. And you got all that missile cloud up so there're no leaks, like you let in that ship to blast Unicephalon. I don't want that to happen again."

"We're under Defcon one," General Tompkins said. "Full war footing, as of six o'clock, our time."

"How about those strategic ships?" That, he had learned, was the euphemism for their offensive strike-force.

"We can mount an attack at any time," General Tompkins said, glancing down at the long table to obtain the assenting nods of his co-workers. "We can take care of each of the seventy invaders now within our system."

With a groan, Max said, "Anybody got any bicarb?" The whole business depressed him. *What a lot of work and sweat*, he thought. *All this goddam agitation — why don't the buggers just leave our system? I mean, do we have to get into a war? No telling what their home system will do in retaliation; you never can tell about unhuman life forms — they're unreliable.*

"That's what bothers me," he said aloud. "Retaliation." He sighed.

General Tompkins said, "Negotiation with them evidently is impossible."

"Go ahead, then," Max said. "Go give it to them." He looked about for the bicarb.

"I think you're making a wise choice," General Tompkins said, and, across the table, the civilian advisors nodded in agreement.

"Here's an odd piece of news," one of the advisors said to Max. He held out a teletype dispatch. "James Briskin has just filed a writ of *mandamus* against you in a Federal Court in California, claiming you're not legally President because you didn't run for office."

"You mean because I didn't get *voted* in?" Max said. "Just because of that?"

"Yes sir. Briskin is asking the Federal Courts to rule on this, and meanwhile he has announced his own candidacy."

"WHAT?"

"Briskin claims not only that you must run for office and be voted in, but you must run against him. And with his popularity he evidently feels — "

"Aw nuts," Max said in despair. "How do you like that."

No one answered.

"Well anyhow," Max said, "it's all decided; you military fellas go ahead and knock out those alien ships. And meanwhile — " He decided there and then. "We'll put economic pressure on Jim-Jam's sponsors, that Reinlander Beer and Calbest Electronics, to get him not to run."

The men at the long table nodded. Papers rattled as briefcases were put away; the meeting — temporarily — was at an end.

He's got an unfair advantage, Max said to himself. *How can I run when it's not equal, him a famous TV personality and me not? That's not right; I can't allow that.*

Jim-Jam can run, he decided, *but it won't do him any good.* He's not going to beat me because he's not going to be alive that long.

A week before the election, Telscan, the interplanetary public-opinion sampling agency, published its latest findings. Reading them, Maximilian Fischer felt more gloomy than ever.

"Look at this," he said to his cousin Leon Lait, the lawyer whom he had recently made Attorney General. He tossed the report to him.

His own showing of course was negligible. In the election, Briskin would easily, and most definitely, win.

"Why is that?" Lait asked. Like Max, he was a large, paunchy man who for years now had held a stand-by job; he was not used to physical activity of any sort and his new position was proving difficult for him. However, out of family loyalty to Max, he remained. "Is that because he's got all those TV stations?" he asked, sipping from his can of beer.

Max said cuttingly, "Naw, it's because his navel glows in the dark. Of course it's because of his TV stations, you jerk — he's got them pounding away night and day, creatin' an *image*." He paused, moodily. "He's a clown. It's that red wig; it's fine for a newscaster, but not for a President." Too morose to speak, he lapsed into silence.

And worse was to follow.

At nine P.M. that night, Jim-Jam Briskin began a seventy-two hour marathon TV program over all his stations, a great final drive to bring his popularity over the top and ensure his victory.

In his special bedroom at the White House, Max Fischer sat with a tray of food before him, in bed, gloomily facing the TV set.

That Briskin, he thought furiously for the millionth time. "Look," he said to his cousin; the Attorney General sat in the easy chair across from him. "There's the nerd now." He pointed to the TV screen.

Leon Lait, munching on his cheeseburger, said, "It's abominable."

"You know where he's broadcasting from? Way out in deep space, out past Pluto. At their farthest-out transmitter, which your FBI guys will never in a million years manage to get to."

"They will," Leon assured him. "I told them they *have* to get him — the President, my cousin, personally says so."

"But they won't get him for a while," Max said. "Leon, you're just too damn slow. I'll tell you something. I got a ship of the line out there, the *Dwight D. Eisenhower*. It's all ready to lay an egg on them, you know, a big bang, just as soon as I pass on the word."

"Right, Max."

"And I hate to," Max said.

The telecast had begun to pick up momentum already. Here came the Spotlights, and sauntering out onto the stage pretty Peggy Jones, wearing a glittery bare-shoulder gown, her hair radiant. *Now we get a top-flight striptease*, Max realized, *by a real fine-looking girl*. Even he sat up and took notice. Well, maybe not a true striptease, but certainly the opposition, Briskin and his staff, had sex working for them, here. Across the room his cousin the Attorney General had stopped munching his cheeseburger; the noise came to a halt, then picked up slowly once more.

On the screen, Peggy sang:

> *It's Jim-Jam, for whom I am,*
> *America's best-loved guy.*
> *It's Jim-Jam, the best one that am,*
> *The candidate for you and I.*

"Oh God," Max groaned. And yet, the way she delivered it, with every part of her slim, long body ... it was okay. "I guess I got to inform the *Dwight D. Eisenhower* to go ahead," he said, watching.

"If you say so, Max," Leon said. "I assure you, I'll rule that you acted legally; don't worry none about that."

"Gimme the red phone," Max said. "That's the armored connection that only the Commander-in-Chief uses for top-secret instructions. Not bad, huh?" He accepted the phone from the Attorney General. "I'm calling General Tompkins and he'll relay the order to the ship. Too bad, Briskin," he added, with one last look at the screen. "But it's your own fault; you didn't have to do what you did, opposing me and all."

The girl in the silvery dress had gone, now, and Jim-Jam Briskin had appeared in her place. Momentarily, Max waited.

"Hi, beloved comrades," Briskin said, raising his hands for silence; the canned applause — Max knew that no audience existed in that remote spot — lowered, then rose again. Briskin grinned amiably, waiting for it to die.

"It's a fake," Max grunted. "Fake audience. They're smart, him and his staff. His rating's already way up."

"Right, Max," the Attorney General agreed. "I noticed that."

"Comrades," Jim Briskin was saying soberly on the TV screen, "as you may know, originally President Maximilian Fischer and I got along very well."

His hand on the red phone, Max thought to himself that what Jim-Jam said was true.

"Where we broke," Briskin continued, "was over the issue of force — of the use of naked, raw power. To Max Fischer, the office of President is merely a machine, an instrument, which he can use as an extension of his own desires, to fulfill his own needs. I honestly believe that in many respects his aims are good; he is trying to carry out Unicephalon's fine policies. But as to the means. That's a different matter."

Max said, "Listen to him, Leon." And he thought, *No matter what he says I'm going to keep on; nobody is going to stand in my way, because it's my duty; it's the job of the office, and if you got to be President like I am you'd do it, too.*

"Even the President," Briskin was saying, "must obey the law; he doesn't stand outside it, however powerful he is." He was silent for a moment and then he said slowly, "I know that at this moment the FBI, under direct orders from Max Fischer's appointee, Leon Lait, is attempting to close down these stations, to still my voice. Here again Max Fischer is making use of power, of the police agency, for his own ends, making it an extension — "

Max picked up the red phone. At once a voice said from it, "Yes, Mr. President. This is General Tompkins' C of C."

"What's that?" Max said.

"Chief of Communications, Army 600–1000, sir. Aboard the *Dwight D. Eisenhower*, accepting relay through the transmitter at the Pluto Station."

"Oh yeah," Max said, nodding. "Listen, you fellas stand by, you understand? Be ready to receive instructions." He put his hand over the mouthpiece of the phone. "Leon," he said to his cousin, who had now finished his cheeseburger and was starting on a strawberry shake. "How can I do it? I mean, Briskin is telling the truth."

Leon said, "Give Tompkins the word." He belched, then tapped himself on the chest with the side of his fist. "Pardon me."

On the screen Jim Briskin said, "I think very possibly I'm risking my life to speak to you, because this we must face: we have a President who would not mind employing murder to obtain his objectives. This is the political tactic of a tyranny, and that's what we're seeing, a tyranny coming into existence in our society, replacing the rational, disinterested rule of the homeostatic problem-solving Unicephalon 40-D which was designed, built and put into operation by some of the finest minds we have ever seen, minds dedicated to the preservation of all that's worthy in our tradition. And the transformation from this to a one-man tyranny is melancholy, to say the least."

Quietly, Max said, "Now I can't go ahead."

"Why not?" Leon said.

"Didn't you hear him? He's talking about *me*. I'm the tyrant he has reference to. Keerist." Max hung up the red phone. "I waited too long.

"It's hard for me to say it," Max said, "but — well, hell, it would prove he's right." *I know he's right anyhow*, Max thought. *But do they know it? Does the public know it? I can't let them find out about me*, he realized. *They should look up to their President, respect him. Honor him. No wonder I show up so bad in the Telscan poll. No wonder Jim Briskin decided to run against me the moment he heard I was in office. They really do know about me; they sense it, sense that Jim-Jam is speaking the truth. I'm just not Presidential caliber.*

I'm not fit, he thought, *to hold this office.*

"Listen, Leon," he said, "I'm going to give it to that Briskin anyhow and then step down. It'll be my last official act." Once more he picked up the red phone. "I'm going to order them to wipe out Briskin and then someone else can be President. Anyone the people want. Even Pat Noble or you; I don't care." He jiggled the phone. "Hey, C. of C.," he said loudly. "Come on, answer." To his cousin he said, "Leave me some of that shake; it's actually half mine."

"Sure, Max," Leon said loyally.

"Isn't no one there?" Max said into the phone. He waited. The phone remained dead. "Something's gone wrong," he said to Leon. "Communications have busted down. It must be those aliens again."

And then he saw the TV screen. It was blank.

"What's happening?" Max said. "What are they doing to me? *Who's* doing it?" He looked around, frightened. "I don't get it."

Leon stoically drank the milkshake, shrugging to show that he had no answer. But his beefy face had paled.

"It's too late," Max said. "For some reason it's just too late." Slowly, he hung up the phone. "I've got enemies, Leon, more powerful than you or me. And I don't even know who they are." He sat in silence, before the dark, soundless TV screen. Waiting.

The speaker of the TV set said abruptly, "Psuedo-autonomic news bulletin. Stand by, please." Then again there was silence.

Jim Briskin, glancing at Ed Fineberg and Peggy, waited.

"Comrade citizens of the United States," the flat, unmodulated voice from the TV speaker said, all at once. "The interregnum is over, the situation has returned to normal." As it spoke, words appeared on the monitor screen, a ribbon of printed tape passing slowly across, before the TV cameras in Washington, D.C. Unicephalon 40-D had spliced itself into the co-ax in its usual fashion; it had pre-empted the program in progress: that was its traditional right.

The voice was the synthetic verbalizing-organ of the homeostatic structure itself.

"The election campaign is nullified," Unicephalon 40-D said. "That is item one. The stand-by President Maximilian Fischer is cancelled out; that is item two. Item three: we are at war with the aliens who have invaded our system. Item four. James Briskin, who has been speaking to you — "

This is it, Jim Briskin realized.

In his earphones the impersonal, plateau-like voice continued, "Item four. James Briskin, who has been speaking to you on these facilities, is hereby ordered to cease and desist, and a writ of *mandamus* is issued forthwith requiring him to show just cause why he should be free to pursue any further political activity. In the public interest we instruct him to become politically silent."

Grinning starkly at Peggy and Ed Fineberg, Briskin said, "That's it. It's over. I'm to politically shut up."

"You can fight it in the courts," Peggy said at once. "You can take it all the way up to the Supreme Court; they've set aside decisions of Unicephalon in the past." She put her hand on his shoulder, but he moved away. "Or do you want to fight it?"

"At least I'm not cancelled out," Briskin said. He felt tired. "I'm glad to see that machine back in operation," he said, to reassure Peggy. "It means a return to stability. *That* we can use."

"What'll you do, Jim-Jam?" Ed asked. "Go back to Reinlander Beer and Calbest Electronics and try to get your old job back?"

"No," Briskin murmured. Certainly not that. But — he could not really become politically silent; he could not do what the problem-solver said. It simply was not biologically possible for him; sooner or later he would begin to talk again, for better or worse. *And*, he thought, *I'll bet Max can't do what it says either ... neither of us can.*

Maybe, he thought, *I'll answer the writ of* mandamus; *maybe I'll contest it. A counter suit ... I'll sue Unicephalon 40-D in a court of law. Jim-Jam Briskin the plaintiff, Unicephalon 40-D the defendant.* He smiled. *I'll need a good lawyer for that. Someone quite a bit better than Max Fischer's top legal mind, cousin Leon Lait.*

Going to the closet of the small studio in which they had been broadcasting, he got his coat and began to put it on. A long trip lay ahead of them back to Earth from this remote spot, and he wanted to get started.

Peggy, following after him, said, "You're not going back on the air *at all?* Not even to finish the program?"

"No," he said.

"But Unicephalon will be cutting back out again, and what'll that leave? Just dead air. That's not right, is it, Jim? Just to walk out like this ... I can't believe you'd do it, it's not like you."

He halted at the door of the studio. "You heard what it said. The instructions it handed out to me."

"Nobody leaves dead air going," Peggy said. "It's a vacuum, Jim, the thing nature abhors. *And if you don't fill it, someone else will.* Look, Unicephalon is going back off right now." She pointed at the TV monitor. The ribbon of words had ceased; once more the screen was dark, empty of motion and light. "It's your responsibility," Peggy said, "and you know it."

"Are we back on the air?" he asked Ed.

"Yes. It's definitely out of the circuit, at least for a while." Ed gestured toward the vacant stage on which the TV cameras and lights focussed. He said nothing more; he did not have to.

With his coat still on, Jim Briskin walked that way. Hands in his pockets he stepped back into the range of the cameras, smiled and said, "I think, beloved comrades, the interruption is over. For the time being, anyhow. So ... let's continue."

The noise of canned applause — manipulated by Ed Fineberg — swelled up, and Jim Briskin raised his hands and signalled the nonexistent studio audience for silence.

"Does any of you know a good lawyer?" Jim-Jam asked caustically. "And if you do, phone us and tell us right away — before the FBI finally manages to reach us out here."

In his bedroom at the White House, as Unicephalon's message ended, Maximilian Fischer turned to his cousin Leon and said, "Well, I'm out of office."

"Yeah, Max," Leon said heavily. "I guess you are."

"And you, too," Max pointed out. "It's going to be a clean sweep; you can count on that. Cancelled." He gritted his teeth. "That's sort of insulting. It could have said *retired*."

"I guess that's just its way of expressing itself," Leon said. "Don't get upset, Max; remember your heart trouble. You still got the job of stand-by, and that's the top stand-by position there is, Stand-by President of the United States, I want to remind you. And now you've got all this worry and effort off your back; you're lucky."

"I wonder if I'm allowed to finish this meal," Max said, picking at the food in the tray before him. His appetite, now that he was retired, began almost at once to improve; he selected a chicken salad sandwich and took a big bite from it. "It's still mine," he decided, his mouth full. "I still get to live here and eat regularly — right?"

"Right," Leon agreed, his legal mind active. "That's in the contract the union signed with Congress; remember back to that? We didn't go out on strike for nothing."

"Those were the days," Max said. He finished the chicken salad sandwich and returned to the eggnog. It felt good not to have to make big decisions; he let out a long, heartfelt sigh and settled back into the pile of pillows propping him up.

But then he thought, *In some respects I sort of enjoyed making decisions. I mean, it was —* He searched for the thought. *It was different from being a stand-by or drawing unemployment. It had —*

Satisfaction, he thought. *That's what it gave me. Like I was accomplishing something.* He missed that already; he felt suddenly hollow, as if things had all at once become purposeless.

"Leon," he said, "I could have gone on as President another whole month. And enjoyed the job. You know what I mean?"

"Yeah, I guess I get your meaning," Leon mumbled.

"No you don't," Max said.

"I'm trying, Max," his cousin said. "Honest."

With bitterness, Max said, "I shouldn't have had them go ahead and let those engineer-fellas patch up that Unicephalon; I should have buried the project, at least for six months."

"Too late to think about that now," Leon said.

Is it? Max asked himself. *You know, something could* happen *to Unicephalon 40-D. An accident.*

He pondered that as he ate a piece of green-apple pie with a wide slice of longhorn cheese. A number of persons whom he knew could pull off such tasks ... and did so, now and then.

A big, nearly-fatal accident, he thought. *Late some night, when everyone's asleep and it's just me and it awake here in the White House. I mean, let's face it; the aliens showed us how.*

"Look, Jim-Jam Briskin's back on the air," Leon said, gesturing at the TV set. Sure enough, there was the famous, familiar red wig, and Briskin was saying something witty and yet profound, something that made one stop to ponder. "Hey listen," Leon said. "He's poking fun at the FBI; can you imagine him doing that *now*? He's not scared of anything."

"Don't bother me," Max said. "I'm thinking." He reached over and carefully turned the sound of the TV set off.

For thoughts such as he was having he wanted no distractions.

WHAT'LL WE DO WITH RAGLAND PARK?

IN HIS DEMESNE near the logging town of John Day, Oregon, Sebastian Hada thoughtfully ate a grape as he watched the TV screen. The grapes, flown to Oregon by illegal jet transport, came from one of his farms in the Sonoma Valley of California. He spat the seeds into the fireplace across from him, half-listening to his CULTURE announcer delivering a lecture on the portrait busts of twentieth-century sculptors.

If only I could get Jim Briskin on my network, Hada thought gloomily. The ranking TV news clown, so popular, with his flaming scarlet wig and genial, informal patter ... CULTURE needs that, Hada realized. But —

But their society, at the moment, was being run by the idiotic — but peculiarly able — President Maximilian Fischer, who had locked horns with Jim-Jam Briskin; who had, in fact, clapped the famous news clown in jail. So, as a result, Jim-Jam was available neither for the commercial network which linked the three habitable planets nor for CULTURE. And meanwhile, Max Fischer ruled on.

If I could get Jim-Jam out of prison, Hada thought, perhaps due to gratitude he'd move over to my network, leave his sponsors Reinlander Beer and Calbest Electronics; after all, they have not been able to free him despite their intricate court maneuvers. They don't have the power or the know-how ... *and I have.*

One of Hada's wives, Thelma, had entered the living room of the demesne and now stood watching the TV screen from behind him. "Don't place yourself there, please," Hada said. "It gives me a panic reaction; I like to see people's faces." He twisted around in his deep chair.

"The fox is back," Thelma said. "I saw him; he glared at me." She laughed

339

with delight. "He looked so feral and independent — a bit like you, Seb. I wish I could have gotten a film clip of him."

"I must spring Jim-Jam Briskin," Hada said aloud; he had decided.

Picking up the phone, he dialed CULTURE's production chief, Nat Kaminsky, at the transmitting Earth satellite Culone.

"In exactly one hour," Hada told his employee, "I want all our outlets to begin crying for Jim-Jam Briskin's release from jail. He's not a traitor, as President Fischer declares. In fact, his political rights, his freedom of speech, have been taken away from him — illegally. Got it? Show clips of Briskin, build him up ... you understand." Hada hung up then, and dialed his attorney, Art Heaviside.

Thelma said, "I'm going back outdoors and feed the animals."

"Do that," Hada said, lighting an Abdulla, a British-made Turkish cigarette which he was most fond of. "Art?" he said into the phone. "Get started on Jim-Jam Briskin's case; find a way to free him."

His lawyer's voice came protestingly, "But, Seb, if we mix into that, we'll have President Fischer after us with the FBI; it's too risky."

Hada said, "I need Briskin. CULTURE has become pompous — look at the screen right this minute. Education and art — we need a *personality*, a good news clown; we need Jim-Jam." Telscan's surveys, of late, had shown an ominous dropping-off of viewers, but he did not tell Art Heaviside that; it was confidential.

Sighing, the attorney said, "Will do, Seb. But the charge against Briskin is sedition in time of war."

"Time of war? With whom?"

"Those alien ships — you know. That entered the Sol System last February. Darn it, Seb; you know we're at war — you can't be so lofty as to deny that; it's a legal fact."

"In my opinion," Hada said, "the aliens are not hostile." He put the receiver down, feeling angry. It's Max Fischer's way of holding onto supreme power, he said to himself. Thumping the war-scare drum. I ask you, What *actual* damage have the aliens done lately? After all, we don't own the Sol System. We just like to think we do.

In any case, CULTURE — educational TV itself — was withering, and as the owner of the network, Sebastian Hada had to act. Am I personally declining in vigor? he asked himself.

Once more picking up the phone, he dialed his analyst, Dr. Ito Yasumi, at his demesne outside of Tokyo. I need help, he said to himself. CULTURE's creator and financial backer needs help. And Dr. Yasumi can give it to me.

Facing him from across his desk, Dr. Yasumi said, "Hada, maybe problem stems from you having eight wives. That's about five too many." He waved Hada back to the couch. "Be calm, Hada. Pretty sad that big-time operator like Mr. S. Hada falling apart under stress. You afraid President Fischer's FBI get you like they got Jim Briskin?" He smiled.

"No," Hada said. "I'm fearless." He lay semisupine, arms behind his head, gazing at a Paul Klee print on the wall ... or perhaps it was an original; good analysts did make a god-awful amount of money: Yasumi's charge to him was one thousand dollars a half hour.

Yasumi said contemplatively, "Maybe you should seize power, Hada, in bold coup against Max Fischer. Make successful power play of your own; become President and then release Mr. Jim-Jam — no problem then."

"Fischer has the Armed Forces behind him," Hada said gloomily. "As Commander-in-Chief. Because of General Tompkins, who likes Fischer, they're absolutely loyal." He had already thought of this. "Maybe I ought to flee to my demesne on Callisto," he murmured. It was a superb one, and Fischer, after all, had no authority there; it was not U.S. but Dutch territory. "Anyhow, I don't want to fight; I'm not a fighter, a street brawler; I'm a cultured man."

"You are biophysical organism with built-in responses; you are alive. All that lives strives to survive. You will fight if necessary, Hada."

Looking at his watch, Hada said, "I have to go, Ito. At three I've an appointment in Havana to interview a new folksinger, a ballad-and-banjo man who's sweeping Latin America. Ragland Park is his name; he can bring life back into CULTURE."

"I know of him," Ito Yasumi said. "Saw him on commercial TV; very good performer. Part Southern U.S., part Dane, very young, with huge black mustache and blue eyes. Magnetic, this Rags, as is called."

"But is folksinging cultural?" Hada murmured.

"I tell you something," Dr. Yasumi said. "There strangeness about Rags Park; I noted even over TV. Not like other people."

"That's why he's such a sensation."

"More than that. I diagnose." Yasumi reflected. "You know, mental illness and psionic powers closely related, as in poltergeist effect. Many schizophrenics of paranoid variety are telepaths, picking up hate thoughts in subconscious of persons around them."

"I know," Hada sighed, thinking that this was costing him hundreds of dollars, this spouting of psychiatric theory.

"Go careful with Rags Park," Dr. Yasumi cautioned. "You volatile type, Hada; jump too quick. First, idea of springing Jim-Jam Briskin — risking FBI wrath — and now this Rags Park. You like hat designer or human flea. Best bet, as I say, is to openly face President Fischer, not deviousness as I foresee you doing."

"Devious?" Hada murmured. "I'm not devious."

"You most devious patient I got," Dr. Yasumi told him bluntly. "You got

nothing but tricky bones in your body, Hada. Watch out or you scheme yourself out of existence." He nodded with great soberness.

"I'll go carefully," Hada said, his mind on Rags Park; he barely heard what
Dr. Yasumi was telling him.

"A favor," Dr. Yasumi said. "When you can arrange, let me examine Mr.
Park; I would enjoy, okay? For your good, Hada, as well as professional interest. Psi talent may be of new kind; one never knows."

"Okay," Hada agreed. "I'll give you a call." But, he thought, I'm not going
to pay for it; your examination of Rags Park will be on your own time.

There was an opportunity before his appointment with the ballad singer
Rags Park to drop by the federal prison in New York at which Jim-Jam Briskin
was being held on the sedition in time of war charge.

Hada had never met the news clown face-to-face, and he was surprised to
discover how much older the man looked than on the TV. But perhaps Briskin's arrest, his troubles with President Fischer, had temporarily overwhelmed him. It would be enough to overwhelm anyone, Hada reflected as
the deputy unlocked the cell and admitted him.

"How did you happen to tangle with President Fischer?" Hada asked.

The news clown shrugged and said, "You lived through that period in
history as much as I did." He lit a cigarette and stared woodenly past Hada.

He was referring, Hada realized, to the demise of the great problem-solving computer at Washington, D.C., Unicephalon 40-D; it had ruled as President of the United States and Commander-in-Chief of the Armed Forces
until a missile, delivered by the alien ships, had put it out of action. During
that period, the standby President, Max Fischer, had taken power, a clod
appointed by the union, a primitive man with an unnatural bucolic cunning.
When at last Unicephalon 40-D had been repaired and had resumed functioning, it had ordered Fischer to depart his office and Jim Briskin to cease
political activity. Neither man had complied. Briskin had gone on campaign-
ing against Max Fischer, and Fischer had managed, by some method still
unknown, to disable the computer, thereby again becoming President of the
United States.

And his initial act had been to clap Jim-Jam in jail.

"Has Art Heaviside, my attorney, seen you?" Hada asked.

"No," Briskin said shortly.

"Listen, my friend," Hada said, "without my help you'll be in prison
forever, or at least until Max Fischer dies. This time he isn't making the
mistake of allowing Unicephalon 40-D to be repaired; it's out of action for
good."

Briskin said, "And you want me on your network in exchange for getting
me out of here." He smoked rapidly at his cigarette.

"I need you, Jim-Jam," Hada said. "It took courage for you to expose

President Fischer for the power-hungry buffoon he is; we've got a terrible menace hanging over us in Max Fischer, and if we don't join together and work fast it'll be too late; we'll both be dead. You know — in fact you said it on TV — that Fischer would gladly stoop to assassination to get what he wants."

Briskin said, "Can I say what I want over your facilities?"

"I give you absolute freedom. Attack anyone you want, including me."

After a pause, Briskin said, "I'd take your offer, Hada ... but I doubt if even Art Heaviside can get me out of here. Leon Lait, Fischer's Attorney General, is conducting the prosecution against me personally."

"Don't resign yourself," Hada said. "Billions of your viewers are waiting to see you emerge from this cell. At this moment all my outlets are clamoring for your release. Public pressure is building up. Even Max will have to listen to that."

"What I'm afraid of is that an 'accident' will happen to me," Briskin said. "Just like the 'accident' that befell Unicephalon 40-D a week after it resumed functioning. If it couldn't save itself, how can — "

"*You* afraid?" Hada inquired, incredulous. "Jim-Jam Briskin, the ranking news clown — I don't believe it."

There was silence.

Briskin said, "The reason my sponsors, Reinlander Beer and Calbest Electronics, haven't been able to get me out is" — he paused — "pressure put on them by President Fischer. Their attorneys as much as admitted that to me. When Fischer learns you're trying to help me, he'll bring all the pressure he has to bear directly on you." He glanced up acutely at Hada. "Do you have the stamina to endure it? I wonder."

"Certainly I have," Hada said. "As I told Dr. Yasumi — "

"And he'll put pressure on your wives," Jim-Jam Briskin said.

"I'll divorce all eight of them," Hada said hotly.

Briskin held out his hand and they shook. "It's a deal then," Jim-Jam said. "I'll go to work for CULTURE as soon as I'm out of here." He smiled in a weary but hopeful way.

Elated, Hada said, "Have you ever heard of Rags Park, the folk and ballad singer? At three today I'm signing him, too."

"There's a TV set here and now and then I catch one of Park's numbers," Briskin said. "He sounds good. But do you want that on CULTURE? It's hardly educational."

"CULTURE is changing. We're going to sugarcoat our didacticisms from now on. We've been losing our audience. I don't intend to see CULTURE wither away. The very concept of it — "

The word "CULTURE" stood for Committee Utilizing Learning Techniques for Urban Renewal Efforts. A major part of Hada's real estate holdings consisted of the city of Portland, Oregon, which he had acquired — intact — ten years ago. It was not worth much; typical of the semiabandoned slum constellations which had become not only repellent but obsolete, Portland had a certain sentimental value to him because he had been born there.

However, one notion lingered in his mind. If for any reason the colonies on the other planets and moons had to be abandoned, if the settlers came streaming back to Earth, the cities would be repopulated once more. And with the alien ships flitting about the farther planets, this was not as implausible as it sounded. In fact, a few families had emigrated back to Earth already ...

So, underneath, CULTURE was not quite the disinterested public service nonprofit agency that it appeared. Mixed in with the education, Hada's outlets drummed away at the seductive idea of *the city*, how much it could offer, how little there was to be had in the colonies. Give up the difficult, crude life of the frontier, CULTURE declared night and day. Return to your own planet; repair the decaying cities. They're your real home.

Did Briskin know this? Hada wondered. Did the news clown understand the actual purpose of his organization?

Hada would find that out — if and when he managed to get Briskin out of jail and before a CULTURE microphone.

At three o'clock Sebastian Hada met the folksinger Ragland Park at the Havana office of CULTURE.

"I'm glad to make your acquaintance," Rags Park said shyly. Tall, skinny, with his huge black mustache hiding most of his mouth, he shuffled about self-consciously, his blue eyes gentle with authentic friendliness. He had an unusual sweetness about him, Hada noted. Almost a saintly quality. Hada found himself impressed.

"And you play both the guitar and five-string banjo?" Hada said. "Not at once, of course."

Rags Park mumbled, "No, sir. I alternate. Want me to play something right now for you?"

"Where were you born?" Nat Kaminsky asked. Hada had brought his production chief along; in matters such as this, Kaminsky's opinion was valuable.

"In Arkansas," Rags answered. "My family raises hogs." He had his banjo with him and now, nervously, he twanged a few notes. "I know a real sad song that'll break your heart. It's called 'Poor Old Hoss.' Want me to sing it for you?"

"We've heard you," Hada said. "We know you're good." He tried to imagine this awkward young man twanging away over CULTURE in between lectures on twentieth-century portrait sculptors. Hard to imagine ...

Rags said, "I bet there's one thing you don't know about me, Mr. Hada. I make up a lot of my own ballads."

"Creative," Kaminsky said to Hada straight-faced. "That's good."

"For instance," Rags continued, "I once made up a ballad about a man named Tom McPhail who ran ten miles with a bucket of water to put out the fire in his little daughter's crib."

"Did he make it?" Hada asked.

"Sure did. Just in time. Tom McPhail ran faster and faster with that bucket of water." Chanting, Rags twanged in accompaniment.

> *"Here comes Tom McPhail*
> *Holdin' on tight to that great little pail.*
> *Holdin' on tight, boys, here he come.*
> *Heart full of fear, faculties numb."*

Twang, twang, sounded the banjo, mournfully and urgently.

Kaminsky said acutely, "I've been following your shows and I've never heard you sing that number."

"Aw," Rags said, "I had bad luck with that, Mr. Kaminsky. Turned out there really is a Tom McPhail. Lives in Pocatello, Idaho. I sang about ol' Tom McPhail on my January fourteenth TV show and right away he got sore — he was listenin' — and got a lawyer to write me."

"Wasn't it just a coincidence in names?" Hada said.

"Well," Rags said, twisting about self-consciously, "it seems there really had been a fire in his home there in Pocatello, and McPhail, he got panicky and ran with a bucket to the creek, and it was ten miles off, like I said in the song."

"Did he get back with the water in time?"

"Amazingly, he did," Rags said.

Kaminsky said to Hada, "It would be better, on CULTURE, if this man stuck to authentic Old English ballads such as 'Greensleeves.' That would seem more what we want."

Thoughtfully, Hada said to Rags, "Bad luck to pick a name for a ballad and have it turn out that such a man really exists ... Have you had that sort of bad luck since?"

"Yes, I have," Rags admitted. "I made up a ballad last week ... it was about a lady, Miss Marsha Dobbs. Listen.

> *"All day, all night, Marsha Dobbs.*
> *Loves a married man whose wife she robs.*
> *Robs that wife and hearth of Jack Cooks's heart.*
> *Steals the husband, makes that marriage fall apart.*

"That's the first verse," Rags explained. "It goes on for seventeen verses; tells how Marsha comes to work at Jack Cooks's office as a secretary, goes to lunch with him, then later they meet late at — "

"Is there a moral at the end?" Kaminsky inquired.

"Oh sure," Rags said. "Don't take no one else's man because if you do, heaven avenges the dishonored wife. In this case:

"Virus flu lay 'round the corner just for Jack.
For Marsha Dobbs 'twas to be worse, a heart attack.
Miz Cooks, the hand of heaven sought to spare.
Surrounded her, became a garment strong to wear.
Miz Cooks — "

Hada broke in over the twanging and singing. "That's fine, Rags. That's enough." He glanced at Kaminsky and winced.

"And I bet it turned out," Kaminsky said, "that there's a real Marsha Dobbs who had an affair with her boss, Jack Cooks."

"Right," Rags said, nodding "No lawyer called me, but I read it in the homeopape, the New York *Times*. Marsha, she died of a heart attack, and it was actually during — " He hesitated modestly. "You know. While she and Jack Cooks were at a motel satellite, lovemaking."

"Have you deleted that number from your repertoire?" Kaminsky asked.

"Well," Rags said, "I can't make up my mind. Nobody's suing me ... and I like the ballad. I think I'll leave it in."

To himself, Hada thought, What was it Dr. Yasumi said? That he scented psi powers of some unusual kind in Ragland Park ... perhaps it's the parapsychological power of having the bad luck to make up ballads about people who really exist. Not much of a talent, that.

On the other hand, he realized, it could be a variant on the telepathic talent ... and with a little tinkering it might be *quite* valuable.

"How long does it take you to make up a ballad?" he asked Rags.

"I can do it on the spot," Rags Park answered. "I could do it now; give me a theme and I'll compose right here in this office of yours."

Hada pondered and then said, "My wife Thelma has been feeding a gray fox that I know — or I believe — killed and ate our best Rouen duck."

After a moment of considering, Rags Park twanged:

"Miz Thelma Hada talked to the fox.
Built it a home from an old pine box.
Sebastian Hada heard a sad cluck:
Wicked gray fox had eaten his duck."

"But ducks don't cluck, they quack," Nat Kaminsky said critically.

"That's a fact," Rags admitted. He pondered and then sang:

"Hada's production chief changed my luck.
I got no job, and ducks don't cluck."

Grinning, Kaminsky said, "Okay, Rags; you win." To Hada he said, "I advise you to hire him."

"Let me ask you this," Hada said to Rags. "Do *you* think the fox got my Rouen?"

"Gosh," Rags said, "I don't know anything about that."

"But in your ballad you said so," Hada pointed out.

"Let me think," Rags said. Presently he twanged once more and said:

> *"Interesting problem Hada's stated.*
> *Perhaps my ability's underrated.*
> *Perhaps I'm not no ordinary guy.*
> *Do I get my ballads through the use of psi?"*

"How did you know I meant psi?" Hada asked. "You can read interior thoughts, can't you? Yasumi was right."

Rags said, "Mister, I'm just singing and twanging; I'm just an entertainer, same as Jim-Jam Briskin, that news clown President Fischer clapped in jail."

"Are you afraid of jail?" Hada asked him bluntly.

"President Fischer doesn't have nothing against me," Rags said. "I don't do political ballads."

"If you work for me," Hada said, "maybe you will. I'm trying to get Jim-Jam out of jail; today all my outlets began their campaign."

"Yes, he ought to be out," Rags agreed, nodding. "That was a bad thing, President Fischer using the FBI for that ... those aliens aren't that much of a menace."

Kaminsky, rubbing his chin meditatively, said, "Do one on Jim-Jam Briskin, Max Fischer, the aliens — on the whole political situation. Sum it up."

"That's asking a lot," Rags said, with a wry smile.

"Try," Kaminsky said. "See how well you can epitomize."

"Whooee," Rags said. " 'Epitomize.' Now I know I'm talking to CULTURE. Okay, Mr. Kaminsky. How's this?" He said:

> *"Fat little President by name of Max*
> *Used his power, gave Jim the ax.*
> *Sebastian Hada's got eyes like a vulture.*
> *Sees his opening, steps in with CULTURE."*

"You're hired," Hada said to the folksinger, and reached into his pocket for a contract form.

Kaminsky said, "Will we be successful, Mr. Park? Tell us about the outcome."

"I'd, uh, rather not," Rags said. "At least not this minute. You think I can also read the future, too? That I'm a precog as well as a telepath?" He laughed gently. "I've got plenty of talent, according to you; I'm flattered." He bowed mockingly.

"I'll assume that you're coming to work for us," Hada said. "And your willingness to be an employee of CULTURE — is it a sign that you feel President Fischer is not going to be able to get us?"

"Oh, we could be in jail, too, along with Jim-Jam," Rags murmured. "That wouldn't surprise me." Seating himself, his banjo in hand, he prepared to sign the contract.

In his bedroom at the White House, President Max Fischer had listened for almost an hour now to the TV set, to CULTURE hammering away on the same topic, again and again. *Jim Briskin must be released*, the voice said; it was a smooth, professional announcer's voice, but behind it, unheard, Max knew, was Sebastian Hada.

"Attorney General," Max said to his cousin Leon Lait, "get me dossiers on all of Hada's wives, all seven or eight, whatever it is. I guess I got to take a drastic course."

When, later in the day, the eight dossiers had been put before him, he began to read carefully, chewing on his El Producto alta cigar and frowning, his lips moving with the effort of comprehending the intricate, detailed material.

Jeez, what a mess some of these dames must be, he realized. Ought to be getting chemical psychotherapy, have their brain metabolisms straightened out. But he was not displeased; it had been his hunch that a man like Sebastian Hada would attract an unstable sort of woman.

One in particular, Hada's fourth wife, interested him. Zoe Martin Hada, thirty-one years old, now living on Io with her ten-year-old son.

Zoe Hada had definite psychotic traits.

"Attorney General," he said to his cousin, "this dame is living on a pension supplied by the U.S. Department of Mental Health. Hada isn't contributing a dime to her support. You get her here to the White House, you understand? I got a job for her."

The following morning Zoe Martin Hada was brought to his office.

He saw, between the two FBI men, a scrawny woman, attractive, but with wild, animosity-filled eyes. "Hello, Mrs. Zoe Hada," Max said. "Listen, I know sumpthin' about you; you're the only genuine Mrs. Hada — the others are imposters, right? And Sebastian's done you dirt." He waited, and saw the expression on her face change.

"Yes," Zoe said. "I've been in courts for six years trying to prove what you just said. I can hardly believe it; are you really going to help me?"

"Sure," Max said. "But you got to do it my way; I mean, if you're waiting for that skunk Hada to change, you're wasting your time. About all you can do" — he paused — "is even up the score."

The violence which had left her face crept back as she understood, gradually, what he meant.

Frowning, Dr. Ito Yasumi said, "I have now made my examination, Hada." He began putting away his battery of cards. "This Rags Park is neither telepath or precog; he neither reads my mind nor cognates what is to be and, frankly, Hada, although I still sense psi power about him, I have no idea what it might be."

Hada listened in silence. Now Rags Park, this time with a guitar over his shoulder, wandered in from the other room. It seemed to amuse him that Dr. Yasumi could make nothing of him; he grinned at both of them and then seated himself. "I'm a puzzle," he said to Hada. "Either you got too much when you hired me or not enough ... but you don't know which and neither does Dr. Yasumi or me."

"I want you to start at once over CULTURE," Hada told him impatiently. "Make up and sing folk ballads that depict the unfair imprisonment and harassment of Jim-Jam Briskin by Leon Lait and his FBI. Make Lait appear a monster; make Fischer appear a scheming, greedy boob. Understand?"

"Sure," Rags Park said, nodding. "We got to get public opinion aroused. I knew that when I signed; I ain't just entertaining no more."

Dr. Yasumi said to Rags, "Listen, I have favor to ask. Make up folk-style ballad telling how Jim-Jam Briskin *get out of jail.*"

Both Hada and Rags Park glanced at him.

"Not about what is," Yasumi explained, "but about that which we want to be."

Shrugging, Park said, "Okay."

The door to Hada's office burst open and the chief of his bodyguards, Dieter Saxton, put his head excitedly in. "Mr. Hada, we just gunned down a woman who was trying to get through to you with a homemade bomb. Do you have a moment to identify her? We think maybe it's — I mean it was — one of your wives."

"God in heaven," Hada said, and hurried along with Saxton from the office and down the corridor.

There on the floor, near the front entrance of the demesne, lay a woman he knew. Zoe, he thought. He knelt down, touched her.

"Sorry," Saxton mumbled. "We had to, Mr. Hada."

"All right," he said. "I believe you if you say so." He greatly trusted Saxton; after all, he had to.

Saxton said, "I think from now on you better have one of us close by you at all times. I don't mean outside your office; I mean within physical touch."

"I wonder if Max Fischer sent her here," Hada said.

"The chances are good," Saxton said. "I'd make book on it."

"Just because I'm trying to get Jim-Jam Briskin released." Hada was thoroughly shaken. "It really amazes me." He rose to his feet unsteadily.

"Let me go after Fischer," Saxton urged in a low voice. "For your protection. He has no right to be President; Unicephalon 40-D is our only legal President and we all know Fischer put it out of commission."

"No," Hada murmured. "I don't like murder."

"It's not murder," Saxton said. "It's protection for you and your wives and children."

"Maybe so," Hada said, "but I still can't do it. At least not yet." He left Saxton and made his way with difficulty back to his office, where Rags Park and Dr. Yasumi waited.

"We heard," Yasumi said to him. "Bear up, Hada. The woman was a paranoid schizophrenic with delusions of persecution; without psychotherapy it was inevitable that she would meet a violent death. Do not blame yourself or Mr. Saxton."

Hada said, "And at one time I loved that woman."

Dolefully strumming on his guitar, Rags Park sang to himself; the words were not audible. Perhaps he was practicing on his ballad of Jim Briskin's escape from jail.

"Take Mr. Saxton's advice," Dr. Yasumi said. "Protect yourself at all times." He patted Hada on the shoulder.

Rags spoke up, "Mr. Hada, I think I've got my ballad now. About — "

"I don't want to hear it," Hada said harshly. "Not now." He wished the two of them would leave; he wanted to be by himself.

Maybe I should fight back, he thought. Dr. Yasumi recommends it; now Dieter Saxton recommends it. What would Jim-Jam recommend? He has a sound mind ... he would say, Don't employ murder. I know that would be his answer; I know him.

And if he says not to, I won't.

Dr. Yasumi was instructing Rags Park, "A ballad, please, about that vase of gladioli over there on the bookcase. Tell how it rise up straight in the air and hover; all right?"

"What kind of ballad is that?" Rags said. "Anyhow, I got my work cut out for me; you heard what Mr. Hada said."

"But I'm still testing you," Dr. Yasumi grumbled.

To his cousin the Attorney General, Max Fischer said disgustedly, "Well, we didn't get him."

"No, Max," Leon Lait agreed. "He's got good men in his employ; he's not an individual like Briskin, he's a whole corporation."

Moodily, Max said, "I read a book once that said if three people are competing, eventually two of them will join together and gang up on the third one. It's inevitable. That's exactly what's happened; Hada and Briskin are buddies, and I'm alone. We have to split them apart, Leon, and get one of them on our side against the other. Once Briskin liked me. Only he disapproved of my methods."

Leon said, "Wait'll he hears about Zoe Hada trying to kill her ex-husband; then Briskin'll really disapprove of you."

"You think it's impossible to win him over now?"

"I sure do, Max. You're in a worse position than ever, regarding him. Forget about winning him over."

"There's some idea in my mind, though," Max said. "I can't quite make out what it is yet, but it has to do with freeing Jim-Jam in the hopes that he'll feel gratitude."

"You're out of your mind," Leon said. "How come you ever thought of an idea like that? It isn't like you."

"I don't know," Max groaned. "But there it is."

To Sebastian Hada, Rags Park said, "Uh, I think maybe I got me a ballad now, Mr. Hada. Like Dr. Yasumi suggested. It has to do with telling how Jim-Jam Briskin gets out of jail. You want to hear it?"

Dully, Hada nodded. "Go ahead." After all, he was paying the folksinger; he might as well get something for his money.

Twanging away, Rags sang:

> *"Jim-Jam Briskin languished in jail,*
> *Couldn't find no one to put up his bail.*
> *Blame Max Fischer! Blame Max Fischer!"*

Rags explained, "That's the chorus, 'Blame Max Fischer!' Okay?"

"All right," Hada said, nodding.

> *"The Lord came along, said, Max, I'm mad.*
> *Casting that man in jail, that was bad.*
> *Blame Max Fischer! the good Lord cried.*
> *Poor Jim Briskin, his rights denied.*
> *Blame Max Fischer! I'm here to tell;*
> *Good Lord say, Him go straight to hell.*
> *Repent, Max Fischer! There's only one route:*
> *Get on my good side; let Jim-Jam out."*

Rags explained to Hada, "Now here's what's going to happen." He cleared his throat:

> *"Bad Max Fischer, he saw the light,*
> *Told Leon Lait, We got to do right.*
> *Sent a message down to turn that key,*
> *Open that door and let Jim-Jam free.*
> *Old Jim Briskin saw an end to his plight;*
> *Jail door open now, lets in the light.*

"That's all," Rags informed Hada. "It's a sort of holler type of folk song, a spiritual where you tap your foot. Do you like it?"

Hada managed to nod. "Oh sure. Anything's fine."

"Shall I tell Mr. Kaminsky you want me to air it over CULTURE?"

"Air away," Hada said. He did not care; the death of Zoe still weighed on his mind — he felt responsible, because after all it had been his bodyguards who had done it, and the fact that Zoe had been insane, had been trying to destroy him, did not seem to matter. It was still a human life; it was still murder. "Listen," he said to Rags on impulse, "I want you to make up another song, now."

With sympathy, Rags said, "I know, Mr. Hada. A ballad about the sad death of your former wife Zoe. I been thinking about that and I have a ballad all ready. Listen:

> *"There once was a lady fair to see and hear;*
> *Wander, spirit, over field and star,*
> *Sorrowful, but forgiving from afar.*
> *That spirit knows who did her in.*
> *It was a stranger, not her kin.*
> *It was Max Fischer who knew her not — "*

Hada interrupted, "Don't whitewash me, Rags; I'm to blame. Don't put everything on Max as if he's a whipping boy."

Seated in the corner of the office, listening quietly, Dr. Yasumi now spoke up. "And also too much credit to President Fischer in your ballads, Rags. In ballad of Jim-Jam's release from jail, you specifically give credit to Max Fischer for ethical change of heart. This will not do. The credit for Jim-Jam's release must go to Hada. Listen, Rags; I have composed a poem for this occasion."

Dr. Yasumi chanted:

> *"News clown nestles not in jail. A friend,*
> *Sebastian Hada, got him free.*
> *He loves that friend, regards him well.*
> *Knows whom to honor, and to seek.*

"Exactly thirty-two syllables," Dr. Yasumi explained modestly. "Old-style

Japanese-type haiku poetry does not have to rhyme as do U.S. — English ballads, however must get right to the point, which in this matter is all-important." To Rags he said, "You make my haiku into ballad, okay? In your typical fashion, in rhythmic, rhyming couplets, et cetera, and so on."

"I counted thirty-three syllables," Rags said. "Anyhow, I'm a creative artist; I'm not used to being told what to compose." He turned to Hada. "Who'm I working for, you or him? Not him, as far as I know."

"Do as he says," Hada told Rags. "He's a brilliant man."

Sullenly, Rags murmured, "Okay, but I didn't expect this sort of job when I signed the contract." He retired to a far corner of the office to brood, think, and compose.

"What are you involved with, here, Doctor?" Hada asked.

"We'll see," Dr. Yasumi said mysteriously. "Theory about psi power of this balladeer, here. May pay off, may not."

"You seem to feel that the exact wording of Rags's ballads is very important," Hada said.

"That's right," Dr. Yasumi agreed. "As in legal document. You wait, Hada; you find out — if I right — eventually. If I wrong, doesn't matter anyhow." He smiled encouragingly at Hada.

The phone in President Max Fischer's office rang. It was the Attorney General, his cousin, calling in agitation. "Max, I went over to the federal pen where Jim-Jam is, to see about quashing the charges against him like you were talking about — " Leon hesitated. "He's gone, Max. He's not in there anymore." Leon sounded wildly nervous.

"How'd he get out?" Max said, more baffled than angry.

"Art Heaviside, Hada's attorney, found a way; I don't know yet what it is — I have to see Circuit Court Judge Dale Winthrop, about it; he signed the release order an hour or so ago. I have an appointment with Winthrop ... as soon as I've seen him, I'll call you back."

"I'll be darned," Max said slowly. "Well, we were too late." He hung up the phone reflexively and then stood deep in thought. *What has Hada got going for him?* he asked himself. Something I don't understand.

And now the thing to watch for, he realized, is Jim Briskin showing up on TV. On CULTURE's network.

With relief he saw on the screen — not Jim Briskin but a folksinger plucking away on a banjo.

And then he realized that the folksinger was singing about *him*.

> *"Bad Max Fischer, he saw the light,*
> *Told Leon Lait, We got to do right.*
> *Sent a message down to turn that key."*

Listening, Max Fischer said aloud, "My God, that's exactly what happened! That's exactly what I did!" Eerie, he thought. What's it mean, this

ballad singer on CULTURE who sings about what I'm doing — secret matters
that he couldn't possibly know about!

Telepathic maybe, Max thought. That must be it.

Now the folksinger was narrating and plucking about Sebastian Hada,
how Hada had been personally responsible for getting Jim-Jam Briskin out of
jail. And it's true, Max said to himself. When Leon Lait got there to the
federal pen, he found Briskin gone because of Art Heaviside's activity ... I
better listen pretty carefully to this singer, because for some reason he seems
to know more than I do.

But the singer now had finished.

The CULTURE announcer was saying, "That was a brief interlude of political ballads by the world-renowned Ragland Park. Mr. Park, you'll be pleased
to hear, will appear on this channel every hour for five minutes of new ballads,
composed here in CULTURE's studios for the occasion. Mr. Park will be
watching the teletypers and will compose his ballads to — "

Max switched the set off then.

Like calypso, Max realized. New ballads. God, he thought dismally. Suppose Parks sings about Unicephalon 40-D coming back.

I have a feeling, he thought, *that what Ragland Park sings turns out to be true.*
It's one of those psionic talents.

And they, the opposition, are making use of this.

On the other hand, he thought, I might have a few psionic talents of my
own. Because if I didn't, *I wouldn't have gotten as far as I have.*

Seated before the TV set, he switched it on once again and waited, chewing his lower lip and pondering what he should do. As yet he could come up
with nothing. But I will, sooner or later, he said to himself. And before they
come up with the idea of bringing Unicephalon 40-D back ...

Dr. Yasumi said, "I have solved what Ragland Park's psi talent is, Hada.
You care to know?"

"I'm more interested in the fact that Jim-Jam is out of jail," Hada
answered. He put down the receiver of the telephone, almost unable to believe
the news. "He'll be here right away," he said to Dr. Yasumi. "He's on his way
direct, by monorail. We'll see that he gets to Callisto, where Max has no
jurisdiction, so they can't possibly rearrest him." His mind swirled with plans.
Rubbing his hands together, he said rapidly, "Jim-Jam can broadcast from our
transmitter on Callisto. And he can live at my demesne there — that'll be beer
and skittles for him — I know he'll agree."

"He is out," Dr. Yasumi said dryly, "because of Rags's psi talent, so you
had better listen. Because this psi talent is not understood even by Rags and,
honestly to God, it could rebound on you any time."

Reluctantly, Hada said, "Okay, give me your opinion."

"Relationship between Rags's made-up ballads and reality is one of cause and effect. What Rags describes then takes place. The ballad precedes the event and not by much. You see? This could be dangerous, if Rags understood it and made use of it for own advantage."

"If this is true," Hada said, "then we want him to compose a ballad about Unicephalon 40-D returning to action." That was obvious to him instantly. Max Fischer would be merely the standby President once more, as he had originally been. Without authority of any kind.

"Correct," Dr. Yasumi said. "But problem is, now that he is making up these political-type ballads, Ragland Park is apt to discover this fact, too. For if he makes up song about Unicephalon and then it actually — "

"You're right," Hada said. "Even Park couldn't miss that." He was silent then, deep in thought. Ragland Park was potentially even more dangerous than Max Fischer. On the other hand, Ragland seemed like a good egg; there was no reason to assume that he would misuse his power, as Max Fischer had his.

But it was a great deal of power for one human being to have. Much too much.

Dr. Yasumi said, "Care must be taken as to exactly what sort of ballads Ragland makes up. Contents must be edited in advance, maybe by you."

"I want as little as possible — " Hada began, and then ceased. The receptionist had buzzed him; he switched on the intercom.

"Mr. James Briskin is here."

"Send him right in," Hada said, delighted. "He's here already, Ito." Hada opened the door to the office — and there stood Jim-Jam, his face lined and sober.

"Mr. Hada got you out," Dr Yasumi informed Jim-Jam.

"I know. I appreciate it, Hada." Briskin entered the office and Hada at once closed and locked the door.

"Listen, Jim-Jam," Hada said without preamble, "we've got greater problems than ever. Max Fischer as a threat is nothing. Now we have to deal with an ultimate form of power, an absolute rather than a relative form. I wish I had never gotten into this; whose idea was it to hire Rags Park?"

Dr. Yasumi said, "Yours, Hada, and I warned you at the time."

"I'd better instruct Rags not to make up any more new ballads," Hada decided. "That's the first step to take. I'll call the studio. My God, he might make up one about us all going to the bottom of the Atlantic, or twenty AUs out into deep space."

"Avoid panic," Dr. Yasumi told him firmly. "There you go ahead with panic, Hada. Volatile as ever. Be calm and think first."

"How can I be calm," Hada said, "when that rustic has the power to move us around like toys? Why, he can command the entire universe."

"Not necessarily," Dr. Yasumi disagreed. "There may be limit. Psi power not well understood, even yet. Hard to test out in laboratory condition; hard to subject to rigorous, repeatable scrutiny." He pondered.

Jim Briskin said, "As I understand what you're saying — "

"You were sprung by a made-up ballad," Hada told him. "Done at my command. It worked, but now we're stuck with the ballad singer." He paced back and forth, hands in his pockets.

What'll we do with Ragland Park? he asked himself desperately.

At the main studios of CULTURE in the Earth satellite Culone, Ragland Park sat with his banjo and guitar, examining the news dispatches coming in over the teletype and preparing ballads for his next appearance.

Jim-Jam Briskin, he saw, had been released from jail by order of a federal judge. Pleased, Ragland considered a ballad on that topic, then remembered that he had already composed — and sung — several. What he needed was a new topic entirely. He had done that one to death.

From the control booth, Nat Kaminsky's voice boomed over the loud-speaker, "You about ready to go on again, Mr. Park?"

"Oh sure," Ragland replied, nodding. Actually he was not, but he would be in a moment or two.

What about a ballad, he thought, concerning a man named Pete Robinson of Chicago, Illinois, whose springer spaniel was attacked one fine day in broad daylight on a city street by an enraged eagle?

No, that's not political enough, he decided.

What about one dealing with the end of the world? A comet hitting Earth, or maybe the aliens swarming in and taking over ... a real scary ballad with people getting blown up and cut in half by ray guns?

But that was too unintellectual for CULTURE; that wouldn't do either.

Well, he thought, then a song about the FBI. I've never done one on the subject; Leon Lait's men in gray business suits with fat red necks ... college graduates carrying briefcases ...

To himself, he sang, while strumming his guitar:

> *"Our department chief says, Hark;*
> *Go and bring back Ragland Park.*
> *He's a menace to conformity;*
> *His crimes are an enormity."*

Chuckling, Ragland pondered how to go on with the ballad. A ballad about himself; interesting idea ... how had he happened to think of that?

He was so busy concocting the ballad, in fact, that he did not notice the three men in gray business suits with fat red necks who had entered the studio and were coming toward him, each man carrying a briefcase in a way that made it clear he was a college graduate and used to carrying it.

I really have a good ballad going, Ragland said to himself. The best one of my career. Strumming, he went on:

> *"Yes, they sneaked up in the dark*
> *Aimed their guns and shot poor Park.*
> *Stilled freedom's clarion cry*
> *When they doomed this man to die;*
> *But a crime not soon forgotten*
> *Even in a culture rotten."*

That was as far as Ragland got in his ballad. The leader of the group of FBI men lowered his smoking pistol, nodded to his companions, and then spoke into his wrist transmitter. "Inform Mr. Lait that we have been successful."

The tinny voice from his wrist answered, "Good. Return to headquarters at once. *He* orders it."

He, of course, was Maximilian Fischer. The FBI men knew that, knew who had sent them on their mission.

In his office at the White House, Maximilian Fischer breathed a sigh of relief when informed that Ragland Park was dead. A close call, he said to himself. That man might have finished me off — me and everybody else in the world.

Amazing, he thought, that we were able to get him. The breaks certainly went our way. I wonder why.

Could be one of my psionic talents has to do with putting an end to folksingers, he said to himself, and grinned with sleek satisfaction.

Specifically, he thought, a psi talent for getting folksingers to compose ballads on the theme of their own destruction ...

And now, he realized, the real problem. Of getting Jim Briskin back into jail. And it will be hard; Hada is probably smart enough to think of transporting him immediately to an outlying moon where I have no authority. It will be a long struggle, me against those two ... and they could well beat me in the end.

He sighed. A lot of hard work, he said to himself. But I guess I got to do it. Picking up the phone, he dialed Leon Lait ...

OH, TO BE A BLOBEL!

HE PUT a twenty-dollar platinum coin into the slot and the analyst, after a pause, lit up. Its eyes shone with sociability and it swiveled about in its chair, picked up a pen and pad of long yellow paper from its desk and said,

"Good morning, sir. You may begin."

"Hello, Dr. Jones. I guess you're not the same Dr. Jones who did the definitive biography of Freud; that was a century ago." He laughed nervously; being a rather poverty-stricken man he was not accustomed to dealing with the new fully homeostatic psychoanalysts. "Um," he said, "should I free-associate or give you background material or just what?"

Dr. Jones said, "Perhaps you could begin by telling me who you are und warum mich — why you have selected me."

"I'm George Munster of catwalk 4, building WEF-395, San Francisco condominium established 1996."

"How do you do, Mr. Munster." Dr. Jones held out its hand, and George Munster shook it. He found the hand to be of a pleasant body-temperature and decidedly soft. The grip, however, was manly.

"You see," Munster said, "I'm an ex-GI, a war veteran. That's how I got my condominium apartment at WEF-395; veterans' preference."

"Ah yes," Dr. Jones said, ticking faintly as it measured the passage of time. "The war with the Blobels."

"I fought three years in that war," Munster said, nervously smoothing his long, black, thinning hair. "I hated the Blobels and I volunteered; I was only nineteen and I had a good job — but the crusade to clear the Sol System of Blobels came first in my mind."

"Um," Dr. Jones said, ticking and nodding.

George Munster continued, "I fought well. In fact I got two decorations

359

and a battlefield citation. Corporal. That's because I single-handedly wiped out an observation satellite full of Blobels; we'll never know exactly how many because of course, being Blobels, they tend to fuse together and unfuse confusingly." He broke off, then, feeling emotional. Even remembering and talking about the war was too much for him ... he lay back on the couch, lit a cigarette and tried to become calm.

The Blobels had emigrated originally from another star system, probably Proxima. Several thousand years ago they had settled on Mars and on Titan, doing very well at agrarian pursuits. They were developments of the original unicellular amoeba, quite large and with a highly-organized nervous system, but still amoeba, with pseudopodia, reproducing by binary fission, and in the main offensive to Terran settlers.

The war itself had broken out over ecological considerations. It had been the desire of the Foreign Aid Department of the UN to change the atmosphere on Mars, making it more usable for Terran settlers. This change, however, had made it unpalatable for the Blobel colonies already there; hence the squabble.

And, Munster reflected, it was not possible to change *half* the atmosphere of a planet, the Brownian movement being what it was. Within a period of ten years the altered atmosphere had diffused throughout the planet, bringing suffering — at least so they alleged — to the Blobels. In retaliation, a Blobel armada had approached Terra and had put into orbit a series of technically sophisticated satellites designed eventually to alter the atmosphere of Terra. This alteration had never come about because of course the War Office of the UN had gone into action; the satellites had been detonated by self-instructing missiles ... and the war was on.

Dr. Jones said, "Are you married, Mr. Munster?"

"No sir," Munster said. "And — " He shuddered. "You'll see why when I've finished telling you. See, Doctor — " He stubbed out his cigarette. "I'll be frank. I was a Terran spy. That was my task; they gave the job to me because of my bravery in the field ... I didn't ask for it."

"I see," Dr. Jones said.

"Do you?" Munster's voice broke. "Do you know what was necessary in those days in order to make a Terran into a successful spy among the Blobels?"

Nodding, Dr. Jones said, "Yes, Mr. Munster. You had to relinquish your human form and assume the repellent form of a Blobel."

Munster said nothing; he clenched and unclenched his fist, bitterly. Across from him Dr. Jones ticked.

That evening, back in his small apartment at WEF-395, Munster opened a fifth of Teacher's scotch, sat by himself sipping from a cup, lacking even the energy to get a glass down from the cupboard over the sink.

What had he gotten out of the session with Dr. Jones today? Nothing, as nearly as he could tell. And it had eaten deep into his meager financial resources ... meager because —

Because for almost twelve hours out of the day he reverted, despite all the efforts of himself and the Veterans' Hospitalization Agency of the UN, to his old war-time Blobel shape. To a formless unicellular-like blob, right in the middle of his own apartment at WEF-395.

His financial resources consisted of a small pension from the War Office; finding a job was impossible, because as soon as he was hired the strain caused him to revert there on the spot, in plain sight of his new employer and fellow workers.

It did not assist in forming successful work-relationships.

Sure enough, now, at eight in the evening, he felt himself once more beginning to revert; it was an old and familiar experience to him, and he loathed it. Hurriedly, he sipped the last of the cup of scotch, put the cup down on a table ... and felt himself slide together into a homogenous puddle.

The telephone rang.

"I can't answer," he called to it. The phone's relay picked up his anguished message and conveyed it to the calling party. Now Munster had become a single transparent gelatinous mass in the middle of the rug; he undulated toward the phone — it was still ringing, despite his statement to it, and he felt furious resentment; didn't he have enough troubles already, without having to deal with a ringing phone?

Reaching it, he extended a pseudopodium and snatched the receiver from the hook. With great effort he formed his plastic substance into the semblance of a vocal apparatus, resonating dully. "I'm busy," he resonated in a low booming fashion into the mouthpiece of the phone. "Call later." *Call*, he thought as he hung up, *tomorrow morning. When I've been able to regain my human form.*

The apartment was quiet, now.

Sighing, Munster flowed back across the carpet, to the window, where he rose into a high pillar in order to see the view beyond; there was a light-sensitive spot on his outer surface, and although he did not possess a true lens he was able to appreciate — nostalgically — the sight of San Francisco Bay, the Golden Gate Bridge, the playground for small children which was Alcatraz Island.

Dammit, he thought bitterly. *I can't marry; I can't live a genuine human existence, reverting this way to the form the War Office bigshots forced me into back in the war times....*

He had not known then, when he accepted the mission, that it would leave this permanent effect. They had assured him it was "only temporary, for the duration," or some such glib phrase. *Duration my ass*, Munster thought with furious, impotent resentment. *It's been eleven years, now.*

The psychological problems created for him, the pressure on his psyche, were immense. Hence his visit to Dr. Jones.

Once more the phone rang.

"Okay," Munster said aloud, and flowed laboriously back across the room to it. "You want to talk to me?" he said as he came closer and closer; the trip, for someone in Blobel form, was a long one. "I'll talk to you. You can even turn on the vidscreen and *look* at me." At the phone he snapped the switch which would permit visual communication as well as auditory. "Have a good look," he said, and displayed his amorphous form before the scanning tube of the video.

Dr. Jones' voice came: "I'm sorry to bother you at your home, Mr. Munster, especially when you're in this, um, awkward condition ... " The homeostatic analyst paused. "But I've been devoting time to problem-solving vis-a-vis your condition. I may have at least a partial solution."

"What?" Munster said, taken by surprise. "You mean to imply that medical science can now — "

"No, no," Dr. Jones said hurriedly. "The physical aspects lie out of my domain; you must keep that in mind, Munster. When you consulted me about your problems it was the psychological adjustment that — "

"I'll come right down to your office and talk to you," Munster said. And then he realized that he could not; in his Blobel form it would take him days to undulate all the way across town to Dr. Jones' office. "Jones," he said desperately, "you see the problems I face. I'm stuck here in this apartment every night beginning about eight o'clock and lasting through until almost seven in the morning ... I can't even visit you and consult you and get help — "

"Be quiet, Mr. Munster," Dr. Jones interrupted. "I'm trying to tell you something. *You're not the only one in this condition.* Did you know that?"

Heavily, Munster said, "Sure. In all, eighty-three Terrans were made over into Blobels at one time or another during the war. Of the eighty-three — " He knew the facts by heart. "Sixty-one survived and now there's an organization called Veterans of Unnatural Wars of which fifty are members. I'm a member. We meet twice a month, revert in unison ... " He started to hang up the phone. So this was what he had gotten for his money, this stale news. "Goodbye, Doctor," he murmured.

Dr. Jones whirred in agitation. "Mr. Munster, I don't mean other Terrans. I've researched this in your behalf, and I discover that according to captured records at the Library of Congress fifteen *Blobels* were formed into pseudo-Terrans to act as spies for *their* side. Do you understand?"

After a moment Munster said, "Not exactly."

"You have a mental block against being helped," Dr. Jones said. "But here's what I want, Munster; you be at my office at eleven in the morning tomorrow. We'll take up the solution to your problem then. Goodnight."

Wearily, Munster said, "When I'm in my Blobel form my wits aren't too keen, Doctor. You'll have to forgive me." He hung up, still puzzled. So there were fifteen Blobels walking around on Titan this moment, doomed to occupy human forms — so what? How did that help him?

Maybe he would find out at eleven tomorrow.

When he strode into Dr. Jones' waiting room he saw, seated in a deep chair in a corner by a lamp, reading a copy of *Fortune*, an exceedingly attractive young woman.

Automatically, Munster found a place to sit from which he could eye her. Stylish dyed-white hair braided down the back of her neck ... he took in the sight of her with delight, pretending to read his own copy of *Fortune*. Slender legs, small and delicate elbows. And her sharp, clearly-featured face. The intelligent eyes, the thin, tapered nostrils — a truly lovely girl, he thought. He drank in the sight of her ... until all at once she raised her head and stared coolly back at him.

"Dull, having to wait," Munster mumbled.

The girl said, "Do you come to Dr. Jones often?"

"No," he admitted. "This is just the second time."

"I've never been here before," the girl said. "I was going to another electronic fully-homeostatic psychoanalyst in Los Angeles and then late yesterday Dr. Bing, my analyst, called me and told me to fly up here and see Dr. Jones this morning. Is this one good?"

"Um," Munster said. "I guess so." *We'll see,* he thought. *That's precisely what we don't know, at this point.*

The inner office door opened and there stood Dr. Jones. "Miss Arrasmith," it said, nodding to the girl. "Mr. Munster." It nodded to George. "Won't you both come in?"

Rising to her feet, Miss Arrasmith said, "Who pays the twenty dollars then?"

But the analyst had become silent; it had turned off.

"I'll pay," Miss Arrasmith said, reaching into her purse.

"No, no," Munster said. "Let me." He got out a twenty-dollar piece and dropped it into the analyst's slot.

At once, Dr. Jones said, "You're a gentleman, Mr. Munster." Smiling, it ushered the two of them into its office. "Be seated, please. Miss Arrasmith, without preamble please allow me to explain your — condition to Mr. Munster." To Munster it said, "Miss Arrasmith is a Blobel."

Munster could only stare at the girl.

"Obviously," Dr. Jones continued, "presently in human form. This, for her, is the state of involuntary reversion. During the war she operated behind Terran lines, acting for the Blobel War League. She was captured and held, but then the war ended and she was neither tried nor sentenced."

"They released me," Miss Arrasmith said in a low, carefully-controlled voice. "Still in human form. I stayed here out of shame. I just couldn't go back to Titan and — " Her voice wavered.

"There is great shame attached to this condition," Dr. Jones said, "for any high-caste Blobel."

Nodding, Miss Arrasmith sat, clutching a tiny Irish linen handkerchief and trying to look poised. "Correct, Doctor. I did visit Titan to discuss my condition with medical authorities there. After expensive and prolonged therapy with me they were able to induce a return to my natural form for a period of — " She hesitated. "About one-fourth of the time. But the other three-fourths... I am as you perceive me now." She ducked her head and touched the handkerchief to her right eye.

"Jeez," Munster protested, "you're lucky; a human form is infinitely superior to a Blobel form — I ought to know. As a Blobel you have to creep along... you're like a big jellyfish, no skeleton to keep you erect. And binary fission — it's lousy, I say really lousy, compared to the Terran form of — you know. Reproduction." He colored.

Dr. Jones ticked and stated, "For a period of about six hours your human forms overlap. And then for about one hour your Blobel forms overlap. So all in all, the two of you possess seven hours out of twenty-four in which you both possess identical forms. In my opinion — " It toyed with its pen and paper. "Seven hours is not too bad. If you follow my meaning."

After a moment Miss Arrasmith said, "But Mr. Munster and I are natural enemies."

"That was years ago," Munster said.

"Correct," Dr. Jones agreed. "True, Miss Arrasmith is basically a Blobel and you, Munster, are a Terran, but — " It gestured. "Both of you are outcasts in either civilization; both of you are stateless and hence gradually suffering a loss of ego-identity. I predict for both of you a gradual deterioration ending finally in severe mental illness. Unless you two can develop a rapprochement." The analyst was silent, then.

Miss Arrasmith said softly, "I think we're very lucky, Mr. Munster. As Dr. Jones said, we do overlap for seven hours a day... we can enjoy that time together, no longer in wretched isolation." She smiled up hopefully at him, rearranging her coat. Certainly, she had a nice figure; the somewhat low-cut dress gave an ideal clue to that.

Studying her, Munster pondered.

"Give him time," Dr. Jones told Miss Arrasmith. "My analysis of him is that he will see this correctly and do the right thing."

Still rearranging her coat and dabbing at her large, dark eyes, Miss Arrasmith waited.

The phone in Dr. Jones' office rang, a number of years later. He answered it in his customary way. "Please, sir or madam, deposit twenty dollars if you wish to speak to me."

A tough male voice on the other end of the line said, "Listen, this is the

UN Legal Office and we don't deposit twenty dollars to talk to anybody. So trip that mechanism inside you, Jones."

"Yes, sir," Dr. Jones said, and with his right hand tripped the lever behind his ear that caused him to come on free.

"Back in 2037," the UN legal expert said, "did you advise a couple to marry? A George Munster and a Vivian Arrasmith, now Mrs. Munster?"

"Why yes," Dr. Jones said, after consulting his built-in memory banks.

"Had you investigated the legal ramifications of their issue?"

"Um well," Dr. Jones said, "that's not my worry."

"You can be arraigned for advising any action contrary to UN law."

"There's no law prohibiting a Blobel and a Terran from marrying."

The UN legal expert said, "All right, Doctor, I'll settle for a look at their case histories."

"Absolutely not," Dr. Jones said. "That would be a breach of ethics."

"We'll get a writ and sequester them, then."

"Go ahead." Dr. Jones reached behind his ear to shut himself off.

"Wait. It may interest you to know that the Munsters now have four children. And, following the Mendelian Law, the offspring comprise a strict one, two, one ratio. One Blobel girl, one hybrid boy, one hybrid girl, one Terran girl. The legal problem arises in that the Blobel Supreme Council claims the pure-blooded Blobel girl as a citizen of Titan and also suggests that one of the two hybrids be donated to the Council's jurisdiction." The UN legal expert explained, "You see, the Munsters' marriage is breaking up; they're getting divorced and it's sticky finding which laws obtain regarding them and their issue."

"Yes," Dr. Jones admitted, "I would think so. What has caused their marriage to break up?"

"I don't know and don't care. Possibly the fact that both adults and two of the four children rotate daily between being Blobels and Terrans; maybe the strain got to be too much. If you want to give them psychological advice, consult them. Goodbye." The UN legal expert rang off.

Did I make a mistake, advising them to marry? Dr. Jones asked itself. *I wonder if I shouldn't look them up; I owe at least that to them.*

Opening the Los Angeles phone book, it began thumbing through the Ms.

These had been six difficult years for the Munsters.

First, George had moved from San Francisco to Los Angeles; he and Vivian had set up a household in a condominium apartment with three instead of two rooms. Vivian, being in Terran form three-fourths of the time, had been able to obtain a job; right out in public she gave jet flight information at the Fifth Los Angeles Airport. George, however —

His pension comprised an amount only one-fourth that of his wife's salary and he felt it keenly. To augment it, he had searched for a way of earning money at home. Finally in a magazine he had found this valuable ad:

MAKE SWIFT PROFITS IN YOUR OWN CONDO! RAISE GIANT BULL-FROGS FROM JUPITER, CAPABLE OF EIGHTY-FOOT LEAPS. CAN BE USED IN FROG-RACING (where legal) AND . . .

So in 2038 he had bought his first pair of frogs imported from Jupiter and had begun raising them for swift profits, right in his own condominium apartment building, in a corner of the basement that Leopold, the partially-homeostatic janitor, let him use gratis.

But in the relatively feeble Terran gravity the frogs were capable of enormous leaps, and the basement proved too small for them; they ricocheted from wall to wall like green ping pong balls and soon died. Obviously it took more than a portion of the basement at QEK-604 Apartments to house a crop of the damned things, George realized.

And then, too, their first child had been born. It had turned out to be a pure-blooded Blobel; for twenty-four hours a day it consisted of a gelatinous mass and George found himself waiting in vain for it to switch over to a human form, even for a moment.

He faced Vivian defiantly in this matter, during a period when both of them were in human form.

"How can I consider it my child?" he asked her. "It's — an alien life form to me." He was discouraged and even horrified. "Dr. Jones should have foreseen this; maybe it's *your* child — it looks just like you."

Tears filled Vivian's eyes. "You mean that insultingly."

"Damn right I do. We fought you creatures — we used to consider you no better than Portuguese sting-rays." Gloomily, he put on his coat. "I'm going down to Veterans of Unnatural Wars Headquarters," he informed his wife. "Have a beer with the boys." Shortly, he was on his way to join with his old war-time buddies, glad to get out of the apartment house.

VUW Headquarters was a decrepit cement building in downtown Los Angeles left over from the twentieth century and sadly in need of paint. The VUW had little funds because most of its members were, like George Munster, living on UN pensions. However, there was a pool table and an old 3-D television set and a few dozen tapes of popular music and also a chess set. George generally drank his beer and played chess with his fellow members, either in human form or in Blobel form; this was one place in which both were accepted.

This particular evening he sat with Pete Ruggles, a fellow veteran who also had married a Blobel female, reverting, as Vivian did, to human form.

"Pete, I can't go on. I've got a gelatinous blob for a child. My whole life I've wanted a kid, and now what have I got? Something that looks like it washed up on the beach."

Sipping his beer — he too was in human form at the moment — Pete answered, "Criminy, George, I admit it's a mess. But you must have known what you were getting into when you married her. And my God, according to Mendel's Law, the next kid — "

"I mean," George broke in, "I don't respect my own wife; that's the basis of it. I think of her as a *thing*. And myself, too. We're both things." He drank down his beer in one gulp.

Pete said meditatively, "But from the Blobel standpoint — "

"Listen, whose side are you on?" George demanded.

"Don't yell at me," Pete said, "or I'll deck you."

A moment later they were swinging wildly at each other. Fortunately Pete reverted to Blobel form in the nick of time; no harm was done. Now George sat alone, in human shape, while Pete oozed off somewhere else, probably to join a group of the boys who had also assumed Blobel form.

Maybe we can find a new society somewhere on a remote moon, George said to himself moodily. *Neither Terran nor Blobel.*

I've got to go back to Vivian, George resolved. *What else is there for me? I'm lucky to find her; I'd be nothing but a war veteran guzzling beer here at VUW Headquarters every damn day and night, with no future, no hope, no real life ...*

He had a new money-making scheme going now. It was a home mail-order business; he had placed an ad in the *Saturday Evening Post* for MAGIC LODE-STONES REPUTED TO BRING YOU LUCK. FROM ANOTHER STAR-SYSTEM ENTIRELY! The stones had come from Proxima and were obtainable on Titan; it was Vivian who had made the commercial contact for him with her people. But so far, few people had sent in the dollar-fifty.

I'm a failure, George said to himself.

Fortunately the next child, born in the winter of 2039, showed itself to be a hybrid; it took human form fifty percent of the time, and so at last George had a child who was — occasionally, anyhow — a member of his own species.

He was still in the process of celebrating the birth of Maurice when a delegation of their neighbors at QEK-604 Apartments came and rapped on their door.

"We've got a petition here," the chairman of the delegation said, shuffling his feet in embarrassment, "asking that you and Mrs. Munster leave QEK-604."

"But why?" George asked, bewildered. "You haven't objected to us up until now."

"The reason is that now you've got a hybrid youngster who will want to play with ours, and we feel it's unhealthy for our kids to — "

George slammed the door in their faces.

But still, he felt the pressure, the hostility from the people on all sides of them. *And to think*, he thought bitterly, *that I fought in the war to save these people. It sure wasn't worth it.*

An hour later he was down at VUW Headquarters once more, drinking beer and talking with his buddy Sherman Downs, also married to a Blobel.

"Sherman, it's no good. We're not wanted; we've got to emigrate. Maybe we'll try it on Titan, in Viv's world."

"Chrissakes," Sherman protested, "I hate to see you fold up, George. Isn't your electromagnetic reducing belt beginning to sell, finally?"

For the last few months, George had been making and selling a complex electronic reducing gadget which Vivian had helped him design; it was based in principle on a Blobel device popular on Titan but unknown on Terra. And this had gone over well; George had more orders than he could fill. But —

"I had a terrible experience, Sherm," George confided. "I was in a drugstore the other day, and they gave me a big order for my reducing belt, and I got so excited — " He broke off. "You can guess what happened. I reverted. Right in plain sight of a hundred customers. And when the buyer saw that he canceled the order for the belts. It was what we all fear ... you should have seen how their attitude toward me changed."

Sherm said, "Hire someone to do your selling for you. A full-blooded Terran."

Thickly, George said, "*I'm* a full-blooded Terran, and don't you forget it. Ever."

"I just mean — "

"I know what you meant," George said. And took a swing at Sherman. Fortunately he missed and in the excitement both of them reverted to Blobel form. They oozed angrily into each other for a time, but at last fellow veterans managed to separate them.

"I'm as much Terran as anyone," George thought-radiated in the Blobel manner to Sherman. "And I'll flatten anyone who says otherwise."

In Blobel form he was unable to get home; he had to phone Vivian to come and get him. It was humiliating.

Suicide, he decided. *That's the answer.*

How best to do it? In Blobel form he was unable to feel pain; best to do it then. Several substances would dissolve him ... he could for instance drop himself into a heavily-chlorinated swimming pool, such as QEK-604 maintained in its recreation room.

Vivian, in human form, found him as he reposed hesitantly at the edge of the swimming pool, late one night.

"George, I beg you — go back to Dr. Jones."

"Naw," he boomed dully, forming a quasi-vocal apparatus with a portion of his body. "It's no use, Viv. I don't *want* to go on." Even the belts; they had been Viv's idea, rather than his. He was second even there ... behind her, falling constantly farther behind each passing day.

Viv said, "You have so much to offer the children."

That was true. "Maybe I'll drop over to the UN War Office," he decided. "Talk to them, see if there's anything new that medical science has come up with that might stabilize me."

"But if you stabilize as a Terran," Vivian said, "what would become of me?"

"We'd have *eighteen entire hours* together a day. All the hours you take human form!"

"But you wouldn't want to stay married to me. Because, George, then you could meet a Terran woman."

It wasn't fair to her, he realized. So he abandoned the idea.

In the spring of 2041 their third child was born, also a girl, and like Maurice a hybrid. It was Blobel at night and Terran by day.

Meanwhile, George found a solution to some of his problems.

He got himself a mistress.

He and Nina arranged to meet each other at the Hotel Elysium, a run-down wooden building in the heart of Los Angeles.

"Nina," George said, sipping Teacher's scotch and seated beside her on the shabby sofa which the hotel provided, "you've made my life worth living again." He fooled with the buttons of her blouse.

"I respect you," Nina Glaubman said, assisting him with the buttons. "In spite of the fact — well, you are a former enemy of our people."

"God," George protested, "we must not think about the old days — we have to close our minds to our pasts." *Nothing but our future,* he thought.

His reducing belt enterprise had developed so well that now he employed fifteen full-time Terran employees and owned a small, modern factory on the outskirts of San Fernando. If UN taxes had been reasonable he would by now be a wealthy man ... brooding on that, George wondered what the tax rate was in Blobel-run lands, on Io, for instance. Maybe he ought to look into it.

One night at VUW Headquarters he discussed the subject with Reinholt, Nina's husband, who of course was ignorant of the modus vivendi between George and Nina.

"Reinholt," George said with difficulty, as he drank his beer, "I've got big plans. This cradle-to-grave socialism the UN operates ... it's not for me. It's cramping me. The Munster Magic Magnetic Belt is — " He gestured. "More than Terran civilization can support. You get me?"

Coldly, Reinholt said, "But George, you are a Terran; if you emigrate to Blobel-run territory with your factory you'll be betraying your — "

"Listen," George told him, "I've got one authentic Blobel child, two half-Blobel children, and a fourth on the way. I've got strong *emotional* ties with those people out there on Titan and Io."

"You're a traitor," Reinholt said, and punched him in the mouth. "And not only that," he continued, punching George in the stomach, "you're running around with my wife. I'm going to kill you."

To escape, George reverted to Blobel form; Reinholt's blows passed harmlessly deep into his moist, jelly-like substance. Reinholt then reverted too, and flowed into him murderously, trying to consume and absorb George's nucleus.

Fortunately fellow veterans pried their two bodies apart before any permanent harm was done.

Later that night, still trembling, George sat with Vivian in the living room of their eight-room suite at the great new condominium apartment building ZGF-900. It had been a close call, and now of course Reinholt would tell Viv; it was only a question of time. The marriage, as far as George could see, was over. This perhaps was their last moment together.

"Viv," he said urgently, "you have to believe me; I love you. You and the children — plus the belt business, naturally — are my complete life." A desperate idea came to him. "Let's emigrate now, tonight. Pack up the kids and go to Titan, right this minute."

"I can't go," Vivian said. "I know how my people would treat me, and treat you and the children, too. George, *you go*. Move the factory to Io. I'll stay here." Tears filled her dark eyes.

"Hell," George said, "what kind of life is that? With you on Terra and me on Io — that's no marriage. And who'll get the kids?" Probably Viv would get them ... but his firm employed top legal talent — perhaps he could use it to solve his domestic problems.

The next morning Vivian found out about Nina. And hired an attorney of her own.

"Listen," George said, on the phone talking to his top legal talent, Henry Ramarau. "Get me custody of the fourth child; it'll be a Terran. And we'll compromise on the two hybrids; I'll take Maurice and she can have Kathy. And naturally she gets that blob, the first so-called child. As far as I'm concerned it's hers anyhow." He slammed the receiver down and then turned to the board of directors of his company. "Now where were we?" he demanded. "In our analysis of Io tax laws."

During the next weeks the idea of a move to Io appeared more and more feasible from a profit and loss standpoint.

"Go ahead and buy land on Io," George instructed his business agent in the field, Tom Hendricks. "And get it cheap; we want to start right." To his secretary, Miss Nolan, he said, "Now keep everyone out of my office until further notice. I feel a attack coming on. From anxiety over this major move off Terra to Io." He added, "And personal worries."

"Yes, Mr. Munster," Miss Nolan said, ushering Tom Hendricks out of George's private office. "No one will disturb you." She could be counted on to keep everyone out while George reverted to his war-time Blobel shape, as he often did, these days; the pressure on him was immense.

When, later in the day, he resumed human form, George learned from Miss Nolan that a Doctor Jones had called.

"I'll be damned," George said, thinking back to six years ago. "I thought it'd be in the junk pile by now." To Miss Nolan he said, "Call Doctor Jones, notify me when you have it; I'll take a minute off to talk to it." It was like old times, back in San Francisco.

Shortly, Miss Nolan had Dr. Jones on the line.

"Doctor," George said, leaning back in his chair and swiveling from side to side and poking at an orchid on his desk. "Good to hear from you."

The voice of the homeostatic analyst came in his ear, "Mr. Munster, I note that you now have a secretary."

"Yes," George said, "I'm a tycoon. I'm in the reducing belt game; it's somewhat like the flea-collar that cats wear. Well, what can I do for you?"

"I understand you have four children now — "

"Actually three, plus a fourth on the way. Listen, that fourth, Doctor, is vital to me; according to Mendel's Law it's a full-blooded Terran and by God I'm doing everything in my power to get custody of it." He added, "Vivian — you remember her — is now back on Titan. Among her own people, where she belongs. And I'm putting some of the finest doctors I can get on my payroll to stabilize me; I'm tired of this constant reverting, night and day; I've got too much to do for such nonsense."

Dr. Jones said, "From your tone I can see you're an important, busy man, Mr. Munster. You've certainly risen in the world, since I saw you last."

"Get to the point," George said impatiently. "Why'd you call?"

"I, um, thought perhaps I could bring you and Vivian together again."

"Bah," George said contemptuously. "That woman? Never. Listen, Doctor, I have to ring off; we're in the process of finalizing on some basic business strategy, here at Munster, Incorporated."

"Mr. Munster," Dr. Jones asked, "is there another woman?"

"There's another Blobel," George said, "if that's what you mean." And he hung up the phone. *Two Blobels are better than none,* he said to himself. *And now back to business* ... He pressed a button on his desk and at once Miss Nolan put her head into the office. "Miss Nolan," George said, "get me Hank Ramarau; I want to find out — "

"Mr. Ramarau is waiting on the other line," Miss Nolan said. "He says it's urgent."

Switching to the other line, George said, "Hi, Hank. What's up?"

"I've just discovered," his top legal advisor said, "that to operate your factory on Io you must be a citizen of Titan."

"We ought to be able to fix that up," George said.

"But to be a citizen of Titan — " Ramarau hesitated. "I'll break it to you easy as I can, George. You have to be a Blobel."

"Dammit, I am a Blobel," George said. "At least part of the time. Won't that do?"

"No," Ramarau said, "I checked into that, knowing of your affliction, and it's got to be one hundred percent of the time. Night *and* day."

"Hmmm," George said. "This is bad. But we'll overcome it, somehow. Listen, Hank, I've got an appointment with Eddy Fullbright, my medical coordinator; I'll talk to you after, okay?" He rang off and then sat scowling and rubbing his jaw. *Well*, he decided, *if it has to be it has to be. Facts are facts, and we can't let them stand in our way.*

Picking up the phone he dialed his doctor, Eddy Fullbright.

The twenty-dollar platinum coin rolled down the chute and tripped the circuit. Dr. Jones came on, glanced up and saw a stunning, sharp-breasted young woman whom it recognized — by means of a quick scan of its memory banks — as Mrs. George Munster, the former Vivian Arrasmith.

"Good day, Vivian," Dr. Jones said cordially. "But I understood you were on Titan." It rose to its feet, offering her a chair.

Dabbing at her large, dark eyes, Vivian sniffled, "Doctor, everything is collapsing around me. My husband is having an affair with another woman ... all I know is that her name is Nina and all the boys down at VUW Headquarters are talking about it. Presumably she's a Terran. We're both filing for divorce. And we're having a dreadful legal battle over the children." She arranged her coat modestly. "I'm expecting. Our fourth."

"This I know," Dr. Jones said. "A full-blooded Terran this time, if Mendel's Law holds ... although it only applied to litters."

Mrs. Munster said miserably, "I've been on Titan talking to legal and medical experts, gynecologists, and especially marital guidance counselors; I've had all sorts of advice during the past month. Now I'm back on Terra but I can't find George — he's *gone*."

"I wish I could help you, Vivian," Dr. Jones said. "I talked to your husband briefly, the other day, but he spoke only in generalities ... evidently he's such a big tycoon now that it's hard to approach him."

"And to think," Vivian sniffled, "that he achieved it all because of an idea *I* gave him. A Blobel idea."

"The ironies of fate," Dr. Jones said. "Now, if you want to keep your husband, Vivian — "

"I'm determined to keep him, Doctor Jones. Frankly I've undergone therapy on Titan, the latest and most expensive ... it's because I love George so much, even more than I love my own people or my planet."

"Eh?" Dr. Jones said.

"Through the most modern developments in medical science in the Sol System," Vivian said, "I've been stabilized, Doctor Jones. Now I am in human form twenty-four hours a day instead of eighteen. I've renounced my natural form in order to keep my marriage with George."

"The supreme sacrifice," Dr. Jones said, touched.

"Now, if I can only *find* him, Doctor — "

At the ground-breaking ceremonies on Io, George Munster flowed gradually to the shovel, extended a pseudopodium, seized the shovel, and with it managed to dig a symbolic amount of soil. "This is a great day," he boomed hollowly, by means of the semblance of a vocal apparatus into which he had fashioned the slimy, plastic substance which made up his unicellular body.

"Right, George," Hank Ramarau agreed, standing nearby with the legal documents.

The Ionan official, like George a great transparent blob, oozed across to Ramarau, took the documents and boomed, "These will be transmitted to my government. I'm sure they're in order, Mr. Ramarau."

"I guarantee you," Ramarau said to the official, "Mr. Munster does not revert to human form at any time; he's made use of some of the most advanced techniques in medical science to achieve this stability at the unicellular phase of his former rotation. Munster would never cheat."

"This historic moment," the great blob that was George Munster thought-radiated to the throng of local Blobels attending the ceremonies, "means a higher standard of living for Ionans who will be employed; it will bring prosperity to this area, plus a proud sense of national achievement in the manufacture of what we recognize to be a native invention, the Munster Magic Magnetic Belt."

The throng of Blobels thought-radiated cheers.

"This is a proud day in my life," George Munster informed them, and began to ooze by degrees back to his car, where his chauffeur waited to drive him to his permanent hotel room at Io City.

Someday he would own the hotel. He was putting the profits from his business in local real estate; it was the patriotic — and the profitable — thing to do, other Ionans, other Blobels, had told him.

"I'm finally a successful man," George Munster thought-radiated to all close enough to pick up his emanations.

Amid frenzied cheers he oozed up the ramp and into his Titan-made car.

NOTES

All notes in italics are by Philip K. Dick. The year when the note was written appears in parentheses following the note. Most of these notes were written as story notes for the collections THE BEST OF PHILIP K. DICK (published 1977) and THE GOLDEN MAN (published 1980). A few were written at the request of editors publishing or reprinting a PKD story in a book or magazine.

When there is a date following the name of a story, it is the date the manuscript of that story was first received by Dick's agent, per the records of the Scott Meredith Literary Agency. Absence of a date means no record is available. The name of a magazine followed by a month and year indicates the first published appearance of a story. An alternate name following a story indicates Dick's original name for the story, as shown in the agency records.

These five volumes include all of Philip K. Dick's short fiction, with the exception of short novels later published as or included in novels, childhood writings, and unpublished writings for which manuscripts have not been found. The stories are arrangd as closely as possible in chronological order of composition; research for this chronology was done by Gregg Rickman and Paul Williams.

AUTOFAC 10/11/54. *Galaxy*, Nov 1955.

Tom Disch said of this story that it was one of the earliest ecology warnings in sf. What I had in mind in writing it, however, was the thought that if factories became fully automated, they might begin to show the instinct for survival which organic living entities have . . . and perhaps develop similar solutions. (1976)

SERVICE CALL 10/11/54. *Science Fiction Stories*, July 1955.

When this story appeared many fans objected to it because of the negative attitude I expressed in it. But I was already beginning to suppose in my head the growing domination of machines over man, especially the machines we voluntarily surround ourselves with, which should, by logic, be the most harmless. I never assumed that some huge clanking monster would stride down Fifth Avenue, devouring New York; I always feared that my own TV set or iron or toaster would, in the privacy of my apartment, when no one else was around to help me, announce to me that they had taken over, and here was a list of rules I was to obey. I never like the idea of doing what a machine says. I hate having to salute something built in a factory. (Do you suppose all those White House tapes came out of the back of the President's head? And programmed him as to what he was to say and do?) (1976)

CAPTIVE MARKET 10/18/54. *If*, April 1955.

THE MOLD OF YANCY 10/18/54. *If*, Aug 1955.
   Obviously, Yancy is based on President Eisenhower. During his reign we all were worrying about the man-in-the-gray-flannel-suit problem; we feared that the entire country was turning into one person and a whole lot of clones. (Although in those days the word "clone" was unknown to us.) I liked this story enough to use it as the basis for my novel THE PENULTIMATE TRUTH; *in particular the part where everything the government tells you is a lie. I still like that part; I mean, I still believe it's so. Watergate, of course, bore the basic idea of this story out.* (1978)

THE MINORITY REPORT 12/22/54. *Fantastic Universe*, Jan 1956.

RECALL MECHANISM *If*, July 1959.

THE UNRECONSTRUCTED M 6/2/55. *Science Fiction Stories*, Jan 1957.
   If the main theme throughout my writing is, "Can we consider the universe real, and if so, in what way?" my secondary theme would be, "Are we all humans?" Here a machine does not imitate a human being, but instead fakes evidence of a human being, a given human being. Fakery is a topic which absolutely fascinates me; I am convinced that anything can be faked, or anyhow evidence pointing to any given thing. Spurious clues can lead us to believe anything they want us to believe. There is really no theoretical upper limit to this. Once you have mentally opened the door to the reception of the notion of fake, you are ready to think yourself into another kind of reality entirely. It's a trip from which you never return. And, I think, a healthy trip ... unless you take it too seriously. (1978)

EXPLORERS WE 5/6/58. *Fantasy & Science Fiction*, Jan 1959.

WAR GAME ("Diversion") 10/31/58. *Galaxy*, Dec 1959.

IF THERE WERE NO BENNY CEMOLI ("Had There Never Been A Benny Cemoli") 2/27/63. *Galaxy*, Dec 1963.
   I have always believed that at least half the famous people in history never existed. You invent what you need to invent. Perhaps even Karl Marx was invented, the product of some hack writer. In which case — (1976)

NOVELTY ACT ("At Second Jug") 3/23/63. *Fantastic*, Feb 1964. [Included in PKD's novel THE SIMULACRA.]

WATERSPIDER 4/10/63. *If*, Jan 1964.

WHAT THE DEAD MEN SAY ("Man With a Broken Match") 4/15/63. *Worlds of Tomorrow*, June 1964.

ORPHEUS WITH CLAY FEET 4/16/63 [published in *Escapade* circa 1964 under the pseudonym Jack Dowland].

THE DAYS OF PERKY PAT ("In the Days of Perky Pat") 4/18/63. *Amazing*, Dec 1963.

The Days of Perky Pat *came to me in one lightning-swift flash when I saw my children playing with Barbie dolls. Obviously these anatomically super-developed dolls were not intended for the use of children, or, more accurately, should not have been. Barbie and Ken consisted of two adults in miniature. The idea was that the purchase of countless new clothes for these dolls was necessary if Barbie and Ken were to live in the style to which they were accustomed. I had visions of Barbie coming into my bedroom at night and saying, "I need a mink coat." Or, even worse, "Hey, big fellow ... want to take a drive to Vegas in my Jaguar XKE?" I was afraid my wife would find me and Barbie together and my wife would shoot me.*

The sale of The Days of Perky Pat *to* Amazing *was a good one because in those days Cele Goldsmith edited* Amazing *and she was one of the best editors in the field. Avram Davidson at* Fantasy & Science Fiction *had turned it down, but later he told me that had he known about Barbie dolls he probably would have bought it. I could not imagine anyone not knowing about Barbie. I had to deal with her and her expensive purchases constantly. It was as bad as keeping my TV set working; the TV set always needed something and so did Barbie. I always felt that Ken should buy his own clothes.*

In those days — the early Sixties — I wrote a great deal, and some of my best stories and novels emanated from that period. My wife wouldn't let me work in the house, so I rented a little shack for $25 a month and walked over to it each morning. This was out in the country. All I saw on my walk to my shack were a few cows in their pastures and my own flock of sheep who never did anything but trudge along after the bell-sheep. I was terribly lonely, shut up by myself in my shack all day. Maybe I missed Barbie, who was back at the big house with the children. So perhaps The Days of Perky Pat *is a wishful fantasy on my part; I would have loved to see Barbie — or Perky Pat or Connie Companion — show up at the door of my shack.*

What did show up was something awful: my vision of the face of Palmer Eldritch which became the basis of the novel THE THREE STIGMATA OF PALMER ELDRITCH *which the Perky Pat story generated.*

There I went, one day, walking down the country road to my shack, looking forward to eight hours of writing, in total isolation from all other humans, and I looked up at the sky and saw a face. I didn't really see it, but the face was there, and it was not a human face; it was a vast visage of perfect evil. I realize now (and I think I dimly realized at the time) what caused me to see it: the months of isolation, of deprivation of human contact, in fact sensory deprivation as such ... anyhow the visage could not be denied. It was immense; it filled a quarter of the sky. It had empty slots for eyes — it was metal and cruel and, worst of all, it was God.

I drove over to my church, Saint Columba's Episcopal Church, and talked to my priest. He came to the conclusion that I had had a glimpse of Satan and gave me unction — not supreme unction; just healing unction. It didn't do any good; the metal face in the sky remained. I had to walk along every day as it gazed down at me.

Years later — after I had long since written THE THREE STIGMATA OF PALMER ELDRITCH and sold it to Doubleday, my first sale to Doubleday — I came across a picture of the face in an issue of Life magazine. It was, very simply, a World War One observation cupola on the Marne, built by the French. My father had fought in the Second Battle of the Marne; he had been with the Fifth Marines, about the first group of American soldiers to go over to Europe and fight in that ghastly war. When I was a very small child he had showed me his uniform and gasmask, the entire gas-filtration equipment, and told me how the soldiers became panic-stricken during gas attacks as the charcoal in their filtration systems became saturated, and how sometimes a soldier would freak and tear off his mask and run. As a child I felt a lot of anxiety listening to my father's war stories and looking at and playing with the gasmask and helmet; but what scared me the most was when my father would put on the gasmask. His face would disappear. This was not my father any longer. This was not a human being at all. I was only four years old. After that my mother and father got divorced and I did not see my father for years. But the sight of him wearing his gasmask, blending as it did with his accounts of men with their guts hanging from them, men destroyed by shrapnel — decades later, in 1963, as I walked alone day after day along that country road with no one to talk to, no one to be with, that metal, blind, inhuman visage appeared to me again, but now transcendent and vast, and absolutely evil.

I decided to exorcise it by writing about it, and I did write about it, and it did go away. But I had seen the evil one himself, and I said then and say now, "The evil one wears a metal face." If you want to see this yourself, look at a picture of the war masks of the Attic Greeks. When men wish to inspire terror and kill they put on such metal faces. The invading Christian knights that Alexander Nevsky fought wore such masks; if you saw Eisenstein's film you know what I am talking about. They all looked alike. I had not seen Nevsky when I wrote THE THREE STIGMATA, but I saw it later and saw again the thing that had hung in the sky back in 1963, the thing into which my own father had been transformed when I was a child.

So THE THREE STIGMATA is a novel that came out of powerful atavistic fears in me, fears dating back to my early childhood and no doubt connected with my grief and loneliness when my father left my mother and me. In the novel my father appears as both Palmer Eldritch (the evil father, the diabolic mask-father) and as Leo Bulero, the tender, gruff, warm, human, loving man. The novel which emerged came out of the most intense anguish possible; in 1963 I was reliving the original isolation I had experienced upon the loss of my father, and the horror and fear expressed in the novel are not fictional sentiments ground out to interest the reader; they come from the deepest part of me: yearning for the good father and fear of the evil father, the father who left me.

I found in the story The Days of Perky Pat a vehicle that I could translate into a thematic basis for the novel I wanted to write. Now, you see, Perky Pat is the eternally beckoning fair one, das ewige Weiblichkeit — "the eternally feminine," as Goethe put it. Isolation generated the novel and yearning generated the story; so the novel is a mixture of the fear of being abandoned and the fantasy of the beautiful woman who waits for you — somewhere, but God only knows where; I have still to figure it out. But if you are sitting alone day after day at your typewriter, turning out one story after another and having no one to talk to, no one to be with, and yet pro forma having a wife and four daughters from whose house you have been expelled, banished to a little single-walled shack that is so cold in winter that, literally, the ink would freeze in my typewriter ribbon, well, you are going to write about iron slot-eyed faces and warm young women. And thus I did. And thus I still do.

Reaction to THE THREE STIGMATA was mixed. In England some reviewers described it as blasphemy. Terry Carr, who was my agent at Scott Meredith at the time, told me later, "That novel is crazy," although subsequent to that he reversed his opinion. Some reviewers found it a profound novel. I only find it frightening. I was unable to proofread the galleys because the novel frightened me so. It is a dark journey into the mystical and the supernatural and the absolutely evil as I understood it at the time. Let us say, I would like Perky Pat to show up at my door, but I dread the possibility that, when I hear the knock, it will be Palmer Eldritch waiting outside and not Perky Pat. Actually, to be honest, neither has shown up in the seventeen or so years since I wrote the novel. I guess that is the story of life: what you most fear never happens, but what you most yearn for never happens either. This is the difference between life and fiction. I suppose it's a good trade-off. But I'm not sure. (1979)

STAND-BY ("Top Stand-By Job") 4/18/63. *Amazing*, Oct 1963.

WHAT'LL WE DO WITH RAGLAND PARK? ("No Ordinary Guy") 4/29/63. *Amazing*, Nov 1963.

OH, TO BE A BLOBEL! ("Well, See, There Were These Blobels ... ") 5/6/63. *Galaxy*, Feb 1964.

At the beginning of my writing career in the early Fifties, Galaxy was my economic mainstay. Horace Gold at Galaxy liked my writing whereas John W. Campbell, Jr. at Astounding considered my writing not only worthless but as he put it, "Nuts." By and large I liked reading Galaxy because it had the broadest range of ideas, venturing into the soft sciences such as sociology and psychology, at a time when Campbell (as he once wrote me!) considered psionics a necessary premise for science fiction. Also, Campbell said, the psionic character in the story had to be in charge of what was going on. So Galaxy provided a latitude which Astounding did not. However, I was to get into an awful quarrel with Horace Gold; he had the habit of changing your stories without telling you: adding scenes, adding characters, removing downbeat endings in favor of upbeat endings. Many writers resented this. I did more than resent this; despite the fact that Galaxy was my main source of income I told Gold that I would not sell to him unless he stopped altering my stories — after which he bought nothing from me at all.

It was not, then, until Fred Pohl became editor of Galaxy that I began to appear there again. Oh, To Be A Blobel! is a story which Fred Pohl bought. In this story my enormous anti-war bias is evident, a bias which had, ironically, pleased Gold. I wasn't thinking of the Viet Nam War but war in general; in particular, how a war forces you to become like your enemy. Hitler had once said that the true victory of the Nazis would be to force its enemies, the United States in particular, to become like the Third Reich — i.e. a totalitarian society — in order to win. Hitler, then, expected to win even in losing. As I watched the American military-industrial complex grow after World War Two I kept remembering Hitler's analysis, and I kept thinking how right the son of a bitch was. We had beaten Germany, but both the U.S. and the U.S.S.R. were getting more and more like the Nazis with their huge police systems every day. Well, it seemed to me there was a little wry humor in this (but not much). Maybe I could write about it without getting too deep into polemics. But the issue presented in this story is real. Look what we had to become in Viet Nam just to lose, let alone to win; can you imagine what we'd have had to become to win? Hitler would have gotten a lot of laughs out of it, and the laughs would have been on us ... and to a very great extent in fact were. And they were hollow and grim laughs, without humor of any kind. (1979)

Here I nailed down the ultimate meaningless irony of war; the human turns into a Blobel, and the Blobel, his enemy, turns into a human, and there it all is, the futility, the black humor, the stupidity. And in the story they all wind up happy. (1976)